The Boy in the Band

KERRI LYNN

PALMETTO
P U B L I S H I N G
Charleston, SC
www.PalmettoPublishing.com

© 2024 Kerri Lynn
All rights reserved.
No portion of this book may be reproduced,
stored in a retrieval system, or transmitted in
any form by any means–electronic, mechanical,
photocopy, recording, or other–except for
brief quotations in printed reviews,
without prior permission of the author.

Paperback ISBN: 979-8-8229-5006-1
eBook ISBN: 979-8-8229-5007-8

To my cherished tribe, who've turned tears into laughter and laughter into tears, and to the boys who've left memories and laughter in their wake, shaping who I am today. Here's to us, the beautiful mess we've created together. You've made me, me, and I'm endlessly grateful.

Contents

Chapter 1: Twenty-Something Friends 1
Chapter 2: Typical Night Out 6
Chapter 3: Ghost of a Girlfriend 23
Chapter 4: Small Bands and Big Burgers 27
Chapter 5: A Typical Sunday 40
Chapter 6: Straight Girl Lunch 48
Chapter 7: A Parker Wednesday 52
Chapter 8: Willy Wonka and the Family Dinner 62
Chapter 9: For The Roomies 83
Chapter 10: Hard Conversations 90
Chapter 11: San Francisco or Bust 97
Chapter 12: I love you, okay? 101
Chapter 13: Friendsgiving 105
Chapter 14: Coit Tower 109
Chapter 15: With A P-H 113
Chapter 16: Bathroom Ain't Big Enough 116
Chapter 17: New Year's Envy 120
Chapter 18: Too Old for MTV 123
Chapter 19: One Year In 127
Chapter 20: Not Your Grade School Recess 132
Chapter 21: Things We Never Said 135
Chapter 22: My Song 137
Chapter 23: Not So New Year 144
Chapter 24: Not Sarah 147
Chapter 25: Miles Between Us 155
Chapter 26: Fast Forward 158
Chapter 27: Engagement Party 163
Chapter 28: Coming Home 170
Chapter 29: Ladies Who Lunch 173
Chapter 30: You, Again. 176

Chapter 31: The Morning After 182
Chapter 32: Spoons 193
Chapter 33: Keep The Music Alive 201
Chapter 34: Three's a Crowd 210
Chapter 35: Christmas on Vinyl... 214
Chapter 36: Hero and a Distressed Damsel........................... 217
Chapter 37: Snowed In 227
Chapter 38: The 100 Acre Ranch 238
Chapter 39: An Embarrassment of Flowers..........................244
Chapter 40: Connections and Constellations 249
Chapter 41: Does Wine Pair with Ex-Boyfriends or New Ones? 256
Chapter 42: Three is STILL a Crowd 261
Chapter 43: Yes to Undress... 267
Chapter 44: Emails Are Like Boomerangs............................ 275
Chapter 45: Disappointing a Friend...................................... 280
Chapter 46: Something Like Closure 288
Chapter 47: The Wedding... 293
Chapter 48: Thirty 301
Chapter 49: Endless Wildflowers 305
Chapter 50: Matching Pajamas 307
About the Author.. 313

Chapter 1: Twenty-Something Friends

In our small, if you lived there, but big, unless you were from an actual big city, neon-lit town, I am back to being single again. Similar to the contrasting beauty of snow-capped mountains in winter or the plain brown ones in any other season, I have two settings, one of which is visually superior. I am a girlfriend girl and I have always liked that look better on me. I have a tendency to see the world through a romantic lens, constantly searching for those elusive sparks of passion. After finally ending a long-term relationship with Peter Pan, and let us not forget the whirlwind rebound situationship with "the love of my life," the guy who couldn't handle being serious with someone as amazing as me because it scared him too much—you know the type. I find myself navigating the chaotic reality of being a twenty-something in a place where the blinding fluorescent lights of windowless casinos and the deafening music from the perpetually open, dimly lit bars can consume your entire existence, making time slip away like sand through your fingertips.

My new roommate, Thomas, a gorgeous Italian with long, silky hair and skin that always looked like it had just slightly exceeded the perfect sun-kissed glow, was the newest column in my support system. Thomas is brilliant, a living encyclopedia, and hilarious. We bonded immediately. Being around him was the easiest and most natural thing I had ever done. The fact that we both liked men was simply the icing on our best friend's cake.

Thomas came with Jessica and Alice. Jessica, with her curly hair and fierce pride in her Jewish heritage, was the kind of no-nonsense person I instantly adored. She and Thomas could set a boundary like no one I had ever met, something I had never mastered as a grown-up. Jessica was never one to trouble herself with impressing anyone. If you wanted an unfiltered opinion, she could deliver it with the directness of an Asian mother. Alice was our quiet friend, unless she was drunk—tall, dirty blonde, funny, someone you could always count on for the fluffier version of Jessica's opinion. While Alice could seem aloof, we all understood that she saw everything. This made her the beacon of truth. Each time she gave advice, it came in the form of a song from a must-listen album.

As part of our fivesome, I brought Heidi, my most reliable and steadfast support column. Heidi was tall, with milky skin and full breasts that should look ridiculous on her slim frame, but they just added to her overall appeal. Her long, jet-black hair and blunt bangs made her bright blue eyes the only feature that might distract you from her chest. As if having a boyfriend since high school wasn't enough of a reason not to shoot your shot, she was often venomous without any provocation. If ever you need someone to remind you that the world should bend for you simply because you're you, Heidi is your gal. Being her best friend was like being powerful by association; you just felt different walking in her confidence.

My heartbreak of a situationship came as zero surprise to all of them. Regardless, they comforted me as devoted friends and then escorted me through a string of one-night stands as we spent our well-earned successful-twenty-something cash on club covers and alcohol. Amid a blurry night at a local band's show, a friend of the situationship introduced me to a two-person team, setting the stage for a boy who would shatter all my preconceptions about love. They needed someone to serve as the face of the local band scene and help raise awareness—enter me, the exuberant drunk girl. Roger, inspired by his well-connected rock star–adjacent magazine editor dad in California, decided to pursue the same path in our smaller city. It goes without saying that I had no interest in any of this because, on one hand, my broken heart sought solace in the attention of men, while on the other, music was my one true love. Combining the two was a no-brainer.

Rock Out Local served as a website and newspaper section for me to write articles, conduct interviews, and curate a guide of local bands' performances. My principal task was to search social media for local bands and contact them about their upcoming shows. After persuading my friends to join me, I would attend the show and extend an offer for interviews on our website.

Perusing social media one day, I ran across a band called Reverberation Breakdown. I begin my typical review of the band's photos, songs, and information. Although not entirely uncommon, I fixate my attention on the lead singer while zooming in on his pictures and imagining him performing the songs from his band's playlist. On the band's profile's friends list, he held the coveted number-one spot. Without a conscious thought, my fingers, of their own accord, clicked on his page. Parker's profile picture showed him with short, dark hair and a goatee in jeans and a button-down shirt with the sleeves rolled to the elbows, screaming into a microphone on a stage.

Some pictures featured girls, but not as many as I anticipated. This suggested that he lacked a serious girlfriend or, perhaps more concerning, didn't prioritize relationships or girlfriends. Once I had my fill of plummeting through the black hole that was Parker's profile page, I wrote him a message.

"Hi, my name is Sarah, and I am with Rock Out Local. I want to meet with Reverberation Breakdown to set up an interview with you for our page. You can find my other videos here. Talk soon."

I finish by inserting our link and hit send. He wasn't online, so I wasn't expecting a quick response, and I closed my laptop and began readying myself for the weekend's debauchery. This usually included dressing up, going out, attempting to force my friends to places my situationship may be, settling for our usual places, getting drunk, and flirting my way through a disastrous amount of also-drunk men.

Because Thomas and I lived walking distance to downtown, we were ground zero for the night's beginning—and sometimes end. Once again, I found myself lingering in my closet, deciding on the perfect combination of jeans, tank top, and heels, knowing that they would ultimately be discarded on the floor, regardless of whether I had a sexual encounter, as my nightly routine of getting naked was not contingent upon having a suitor.

I am not tall and definitely not considered thin, especially in this day and age. When you're not retired because you never made a thing of it, gymnast, certain stocky features remain intact, causing people to sling insults about how fat you are. In addition, my decision to give up the sport after high school resulted in a persistently disappointing delayed puberty and a smaller chest. I grew up in the Pamela Anderson era, so while having a butt that filled out everything gave me an enviously curvy shape, all I desired were boobs that filled more than one hand. So each night I would push up, and together, those girls in every Victoria's Secret bra I could buy. Another quality that firmly placed me in the cute-versus-hot-girl category, and would ensure that I would be IDed well into my forties, was my heart-shaped face. If I didn't follow a strict diet, my soft face would lose its cheekbones and chin. Strikes two and three against the blonde-haired, blue-eyed beauty standard that Hugh Hefner and his girlfriends set. I had wide green eyes and long brown hair, which I almost defiantly dyed jet black.

Chapter 2: Typical Night Out

So now here we are, walking in the frosty night air after I was once again vetoed on a night that would start at my ex's regular hangout. Heading into the first stop of the night, we entered a dark, compact, longer-than-it-was-wide bar called The Narrow Room, where we all greeted the bartender we affectionately referred to as Narrow Garth and grabbed our first round of drinks before squeezing into the only available table that only appeared clean because of its dark lacquer and the dim lighting.

"Are you upset we didn't stage a run-in with Zach?" Heidi leaned into me, laughing.

"I wasn't staging a run-in; I like that place," I object defiantly. She looked at me as if to say, now we're going to start lying to each other. "What?" I assert again.

"Look," she began, "all I'm saying is that guy is a fucking asshole, and you shouldn't fixate on that fucking asshole when there are plenty of dudes right here who want to put their penis in you."

I scoff. "What makes you think I want any of these dudes to stick their penis in me?"

Thomas leans in, his voice loud enough that I'm sure the entire bar can hear. "Because you are always looking for some dude to stick their penis in you. Besides Heidi here, who will let that boring bird-chested man of hers do it to her later. We are all just trying to find a penis that wants to stick itself inside of us."

Alice, scanning the seat she was about to take, wiping away at not-so-imaginary germs, remarks, "I'm not looking for a penis."

Thomas bellows to the bar, "we are all just looking for penis!"

"Thomas!" Heidi screeches. "Brian is coming back from the bathroom. Could you please not get me in trouble by screaming that in my presence?"

"Remind me again why we all pretend to like your boyfriend. Including you?" Thomas questions with a look of utter disdain.

As Brian sat beside Heidi, we all fell silent and smiled at him. If he felt the tense awkwardness, he didn't respond to it. Alice grabbed us another round from the bar while Heidi and I made our way onto the dance floor. With our bodies slowing making their descent into the delightful haze of alcohol-induced buzzing, we ground on each other, scraping up each other's bodies and then skimming our hands over one another, giving the sense that we were either: 1) very into each other or, 2) putting on a show that would entice male onlookers. Like clockwork, Brian would seek out Heidi's backside whenever he sensed a surge in male attention, leaving me as the sole viable option in our passionate pair.

"Sarah," came a husky voice from behind me. Turning, I almost locked lips with Jake, who was leaning to whisper into my ear. Laughing, he leaned away from me. "Good to see you; no shows tonight?"

Standing on my tiptoes using his shoulder for balance, I shout into his ear, "Not tonight, but I'll probably catch one tomorrow at the Knit."

"Oh?" he teases, one eyebrow raised.

"Yeah, I hear they're okay, but could use a bassist that actually knows their chords," I tease.

He smiles and wraps his arms around me, his hand finding its place on my backside. "How about a drink?"

"I think I have one at my table."

"Grab it and come say hi?" He gives my butt a small squeeze.

"Sure, give me a sec." I float away, levitating from the attention.

While absentmindedly rummaging through my purse for gum, I yell to my friends at the table, "Jake is here!" "He asked me to come say hi to the band." Retrieving a lone gum with nicotine from my purse, I dust it off, unwrap it, and pop it in my mouth. "Good?" I shout and gesture at myself.

"You look sexy as hell," comments Alice while raising her beer to me.

I smile with gratitude and begin my walk toward Jake and his bandmates. Jake was smoking a cigarette and greeted me with a cheeky grin, holding his arm out wide to let me join the table. Jake is toweringly tall, one of the tallest people I'd ever stood next to, but I made a show of concern that the cigarette would make its way to my hair, so I plucked it from his hands and took a drag while stepping into their circle. They reintroduce themselves and skip the girls who accompany them, predictable; I think. Before leaving, I traded jokes and casual conversation, assuring them that I would definitely attend their show tomorrow.

Upon returning to my friends, Thomas is the first to comment, "you going home with that, or may we continue on?"

Shooting him a sideways glare, I respond, "we can continue on, sir."

"Good, Jessica is at Five Queens, and I am dying to be in a place where someone may want to stick their penis inside me." Heidi shoots him a threatening look, to which he shouts, "I said IN ME, Heidi!"

Heidi turns to Brian, and they whisper back and forth before she announces, "Guys, I think Brian is going to call it a night." We all fake devastation at the loss of our saddest, most boring wheel.

"Are you sure you want to go, Brian? You always get so many compliments at Five Queens," I protest. My responsibility as Heidi's best friend requires me to make Brian feel included and secure, regardless of my own feelings towards him. Besides, there's a reason Heidi has stayed with him all these years, right? Thomas shoots me a cautionary look, signaling me to stop talking and let him leave. Once we had one last round and made a few half-hearted pleas for Brian to stay, we got him into the first cab of the evening and set off for Five Queens, just two blocks away.

Despite the slight buzz, I managed to effortlessly keep up with my taller friends in my too-high, tight heels, but I'll definitely regret it later. Observing our smoke merge with our warm breath, we witness the formation of voluminous white clouds in the cool air. Huddled together once we've reached our destination, IDs displayed in outstretched arms. One by one, we pay our covers, then receive the stamps identifying that we are over 21—a job performed exclusively by the effortlessly funny masculine lesbian staffing the sad-looking carnival-style ticket booth. When the door to Five Queens opens, we are besieged with smoke, humidity, and the loud stereo mix of something with Britney Spears. Jessica is seated at the bar in front of the Five Queens glittery stage, which includes two stripper poles and a "use at your own risk" sign posted in Comic Sans to the side.

As we collide into a hug, Jessica, without relieving my ear from her proximity, shouts, "Lemon drops!?" After slugging them back and making puckered faces, we get our usual drinks. We mingle with the other familiar patrons, smoke more cigarettes, and shout over the music. When "Lollipop" by Lil Wayne starts its familiar intro, I proclaim, "This is my song!" Then I make my way to one of the two chrome poles to use, at my own risk.

Dragging my heels and shimmying my hips, I begin a sultry dance for Heidi, Thomas, Jessica, Alice, and whoever else as they hoot and holler obscenities my way. Dropping into a squat with the pole centered between my open legs, I gradually make my way up, locking eyes with a freakishly tall, muscular blonde walking into Five Queens. Jake... Jake is now nodding at me appreciatively. I maintain eye contact while I gracefully wrap my leg around the pole, gradually maneuvering into a position where I arch my back and press my pelvis against the pole. I perform a deliberate movement, flipping my hair into my face, rolling my body, sticking my butt out, and finishing in a squatted position with my hand still on the pole.

Alice was the first to track my gaze, enticing her to see what was on the other end. She clocks Jake in his predatory approach, then shifts back to the group with a wide-eyed expression, tilting her head in his direction. They take turns surreptitiously looking over their shoulders. As the song ends, I jump down from the pole, head to the table, and take a long drink from my glass. Meanwhile, two bandmates and one of their girlfriends follow Jake, or at least that's what I assume. "Anyone using this?" He points at the primarily empty table in our vicinity. We all shake our heads while they move empty bottles around and scoot chairs in. Disregarding the familiar pull in my jeans center, I introduce my friend group to his, reminding my friends through slightly gritted teeth they are three of the five-piece band we will see tomorrow at the Knit.

Making bands on our page feel important is essential, so having my friends look confused doesn't speak favorably of us. Once they recall or don't, it's hard to tell. They nod and chorally make sounds like "ah," feigning amusement or admiration. I rush us along to prevent the band from noticing how unenthusiastic my friends are. The discussion veered off into unimportant topics like whose hands are bigger. Alice held up her small hand with her fingers outstretched in an attempt to make them longer. While conversations overlap, drinks are refilled, shots are raised, and lust fills the air, Jake edges his chair closer to mine.

"Hey," he whispers against my ear, the sound less perceptible than the tingle it shoots down my spine.

"Yes?"

"Is this it for you, or are you interested in one more stop?"

Our evenings usually ended at Five Queens, and depending on factors like weather or intoxication level, we'd either walk or take a cab back to our town home. However, his deep voice and enormous hands, thanks Alice, captivating my interest. "What were you thinking?"

He recommends a spot close by that has dim lighting, a jukebox, pool tables, and less obnoxious pop music. "We can actually talk." Jake's smile reveals his desire.

"If I take Thomas to a place with pool tables, he'll murder me."

"Five Queens has a pool table," he responds in amusement, shooting a look at the lone pool table.

"Also, gays in each corner," I quickly point out.

"Can we find him a gay to tag along?"

"You really want me to go to this dark, seedy bar, don't you?"

"Yes, more than almost anything."

"Thomas!" I shout across the table. "Are we getting any closer to finding someone who wants to stick their penis in you?"

"In fact," Thomas shouts back, "There's a tall, dark, handsome type over there that I've been exchanging eye contact with all night."

"Great!" shouts Jake, whirling around in his chair, headed for the bar.

Thomas, Heidi, and I exchange confused glances as we watch Jake approach the stranger. "What the hell is he doing?" asks Heidi, mildly amused.

"I have no idea," I offer, still confused by the sudden jerk of his attention from me to the stranger.

"If this works and Dark Handsome returns to our table, I don't care; Jake is a God," Thomas affirms, clasping his hands together in prayer.

Sure enough, after a few glances back and forth amid prominent discussion, Jake was heading back to our table with tall, dark, handsome, and hopefully gay.

"Everyone!" he shouts above the Madonna remix that seems to play louder than the last few songs. "This is Felix; we got to chatting, and it turns out he's been waiting for the only pool table to open up and has yet to get a game in." Heidi, Thomas, and I again exchange glances. "I told him there's a place around the corner from here where he is guaranteed to get a game in with me and my buddies. He's agreed to come with us with the stipulation that Thomas goes." Jake winks at Thomas who stands abruptly. Bottles and empty glasses clink together noisily.

"Is there a reason we're waiting? I've been dying to see this dark, seedy bar all night." Thomas says, waving us all to hurry.

Alice and Jessica, as if rejoining the conversation, put down their drinks and began gathering their belongings off the chairs.

Heidi looks at me almost sadly before finally announcing, "Hey guys, I'm going to head home. Cabs are already outside."

I look at her disappointed, but we both know that this will entangle me with Jake at the next bar, and she is tasked with maintaining her happy relationship. Also, the earlier she heads in tonight, the longer she can stay out tomorrow.

Outside of Five Queens, the crisp night air gently caresses our skin, carrying with it a hint of dewy freshness. Laughter and music from nearby establishments mingle in the background, creating a vibrant symphony of sounds. With bittersweet embraces, we bid Heidi farewell, feeling the warmth of friendship radiating through each hug. Guiding her unsteady steps, we carefully guide the slightly disheveled yet still captivating Heidi into the waiting cab.

Heidi is my anchor, a constant source of support. Thomas and I may be physically closer as we live together, but he allows me to fall apart when left alone. In contrast, Heidi always pulls me away from self-destruction and heartbreak. It's bittersweet to watch her leave, as I am pleasantly intoxicated. If I were to go home now, I could replenish myself with sleep, water, and nourishment for the upcoming night. A night dedicated to the darkness of the Knit to watch four bands clang together, their instruments mostly pleasantly. Despite the allure of going home, I cannot resist the temptation of Jake and stay.

Jake interrupts my thoughts and the loss of Heidi. Hooking his arm around my shoulders; anywhere else would be comical, given our height difference. He leads me while shepherding the rest to Tipsys. Jake was right; Tipsys is much quieter than Five Queens, darker, and smells more like cigarettes and stale beer than the mix of vanilla, axe, and cotton candy at Five Queens. The floors are a mix of green carpet and speckled linoleum with the only light coming from the ones hanging over the pool tables advertising various domestic beers and the three yellow gold hanging lamps above the bar. In short, it's not a gay bar and not a club, either. People at Tipsys are coming to sit, play billiard games, and drink beer or various whiskey varieties with Coke.

We find a couple of high tops stationed near one of the three pool tables. My shoes struggle to not stick to the floor in an area as we pass, and I force myself not to think about it. Felix and Jake announce they're teaming up to take on his bandmate, Kyle and Alice, whom Jessica volunteered to play if only to ensure they would not cast her as pool player number four.

"Drink?" Jake asks, placing his hand on the small of my back.

"Raspberry press," I respond.

With a smile dripping honey, Thomas requests a Jack and coke, and I give him a suspicious look. He NEVER likes the guys I bring home.

"Anyone else?" Jake announced loudly to the remaining group, who settled on another Jack and Coke for Felix and a pitcher of beer for the rest of them.

I flash a smile and raise an eyebrow as I sit across from Thomas. "Your anticipation of seeing this place was uncontrollable, wasn't it?" My words dripping with sarcasm.

"Please, you're here for one tall blonde reason. I don't want to hear it."

"You're here for a handsome black man who clearly has a thing for the bar game you find most atrocious. Where do you think that will lead—long term?"

"Long term?" Laughter escapes from him. "The longest term I see is Felix joining our cab back home. Then we will go at it for about an hour before I wake up tomorrow and he is gone. That's about as long term as I am willing to go."

I roll my eyes and look toward Jake, who has clearly become the drunk fantasy of a small group of scantily clad girls vying for his undivided attention. For a moment, I feel the pangs of jealousy, the need to stomp over and claim my territory. The impracticality of the move is clear in the many reasons that stop me. This marks my third time being in Jake's presence. While there's undoubtedly enough attraction and flirtation to go around, there's been no talk of anything between us, no exchanged messages, no date nights. This is the first time we've hung out without the website's two-person crew of producers formally filming for Rock Out Local. The reality is, I feel this way because despite my confident facade of being single, I sincerely enjoy the feeling of belonging to someone. I am the queen of pretending to be the cool girl. Well, most of the time, anyway.

Jake returns to the table in several trips, dropping off everyone's drink order. When he slides mine to my front, he bends just enough to be eye level with me at the tall table and winks. I smile a little, confused, and wonder if he just drugged me. Shrugging away the thought, I remind myself there would be no reason to work this hard to drug me. Besides, I've been around him enough that I don't get the drugging girl's vibe; I mean, look at him. He's a statue that belongs in a museum. But why wink? What am I not in on? I search around our groups to determine if anyone is glancing at me as if to answer the looming question of what I am missing. I see the group of girls Jake was talking to, and they are looking over, but nothing out of the ordinary; there aren't many people in the bar, so because Jake, Felix, his two bandmates, and Thomas are all attractive, they may consider how they could score one of them for the night. They are oblivious to the fact that two of them are gay, one is practically married, and Jake's status is uncertain, although they should assume he's with me. The only thing that makes Tyler attractive is his skill behind a drum set. He is definitely single, but as of now, Alice continuously bombards him with deafening screeches whenever they make a decent play at the table. So is off-limits.

I lower my gaze to drink and notice writing on the napkin. **Kiss me** it says. Nothing else. I flip it over back and forth, and still nothing explains the note. Kiss me? I ponder and resume scanning the room. Kiss who? I think. Is this a joke? Did someone slide this over to me by accident? I give Thomas a nudge, shaking the napkin towards him from across the table. I receive a rude glare from him for daring to interrupt his conversation with Felix. Taking a closer look at the napkin, he and Felix examine it. Then Thomas, just like me, begins to scan the room.

"He wants you to save him from the bimbo," Felix provides.
"Who?"
"Jack."
"Jake?" I correct questioningly.
"Oh, is that it? Whoops, I've been calling him Jack."
"What do you mean, save him?" I ask.
"That blonde over there," he gestures with his pool cue, "apparently he met her at a show or something, and now she basically follows him everywhere."

I silently feel sorry for her. Understanding the longing for someone's attention and wanting them to feel the same way.

Thomas loudly urges me to kiss him while Felix watches eagerly, encouraging me with an excited expression. Blinking rapidly, I look over at Jake, who is analyzing the pool table for his best move, while Alice and Tyler smoke a cigarette, appearing to disregard his consent.

"Sarah!" Thomas interjects into my thoughts. "Why are we here if you weren't remotely interested in seeing him naked and on top of you?"

"Hell, I'm interested," affirms Felix as Thomas shakes his head in agreement.

With a chuff, I spun on my stool and landed on the ground, my eyes cast downward. When I look up, I see Jake holding out his pool cue in conversation with his married bandmate, apparently waiting for Felix to take his turn. I slide between him and the pool table, hearing his married bandmate's conversation cut short at the site of me leaning back against the table, staring upwardly at Jake. His surprise shows for a mere moment as he understands the intent of my sudden attention and leans down, wrapping his free arm around me, pulling my body into his before landing his lips on top of my own. As he presses his lips against mine, he holds his breath and draws me nearer. Pushing my lips apart, his tongue brings the flavor of stale beer into my mouth, along with his. While we keep kissing, the sounds of the bar gradually return to my ears. Jake pleasantly surprises me with his politeness, pulling back and grinning before his gravelly voice murmurs, "thanks."

"Alright, darlings," I hear Felix break in. "I have a game to win, and you are all blocking my shot."

With bashful laughter, we both step away from the table, and I resume my place on the stool where Jessica and Thomas are engaging in a conversation about the movies they have seen lately and Jessica's plan to stay at our place. This leads to a further discussion about Felix coming to the townhouse tonight. The night proceeds as usual: a couple more shots, Jessica, Alice, and I taking over the bar's jukebox and roaring with laughter at whatever ridiculous conversations pass between us. Jake's bandmate and his girlfriend leave telling no one, which is normal, says Jake. Tyler's intoxication prevents him from steadying himself and continuing to play pool. Glancing at my phone, I realize it's 2:30 AM, later than I thought we'd stay out tonight. Alice and Tyler agree to split a cab, and the rest of us walk to our townhouse.

Amidst laughter and cigarette breaks, we finally shed our jackets upon entering our two-story townhouse. Jessica secures her place on the couch as Felix and Thomas go upstairs to his room. This left Jake and me awkwardly standing by the front door, the tension growing with each passing second. "Do you want some water?" I muster.

"Yeah," he answers, "that would be great. Some gum, too, if you have it. I hate the way my mouth tastes after cigarettes and beer."

"There's a fresh pack upstairs in my room. If you head up, I'm on the left. Thomas' door will probably be closed, but I wouldn't want you to walk in on that." I quip.

Jake agrees, "Good call," then inquires, "Mind if I head up without you?"

"No," I respond, "there is not much up there, and I doubt you're in the market to steal my shoes." I let out an awkward laugh, and he responded with a polite smile.

While I finish filling glasses of water, I place one on the table in front of Jessica. She's clicking through the TV channels we've swiped from our neighbor's cable while I sneak a quick look at myself in the downstairs bathroom mirror. When I glimpse at my reflection, I realize my hair is flatter and my makeup is a bit smudged, yet I don't look as drunk as I truly feel. I seize this opportunity to clean up eyeliner smudges using wet toilet paper. Additionally, I spray body spray in the air, walk through it, and apply some to my underwear.

When I finally make it to my room, balancing the cups of water, I catch Jake's curious gaze on my wall adorned with posters, causing my cheeks to flush. Walking into my bedroom, the first thing you notice is the low-lying bed on its box spring, accompanied by a vintage blush pink velvet recliner and a standing chain lamp from the 70s. I adorned my walls with cutouts of rock bands from the last six decades, giving the room a nostalgic atmosphere. I couldn't help but feel a wave of embarrassment, like I had been transported back to 1982 as a teenage boy.

"My Dad." I provide as if answering a question.

"Your Dad?" Jake responds, his confusion clear.

"My Dad is the reason I love rock music so much. Well, all music, actually. I remember being little, and he had these enormous suitcases that were made to carry cassette tapes, and we would listen to them all in our garage. He told me stories about where he was when he listened to certain ones or girls he was dating; it was like sharing my dad's history through music." I pause. "Anyway," my words catch in my throat as I struggle to overcome the embarrassment. "He's the reason I plastered my walls with all these poorly kept magazine cutouts."

"I see," he says, nodding and removing the full cup of water from my hand. Then changing the subject displays my gum pack in offering. "Found the gum,"

"Thanks," I reply casually. I dislike the taste of cigarettes and alcohol in my mouth at the end of the night, too.

When I tug the chain on my standing lamp, my nerves start to tremble. With a deep breath, I mustered the courage to walk back and turn off the bright 100-watt bulb in the center of my ceiling. Next, I carefully close the door to my bedroom. Jake places his water on my nightstand, the sound of glass against wood shattering the quietness.

Although his face is mostly obscured by shadows, I catch a glimmer of curiosity and amusement as he observes the performance he eagerly expected. I place my water next to his, feeling a sense of anticipation building inside me. As I turn to face him, I can sense his presence, and I take slow, deliberate steps until I am perfectly centered between his legs. With a hand on either side of my hips, he meets my gaze, our eyes aligned because of my height. I gently hook one bent leg over his and align my knee with his hip, repeating the action with the other leg until I find myself comfortably seated on his lap, my arms wrapped around his neck. I don't make a sound as I remove both arms and drag my shirt over my head. Jake sighs and plants his lips along my collarbone, descending to my chest.

As I lean my head back, I feel his lap beneath me, and I begin to move my hips in a slow, sensual motion. Jake releases my hips, and I catch a glimpse of his toned torso as he takes off his shirt, then he digs into his pocket. Once he's retrieved his prize, he holds up a single condom, its wrapper crinkling in his hand, before placing it on my nightstand. As we kiss again, our lips move with familiarity, while I sway gently in his lap, sensing his desire rising beneath me. He slowly pulls and lowers my bra straps, kissing the skin where they used to lie, then reaches behind me and unclasps it all together. My bra falls between us, and he shifts his weight to one side, allowing him to wrap his arm around me in one motion, flips me to my bed.

Exposed and on my back, and a wave of self-consciousness washes over me. My breasts flatten against me and don't look their best in this position, but I remain patient as he struggles to remove his jeans and boxers. Beside my bed, Jake stands confidently, his naked form captivating and breathtaking. In that moment, heat and a familiar tug reach my center, and I unbutton and shimmy free from my jeans and heels, carefully shucking them to the floor to meet my shirt and bra—there's the inevitable pile of clothes, I think to myself.

Jake sheaths himself before lowering over me on my too-low bed. Opening my legs wider, I make space for his body, and he wets his fingers with his tongue before sliding them inside me. Then I feel his firm grip on my legs, spreading them wider as he positions himself and enters me. A barely audible moan escapes me, prompting him to increase the pace of his movements, revealing his familiarity with this act. I roll up my hips into him and grip his shoulder blades, pressing my fingers hard into him, and his rhythm and breathing increase. As I tilt my head back and stretch my arms overhead, his teeth sink into my neck, causing me to cry out in abrupt agony. He confuses this sound as my reaction to intense pleasure. His passion grows stronger, making me seem invisible, and my orgasm fades into oblivion. With every motion, I mimic his rhythm, creating the illusion that I am on the brink of orgasm, all to expedite his release.

"Fuck me." I utter into his ear, and it seems that's all it takes for him to finish. He moves away from me, wrapping the condom in a tissue and disposing of it in the trash can next to my recliner. I bolt out of bed, throw on my robe, and eagerly head to the bathroom. The grunts and the shifting of furniture from Thomas' room reach my ears, hinting that his night will be livelier than mine. I close myself in the bathroom, the cold tiles under my feet providing a sharp contrast to the warmth of the room, and clean myself. "Oh god," I proclaim, taking the chance to splash cold water on my face and hastily tie my hair into a messy bun before leaving.

Upon returning to my dimly lit room, I find Jake already settled on my side of the bed, softly snoring. I study him for a moment and can't help but admire his handsome appearance. His pale blonde hair, which has a slight wave to it, enhances the surfer vibe. The scattered tattoos of ships and women on anchors on his muscular arms, along with the faint stubble on his cheeks, contributed to his intriguing presence. Was he the one in the Navy? Reflecting internally, I contemplate. Perhaps that was another one of them, or it could have been both. Unable to fall asleep, I end up tossing and turning and ultimately decide to go downstairs for a cigarette.

Jessica is nowhere to be found on the couch where I left her; instead, I spot her outside engaged in conversation, a Marlboro red between her fingers. As I grab a cigarette from a spare pack lying in the kitchen, I step outside and notice Felix occupying the second chair on our porch. The sky's deep hue serves as a reminder that dawn is near, and a sense of impending regret washes over me. With caution, I descend the step, ensuring my robe remains securely fastened to maintain any modesty. With a flick of my lighter, the flame illuminates the tip of my cigarette, adding a flicker of warmth to the chilly air. Felix and Jessica are both staring at me, and through one eye, I manage, "Can I help you two?"

Jessica's shrug is met with a deep breath from Felix, his lungs expanding with anticipation. "Is he a god?"

"Jake?" I inquire, already aware of the answer, but buying myself a moment to think before formulating a courteous reply.

"Oh, bummer," Felix answers without waiting for my response. "You know, it's always the ones built like Greek sex heroes that are disappointing."

"He wasn't disappointing," I offer tentatively. "He's just a straight, very attractive male in a band, unable to divert his focus from his own wants." Once I finish, I half remember that it is Felix sitting here, not Thomas, and I am momentarily frozen by my honesty.

"That's gay men, too, honey," Felix answers in a matter-of-fact tone while slowly taking a drag from his cigarette.

We fall into more casual conversation, and I learn Felix has just moved here from Seattle to finish grad school at the University of Nevada (UNR); he's hoping to become a nurse practitioner and works as a bartender on weekends at the Knit, as well as other odd jobs during the week. Being a regular at the Knit, I didn't recognize him because he was new. Felix tells Jessica and me that he'll be slinging our drinks tomorrow and promises to get us some deals, but I inform him that it's not required.

My pounding head and unsatisfied body tell me it's time to sleep to survive tomorrow's 8-hour endeavor. I let them be and make my way back upstairs, the stairs creaking beneath me. As I lay on the wrong side of my bed, I was delighted to find sleep embracing me effortlessly. I am once again comforted by the weight of someone sharing my bed.

Chapter 3: Ghost of a Girlfriend

After a long night out, I can never get the recommended 7-8 hours of sleep. Blinded by the harshness of the sun, I wake up to find Jake occupying my recliner. Jeans on, no shirt. He's quite the spectacle to admire.

"Good morning," he says with a smile that leads me to believe that of the two of us, I had a lot to drink, and he did not.

"Morning?" I question, my voice thick with too many cigarettes.

"Yeah, it's only 10 o'clock; I rarely sleep in, even if I've been out late."

"Me either." I grumble and shuffle out of the blankets. I dimly realized I was thoughtful enough to wear an oversized t-shirt, avoiding the need to greet the morning after naked in the harsh light.

"Your friends are downstairs making quiche and drinking mimosas. I wasn't sure if you were a hair of the dog kind of girl, so I didn't steal you one. Do you want me to?"

"That's ok," I respond, "I probably shouldn't, considering I have another long night ahead of me tonight."

"About that," he mumbles regretfully. "I know you and all your friends will be out tonight, but I was wondering if we could keep this under wraps." He circles the air between us.

"Sure," I say, hoping the subtle pulse I feel behind my eyes doesn't evolve.

"The thing is," Jake goes on, "I sort of have someone coming tonight." He pauses and takes a deep breath before going on, "my — my girlfriend will be in town; she goes to school in Florida and will be here for this show because she's on break and this show was important to me."

He keeps explaining, but his voice becomes faint, and my memory of our interview rushes at me like a volley of cannonballs: Navy, he and Kelley, the other bandmate from last night, five years, honorably discharged, Florida hometown, girlfriend since high school, moved to Reno for work and started the band, the girlfriend would come after college. Immediately, the urge to vomit overwhelms me, a desperate attempt to break free from this conversation. He must have noticed the pained expression on my face, prompting him to move closer, his weight sinking into the edge of my bed. Engaging in one-night stands is one thing, but getting involved with a guy who already has a girlfriend? "This is unbearable," I mutter under my breath, the pulsing sensation in my head becoming more pronounced. Placing my fingers into my temples, I stammer, "Jake — ha — how many girls will be there tonight keeping this very same secret?" His face twists into a grimace, and I can't help but laugh, shaking my head in amusement. "I think you should probably go," I say, propping myself up to my elbows. He gives me one last glance before grabbing his remaining things and leaving, the door softly closing behind him. Before heading downstairs, I make a quick pit stop at the bathroom to relieve my bursting bladder and refresh myself with a splash of water on my face.

"Mimosa?" Jessica proposes as I enter the small kitchen.

"Please," I reply, taking it and then downing it like a glass of water.

"Jake just left before I could formally declare him a God." Thomas says, pointing his head to our patio containing one Felix talking on his cell phone.

"Yeah, well, I might keep that comment hidden away for a lifetime." I convey grimly. Pulling another cigarette from the pack on the counter, I continue. "Jake's long-time girlfriend will join us for the show tonight." I pause, then finish sarcastically. "We wouldn't want her getting any sordid ideas about her precious boyfriend."

Jessica and Thomas turned to me, their faces a canvas of shock. I give them a closed lipped smile, hinting that I'd rather not delve deeper into the topic, and accept the outstretched quiche from Jessica with my free hand, away from the cigarette.

Settled now at our kitchen table, which takes up so much of the kitchen, we have to strategically arrange some chairs before others so that we all fit. The simple conversation between us dances in the air as we recount the evening's depravity with animated gestures. Whether it's the lingering alcohol in my system or the sheer comfort of this present moment, I felt an overwhelming urge to take a nap. I express my gratitude to Thomas for breakfast, while Jessica playfully feigns horror, insisting she prepared the meal. Felix gives me a brief kiss on the cheek and says he'll see me tonight.

As I head into my room, closing the door behind me, I stare at my bed as the memory of Jake fills my senses. Except this time, instead of sending the heat to my center, it sends a wave of nausea over me. I shake it away, open my window for the breeze, but carefully shut my curtains to lessen the brightness from the fall morning outside. I let my finger trace over my stand of DVDs and choose a familiar rom-com to throw in the player while I coax myself back into my sheets for what will hopefully be a long nap to prepare me for the evening. As I settle in, I grab my laptop from its usual space between the wall and my bed and place it on my lap. I opened it to my Myspace account when I saw I had an unread message.

Sarah!!!!!!! This is so cool. I seen your stuff on YouTube and wondered if I would ever be deemed worthy. Hahaha! We would love to have you meet us and listen to our set! I know it's short notice, but we're actually playing at the Knit tonight because a band had to drop at the last minute. If you're interested, I'll leave a few tickets at will call.

I read it two, three, five times before working through a response that doesn't come as quickly, thanks to the looming hangover.

Parker! Glad to hear you are so enthusiastic about our little gig. LOL, I'd love a few tickets at will call and will certainly be there tonight. Can't wait to see your show.

Send.

I linger on the message and scroll over his profile before shutting my laptop and checking my phone.

BITCH! Flashes in a text message, and I notice I missed a few messages from Heidi.

You will not believe all the shit I am going to tell you; too tired now and need sleep for tonight. See you in a few. <3

Her response comes quickly.

Ugh fine. Less than 3 you too.

I laugh and plug my phone in before turning over and hugging my cold satin pillow to my hot face. "Ew," I remark aloud in disgust. It smells like Jake, and that's enough to make the quiche turn sour in my stomach. I toss that pillow on the ground as if it has personally offended me and grab another one, inspecting it for smells of old spice, aftershave, and beer. Nothing. I close my eyes.

Chapter 4: Small Bands and Big Burgers

Making our way along the dingy alley, its unkempt appearance reflecting its uninviting nature, we eventually reach the entrance of the Knit. Next to it, the back entrance of Big Burger Guys stands, the probable next destination for our group. Big Burger Guys is our favorite end of "the Knit night," usually for burgers and fries to soak up whatever the "locals" special is that evening.

After confirming I have four tickets at will call from Parker, plus the ones set aside for Rock Out Local, we conclude no one will have to pay to get in, so we skip the wait in a line that wraps around the outside of the alley. There are four bands, I think; the opener is at 7 PM, and we're here right at 6 PM so I can head backstage and meet with some bands before they go on. Will and Roger are already inside, acting as the two-person light and camera crew for Rock Out Local. Will never stays for shows, and Roger only remains as long as Will does. So, as soon as the lights dim and the music plays, I'm free to hang with my friends. I vaguely recall Jake asking me to wear a skirt to his show last night when we were at Tipsys, and because of this, I am wearing jeans. I will in no way act as if I remember anything about him. Asshole. Another, in the lengthy list of assholes I have been keeping for years.

This reminds me that the chances of a run-in with Zach, situationship, are basically less than negative because we will remain inside the Knit for the evening, which he has and will never enter. He hates crowds; in fact, it occurs to me in this very moment as I stand at the will-call counter that other than all the things I pretended to be; we had nothing in common. Like tofu, I was just trying to absorb all his flavor in order to gain his liking. Upon ending my long-term relationship, I quickly rebounded into him with such speed that a part of me recognized my desperation for someone to love me, to love me in a way I deserved. Squeezing my eyes closed I let the thought pass. Desperate... what a terrible thing to be.

"Name?"

I blink frantically as if completely forgetting where I am. "Huh?"

"Do you have a name for will call?"

"OH, uh yeah, Sarah. I should have four from the band Reverberation Breakdown and one from Rock Out Loud."

"You're Sarah?"

"The one and only," I respond brightly, immediately wondering why I referred to myself as the one and only. He looks at me unimpressed and passes me the five tickets, plus a lanyard, allowing me to get backstage with Rock Out Local. With an hour remaining before the show, the venue is mostly vacant. The line to get in the doors contains most of the patrons, who have only just now started being allowed in. Thomas spots Felix immediately. He hooks his arms through Jessica and Alice's and makes his way to the bar. Heidi follows them and turns to blow me a kiss as I look for Will and Roger. We tend to hang out in the same areas where we go, so I know I'll find them later, even through the crowds. I head to the small, roped section for VIP guests, which usually includes band wives, girlfriends, or family members and spot Will and Roger. Roger waves at me like an eager toddler and I smile as I head in for a hug.

"You look great! As always," he proclaims, holding my arms to my sides to examine the jeans, tank, and heel ensemble that could be a copy-paste of last night's outfit.

"Thanks," I glean, appreciating the compliment. "Are we ready to head in?"

"We're all set; just waiting on the big guy over there to let us in," Will says, hooking a thumb at the sizeable bald man in front of the door.

I fuss with the microphone in my shirt, and the one I'll hold so we can get the best sound quality from the interview, and I do a couple of test phrases in each while Roger listens on his headphones. He gives me a thumbs up while Will collects the one mobile light we'll take with us, as well as the extensive professional camera. Many other people do these things on smaller devices and even phones, but these two like to class it up with good equipment. The concert hall, hosting mainly alternative bands, lacks visual appeal. It resembles a movie theater with its black walls and sleek, easy-to-clean floors. Standing out are two grand red velvet curtains that remain perpetually open. The abundance of lights overhead gives the impression that this place serves as both a regular establishment and a seedy warehouse. No one is looking at the decor, of course. We're all here for the bands.

"Rock Out Loud?" The bald man shouts near the door, and we make our way backstage. We pass through the hall of doors until we get to the show headliner, and out of the corner of my eye, I see Jake and his band. I roll my eyes to myself as we're let into their room. The band is called Trapdoors, and they've been slowly increasing in popularity, but not so popular that we are unqualified to interview them for their first show in Reno. Like our local bands, they started in their hometown of Tacoma, Washington, and have slowly made their way down the coast, landing a headlining gig here at the Knit. They will play with another band that hails from Sacramento, California, and then our two local Reno bands, Squalor (Jake's band) and Reverberation Breakdown (Parker's band). As I ask the questions that people love to hear, I can't help but plaster on my most amused and shimmery smile. "Who inspires you?" I inquire.

We wrap up, and all exchange handshakes before we do our signature photo of me with the band in a pose of their choosing. Some bands get creative, and we do something fun, while others stand beside me awkwardly. Trapdoor has enlisted their tallest bandmate to hoist me on his shoulders while the rest stand around him and pretend like I'm going to fall off. The proof capture on Rogers's small screen is hilarious, and I can't wait to put it on the site.

"Sarah, right?" a voice calls from behind me as we head out the doors.

"Yeah?" Turning into the face of lead guitarist Jayson with a 'y.'

"Are you staying for the entire show?"

"I wouldn't miss it; what would I write about y'all if I didn't stay?"

He smiles and turns back to his room. In no mood to track down Jayson with a y to understand the intent of his outreach, I keep in step with Will, who couldn't be in more of a hurry to get out of there. Once we returned to the small, roped VIP section, Will and Roger promptly packed up and took their leave. The first band is already testing their sound and preparing to play on stage. I find my friends standing at a stable nearest the stage but far enough away from where people will probably dance and mosh as the night gets underway. Heidi eyes me first and waves me over while the rest turn and see me coming. I informed them of the interview and its insignificance overall but remember to point out that they chose a fun pose that garnered the band additional cool points. They all nod in agreement, and I ask if anyone needs to head to the bar. Thomas offers to join me only to have more face time with Felix, and we approach his section. The locals special Felix shouts at me is a can of Pabst Blue Ribbon and a shot of Jägermeister. I make a face that communicates absolutely not and instead shout, "raspberry press." Felix shrugs and Thomas orders the special, which gets him a wink.

Returning with my assumed boring choice, he gives me a signal that says it's on him. So I pass him my 5-dollar bill as a tip. He blows me a kiss and sticks it in his pocket. Their conversation is muffled by the band that has just started playing, leaving me unable to make out any words. Thomas nudges me, urging me to go back to our table, but I can't help but pause for a moment to listen to the singer's soulful voice as he delivers his lyrics with heartfelt passion. A slightly high-pitched voice accompanied his unpolished performance, possibly because of nerves, yet there was an undeniable charm hidden within. Once we get to the table, I look at the stage and watch a small crowd form around it. People are swaying and pumping their fists to the music. By the time the second song starts, the singer has settled into his rhythm, and though not a seamless match, he's sounding more suited to the songs. Amidst our typical banter, Heidi yells across the table, inquiring "What happened with Jake?"

"A huge mistake." I respond, "he has a girlfriend floating around here tonight for his big show." I mimic quotation marks with my fingers as I speak.

"Seriously??" Alice shouts.

"Yep." I insist, popping the p sound.

"Wow," Heidi states exaggerating the word and dragging it out over several seconds, "Another asshole for the list!"

"I'm a collector," I sneer, not entirely joking while raising my drink.

Seeing Heidi's mock sad face, I tactfully redirect the conversation to focus on Thomas' evening with Felix. Exclaiming, "Oh, I heard something going on!"

Amidst our shouted conversation, Alice, Jessica, and Heidi closed in on Thomas, their eyes filled with curiosity as they demand to know every detail of his night with our new favorite bartender. I notice the music slows, and the guitar emits a beautiful melody that resonates with my soul, transporting me to a different world. I turn and face the stage and realize that I'm looking straight at Parker with his band Reverberation Breakdown all blurred around him. Immediately I'm entranced, swaying to the melancholy tune, and taking in the man whose voice is singing the spell I'm currently under. Parker's voice melds seamlessly with the melodic ballad, transporting me to this very moment, where I hear the music, sense the speakers' vibrations, and witness his guitar strumming and vocals flowing into the microphone. His eyes switch from closed to searching the crowd and back to closed again; his shirt pulls tight against his chest, and the veins in his neck strain as he continues to belt out the lyrics. He is good-looking, yes, but watching him right now, at this moment, makes him something else entirely, something beyond good-looking, something more profound. As the song wraps, I notice I haven't moved, except for the gentle swaying I've been doing during the song.

"Helllooooo," Heidi remarks, her fingers snapping in front of my face, bringing me out of the trance induced by the mesmerizing three-plus minute song. "I have to pee! You coming?" She shouts and I nod, peering over at the stage as they ramp up for another upbeat song, starting with a loud drum solo.

We head to the upstairs bathroom as those stalls are notoriously less dirty because it is the 21 and up section of the two-story establishment, but the sound of the music is better on the bottom, which is why we usually hang there for shows. Still recovering from the spell, Heidi guides me into the also dark-colored bathroom, where we both take an open stall and empty our bladders. We exit almost simultaneously and wash our hands. As I hold my hands under the dryer, the sound of heels clacking grows closer, leading me to assume it's Heidi. Remembering we're wearing matching converse, I whirl around and am startled by the upbeat platinum blonde standing before me. Dressed in a leather top that accentuates her ample chest and showcases her toned mid-section, she pairs it with a coordinating leather skirt. For a refined twist, she opts for boots that incorporate elements of combat boot design. My first thought: what was that 90s movie starring Pamela Anderson in all the leather?

"Hey," she drawls with an accent I can't quite make out.

"Hey?" I murmur unable to decipher if I should know who she is as Heidi approaches from behind the leather wearing blonde.

"You're that girl from the website, right? Jake sent me something, and I remember your face." Her eyes leave mine briefly when Heidi takes her place by my side.

"I am," I respond curtly, not bothering to hide my disinterest. Two thoughts collide in my brain. The movie was called Barb Wire, and this is Jake's girlfriend.

"I think it's so cool you do that for the bands, you know? They deserve recognition and I think it's really cool for them."

"Yeah," I reply, my head bobbing up and down robotically.

"Are you staying the whole show?"

"I am," I answer, my voice pitching oddly, so I clear my throat and offer more detail. "I have to do a piece on the headliner, so I'll be here for the night."

"Oh, you poor thing, listening to this music all night long has to get old. I mean, I love that Jake has something he's passionate about, but I am hoping he grows out of it, eventually; I'm not sure I can listen to rock music forever, you know. I mean, we're going to have a baby soon." Instinctively, my eyes dart to her stomach. "Oh, I'm not pregnant right now, but when I came in today for the show, Jake said he wanted us to get more serious about planning for the future: marriage, kids, you know, all that."

Heidi, who has fully caught up to the train wreck of this conversation, nudges me to end this conversation by any means necessary.

"That — That is great." I manage, "I hope everything works out. Nice meeting you —"

"Kaylee," she inserts.

"Kaylee," I repeat, "Heidi and I need to head back downstairs."

Heidi and I whirl around and head toward the exit while she hooks her arm through mine. "Well, that was fucking awkward." She declares, loudly.

"No kidding," I snicker as we turn abruptly to head down the stairs, feeling the familiar nausea from last night creeping in. I shake the memories and take a deep breath. "Cigarette?" I propose and Heidi nods.

We make our way to the table and grab the others for our cigarette break, which has to be taken outside in a designated smoking area. Circled together, we all light our cigarettes. Thomas continues to get pressed about Felix, to which all his responses have the same theme of low expectations and nothing long-term. Startled by an unexpected laugh at one of his rants, I stumble backwards, colliding with an unsuspecting person. They quickly catch me, preventing me from hitting the ground.

"Thanks," I express while laughing. "Sorry about that!"

"No problem, Sarah."

I make eye contact with the stranger to find it is Jake, who has his hands steady on my arms, holding me upright. I jerk away as if he is made of wasps, and the unexpected sight of him staring down at me swallows my laugh. Kaylee joins him, and the five of us stare at them silently.

"Sarah," he starts, "this is my girlfriend —"

"Kaylee," I finish, and I see a faint twinge of panic cross his face. "We met earlier in the bathroom."

"Oh," he notes, still searching my face for what I may have said to her.

"Yes," I continue, the words falling out of me a bit maniacal. "She told me how you guys are getting ready to take your relationship to the next level, and I believe mentioned something about not wanting to hear rock music forever since you're going to have to grow up or something." Kaylee's face turns crimson as she looks up at Jake, shaking her head in disagreement. Jake laughs it off, not wanting to have what is likely a revolving argument in his relationship, and hoists her closer to him.

"She is from a big family," he explains cooly, looking at her still-blushed face, "and, of course, wants to get started right away."

"Well," I asseverate louder than I mean to flailing my arms in a wild circle, "I hope all that lasts longer than you do." I swivel immediately to head back inside, no doubt my friends trailing behind me. I make a beeline for the bar and find Felix finishing up with his customer.

"Shot, please," I shout.

"Any preference?" he asks.

"No whiskey and another press, please."

"Liquid courage?"

"Too late for that." I indicate with an eye-roll.

Heidi finds me first with Thomas closely in toe. The second band is already playing, and I am deaf from the ringing in my ears that is only slightly drowned out by the rapid beating of my heart. Thomas fills Felix in on current events. Heidi downs one of the red-colored shots that land before us. I tilt my head back while swallowing the sweet alcohol in one gulp, then spin around and ask Heidi for the time. She tells me it's almost 9 o'clock, and I mentally calculate how long I need to stay here or if I could leave and return after Jake's band plays. Heidi seems to work out what I am doing and offers, "we can go if you want, but I think that would give him too much credit. You barely knew him, and he is obviously a fucking asshole."

"I'm a little embarrassed," I admit.

"About what?" Heidi scoffs. "That little speech out there? Other than it being wildly entertaining, they both needed to know that their relationship wasn't where they thought it was, and frankly, leather Barbie should know that he's slept his way through most of Reno and probably her friends, too."

"I barely knew him!" I screech, the words flying out. "I totally gave off crazy ex-girlfriend when I should've kept my mouth shut."

She places my drink in my hand and gives me a half smile. "Okay," she concedes. "It was a bit crazy ex-girlfriend of you, but I'm sure some of that had to do with the fact that Zach had like a secret relationship the whole time you were together, and you never really got to yell that at him," she pauses and tilts her head finishing, "clearly Jake paid penance for that, an asshole is an asshole whether Jake or Zach shaped." She breaks again as she searches my face for anything that shows what she's telling me is helping.

"It made me look crazy," I suggest, exhausted.

"Eh," she responds, shrugging her shoulders, "Who cares? Let's forget it and have fun!"

With that, she grabbed my drink free hand in hers and led me back to our spot; after a bit, we were having our typical brand of fun while I more or less attempted to forget about the embarrassment of my run-in with Jake and expensive leather Barbie. You see… My brain is simply incapable of letting myself off the hook for anything. I will reel and cross-examine this incident for years to come, undoubtedly. Sometimes, it will present itself at other awkward times, doubling down on the embarrassment trauma in which I will simply invert and lose all sense of speech, movement, and time. This, of course, may be an over-exaggeration of the events and definitely highlights the unnecessary amount of time I spend worrying, but here we are, and this is who I am.

The night continues incident-free mainly, and the remaining bands prove why they are co-headliners in tonight's show by being extraordinary. People crowd the floor as we move upstairs to the over-21 area and watch the sea of people come alive and mosh and sway in time with the amplified electric guitars and drums. It's a reminder that I do, in fact, love this. I love how the hard-edged music swims through my veins and becomes a part of my energy. Only a few things I've experienced in life impact me this way. I see my friends, who are also in and out of swaying and dancing and cheering on the stage below. All things considered; this is one of those nights that will eventually be something I look back on fondly.

We leave just as the last band has returned to the stage for an encore performance and go next door for our "end of The Knit night," shared burgers and fries. The burgers at Big Burger Guys are legendary for their enormous size, leaving us unable to consume them entirely. Also, they pair the burgers with an overflowing basket of salty shoestring fries. Because of their monstrous portions, we order three and have them all split, which is usually perfect. However, because Boring Brian has not joined us tonight, we will give one-half to a drunk patron. Thanks to our decision to leave the show early, our order came quickly. Thomas and I carried all the baskets carefully, winding through the crowds of people gathered in a small casino slash burger joint at our shared table. The five of us take our half burgers, touch them together in a sort of end-of-night cheers, and eat while exchanging conversation about our plans for later today, as it is officially Sunday.

"Sleeping in and getting laundry done before the workweek are my only concerns tomorrow," I announce. Everyone agrees that laundry and sleeping in are also on their to-do lists for the day and agree that it will be nice to have some time to recover with no pressing engagements. We like going out together and hanging out, but the time spent with ourselves is equally important and enjoyable. Thomas and I walk home again. This time our walk home is considerably longer as we were further into the city, so we make idle conversation to pass the time. The night air is delightfully cool, providing a stark contrast to the warm interiors of both the Knit and Big Burger Guys. As we keep in step, we savor the sensation while indulging in our cigarettes.

While staring up at the sky, whose stars are barely visible thanks to the competing neon lights from the city, I inhale deeply and blow all the air out slowly through my mouth. It feels cold going in and causes a slight burn at the back of my nose, making my eyes tear up. I giggle and briefly look down before making eye contact with Thomas, who looks confused, and comment, "tears are odd." He lifts one eyebrow. I continue, "I inhaled air through my nose and it made me cry, no joke."

"That's just your tear ducts being triggered to release tears. It's not crying, don't be so dramatic."

"I'm all about the drama, Thomas. You know that; it's why I have such a stellar track record for relationships."

"But all the nice guys are boring, and you have proven to be a little too mean for that."

"Ughhhhhhh," I say frustratingly. "So I'm destined to be lonely forever???"

"You're not alone; you're just not in a couple, which is also a very different thing, like crying and tearing up."

"What about you? Is Felix the guy who's going to make you settle down and be a one-man, man?" With an awkward tilt of my head, I contemplate if what I said makes sense.

Laughing boisterously, Thomas tilts his head upwards towards the sky. He replies with a matter-of-fact "No."

"Why not?" I ask, and continue "he's smart, funny, good-looking, unavailable on weekends…"

"Sarah, I did not come from a family that would have formed me into the kind of person who could commit to another person long-term. Relationships with my family are so messy that the idea of condemning myself to something like marriage seems not only unreasonable, but like a punishment. They're all cautionary tales, the lot of them."

"That's a little sad," I respond quietly.

"It's only sad if I were unhappy; I am not unhappy. I enjoy the current trajectory of my life and relationships. I wish I had a little more money and a little less fat, but nothing stops me from being happy. That's the problem with most people, they are allowing their expectations of life to dictate their happiness instead of just being happy."

I let the weight of Thomas' words sink in and imagine a stretch of time when I wasn't infatuated with a goal or relationship and allowed myself just to be and enjoy it. None comes to mind, and I'm a little ashamed of myself, so I silently promise myself that I will stop missing the point and enjoy my life. I extend my fist to Thomas in an agreement to seal our happiness discussion with a fist bump and he eyes it speculatively, "I will not be doing that; put it away." I cackle wholeheartedly, and we make our last turn to our row of townhomes overlooking the river. As I first walk up the stairs to my room, I make a mental note to grab all my bedding for tomorrow's laundry mat trip. I do not need the reminder, or smell, of Jake to last any longer on my sheets.

Chapter 5: A Typical Sunday

"RISE AND SHINE BUTTERCUP!" I blurt out in a singsong voice as I open the curtains in Thomas' room.

"Go away, you demented Snow White!" He mumbles, pulling his blanket over his face.

"I thought we could hit our brunch spot before the laundry mat; my treat!"

Thomas groans and removes his blanket from his face, revealing his messy, wavy locks and olive skin. "Since you're buying, I'm in. Can I at least shower?"

"Of course!" I chime, bounding out of his room toward my own.

Our townhouse has a straightforward layout with two bedrooms upstairs, connected by a full bathroom, and a convenient half bathroom downstairs, between the kitchen and the living room. From our patio, nestled beneath Thomas' room, we can hear the soothing sounds of the river flowing nearby. The warmth of the sun fills my room throughout the day, creating a stark contrast to the cool and dark ambiance of Thomas, which only brightens up in the early morning. Our furnishings were a mix of donations from my parents and grandparents or secondhand finds from a thrift store. We certainly make enough money to buy new things, especially with how little rent we pay, but we prefer nice clothes, nights out, and having other people prepare our meals, which is the primary drain on our budget. It's like we emulated Carrie Bradshaw, without living in New York City and having access to high-priced stores like Bergdorf's.

Standing in my usual position in my closet, I decide on a loose, long-sleeved cotton shirt on top of a sports bra with black yoga pants. I put on my bright purple Converse and grab a sweater in case the fall weather takes a cold turn today, as it inevitably will in October. Hearing the shower begin, I noticed I had a little time to waste before we were ready to leave, so I opened my laptop and logged into MySpace. I have three messages: one from Roger reminding me to have my piece written for the site by Thursday, another from Alice telling me how horrible I am for posting our pictures from the last couple of nights, and then I see one from Parker.

I don't remember getting a Thank You for the tickets or a great show or anything, which can only mean two things: we were terrible, in which case please don't tell me so I can remain blissfully unaware, or you are just a rude person. I am going to assume it's the latter.

The message box informs me that Parker is online, so I send him an IM.

Well, I wouldn't want to be the person who damages your ego, so we'll just say I am, in fact, a rude person.

Wait....What do you mean by that?

Parker, you guys were good! I am just a jerk.

Swear it?

Cross my heart.

Curious then, why you didn't introduce yourself?

Honestly??? I was kidnapped immediately after your ballad and just escaped my captor before responding to your message.

Funny.. ok.. well then when can we meet? Do the interview?

I'm pretty free anytime during the week after 5. Today is my get my shit together day, so I prefer not to do any band stuff.

Got it.. How about Wednesday then? We have band practice at 6. I'll give you the address, and you can meet us there?

Sounds good to me; shoot me the address in my messages so I don't lose it.

K, see you then, Sarah.

Closing my laptop, I stand from my recliner and find Thomas in my doorway.

"What was that?" He questions.

"What?" I state, confused.

"Your face, it's all smiley and glowing and a bit nauseating." He indicates tracing a circle in my direction.

"I just —" I stammer, blushing. "I am meeting that Parker guy on Wednesday to get his band prepped for an interview. We were making the plans."

Thomas skeptically nods his head, implying that he's suspicious of my intentions. I brush past him and remind him we only get to go to Benedicts on weekends when we wake up early. Benedicts is a small brunch place around the corner from our townhome that closes at 1 o'clock. They have the best coffee, mimosas, and breakfast foods of any place I've ever been, and because they're tucked away, you can usually get a table if you're a small party. Thomas and I have kept this place to ourselves. This hasn't been a rule so much as it is only ever visited on days when we wake up early, which only happens when no one stays the night.

Inside Benedicts is warm and smells like freshly brewed coffee and syrup and is wall-to-wall wood or brick. Based on its layout, I imagine it was once a home that held a family in the 40s or 50s back when this area was railway workers and farming along the river. The large windows allow the sun to cascade in, casting a soft orange light with a tinge of yellow. The view from the windows, which would have been towards the river, is now obstructed by the apartments built almost specifically to obstruct its view. It has a real working fireplace that is always lit in the colder months, but today, it just provides the surrounding tables with a steady draft of cold air. As luck would have it, and the reason I brought my sweater, they seated us next to the fireplace that doesn't have a fire. Thomas, who comes fully equipped with a personal heating system, appreciates the location and removes a layer before sitting across from me. In contrast, I pull my hoody over me, fixing my hairs loosely knotted top bun before taking my seat.

After drinking our coffee and eating our perfectly cooked meals, we walk back to our townhome to load up our laundry baskets, and I haul a large wad of bedding down our stairs. Thomas decides if we're going to wait for mine, he may as well do his, and after a quick discussion regarding whose car to take, we load the blanket bushels into the back of his car, deciding we don't want to lift them into the back of my tall truck. Laundry goes as usual. We return to the townhome with some Chinese takeout and our now clean bedding and laundry. We sit on the downstairs couch that we both decide needs to be cleaned, but that'll be another day, and we fill our plates with piles of different Chinese dishes. We watched the Food Network on our stolen cable for a few hours before finally deciding to put our beds back together. It's the hour before the world darkens, and we go down by the river for our cigarettes.

A man on the opposite side tosses a floating object into the river for his dog, which is excessively enthusiastic and barking. We can't make out any of his features, but pretend that he is an excellent-looking business executive with a flashy car who is a passionate lover and takes extra care to make sure his beautiful girlfriend or wife always orgasms before he does. He says things like, "Are you close?" "Do you like that?" and she doesn't even have to lie because he's so particular about her each and every need. Continuing our made-up story all the way back to our house, we divided up the remaining Chinese and watched another couple of hours of The Food Network.

"We should cook more," I announce while forking my chow mein into my mouth.

"We're in our 20s," Thomas mumbles with a mouth full of food. "This isn't the time to perfect our cooking skills. This is our time to perfect our finding rich husband skills."

"I thought we didn't believe in marriage."

"As an institution, no, as a lifestyle? Absolutely."

My phone buzzes on the table and I see Heidi's name on the screen.

Tomorrow, the big bosses are coming in for quarterly reviews; wear the blazer and pant combo we picked together. You're definitely getting your bonus, and we both know I always get mine. SF Trip to celebrate? Night <3

I check the time cautiously, afraid it's late; you can never tell when darkness descends around 630 PM. Only 8 PM, I see, plenty of time to prepare before the workday.

Less than 3 you, I return.

Thomas and I clear our plates and head to our respective rooms, where I immediately head to my closet and check on the suit Heidi is telling me to wear. Heidi has been with our company four years longer than I have and is a company favorite, so by proximity, I am too, but I have yet to achieve her goal-crushing habits. While she mentors me personally, which creates some jealousy among the other employees, the fact of the matter is without her, I wouldn't be in line for this bonus at all. It is because of her dedication to me I am even half as successful as she is; she has a knack for leadership, and I am all the better for it. I find the blazer with the pants tucked neatly underneath and observe I've left the tags on, which I remove before I forget. My phone buzzes again, and I assume it's Heidi with more follow-up advice as she's doing her nightly cleansing, cleaning, masking, and whatever she does routinely before bed. I know it's long, and I think it's just a way to have more time away from Brian. It keeps buzzing. It's a call. I think as I head over to its place on my nightstand. Zach is flashing up at me. I take a deep breath and make a split-second decision to hit the ignore button, then regret it immediately. It rings again, Zach. NO, NO, NO, I say to myself, do not answer that call.

"He—Hello," I answer with more hesitation than I like.

"I'm outside," Zach responds, his voice echoing like an alarm in my brain. "Let me in, please."

"Not a chance! Zach, are you kidding me!"

"Look outside your window, please."

Holding the phone to my ear, I look out my window and see him leaning against his car, waving up at me. Shaking my head, I say into my phone. "I have a pretty important day tomorrow, Zach; I cannot do whatever this is right now."

"I know," he says, still looking at me, his lips slightly offbeat with the sound in my ear. "Quarterly reviews, I remember." I hate that he remembers.

"It's probably unlocked," I divulge, watching him walk to and through my front door. I hang up and wait for him to come up the stairs.

"I locked it, I hope that's ok."

"Fine," I squeak.

"Sarah, listen, I need to apologize to you for everything, for being so complicated and so scared of you." He looks at me for something, and I say nothing. I don't even change my face. "The thing is, I don't know how to be with someone who loves me, and I know you love me." I snort at this, and he goes on, "Do you know how gorgeous you look standing here in front of me? You're practically shooting lasers at me, and I can tell you're tense, but you're just so beautiful that I can't remember the rest of my speech." This is the thing about Zach. He is prince freaking charming with the wit of Robert Downey Jr. playing Tony Stark. It's not my fault my legs turn to jelly, and I swoon when he speaks. I'm chromosomally predisposed to like this - it's biological for crying out loud! He approaches me slowly and places a hand on either side of my waist, pulling me into him. He's so close now that if I look up, there will be no stopping me from throwing my arms around him and kissing him until we're inevitably tangled in my bed together — my clean bed, I remind myself. Without looking, I can see his ice-blue eyes surrounded by his dark brown, almost black hair. I can see the stubble on his cheeks lining his square jaw that juts out from his face as if carved from stone. He dips his lips to my ear, and my heartbeat quickens under my shirt.

"Please," he whispers.

I feel yes creeping into my throat then realize I'm not even sure what the question is. "Wait, what?" I mumble while staring at the ground.

"Please let me back in," he replies, using one hand to cover my heart.

At this, my pulse skyrockets, and I'm confident that my underwear and yoga pants have disintegrated from the heat generated between my legs. Instinctively, I squeeze them together, a feeble attempt to stop them from opening on their own accord. I make a conscious effort to remember the tears and the crushing feeling in my heart when I realized he didn't love me, and never would. He is not the person who can love me or anyone else, not at 27 at least, maybe not even at 35, maybe in his 40s. Yes, when Zach hits 40, he will love some girl with everything he couldn't love me with, and by then, I will be long gone.

"I can't," I remark as the familiar feeling of tears forming hits the backs of my eyes. "I can't, Zach. You broke my heart, and you didn't even mean to. You were just being who you are, and I got confused, and it broke my heart." In an effort to remain composed, I pause and take a deep breath, willing myself not to cry. "You also were having a full adult relationship with another person who has a child."

His eyes convey understanding, yet lack remorse. "I'll call you tomorrow. We'll do the proper date thing, ok?" He moves closer to me and cups my face with his hands. "I'll be a proper gentleman, I promise." With a nod from me, he plants a kiss on my forehead and proceeds down the stairs. "Lock the door, please! I need to know you're safe." I move behind him, and he comes to a halt by my door. His words, "Kiss me," instantly trigger the memory of the note from Tipsy's. I lightly peck his mouth and lock the door once he goes away. Upon reaching the top of the stairs, Thomas awaits me.

"I will not pick you up from another Zach fall."

"I don't want to have another Zach fall," I respond tersely.

Although he can sense my tension from the remark, neither of us continues the conversation. We retreat to our opposite sides of the townhome, and I begin the night with restless tossing and turning.

Chapter 6: Straight Girl Lunch

Monday goes precisely as planned. I wore the pantsuit Heidi picked out and received word that I'm excelling beautifully and will receive a full bonus, plus a trip to Chicago in a few months with the other goal-crushing team members across all our states. When I leave the office, Heidi sends me a message indicating when and where we will meet for lunch, and we avoid giggling together until we're seated at our favorite soup and sandwich spot.

"I'm going to Chicago, too!" Heidi exclaims with absolute delight, "The best part is because we will be at the conference, Brian can't come, so it'll be like a free girl's trip. Isn't that great?"

"It's honestly unbelievable; I can't believe we will be together for six full days in Chicago! I can't thank you enough for all you do to help and coach me. I really do love you. Sometimes, even in a gay way."

"Don't do that," she remarks, smiling. "We both know we can't be together because we like penises and wouldn't eat each other out."

I laugh into my sandwich while the mildly conspicuous lesbian couple seated next to us gives Heidi an impolite look. She peers over at them and blurts out, "I don't have a problem with that sort of thing; I just don't want to do it to her." She declares this, waving a forkful of salad in my direction. I shrug uneasily at them, and with that, they seem to reengage in their own conversation. We use the rest of lunch to eat, talk about our upcoming trip to Chicago, and make tentative plans to celebrate our reviews in San Francisco.

The rest of the workday flies by, and I am in an excellent mood from the morning, so everything seems to go my way. Thomas shoots me a text on his break saying that he'll be meeting Felix tonight, so I'm on my own for dinner. I shake my head and write back: **I thought you were the non-committal type, and now I have to fend for myself?** He sends a group of symbols I assume are a middle finger in return. With a smile, I put my phone down. It's not a big deal. I've neglected my runs by the river and have a lot of writing to catch up on, so tonight is the perfect night to get a salad from Franks near the townhouse and catch up.

As the workday comes to a close, we gather with the bosses in a dimly lit lounge, the air thick with the mingling scents of freshly poured drinks and subtle colognes. Laughter and chatter fill the room, blending with the clinking of glasses and the soft music playing in the background. Heidi and I, eager to make a professional impression, ordered a Pinot Noir. No need for sordid dances and loud activities here.

With exchanged congratulations and a few excited giggles, we say goodbye to our colleagues, the sound of our heels clicking on the polished floor as we go. As we step out into the cool evening, a sense of accomplishment and determination lingers, guiding us toward our respective homes.

When I stop in at Franks, Frank Senior (its namesake) is nowhere to be found. His wife, Aldina, shouts that I need pasta between Italian phrases I can't understand. I grab my regular salad and favorite Italian soda, where Aldina adds real cream, and promise her we'll get her pesto special when Thomas is home another night. "Yes, Aldina, we love pesto, so I'm sure it will be delicious."

She grabs my elbows while Frank Jr. rings my items and smiles while imparting something else in Italian; at least, I assume it's Italian because I don't understand a word. Without further clarification, she returns to her restocking. The sky lost its final hues of orange and pink as I arrived at my peaceful townhome. I consider my running routine and make the decision to wake up early tomorrow to catch the sunrise while jogging, rather than going in the evening. There are lots of joggers and it's a safe neighborhood, so I'm not afraid of going out in the dark. However, tonight feels different, so I think it's best to stay in. I put the dressing on my salad and set up my laptop downstairs to watch HGTV and type.

Just as I start eating my fresh salad, I see a flashing IM on my profile and quickly open it.

Still on for Wednesday?
Yes, sir, I return to Parker
Sir? Ouch, sir, is my father
Mister?
Better, I guess
Well, it sounds weird not knowing your last name
Pagano
Italian?
Sicilian
Ah, my mistake
Forgiven
What are you up to?
Writing my articles and eating a salad.
I'll leave you to it, Sarah.
Thanks Mr. Pagano, see you Wednesday.

You too Miss?
Gillespie.
Miss Gillespie.

I lock my eyes on my name for a brief moment, only to be interrupted by the sound of my buzzing phone and realize it's Zach who's calling.

"Hello?" I answer.

"I'm not outside, but I wanted to see how today went."

I happily declare, "It went really well," savoring the joy of sharing. "The review went really well, and I'm even going on a special trip to Chicago in March or April. Now I can't remember, but Heidi and I get to go together, so I can't wait."

"That's so great, Sarah. I'm really proud of you."

"Thank you. It's nice to hear someone else say it." Because it is nice to hear someone else say it.

"Well, hey," he changes the subject. "You free Wednesday?"

"No, actually, I'm not. I have a band thing."

"Oh, well, I leave Thursday and won't be back until Monday, so I was hoping to see you before."

"Oh?" I question.

"Nothing big. A couple races over in Utah, we're making a trip of it."

I don't want to know who "we," is, so I don't ask. "Well, I guess we'll have to try again when you're back."

"It's a date." He says, "And Sarah," a pause, "I mean it. This time will be different."

"Okay," I say, absolutely certain that this time it will be exactly the same, and then I hang up.

Chapter 7: A Parker Wednesday

I head home before my Parker meeting and throw my work clothes into a heap in my closet while standing in my bra and underwear, trying to decide on an outfit before vetoing everything in my closet. Thomas isn't home again, and I assume he's having his noncommittal meet-up with Felix, which leaves me now running late and still not dressed, with no one to ask for help. "Fuuuuuck," I hiss and grab a sweater, toss it over my head, and a pair of jeans that are all buttons in the front, which take me three times as long as they should to button up because I am in a hurry. Instead of my go-to chucks, I would have to lace. I opt for a boat shoe with no socks that I will undoubtedly regret later and run out the door. I hurled myself upward into my too-high truck and headed to the address Parker sent. When I arrive, I key in the code he gave and look for his studio space, noting a few other bands I recognize, and I slog my way to his. I pull into a parking space across the closed door and think how ridiculous I am to assume they would be on time. Resigning to this, I hop out of my truck and open my tailgate. I have a few cushions in the back from an old outdoor patio set of my parents, and I use one to sit on, swinging my legs back and forth while scrolling on my phone.

"Sarah?" I hear a voice from in front of me

I look up and see real-life Parker walking toward me. He is maybe six feet tall, the same height as Felix, based on my vantage point, and has thick, dark hair cut close to his head. His eyes are dark and intense, and he has a bit of a beard, more than a five o'clock shadow but less than a full beard. I can tell he's in shape because his arms flex as he enthusiastically waves at me and jogs in my direction. Even with no standout features, he manages to be handsome and is clearly of Italian descent. He could very well be part of Thomas' family.

In my clumsy attempt to get down from the truck bed, I miscalculated the distance and ended up jerking forward. Expecting an awkward landing, I close my eyes and tense, but Parker reaches out and firmly holds onto my shoulders. Even though the impact was more painful than anticipated, I remain upright with the help of Parker. Nevertheless, I was glad to be standing, escaping the worst-case scenario that was running through my head. Once I steadied myself, he loosened his hold on me, and I could still sense the impression and warmth of his hands on my body. Stepping aside, he allows me to dust myself off before I hesitantly reach out my hand, "Mister Pagano, I want to express my gratitude for rescuing me. I'm Sarah from Rock Out Local, and usually, I'm much more coordinated than whatever that was," I explain, gesturing with my hands.

"Glad I could help, and can I say that truck seems a little too big for you?"

With a laugh, I raise my tailgate and close it again. "I get that a lot, but I love it, so I don't know what else I'd drive."

"Fair enough. Come meet the band."

Hours later, as we finally leave their practice space, Chris, a member of the band, stays with me and Parker in a tense silence before announcing he's off to work the graveyard shift.

I experienced an overwhelming sense of awkwardness as they engaged in a lively conversation, talking over one another about different matters, while I stayed secluded in a corner, practically unnoticed. Instead of asking them questions and getting to know them, I ended up just sitting and observing.

"So, what did you think?" Parker asks.

"I think you guys are on to something! If I'm being honest, I have no technical opinions. This is all purely subjective."

Chuckling at my response, he asks, "How did you get into all this, anyway?"

"I was a lucky pick and I love music." I say honestly, shrugging my shoulders. "I don't really know much about music other than how it makes me feel when I hear it. Like, a good song? A good song can do things to me I can't explain it, it's like I can feel it inside me."

"Name one." He says.

"23," I say.

"Jimmy Eat World?" He says, surprised. "Do you have it?"

"What do you mean? Do I have it, like, in the truck?"

"Yeah, I haven't heard 23 in a long time."

"Uh, yeah, I'm pretty sure I do."

"Can we listen to it?"

"You want to get in my truck and listen to Jimmy Eat World?" I inquired, baffled, as if he had just proposed a collaboration in a pyramid scheme.

"Yes." He says, nodding. "It's the only thing that makes sense to do right now. Besides, it'll give me time to call a cab."

As I glance around, I notice that there are no other vehicles near Parker's studio space. "You don't have a car?"

"I do," he says, "but I'm fixing it, and it's taking longer to get the parts and things I need to get it running, so I've been getting rides or taking cabs. It's not great, honestly, and costing me a small fortune."

"How about you don't call a cab? I'll give you a ride, and we can listen to it on the way."

"No," he snaps. "We cannot be moving and listening simultaneously. I need to see your face when it plays."

I laugh. "These rules are getting oddly specific for song listening."

"It's important." His face is serious.

"Okay," I say, "I'll play along, but if you need to see my face, we need a better backdrop than this parking lot."

"I agree," says Parker.

"Rooftop parking garage," I declare.

"Okay," he nods.

Parker swiftly hops into my truck, effortlessly assuming ownership, as if it were his own. I follow suit, settling into the driver's seat, and embark on the journey towards downtown. The familiar route leads us to my cherished destination - a rooftop parking haven. The last of its kind with no roof on the top floor, the open-air structure allows a breathtaking view of the dazzling lights emanating from the nearby casinos. As we enter, the sight engulfs Parker, his eyes widening in awe, as though this magical panorama were unveiled before him for the very first time.

"Wow," he breathes.

Oozing with satisfaction, I reply, "First time?"

"It is. I am a rooftop parking garage virgin."

"Well then, let me set us up properly." I steer my truck to reverse so we can sit in the bed and have more space to enjoy the view. I open the sliding window at the back so we can hear the speakers and connect my iPod to the aux port. Parker and I both step out, and he lowers my tailgate and kindly offers to assist me in getting into the back. I take it because I don't want to embarrass myself again, and he lifts himself up right after. After gathering my scattered cushions, we arrange them like small chairs, and Parker, with his longer arms, starts playing music on my iPod. The open guitar rift of 23 by Jimmy Eat World fills the silence.

"I felt for sure last night that once we said goodbye
No one else will know these lonely dreams
No one else will know that part of me
I'm still driving away, and I'm sorry every day
I won't always love these selfish things
I won't always live not stopping"

With each note I sing, my eyes are fixed on the dazzling neon lights that hover above the familiar streets where Thomas, Alice, Jessica, Heidi and I wander every weekend. The sensation of this moment is overpowering, causing me to briefly disregard the fact that I am here with Parker, who is essentially a stranger. To my surprise, he has taken hold of an acoustic guitar, delicately strumming it while I sing along.

"You'll sit alone forever if you wait for the right time. What are you hoping for?"

He continues to match the keys, and I stare into the lights, feeling my heart thrumming in my chest. A breeze blows, making me absentmindedly rub my arms. I hear the strumming stop and realize the song has stopped, and The Pretender by Foo Fighters has started to play. I reach into the truck window, grab a blanket, and stretch it across us silently. We are both perfectly happy, silently gazing at the night. I observe as Parker strums his guitar and plays along to the Foo Fighters for a brief moment before placing it back in its spot, where I realize there's an entire case I didn't notice.

Without looking at me, Parker explains, "When you listen to something, you really listen to it. It's like — it's like you're not even here anymore. You're wherever that song takes you."

My face breaks into a smile as I stay quiet. The icy wind motivates me to seek refuge from the cold by concealing my hands under the blanket. Our hands connect under the blanket, and

Parker intertwines his fingers with mine, a tender gesture that is observed by both of us. He looks at me for a reaction that would tell him to stop, and I again say and do nothing but fix my gaze on the city.

While we remain in that position for another song, Parker scoots closer and brushes my stray hairs away from my face, placing them behind my ear. Even after his touch is gone, I still feel it lingering on my skin. As I turn towards him, our closeness causes our noses to touch, and although I feel the urge to look down, I don't pull away or let go of his hand. He leans into me, and now I can smell his cologne, sandalwood, and something like cedar, maybe something citrus. I breathe it in and lean against him, continuing to inhale him until I am intoxicated.

The closeness, the smell, the music, the view, and the breeze are the ingredients of my lust, and this moment has been designed to make me feral. I raise my gaze, finding his eyes filled with desire and curiosity. The pace of my heart quickens, and I'm sure he can feel it because of his sheer proximity to me. I see his chest heave, and I know what's about to happen, so I close my eyes to prepare for it. "BEEP BEEP BEEP BEEP!" Abruptly, a car alarm wails, prompting me to jerk away and sit up straight. My face awkwardly grazes his prickly cheek, which feels coarse against my soft skin.

Parker laughs hysterically, and so do I. We laugh until it's silent, and my belly aches from the contractions.

"Oh…. my…… gosh….." I say, gasping for air. "That scared the shit outta me!" Parker can't find words, so he focuses on taking gulps of air while holding his stomach in agony. Once we regain control of ourselves, I check the time. "Damn." I say, "I really gotta get going. where can I drop you?" Parker explains where he lives and gets out of the truck bed first. He then helps me down, and we return to our spots inside.

"Where do like, other people sit?" asks Parker.

"Nowhere," I say matter-of-factly. "If we all go somewhere, we take someone else's car, usually my friend Heidi's or Thomas' this gal is a two-person max only," and I pat the dashboard as if the truck is my pet.

"But there's a cab." He points out while looking over his shoulder.

"Yes, but that is where I keep blankets and other things. I'm not totally sure what's all back there, and I don't know if I want to find out." I feel a momentary embarrassment as Parker peers into the dark emptiness of my small cab, wondering what else might be hiding among the sweaters and blankets.

"Do you take all the boys you meet there?" He asks, but I sense he's been eager to ask because his confidence doesn't match his usual tone.

"Actually," I say honestly, "That's where I go when I need to forget them."

He nods, and I see a small grin form on his face, simultaneously exposing a dimple I didn't notice before. The small indent on his cheek makes me long for something intangible, and looking back at the road takes genuine effort. During our winding trip out of the parking garage and on the drive to Parkers, he plays songs from my iPod, and we banter back and forth about the ones he likes, the ones he hates, the ones he can't believe I do, or don't have, and even goes as far to question my sanity for a few of them.

Following his finger to a one-story house, I pull my truck along the curb, so his passenger door faces the front door. Parker leans over and kisses me on the cheek. "Thanks for tonight," he says, and then, before jumping out, "don't pull away until I have my guitar, okay?" I signal my agreement, and he hops effortlessly to the ground. While I close the small window to block the increasingly cold air, he reaches into the back of my truck. Making his way to the door of the small house, he turns and gives a swift wave. I begin retracing my steps towards the city and my townhouse, my heart beating deliberately in my chest. While "I Miss You" by Blink-182 plays, I reminisce as I strum along on my steering wheel, recalling that this was my profile song for two entire weeks after Zach shattered my heart. I finally gave in to Heidi's persuasion and changed it.

"*Like indecision to call you*
And hear your voice of treason
Will you come home and stop this pain tonight?"

When I arrive home, I swiftly shed my clothes and eagerly step into the steam-filled shower, enveloping myself in a cascade of thoughts about the evening. As the scalding water cascades over me, I hear Parker's voice reaching deep into my stomach. Stepping out, I reach for a soft cloth and gently clear a small patch on the fogged-up mirror. Through the mist, my reflection reveals reddened skin, hair clinging damply to my shoulders and arms. As I wrap the towel around me, I gaze at myself in the mirror, making sure it stays secure by tucking it into itself. Observing my face in the mirror, I follow the trail where Parker's fingertips lightly caressed my skin, easing aside my hair. As I fell from the truck bed, his fingertips gripping me still linger in my memory. Why did it feel like his touch left permanent traces of himself on me, and why were my thoughts filled with him, his deep brown eyes, his laugh, and the dimple I saw in a flash of streetlight? I exit the bathroom, and the steam billows out behind me; the contrast in temperature from the bathroom to the rest of my place makes me instantly freeze, and my skin prickles with goosebumps as I dash the 5 feet to my bedroom. I grab my warm pair of matching pajamas sent from my mom last Christmas, quickly throw them on, and wrap my wet hair up in my towel to stop any part of me from getting dripped on. A brief sequence of knocks comes from my door before it's being pushed open, and I see Thomas tentatively entering my room.

"Wanted to see how the band thing went?"

"I think I'm in love with him." I blurt out.

"Uhhh, that's a little soon, even for you."

"I know," I drag out. "I can't even explain it; it's like so crazy I don't even know what to do with myself."

"Ooohhhkay, so he was just outstanding in bed, and you've confused that for deeper feelings; we can work past that."

"No, Thomas, I don't think you understand the gravity of what I am trying to tell you. We didn't even kiss! We held hands for like 10 minutes!"

He blinks at me. "You do recognize you sound nuts, right?"

"YESSSSSS," I yell while throwing myself back onto my bed while smashing a pillow over my face. "UGHHHHHH."

"So, when do you see him again?"

"I don't," I say under the pillow.

"You don't?" Thomas questions, clearly confused.

Sitting back up, I rant, "I am a train wreck. It is impossible for me to be in love with someone I don't know and still pine after the rebound guy I thought I loved. I am a love disaster! I am just falling in love with anyone I meet at this point. This is INSANE! I am insane."

"Listen," Thomas says calmly, "This isn't my area. This is clearly a Heidi problem, so I'm not sure what to do for you other than say, I think you should remain calm and focus on being happy. You'll be ok."

I stare at him, bemused, "You're the least helpful roommate on the planet!"

He shrugs, holding up a hand to display one and then two fingers. "First, I am a gay man, and second, you know my backstory. Which of those things tells you I would be any help here?"

Changing the subject, I say, "Aldina would like us to come in for pesto soon."

"That's a discussion I fully support," he chuckles, "what do you think about Friday?"

I give him a thumbs up and lay back down.

Chapter 8: Willy Wonka and the Family Dinner

Halloween weekend rolls around and the five of us crowd into our small bathroom, taking turns in front of the mirror, getting ready. I am Penny Lane from Almost Famous, hair spraying and spiral curling my straight-as-a-board hair while grunting in frustration. Heidi, resembling a deer, finishes applying her face makeup while Brian, who chose to put in zero effort and is dressed in his actual mossy oak hunting gear, sits on my couch with Felix. Felix, dressed in navy dress whites, complements Alice, Thomas, and Jessica. Jessica is dressed as a cowgirl, Thomas is a construction worker, and Alice is a Indian. Together, they make four out of the six village people. They've resolved to recruit strangers throughout the night to complete their ensemble, which strikes them as undeniably amusing, as though it were the intended strategy from the start. Chase strolls in, and Brian gets up from the couch to welcome his friend, who is sporting his usual attire plus a cowboy hat that seems to be part of his regular wardrobe, in contrast to Jessica, whose hat looks brand new. He tips his hat to her, and she tips her back less gracefully while Alice berates him for also choosing "cowboy" when they're down two of the six village people. He explains he isn't in their group costume, which only frustrates her further.

We head out to the Knit, which promises to have the best Halloween party that is by invite only, and, instead of having their usual band line up, will have a DJ. Zach and I have been slowly integrating ourselves into our regular no-sleepover, only hanging out when he wants to pattern, meaning a Halloween party is by no means his thing, so I will be dateless once again. I acknowledge that the first time this happened, which was almost exactly one year ago today, I cared a lot more. It ruined my evening, forcing me to leave that Halloween party early and go to his regular hangout to find him playing pool with his friends and her, the girl who would always be in the background. Zach is four or five years older than me, depending on the month, and promises almost daily that I will understand him when I reach my 30s. I don't know how I will appreciate him cheating on me constantly; better at 30, but ok. I don't know why I am even talking to him again, if I'm honest. Maybe because his familiarity and companionship make me feel more grounded? Is it because the sex is good enough? Because I enjoy having someone to call and tell about my day and have the odd date with? All question marks I don't spend nearly enough time and energy answering.

We grab drinks and shots at the bar and fall into the swaying and bouncing crowd. We dance and laugh while the Village People foursome poses with strangers to make up the rest of their band, but instead of finding costumes that match the two missing members, they settle for dinosaurs, zombies, Ketchup and Mustard.

"OH EM GEE!" Alice shouts while pointing toward the crowd. "We have to get a picture with them. I look at the purple crushed velvet jacket with a brown top hat and a gigantic candy bar leaning against a table. We go in their direction, and Felix taps the Willy Wonka-dressed man on the shoulder, asking if he and the chocolate bar will be their two missing village people.

"Of course!" I hear the man's voice shout back.

"Sarah, take the picture!" Alice shrieks, and I spin around compliantly to take their photo for the hundredth time. I placed my round sunglasses on my head to better focus the image and immediately locked eyes with Willy Wonka. My stomach does a flip-flop as Parker, and I nod in recognition of one another.

"Say Party!" I shout, and everyone shouts back, "Party," while I snap the picture.

"Sarah," Parker chirps in surprise "Or should I say, Penny Lane?"

"Mister Wonka." I say admiringly, "These are my friends," Each introduces themselves, and Heidi and Thomas exchange a look when they shake Parker's hands. It's discreet, but I notice it even if they try to be secretive and immediately regret that he is standing before them.

"Parker," Heidi says with a gleam in her eye, "We are actually getting ready to finish our night at Thomas and Sarah's place. We've already placed our late-night pizza order, and if we go now, we'll beat it there. Do you and your friend here want to come? It's a Halloween party tradition."

Parker eyes me, and I shrug, suggesting they can do as they want. "Sure," he responds. "I'll ask Chris if he's down."

We get the nod of approval and make our way through the doors. As we are leaving, I saw Brian wave a hand to Chase, who waved back and then returned to a sexy Catwoman teasingly wearing his cowboy hat. I'm grateful I chose a costume that required a fur-lined jacket because it has officially reached the cold weather season. No more crisp nights, just cold. Because Halloween parties are happening everywhere tonight, we walk to our place, and surprisingly, our pizza guy pulls up just as we do. Heidi and Brian paid the delivery driver, and we head inside. Alice turns on our TV to The Food Network, and we open the pizza boxes and pull out our two decks of cards to begin the end-of-the-night game of gin rummy. Parker knows how to play; we must explain the rules to Chris. Brian, as usual, opts to watch and hold Heidi around the waist while eating pizza and watching a rerun of Rachel Ray.

Between chewing pizza and drinks of soda, water, or beer, we shout at each other in competitive gameplay, laughing and screeching in horror when someone has a good hand. The night turns to very early morning, and Brian and Heidi are the first to head home in a cab while Chris and Alice, who are making out now, leave shortly behind them. Jessica takes up her space on the couch, and Felix and Thomas head upstairs, leaving Parker and me out on the patio finishing our cigarettes.

"So, Alice and Chris, huh?" He asks.

I laugh and say, "She works quickly."

"Do you mind if I stay here?" he asks. "I can sleep on the floor. I don't feel like heading all the way home at this time."

"Sure, you can come up to my room," I suggest, and then I quickly add, "I have lots of blankets and floor space. I'm not suggesting —"

"It's okay, Sarah, I won't accost you." He teases and winks.

Why? I question silently. I lead him upstairs and open my bedroom door. He walks in and immediately bounces from wall to wall, looking at all my posters. "Sarah, these are incredible. Look at all these bands! ACDC, Steve Miller Band, Poison, The Beach Boys, Metallica, The Doors! You like all of them?" he asks without turning to me.

"I do," I laugh. "They make up the soundtrack of some significant memories with my dad."

He looked back at me and looked over my costume, then says, "You should be the enemy, not Penny Lane."

"Ha!" I respond.

"So where do you want me?" he asks.

On top of me, beneath me, inside of me, I think before responding, "my bed is huge."

He fixes his eyes on me, silently urging me to continue my statement.

"What I mean is," I correct, "I have a king-sized bed when a twin would be sufficient; I can share, so you don't have to sleep on the floor. I won't accost you either," I joke, putting my hands up in a show of surrender.

"Okay," he says quizzically. "If you're comfortable with it, of course, I wouldn't want you to be uncomfortable."

"We can share a bed, Parker. We're adults." I state this as if I'm daring us not to sleep together.

He removes the purple crushed velvet coat and pulls the green tie held on by an elastic band over his head. He's left with a brown tightly fitted t-shirt and brown khaki pants. I walk into my closet, remove my coat and my bra, and look down at the white tank top, which is showing entirely too much of my breasts for a platonic sleepover. I swap it out for a tank top with a built-in bra and some soft PJ bottoms, wondering how I'll sleep in so much clothing since that isn't my usual get-up. As I step out of the closet, I find him already in my bed, shirtless, and his pants and jacket thrown in a heap. I must have a look on my face that forces him to explain, "I have my boxers on." "I assumed," I retort, even though I didn't. Since my bed is pushed against the wall and Parker has chosen the outside, I have two options: I can climb into my covers by climbing up my bed from the bottom, or I can climb over Parker. I opt for the ridiculous crawl up from the bottom of my bed and then maneuver myself under my covers, deliberately leaving a vast space between us. "Ugh, my light," I say, looking longingly at the light switch by the door. Parker looks in the same direction and swings one leg out before rising to a stand and crossing the room. I feel the heat rise in my cheeks as I watch him cross my room in just his boxer briefs, and before he turns back, I stare into my lap. He smoothly slides back into the covers, and we shuffle to lie down.

"I can't see your face, Sarah." Parker's laughter makes it seem like we're the closest of friends at our very first sleepover.

This makes me blush and I'm thankful for the darkness. "I can't see yours either, Parker."

He stretches his arms out and firmly plants his palm on the center of my face. Laughter fills the air as I shift his hand from my face to rest on my shoulder. "Here, now you know where I am."

His breath hitches, and he says in a low voice, "Tell me about you."

I can't explain where his voice travels inside me. "What do you want to know?"

"All of it."

We exchange stories about our lives, and he informs me he's currently living with his parents while getting back on his feet from a few poor decisions that led to him having some legal trouble; this is why he didn't want to go home late. I tell him that my parents are in Washington, and I haven't seen them in over a year now. I tell him about my job and the bonus and trip to Chicago, how I got started with Rock Out Local. Surprising myself, I tell him about the four-year relationship I ended and the relationship with Zach that consistently proves it's doomed to fail. Parker listens attentively, asking questions to clarify my feelings about some subjects. He tells me about his last relationship, how she is now with his ex-best friend, and how betrayed he was when he found out they were together. He doesn't think she cheated but can't help feeling like she did. That's what led him to legal trouble, a string of poor decisions fueled by a broken heart and alcohol. He also tells me how much better he feels getting back on his feet and how grateful he is for having supportive but strict parents. As far as I know we fall asleep mid conversation.

Late Morning is peeking through my curtains, and I wake to find myself alone yet so well-rested that I can hardly bring myself to care. The pizza-soda water combo in the hours after we got home seemed to have stifled what could have been a hangover and, let's also give credit to the late conversation and weight in my bed. I stretch across my bed, grab my phone, and flip it over to check the time: 10:03 AM. Because I can't recall Parker waking up and leaving, I assume he's at home. I shuffle to my usual side of the bed and kick one leg out, then my other to free myself from the blankets. As I stand up too fast, the room spins. I hurriedly sit back down, closing my eyes tightly to combat the dizzy sensation. When I finally regain my balance, I notice a heap of Willy Wonka next to my recliner. I'm confused; Parker isn't in here, but wandering somewhere in boxer briefs?

When I go downstairs, I see Jessica and Felix both wrapped in blankets on the couch. Jessica unfurled her blanket, and I nestled up against her as she cocooned me in her comforting heat. It's Saturday morning, and they're gathered together, quietly watching Golden Girls, while I overhear expletives, laughter, and a slightly argumentative conversation coming from the kitchen. I lean forward to look into my kitchen and see Parker armed with fresh mozzarella that he is taking full bites from like an apple while Thomas is trying and failing to stop and shoo him from the kitchen simultaneously. I now realize that he is clearly dressed in someone else's clothes.

"They've been like this for almost an hour." Felix, glued to the TV, comments on Parker's insistence on taste testing all the supposedly fresh ingredients from Franks before Thomas can make his quiche.

"We're HUNGRY!" Jessica shouts into the kitchen, "and THIRSTY!" she finishes.

I cover the ear she's yelling into and see Parker whirl around to see me. He smiles and waves me outside, making a cigarette-smoking motion; I give him a "one-sec" signal and remove myself from Jessica's warm blanket before opening our jacket closet for a sweater. We head out the back while Thomas cries, "Thank heaven you came to distract him."

The weather has taken an unexpected turn as dark clouds roll in, obscuring the sun and signaling a looming storm. As I settle onto one chair, Parker snatches the remaining seat and positions himself directly across from me, ensuring our eyes meet. I offer him a cigarette, and he takes it, lights it, and then holds the lighter in an offer to light mine, which I allow.

"You know what?" he starts.

"What?" I ask.

"I think we like each other."

"Oh?" I say amused.

"Yes," he continues, "We have a thing, I think."

"A thing?" I say, raising an eyebrow.

"Sarah." He meets my gaze, and his tone turns serious. "Are you prepared to tell me right here and now that you do not want to kiss me?"

I feel my mouth open, but not a single sound escapes my lips, and then finally, I manage to squeak out, "I —"

His eyebrows rise flirtatiously, and he breaks into a wide grin as if he had just confidently blurted out the correct answer to a math quiz with no prior knowledge. I chuckle timidly, and my cheeks are burning with hot embarrassment as I struggle to find sentences or words or thoughts or anything to pull me out of my speechless blunder. Suddenly feeling very self-conscious, I tug at the collar of my sweater and groan into it. Parker is still grinning, and now I see he has a dimple on both sides of his face, which makes him go from good-looking but mostly unremarkable to charming and desirable in a way that makes me feel if I don't close our distance immediately, I will explode with unfulfilled desire. Still, I can't move. I'm not even sure I'm breathing until I do it voluntarily.

"I'm messed up," I mumble.

"Me too," He says, "and I shouldn't bring you into it, which is why I never reached out after that first night, but now I don't think I can stay away."

"So then what?" I ask, my voice filled with curiosity. Without hesitation, he clutches my hand, his touch sending a jolt of excitement through me. We rush through the creaking door, the sound echoing through the hallway, and ascend the stairs with hurried footsteps. My heart slams in my chest, and again, I breathe voluntarily to ensure I'm actually breathing. There's heat building in my face, chest, and, most notably, between my legs. It takes me a minute to remember how to move my legs once we're in my room and he's no longer pulling my hand. He closes my door and spins around to find me standing in the center of my room where he placed me, and all I hear is hammering heartbeats, mine, his, or both. He advances toward me slowly, like a predator stalking prey, and instinctively, I am backing up, which causes him to stop progressing. "Stop?" He asks. "No," I say, and almost imperceptibly shake my head. He advances again, and this time, I don't move. He cups my face and angles it toward him. My breathing shallows, and he dips his face to mine, crashing his lips to mine. Our tongues dance, and fingers slide up and down our bodies, gripping and digging into each other, trying to bring ourselves even closer so that my chest flattens against him.

We come apart, both making full gasps for air while he grabs the bottom of my sweater and yanks it over my head. He then removes his borrowed shirt and tosses it with the rest of his pile. He grabs my face again and lands another forceful kiss on my mouth before grabbing my two tank-top straps, yanking them down my arms, exposing my breasts. Kissing me again, he palms one of my breasts, squeezing and rubbing me, which forces me to do something akin to a moan into his mouth. He pushes his borrowed pants to the floor, and on a break from our kiss, I can see the erection in his boxers. He places one hand in the center of my chest and eases me back onto my bed, where I shimmy my arms free of my straps, leaving my shirt around my middle. The exposure of my cold sheets prickles my skin, and my nipples harden. Noticing Parker grins while he places a knee on my bed to take a position of hovering over me, then lowers his lips to one nipple, then the other, a real moan this time. I arch into his mouth while he uses his other knee to open my legs. Then he settles his bent leg between mine and frees one hand to cup my center, sending shockwaves through my pajama pants' thin fabric. I will orgasm right now, I think, and he hasn't even done anything. My center heats and throbs as I arch and rock my hips to put more pressure on his hand. He responds with more pressure against my pajamas, and I wonder why they are still on, for goodness' sake! Parker seems to read my wishes and snakes his hand into the band of my pajamas and feels around, moving the moisture collecting at my slit around my lips before sinking one finger inside me and using the heel of his palm to rub the outside. I am fully arched back and moaning desperately.

The temperature has shifted from cold to unbearably hot, and I am swallowing gasps of air and chanting his name with pleas for release. I sit up on my elbows, take his mouth to mine, and wrap one arm around his neck, using him to keep me upright so I can push past the waistband of his boxer briefs and fully grip him in my hand. He pulses against my hand and is bigger than I was expecting, so I feel a fleeting nervousness about taking him inside of me. "Condom?" he asks into my ear, and I shake my head no. He groans and removes his fingers from inside me. I make another more pitiful pleading sound as he frees me from my pajama bottoms and sinks further down me, planting kisses and biting down my torso until he reaches between my legs. He hoists one leg over his shoulder and kisses my center long and hard, sucking me into his mouth. I gasp and scream and grind against his mouth, fighting for the release which comes thunderously. My body shutters and convulses involuntarily. I see him come up, and I can see he's holding himself with his free hand, so I use both hands to guide him on top of me. He sputters, "I can't without a condom." I move him aside and put my hands on his muscular and hairy chest, gently pushing him back. It's my turn now to kiss and bite his midsection, while admiring his toned abs. I grip him, teasing him with my tongue and feeling the relief in his breath. As I take him into my mouth, a small droplet of semen forms at his opening, while my hand completes the rest. I move in a rhythmic motion, observing his muscles, tightening and relaxing, and listening for signs of approval. I feel his hand come down and tenderly take a bundle of my hair, pulling it and releasing it as if to guide my motions up and down his shaft. As I continue to move up and down him, being careful to breathe through my nose, I notice the intensity quickening, his legs becoming taut, and his hips arched. His sounds intensify, and I knew I would need to decide soon. He releases my hair as if reading my mind, and I take him further into my mouth whilst his release explodes. I feel him jerking and I swallow quickly before gagging on the length of him, letting him slowly retreat from my mouth and then move to a seated position. Before I can turn off the bed, he grabs my arm and pulls me toward him. He wipes my mouth with my pajama bottoms and drags me next to him, kissing me deeply, unafraid to have his tongue swirling in my mouth, filling me with gratitude.

We lay next to one another, transfixed as our breathing slowed, making way for steady, equal rises and falls of our chests. The air becomes cool again, and I grab the rumpled blankets, pulling them over us after I remove the tank top still wrapped tightly around my waist. It feels like an itch that hasn't been sufficiently scratched, but I am also in a wondrous haze of contentment when I hear someone calling "BREAKFAST YOU HEATHENS" from what I assume is the top of the stairs.

Parker rolls over the top of me and gently kisses me. Then we lock eyes for a moment before he dashes for his borrowed pants, unsure where his boxer briefs may have disappeared. Not feeling the confidence of someone who wants to be completely naked in front of this man, I take my comforter and wrap it around me as I step into my closet. I catch sight of myself in my full-length mirror, and my tightly curled and hair-sprayed hair looks absolutely insane, so I grab a stray scrunchie from my floor and quickly throw my hair up in a messy bun. Next, I find another tank top with a built-in bra, throw it on with a loose sweater over the top, and grab some yoga pants before emerging to find Parker standing in his khakis and brown shirt. We exchange bashful smiles, and he takes my hand in his own. "Shall we eat? I tasted all the ingredients from Franks. I think... and they were fresh and delicious."

"I'm going to go use the bathroom... and stuff..." I say.

He nods. "Mind if I borrow some mouthwash?"

I look at him embarrassed, and he clarifies, "Not because, you know—just because morning and everything, I just don't want anyone to—"

I raise my hand, nod affirmatively, and pass him the mouthwash before isolating myself. As I opened the door, I'm surprised that he stayed in the hallway, sloshing mouthwash around and shoving past me to spit it in the sink. He exclaims in exasperation, "Damn, that was intense."

"You waited this whole time?? We have a bathroom downstairs!" I laugh in disbelief.

He rinses his mouth two, three, four times before finally saying. "I didn't notice."

We then head downstairs and judging by the quiet, I am guessing everyone heard us. As we stepped to the bottom of the stairs and began crossing the living room, I noticed everyone's eyes dart around the room besides Thomas, who gave me a knowing nod. I know I am blushing and give him a silent plea to say nothing. Felix breaks through the silence and announces the quiche is on the stove. "There are different infusions of balsamic vinegar for a drizzle, unless you had enough drizzle already, and Prosecco with peach nectar for the drinks." My eyes widened, and everyone stifled a laugh, including Parker, who gently squeezed my arm to make it known the comment did not embarrass or bother him. "Thanks." Parker returns and heads to the kitchen. I grab him a plate from our cupboard, and we help ourselves to the two different quiche options, pour our bellinis, and sit at our obscenely large table that housed pizza and gin rummy just a few hours ago. Parker and I exchange glances while eating and drinking, and finally, normal conversation reoccupies the kitchen slash dining area.

Felix pressures Parker on the details of his life, a job typically reserved for Heidi, while Thomas makes obscene remarks about keeping it down while clapping my cheeks. I could die. Parker takes it all in stride and makes easy conversation back and wisecracks about the competition to see who's louder. We clean up and stand side by side at the sink, rinsing and organizing dishes in the dishwasher. I think it shouldn't be this easy; things are never this easy; relationships are so complex, and no one is ever quite happy; that's been my experience so far. When everything has been cleaned up, I say, "So, home then?"

"I'm in no rush," responds Parker. "I could go for a nap."

Standing still, I am unsure of what to say. I'm used to Zach barreling out to do whatever and having most of my time to myself.

"Or, I guess you could take me home; I could use some clean clothes and a shower."

"I have some clothes you could wear," shouts Felix from the couch. "Probably the best dressed you've ever been, and there's plenty of MAN smells in the shower," he says, deepening his voice as if Parker would take offense to smelling like a gay man, whatever that difference may be.

He looks over at me, and I'm still stuck in pause as I think over the options in front of me. "I, uh, I don't have any other plans." I finally squeeze out with a half-smile.

Thomas also pipes up from the couch and announces, "don't be offended, Parker. She's used to shitty boyfriends who leave to see their other girls or hang with the boys."

Flustered and somewhat ashamed, I walk to face Felix. "If you could pull those clothes out, that would be great."

"We should shower," I spin around and say to Parker before heading too quickly up the stairs. I feel him following behind me, and when we reach the top, he grabs my hand, forcing me to turn and face him. "I can go if this feels uncomfortable or fast for you. I'm not here to complicate your situation."

"You're not complicating anything; you are so uncomplicated that I am making things complicated." I sigh. "I told you; I'm messed up."

"I can handle whatever pace you set. No pressure. I'll even shower after you." He says with both hands up in surrender.

I smile up at him and pull him into the bathroom with me. "No, I don't think that's what I want."

The shower is hot, and when Parker follows me in, he screeches and steps out of the water. "Holy shit, lady, how is your skin not melting off your body?" I laugh and turn it down to a temperature he can step into, and we shower, regularly taking turns under the water. I notice how the water cascades down him, following the striations of his muscular body. As if by someone else's control, I touch his chest and trace my fingers down his abdomen and then, using both hands, trace his obliques until his body slants inward, leading to his pelvis. He brings my hands back up to his chest and says, "I don't think I could do anything without being inside of you, so we're going to have to keep these up here," and pats my hands against his chest. I snort, which surprises both of us, and then I laugh at the absurdity of snorting naked in a shower with this man in front of me.

Once done, we wrapped towels around us and dashed into my bedroom, which had cooled significantly because of the loss of the sun. With my free hand, I point to an electric fireplace, and Parker turns it on while we both continue to dry off. Now ridiculously choosing modesty, I step inside my closet and throw my hair in a towel to dry. Digging through my drawers for lounge wear, I see the bag. I pull it out and open it, revealing the Abercrombie & Fitch jogger sleep set I bought for Zach, who once told me he got too cold sleeping in my room when I asked him to stay overnight. Taking them out, I examine their packing for any notes I may have tucked inside them. Finding none, I glance out of my closet and see Parker has remade my bed and is sitting on my recliner with his towel wrapped around his waist and the fireplace turned just so that it's blowing heat onto him. I clear my throat, handing him over the jogger set. "They were always meant for someone who thought I was important enough to stay the night, that's you. Hopefully, my futuristic purchasing decision is in your size."

While inspecting the packaging for any sign of it being opened, he takes the brand-new joggers and notices that someone has removed the price tag. "These will do, thanks," he says, nodding politely. "I am a little cold, and Felix gave me something very bright orange." He stands, and the towel stays draped across my recliner. I watch as he drags the pants up, his legs crossing over his knees, stretching over his muscular thighs, and finally stretching the waistband over himself and securing them low on his waist. He pulls the shirt on and rubs the fabric everywhere over and over. "These are the softest pieces of clothing I've ever had on my body before." he looks at the packaging again. "Abercrombie & Fitch, job well done."

The clouds outside have finally released their contents, and the rain comes in sprinkles, then gradually builds to a steady pattern of knocks and bangs on the glass of my window. Parker and I continue in a steady conversation between music, family, and five-year plans as he interlaces his fingers with mine, then releases, then twists his fingers with mine again. We continue this leisurely act until an unfamiliar tone fills my bedroom; Parker jumps to attention and shakes his phone loose from his khaki pants.

"Hey Ma," he says into the phone. "Yeah, yeah, I'll be there. No, I just didn't want to spend the cab money. Uh..." Looking behind me, he says more quietly, "I'm with a girl.... Ma, too soon Okay, okay... I'll ask. Okay, I love you too."

"Was that your mom?" I tease.

"It was," he says tentatively. "It's Sunday, which means family dinner night. It's a big deal for us Italians, you know... Family and eating."

"I do," I respond. "Thomas suffers the same affliction."

"Well," he says, "I was trying to get her off the phone, and now she knows you exist and insists I have you over. I know it's early, so you can say no; I won't be offended."

"Are you asking me to meet your parents?" I tease again.

"No," he says thoughtfully, "Practically, my whole family."

"I'm in," I say, surprising him. He sits back on my bed, looks me in my eyes, and beseeches me to confirm my invitation. I do, and he kisses me deeply, then tells me I should probably get ready unless I want to wear pajamas, which would be totally fine if I wanted to. Gesturing my disdain for that idea, I inform him that is not the first impression I intend to make and go to my closet to pick out jeans, calf-high boots, and a nice woven sweater with a bralette underneath. I twist my hair into a low-side bun and throw on some hoop earrings.

I exit my closet, open my arms wide, and say, "Done!"

"Beautiful, but so much clothing." He says with a wink.

I shake a finger at him and say, "oh, Mister Pagano, do not start something you don't intend to finish. Again."

He stands and grabs me around the waist, and pulls me into him. "Let's go before we don't make it."

I drive us to Parker's parent's house, and suddenly, my heart thumps before we step out of the truck. I remember frequently begging to meet Zach's parents and him explaining to me how it wasn't time yet, or maybe in another month or so. When, in reality, the entire time, he was hiding me from anyone who wouldn't keep his secret from her. Parker jumps out and comes to my side before I have a chance to open my door. He lifts the handle, opens it wide, and holds his hand out in this very prince-like gesture that makes me giggle. Walking up the path to the front door, he says, "Wait, I want to show you my car!" He steers me by my shoulders across the grass to the driveway and punches a code into the garage door. It lifts, and I see a black Ford Mustang; in my head, I guess it is a '60s model year, but my secondhand knowledge passed down from my dad isn't always the most reliable. I see the hood is propped open and someone has spread parts over a rolling cart.

"It was my grandpa's." He says proudly. "he's inside; you'll meet him. I'm almost done, but I borrow my mom's car when I go to work or school."

"School?" I question.

"Oh yeah," he says. "I guess in all the other talks, I forgot to mention I'm taking classes toward a degree in marketing. I can't give it a lot of time yet, so it's going slow, but I definitely enjoy it, and I figure it'll push the band stuff along one day."

"Wow." I say, "You have it much more together than you led on."

He nonchalantly lifts his shoulders and repositions the stack of garments cradled in his arm. Together, we stride towards the entrance, whereupon swinging the door open, an overwhelming wave of aromas and boisterous merriment engulfs my senses. The air is thick with the savory scent of food being prepared, while a cacophony of laughter and animated banter fills the space, vying for dominance amidst the lively ambiance. I hear glasses clinking and metal pots shuffling, and then comes an unmistakable Italian accent. "Parker, how nice of you to join us with your lady friend this evening."

"Sarah," he says, and I am greeted with handshakes and names flying so rapidly that I can barely hang on to them. Carla, his mother, is last and is bustling around the kitchen in a white chef's coat. She kisses Parker on both cheeks, greets me pleasantly but quickly, and turns to continue manning the many bubbling pots and pans.

Parker leans into my ear and says, "I'm going to change into something more appropriate for dinner, but you'll have to stay out here. My parents are old-fashioned like that." He steers me again onto a bar stool overlooking his mom's methodical cooking, and I am then joined by a girl around my age who introduces herself as Addy, short for Adrienne, who is Parker's younger sister by two years, one year behind me. I know a few things about myself: I am GREAT with parents and have never been great with sisters; abruptly, I sit up, straightening my back and silently pray that I don't give her any hints that I am broken and flawed in relationships that may cataclysmically destroy my brand-new relationship with her brother. She informs me she is taking psychology classes hoping to become a marriage and family therapist, and this creates an uneasiness that goes beyond the sister problem I have. I hope I am not noticeably sweating, although I can feel it in my armpits. Her dominant talking held our conversation up and me filling in one-word answers. She doesn't seem bothered by this, so I happily take the job of being an excellent listener to avoid anything spilling out of my mouth that I don't mean to say.

Parker returns, and his hair is damp.

"Did you shower?" I ask, confused.

"I had to," he whispers, and the question mark plastered on my face forces him to bend lower and whisper even softer. "I'll tell you later."

Raising an eyebrow, but ultimately letting it go, he parades me around to everyone again, and we answer questions about where we met, what I do, where and who my family is, etc. "Is that Scottish?" they ask. "And British," I answer politely. "I think there's some historical weirdness there, battles and such; my dad knows, he's an English professor with a minor in World History." His mother calls out that it's time to eat, and Parker leads me to their formal dining room, which has a table that rivals the length of tables I used to see lining the school cafeterias of my youth. Parker's father asks if I drink wine, to which I reply I do, and he gives me a couple of options. I choose the noir, avoiding anything heavier, and he compliments my choice while winking at Parker in approval. Parker squeezes my hand, and I try to settle my nerves.

Dinner is SENSATIONAL! How does that woman cook all of that and make it taste so good, I think to myself? It's like a superpower. I mean, Thomas' mom is good, but she's always busy with grandchildren, so more often, she cooks a vat of one dish, which is it. My mom just had my dad and me to feed, so the time spent in the kitchen was always efficient and usually included a gravy. My Mom also grew up in the era before microwaves, so once the microwave was invented, it became her primary mechanism for cooking anything.

We finish the evening with dessert and espresso, which I pass on because I will never get to sleep if I don't. I say my goodbyes to the house full of people as Parker walks me out, gripping my hand gently, then spinning me as we hit the wood porch and pulling into a sort of dance, placing one of my hands on his chest and holding the other as if we're priming to waltz. We sway effortlessly on the porch, and I try to mimic his steps when he says, "You're trying too hard," so I return, "I don't think I know how to dance." he pulls me closer so I can't look down at our feet and instructs "the first step is to relax." We sway like this a few minutes more, and then he pushes me out and spins me again so that my back is against him.

Curiously, I turn back to him and inquire, "What made you decide to shower?"

Parkers head hangs following a long breath of air pushing through his lips. "I was hoping you would forget."

"I don't forget anything," I say. "I'm incapable."

"I'll keep that in mind."

"So?" I say, urging him to continue.

He looks down, kicks at a stray couple of leaves on the porch, and expels more air before saying. "It was a cold shower."

"What?" I question, thoroughly confused.

"I had to take a cold shower," he groans and kicks at the leaves again. "Okay," he says, hands up, readying himself to provide an explanation. "When you were changing in your closet, I could see you in that long mirror you have and —" he pauses and looks at me, "I just—see, ever since that first night, all I could think about was having sex with you, what it would be like and you know we still haven't but watching you naked made me think of the shower and the time before and just how much I still want to so I needed to cool off before someone in my family pointed at my pants and yelled PARKER HAS A

BONER." He doesn't look up, and I can't stop myself before a snorting laugh escapes me. This causes me to double over trying and failing to stop snorting and laughing.

"I —" I stammer, "I can't believe you had a boner at your parent's lovely dinner party." I finish.

"I didn't," he explains defensively. "Thanks to the cold shower."

Changing the subject, I quickly say, "Thank you for bringing me to your parents' house," as I gently wrap my arms around his neck.

He spins me again, this time toward my truck, and walks me to the street side, where he then swings my driver-side door open and hoists me in. "Don't run off, Sarah; the good parts will just get better." I smile and lean down from my truck to meet his lips and then start my vehicle and switch from aux to the radio, catching the first chords of You & Me by Lifehouse.

"Cause it's you and me and all of the people with nothing to do
Nothing to lose
And it's you and me and all other people
And I don't know why, I can't keep my eyes off of you."

Chapter 9: For The Roomies

In the next couple of weeks, Parker and I will continue to fuse and steal time from friends, family, and band practices to be together. We still haven't had sex, which doesn't come as a surprise because our lives were already busy, and now we are finding and scraping together moments to see each other. He spends his weekends either studying or playing gigs, while I watch gigs and write articles. I fill extra time with Heidi on runs or hosting "grown up" dinner parties for Brian, Chase, and Brian's uptight work friends. Parker comes to one of the dinner parties with me and is a natural thanks to his Sunday dinners. Every time he has to leave early to prepare for a show, we linger in Heidi's doorway, panting on each other in a desperate plea for more time.

Between short run-ins with Parker, my busy schedule, and dinner out with my friends, I keep Zach at bay long enough that he loses interest or takes a hint. Who knows for sure, but if I am honest, he was just familiar, and I was just a shiny plaything he liked to keep in his back pocket when he got bored with his adult girlfriend. He liked me for fun and drunk dancing on poles; he never stuck around for dinners, dates, or hikes on the weekends. I was like his vacation, and now that I had felt something like what Parker and I had, I knew I could never meet someone and be their vacation girl again.

At long last, our schedules aligned, and I could go to his show with all my friends. Roger and Will arrive to do their taping, preparing Reverberation Breakdown to be featured adequately on our site as the next hot band for December. We arrive individually, as Parker always arrives early to test sounds and ensure everything is perfect for their show. We have our IDs checked by the loan grumpy bouncer on the stool, acquire our wristbands, and head into the small dark bar to grab a table. I recognize Parker's sister sitting with two girls. I assume these are her friends along with a man who's on the taller side that has a small child-like face. She waves politely at me, and I wave back as we circle our table to get settled. We sit at our table and need one more chair. Addy and her group are at the closest table, so Heidi asks if she can take one. The girl closest to Addy with blonde golden hair turns kindly to her and announces, "It's taken." Heidi stalks back to our table and shrugs, so Brian offers to stand; I also opt to stand so I can move around with Will and Roger.

I spot Parker, and he waves, but it's not at me; it's directed at Addy's table. I wait for his view to carry its way to me, but it doesn't. He spots Roger and the camera next, giving him a thumbs up, and does another test into the microphone. Trying not to feel forgotten, I take a breath and make my standard passes as I would for any other show except—I am getting increasingly irritated at the fact that the chair that was allegedly taken still sits empty at their table. It is even more frustrating that the girl with the blonde golden hair, who sweetly announced it was taken, hasn't taken her dreamy look off of Parker. Lastly, He has paid little attention to me. As my anger escalates, I unsuccessfully try to lubricate myself with alcohol, hoping that it will calm me. Instead, I am pouring gas on the raging inferno of my bottled temper.

After consuming four beverages and numerous shots, I notice Brian positioned behind Heidi. With a swift glance, I shift my attention to the unoccupied chair. Determined, I stride purposefully towards the table, exhaling sharply through my flared nostrils. Grinning, I seize the chair, not quite slamming it, but causing a raucous noise as it meets the floor near Heidi. I nod briskly, only to discover both Heidi and Brian staring at something behind me, their expressions filled with alarm. In that moment, I am engulfed by a frigid, sticky splash that covers my entire face, seeping into my ears and trickling down my chest, penetrating my shirt and bra. Noises reverberate from all directions, echoing through the air, but their presence is muffled as the cap containing my temper bursts open. My body swings wide from the right, hoping to ensnare someone with my hook. The world around me seems to slow down, like a dream, as I sense the waist of my pants being forcefully yanked backward. An arm wraps around my chest, constricting my breath. Desperately, I reach behind me, struggling to break free, but my assailant's strength is overpowering. A child-faced man, I think, as I feel two formidable arms encircle my torso, lifting me off the ground. Helpless and vulnerable, I thrash my feet wildly, fighting for release. It's an unbearably long minute of standing outside in the chilling cold weather to notice that I am no longer in the bar. Heidi stands before me, lighting two cigarettes at once with my purse and hers hanging on one arm. She hands over one of the lit cigarettes, and I take it with a shaking hand, I feel a jacket wrap around my shoulders, but I can't be sure that I am cold at all. Aberrant, yes, mad still, absolutely, but not cold. I turn, and it is Will behind me and whose jacket I am wearing; there is no child-faced man who has led me to the conclusion that Will was my assailant but more likely my savior. No one is speaking; Heidi and Will are apparently standing guard until I decide my next course of action. Feeling the sticky drink drying on my now bitter face, I turn to Heidi. "You got any of those makeup wipes in your bag?" she shakes her head solemnly, and I look toward my truck. "Well, time to go then," I say, digging into my purse for my keys.

"Sarah," Heidi says softly, "you're not driving home, not drunk, not with snow on the ground, and not with whatever the hell that just was."

I take micro steps to bring feeling to my legs and growl at the ceiling. "I just want to go home."

"Oh, that's where we're going," says Thomas, clamoring out the door with the rest of our group. "Cabs on the way, and just so we're all clear here, he circles the air, my hetero life mate here," he slaps my back a little too hard, "could've taken that pencil-built bitch!" Thomas has apparently also had a little too much to drink and is all for fueling my already-stoked fire. The man who checked our IDs is standing completely in front of the door now, preventing me from entering or the gold-blonde girl from leaving. I peek behind him to see if I can make out anyone on the other side. I can't.

Our cab pulls up, and I hug Heidi, Alice, and Jessica before handing Will back his jacket. Brian nods at me respectfully, and I notice that he, too, has positioned himself nearest the door. Thomas comes crashing down beside me and plops my purse into my lap. We head home, and Thomas asks the cab to wait 15 minutes.

"Leaving?" I ask.

"Yeah, we are," says Thomas, not pausing on his way out of the cab.

"Wait, what?" I say, hurrying after him.

"You are going to wash your face, change your clothes, re-apply the least amount of makeup you can, and WE are going to Five Queens. This night will not be ruined by that skinny brassy haired twat."

I hold up my hand to counter and then think better of it. It's merely 10; why would I let some strange horrible girl ruin my night? Flinging my door open, I bolt inside, throwing my soda-filled clothes onto the floor of my closet. I dash topless and in underwear to the bathroom and swiftly wash my face, ears, and chest wetting most of my hair, then throw it into a messy wet whatever on top of my head. I go back to my closet, smelling more like soap than soda and feeling less sticky, and select my silver shimmery halter dress and black thigh-high pleather boots. Scurrying into the bathroom once more, I try to get my hair into a more flattering style before giving up and throwing on some mascara and lipstick. I am back in the cab, and Thomas shouts, "Yaaassss BITCH!" as he looks over my choice of outfit. He tells the driver we are heading to Five Queens and getting released to the curb a few minutes later. Once inside, my mood is instantly fixed by gay men cat-calling me over Ushers, Yeah, blasting.

We order our usual drinks and declare the night "FOR THE ROOMIES" while clinking our glasses with everyone in our radius. We dance and drink and clink drinks with patron until the blonde gold girl becomes a minor blip on the evening unless we tell our fellow patrons the story; after hearing me and Thomas take turns recalling the events, they swear their allegiance to us, and we toast and drink more. The story even gets us most of our drinks for free, and several of the good-looking drunk gay men tell me how hot I am in my ensemble. When we leave the bar, Thomas steadies me around the waist and must support himself and my total weight while trying to guide me into the cab seat. Normally we walked home, but our drunkenness and the extreme cold made it too risky to attempt without sustaining an injury. As the driver makes the few turns to our townhouse, I am slurring my appreciation to

Thomas for his friendship; he pats my head and chuckles at the sight of my impairment. When we pull up to our place, I hear a soft "uh oh." I try to say what or huh, but something more like a grunt comes out; I hear a cab door open, and Thomas is exchanging what sounds like a hushed discussion with our driver. Then I hear a third low voice coming from the driver's window, and cash is being counted; leaning toward Thomas' side, I hold my arm out, hoping Thomas will help me, but the door swings slightly, revealing my parked truck and no Thomas. To my surprise, my door opened, and a more coordinated person, Parker, hoisted me upright and then out of the door. Parker walks and mostly carries me to my door as Thomas holds it open before I slam my hand against the door frame.

"Who was she?" I taunt fiercely as he steadies me on my heeled boots.

"Later," he says, annoyed.

"I—" I hiccup, "deserve an examp—exclamp—splation,"

"I know," he says, still annoyed. "Tomorrow, okay? Let's get you upstairs."

Dizzying in the night's air, I abandon my attempts to fire questions at him and let him lead me to my room where, utterly defenseless, I flop backward onto my bed, and the walls became opposing motions going up and down. I try to rise, but instead, I fall short and find myself on my side. Parker places a cup of water on my nightstand and sits me upright. I stare at him mournfully before announcing, "I'm going to puke."

"Alright," he says and helps me to the bathroom, where I heave the contents of my stomach into the toilet, once, twice, three times, before groaning and sitting backward until my back hits the wall. Parker turns on the shower, helps me with my boots and tiny dress, and gingerly removes my bra and underwear. I feel his fingers grazing, leaving stinging paths everywhere he touches me. Parker then stabilizes my balancing act from outside the tub, and he takes a surprising amount of effort to keep me upright. At the same time, I attempt to wash my hair and body. I point to my toothbrush, and he obliges. Once I give him a nod, that signifies I've done all I can do. He meticulously helps me lift my legs over the tub wall, wraps a towel around me, and leads me with my shoulders to my bed. "Nooo," I cry, "I'm too wet to get in there." He sits me in front of my fake fireplace and turns it on. While I rock from the effort of keeping myself seated, he hands me vitamin B and water.

"Thomas said to give you this."

I raise a fist to the sky. "It's a trick," I burp.

"Okay," he says.

I stare at him seated in the adjacent recliner, and he meets my gaze. "You know what," I say assertively, "I loved you from the moment I met you, and that is a big fucking problem." He says nothing, his mouth agape, his eyes searching my face. Moving to stand I clumsily let the towel fall away and get into my bed. I feel his weight gracefully join me and pull me into the curve of his body that mine fits exquisitely in. Sleep arrives swiftly.

Chapter 10: Hard Conversations

Morning and a pounding hangover keeps me from opening my eyes or attempting to lift my head. My blankets are hot, and the texture feels like it's scratching my skin. Sunlight peeks in through the brown tweed curtains, blinding, like the soft rays are burning my dry eye sockets. I feel something heavy across my abdomen, which is just enough pressure to make me feel nauseous. Gently feeling across me to avoid further pressure, I realize it's an arm across me and turn my head to see Parker sleeping peacefully. Despite feeling sick, I refuse to remove his arm and instead inch closer to him until our faces are only an inch apart. He doesn't stir. I firmly kiss him, parting his lips with my tongue, and I feel the familiar return of his tongue to mine. He adjusts his position to get a better angle, then lifts himself up, deciding to float over me as we continue kissing. I feel my way up the curve of his muscular arms and sigh into his mouth. He lifts from me, looks down toward our converging groins, and sighs, "I owe you an explanation, and quite frankly, you owe me one, too." I half smile as he pushes off me, returning to his shoulder, and I flip to face him.

"Parker." I start, and my voice is hoarse, which is unexpected, causing his name to come out in a cough. "This is one of those times—" I clear my throat again. "I am not good at complicated feelings; I tend to shove them down and breeze past the hard conversations."

"Sarah." He says softly, "We are going to have to be better at the hard stuff if we want to be better at being together."

"This is usually the part where I pretend I'm blissfully unaware of the complications."

"Not today," he says, and I strain to keep my eyes on him. "Then you start and hand me that cup of water." I resign to sit up and let the collective force of the night cascade onto my already throbbing head, neck, and shoulders. "Savannah," he starts, and I immediately throw the name to the top of my names for horrible bitches list while I tense at the fact that golden blonde girl now has an actual name and not all the colorful things I've been calling her for the past 16 or so hours. He continues, "After the breakup, Addy convinced me to go on a date with her friend Savannah because she always had a thing for me. I agreed even though I wasn't looking for anything. I was still messed up; I am still messed up." He shakes the thought. "Anyway, we go out, and she tells me all the things that will make a guy feel good about himself, so I sleep with her, and then after I sleep with her, I can't exactly find the right way to explain to her that the only reason I slept with her is because she made me feel special, but I don't actually like her." He lets out an exasperated breath. "I sound like an asshole."

He does, but I don't care. She aggressively threw a drink in my face less than 24 hours ago, so she's enemy number one and fully deserving of whatever he thinks he did to wrong her. "So, I continue to see her, and the more I see her, the more I realize there's no way I could ever be with her. Seriously, she's my sister's age, but she's practically a thirteen-year-old when it comes to her maturity, and worse, she's COMPLETELY obsessed with me, which makes me dislike her more. Then I meet you, and we spend those few hours together. I'm even MORE confused because all I've been trying to do is escape a relationship, convincing myself that I need to be alone for a while, you know, to work out why I can't like someone who clearly likes me. Still, you, you make me feel like I need to handcuff myself to you so that I never lose you after a couple hours! Like what the fuck Parker!?" He shoots his hands out in front of him, expressing his confusion. "So I call her," he continues. "I tell her that I'm just not in the right headspace for anything serious, and I need to stop seeing her. She cries, and I'm disappointed that I obviously led her to believe I cared more than I did. Despite her begging and crying, I tell her I will not be taking her as my plus one to the Halloween party. I hate myself, of course, but I have already committed to the Halloween Party with my friend and am desperate for a distraction, and guess what?" he asks, baffled. "You're fucking there, Sarah! You're FUCKING there." He laughs, disbelieving, like he's reliving the shock of it all.

"I'm sorry?" I say, perplexed. He lets out another disbelieving laugh and goes, "I took you to my parents the day after, THE DAY AFTER, and you know who completely missed the part where she's supposed to have my back? Addy." He finishes without pause. "Addy texts her immediately." He laughs again, sounding a little crazy. He scoots up to a seated position and looks over at me. I am actively trying to sift through everything he told me and organize it in a manner that will make it all make sense, but I am perilously hungover, so thoughts are coming slowly. As the silence lingers, I come to the realization that she may have believed our relationship was deeper and more significant than it actually was. Where I would naturally empathize with the poor girl, the memory of cold Coca-Cola stinging my face stops me. "Say something." He pleads.

"I would've done more than throw Coca-Cola in my face," I say honestly, then let out a long exhale. Raising my shoulders in a silent gesture of understanding, I reach for his hand and turn it upward so I can trace the lines of his palm.

"I called you like three hundred times." He says, "I didn't know where you went. Heidi said you were going home, but you weren't here, and all I could think is that you were out doing something stupid." I snatch my hand away and face him straight on.

"What's stupid?" I ask defensively.

He looks down, ashamed. "You know so many people, so many guys—I just thought."

I become more conscious of my nudity and quickly reposition the blankets to provide more coverage. The comment stings and I can't respond because if I do, I will be mean, a response I often display in these situations.

"I'm sorry, Sarah, I told you I'm messed up and way too insecure. When I saw Thomas get out of the cab with you, I was so relieved."

I wish I had clothes on because all I want to do is get out of my bed and have a cigarette. Sure, I do my share of flirting, and sure, I've been with my fair share of guys to cure the sting of Zach's betrayal, but I've never given Parker the idea that I would run away and cheat on him. Have I? He grabs my hand, and I miss pulling it back thanks to my slower-than-usual reaction time.

"I know you're mad, but I had to tell you everything, so you knew." A pause. "You know how messed up I am. So, you know now how hard it is to be with me." I look at him, and my anger dissipates, seeing the sincerity and apology on his face.

I relax my shoulders but keep a tight fist on my blanket over my chest. He notices the relent in my posture, and I see relief in his features. "Okay," I say professionally, treating this like a business transaction, which is my default in conflict and requires something more than my attitude. "We're both unquestionably messed up, and I am horrifyingly bad at conflict management, especially when alcohol is involved." I check for recognition, and he nods. "In what world will this translate into a relationship that is anything but volatile?"

He nods again. "I don't know how to tell you this without scaring you," he interjects quickly, like ripping off a verbal band-aid, "but thanks to something you said last night, I think you'll understand." He pauses and faces me again, cupping my face in his hands. "Sarah, all I know is how I feel, and I feel like I couldn't possibly feel this way about anyone else." he takes another full breath in and out before finishing, "I am in love with you."

Trying to remember what I said last night, it occurs to me I may have told him I loved him, although my delivery was harsh and said more like an insult. Drama aside, I believe we could truly love each other, and every muscle and bone in my body melts against him. I feel tears sting my eyes, and he's wrapping his arms around me. "Everything has changed, Parker," he squeezes me tighter. With sudden recognition, desire overwhelms me. "Parker," I lean back from him and meet his eyes with sudden seriousness, "I need you." His breath hitches. I steady my eyes on him. "Please, I need you." With a nod of understanding, he jumps from my blankets and darts to open my door, shutting it behind him; he then returns in what feels like a millisecond, holding a square shiny packet. "Did you know Thomas had a cup of these??" he says, and I think of how silly I am because I did know that. He shoves his boxers down his legs, revealing he will not need any encouragement to perform, and rejoins me under the covers, placing the condom on the nightstand.

Using zero effort, he grabs around my back and shifts me underneath him, forcing my fist full of covers to retreat around his back, and my arm is now pinned at my side. He kisses me with overwhelming gratitude, hastily, and marginally sloppy, wetting the area around my mouth. He stops and retrieves the condom, rips it open, and wraps himself while I try to free my arms from my sides; stopping my struggle, he grabs both of my arms and pins them above my head, using one arm to hold them. My nipples harden, and my muscles tense at the sudden forwardness of his actions. He moistens his fingers and inserts them into me, widening my legs and eliciting an unexpected gasp of pleasure. Parker firmly rubs his palm against me, using his tongue to flick each of my nipples, and I cry out, "Please!" With that, he removes his hand and replaces it with the length of him, deliberately entering at a measured pace, ensuring to wait for any signs of discomfort. He feels like an answer to a prayer, a wish fulfilled, an itch scratched, flooding my body with euphoria. Our bodies become so entangled that I can't tell where one of us ends and one of us begins; the only thing I am sure of is that his weight atop me must mean that I am underneath. Between gentle scrapes along his chest with my teeth, finding the firm muscle of his chest, I firmly clamp my teeth into him, intensifying the pressure, something not more than a tender bite, while I persistently struggle against the pressure of his hands around my wrists. He confidently thrusts against me in perfect rhythm with the moans and trills, sounds I'm not trying to hold back and will definitely hear about later. He releases my wrist and straightens upward, gripping my hips now, pulling me against him as he thrusts. This is it; I think I'm going to die from the intensity, and then, as if a nuclear bomb detonates, my orgasm forces me upward, digging my nails into his back forcing him to place his ample weight on top of me as he, too, writhes with his own impending release. I place back pressure on his chest, trying to find air, but he thrusts into me once more deeply, and I feel him throbbing inside me as he gasps with his finish. He eases back, giving me just enough space to gulp air. Leaning down so that his lips brush against my ear, he whispers, "I will never be the same now." I hugged him to me, and we stayed tangled that way. No more words needed to pass between us.

Chapter 11: San Francisco or Bust

It's the week after Thanksgiving. I decided to spend the holiday with Thomas and his family, not with Parker's. Despite Addy apologizing and acknowledging her misplaced hope in Parker and Savannah's relationship, which led to her lapse in judgment. The apology lacked sincerity, leading me to believe that we would never form the close bond of chosen sisters. I skillfully played nice, though, serving us both, since I would always have to be the bigger person.

Due to Heidi's insistence on group travel, we found ourselves crowded around my doorstep. Brian, the most responsible among us, and his friend Chase had to rent a spacious passenger van for the four-hour journey to San Francisco. Chase and Brian take the front, Heidi, Alice, and Jessica take the first row, Parker and I take the middle, and Thomas and Felix take the last row. We're about an hour in when Chase and Heidi are switching because after pulling over to let Heidi forcefully hurl the contents of our gas station snack, we learn that evidently Heidi gets actual car sick and has to be in the front seat. Chase, who is predominantly quiet but resolutely polite, offers to buy her some Dramamine at our next stop and gives her his remaining Coca-Cola to settle her stomach. As we navigate through the snow-laced mountains, the sound of crunching snow beneath our tires mingles with the sight of Douglas fir trees lining the highway, providing fleeting glimpses of the awe-inspiring elevation. The sun comes through the cloud-dotted sky in intervals, cirrocumulus, my mind wandering to that young age when we learned about weather and cloud formations using cotton balls and tissue on blue cardboard to design each one. I imagine the denseness beyond the trees, feeling the crisp air through the poorly sealed windows. We often stop to use the restrooms at varying degrees of kept rest areas, which none of us can seem to do concurrently. Some are clean, smelling of pine and lemon, with abundantly stocked vending machines and handouts about the area, while others are putrid and cold, forcing us girls to test our balance while hovering over the stainless-steel toilets. Finally, we are sitting on the bay bridge in traffic, surrounded by the cacophony of car horns and exhaust fumes, while Alice paints vivid pictures of the horrifying scenarios that could unfold, instilling a sense of dread in all of us. After enduring approximately forty-five minutes of Alice's anxious ramblings about bridges, the tension in the van reaches its breaking point and we all erupt in unison, shouting, "SHUT UP ALICE!" The sudden outburst plunges the vehicle back into silence.

We arrive at Felix's family's Timeshare, an impressively well-laid-out four-bedroom, two-story home in Pacific Heights. The house is painted in different shades of gray-blue paint, a color combination which only works alongside the vertical streets of San Francisco. The front door is a bright yellow. Upon entering, I'm abruptly hit with the sense that we shouldn't touch or sit on anything. Shades of white dominate the scenery, with touches of blue and occasional pops of red adding contrast. As each of us enters, we can't help but notice the polished pine floors, prompting us to remove our shoes and place them by the entrance. The bedroom gifted to us by Felix on the top floor overlooks Alta Plaza Park and a sliver of the bay; it includes an adjoined bathroom with a deep claw-foot tub and a four-post bed adorned with soft white linens. He and Thomas take the master, Brian and Heidi take the room on the bottom floor, and Jessica and Alice share the last room. Chase informs the entire house that he'll switch between Alice and Jessica's beds, and none of us can tell if he's joking. Parker and I have never spent more than one night together, and it doesn't come often, so having five nights with him in this beautiful city in this gorgeous fairytale house makes me feel overwhelmed and giddy. To settle my excitement into a manageable state, I'm focused on the wide range of activity at the park below: dogs running, children playing, a few joggers making their rounds, some couples just seated on the grass. Startled, my heart skips a beat as the sharp thud of bags hitting the floor makes me leap into the air.

"What the hell did you bring, lady?" Parker says heavily and falls stomach-first onto the bed. "I thought you were some big, strong muscle man who could carry all my stuff," I say, teasing, and he turns to look at me and glare. "Looks like I'll need to find a more capable guy to carry my belongings," I comment, glancing towards the park, and without warning, Parker hooks his arm around my waist, swiftly turns me to face him, and effortlessly lifts me over his shoulder. "Put me down!" I scream and laugh as he uses his other hand to tickle my sides. Hopelessly, I thrash and bang on his broad back while fighting his one arm to free me and his other hand to stop tickling me. Howling with laughter, the pain of it deepening in my gut, I am relieved as he throws me onto the bed and pins my wrists at the sides of my face. He looks at me coolly with one eye raised. "Just testing my strength," he teases. Meanwhile, I am still trying to catch my breath, and I can feel my hair strewn across my face, but I have no hands to fix it, so I am just attempting to shake and blow it out of my face. "Okay, okay," I sigh breathlessly. "You've made your point now. Unhand me, you brute." He looks up and down at me. "No, I don't think I will yet."

"Parker," I plea, still trying to free my wrists. His eyes were still on me, and my breath hitched before he aggressively blew a raspberry into the middle of my chest. I guffaw and curl up at the surprise gesture. He releases my wrist, and I clench my stomach, trying to hold in the laughter that bursts out like bubbles escaping a freshly uncorked champagne bottle. Parker becomes quiet and somber as he's looking out the window. The sun is setting, and the sky is changing shades of pink and orange. I stand beside him and lift his arm over me so I can lean into him. He pulls me to his side and exhales. "I never knew someone could mean so much to me in this short of a time; I feel like a fraud." I squeeze around his waist but can't find the words to match his. Instead, I pull myself closer to him, trying to see if I hold hard enough to sink into his skin and curl up there. My heart aches at the enormity of my love for him, and the sting behind my nose forces me to look down and blink through some tears. A love story, my love story, is playing out right in front of me, and I can't find the right words to tell him how much he means to me.

Chapter 12: I love you, okay?

Heidi, Thomas, and I take a cab to the nearest grocery store, and upon entering, Thomas whispers to us both, "It's very expensive. Please leave." Heidi gives him a playful shove while shushing him, and we grab a cart; it's worth mentioning that this cart might as well be self-propelling; it is the most excellent, smoothest, quietest grocery store cart I've ever put my hands on and I check in with my two best friends to confirm that we cannot, in fact, be asked to leave because we are clearly not in the same median income category as their regular shoppers. Heidi gives me a look that implies if the subject is mentioned again, she will shop alone, and Thomas and I will wait outside like her incorrigible children.

We purchase everything we need to spend all day tomorrow preparing a Friendsgiving masterpiece; well, they will be, and I will be tasked with retrieving whatever they need and may do some chopping. The store is the kind that will package all the fresh ingredients in such a way that we couldn't conceivably crush anything, and they also happen to be doing a complimentary wine tasting, which we simply cannot refuse.

As we sat for the first pour, the clerk told us they would keep our items cold. What is this place, honestly? Heidi looks at me and says, "Sooo Sarah, you and Parker are like, real serious already."

Thomas pipes up, "She told me when she very first met him, she loved him, and I thought she was being crazy, like the crazy you would commit, you know?"

"Thanks, Thomas," I say defensively. "We're just—" I start. "We have a lot in common."

Heidi throws her head back with laughter and then playfully slaps me. "Oh my GAWD! You're totally in LOVE with him!" she squeals. "Does he know? Have you told him? How's the sex? Tell me everything!"

Seated between my two best friends, the alarm bells in my head are sounding at maximum volume, and I squeeze my temples with one hand. Heidi, propped on her knuckles like an expectant gossip queen, eyes me until I finally give in.

"I'm having a hard time compartmentalizing it all." I finally say, "It's overwhelming. I feel like I am connected to him in every existence that matters. Like in a hundred lifetimes, I will always search for him."

"Say it right now," demands Thomas,

"Excuse me?" I scoff.

"Say the words, just say them out loud. Get it out; maybe it will somehow cleanse you to admit it to us," he pressures.

Putting my face in my hands, I whisper, "I think I really do love him."

"What was that?" Heidi sing songs.

Still muffled by my hands I proclaim louder "I love him!"

"I'm sorry, Sarah, we can't seem to make out anything you're saying, but it sounds like you said, I'm a chickenshit."

"I LOVE HIM, OKAY!?" I yell and immediately flush at the number of patrons looking directly at me.

Our wine pourer claps proudly, and most other patrons chime in while I sink lower onto my seat, hoping the earth will crack open right where I'm seated and swallow me whole.

"Our girl is in love," Heidi says, holding her heart. Once we're sufficiently drunk from the wine tasting that turned into a wine gulping contest with one competitor: me, we make our way back to the breathtaking home over the park. Parker, Chase, and Brian meet us at the curb and help haul the groceries; Brian sniffs over me and goes, "Did you spill wine on yourself, Sarah?" "No," I say, but offer no explanation, which causes Parker to give me a sideways glance. Trusting that someone else will put the groceries away, I head upstairs to brush my teeth, change my clothes, or do something that makes me smell less like a winery and feel less like a person carrying a secret.

"Hey," Parker knocks, "Everything ok?"

"I need you to hear it from me first, okay? Before anyone else tells you this week." I blurt out, and Parker immediately freezes, turning a shade of pale reserved for someone who is going to panic. "I love you, alright? But I'm not good at it; you need to know that. I've never been good at it; I've only loved people who didn't love me back, and I think I did that because then I knew that I would get hurt in the end. So because I knew the ending, it was okay — I'm rambling now and sound frantic. But you aren't the same; we aren't the same. We are in love, and I do not know what to do about it."

He comes forward and takes both my hands in his. "Let's just figure it out together, no pressure. We don't even have to say it out loud ever again." He pauses and finishes with a smirk. "It would be nice to hear it from you without sounding terrible."

We head back downstairs and discover that someone has put away the groceries. Everyone snatches blankets, and enthusiastically Alice shouts, "We're going to the park to watch the sunset!" Parker runs back up the stairs to grab his and my sweaters. We take a blanket from Felix and walk across the street to the park. Once we line the grass with our blankets, Thomas and Felix surprise us with plastic cups and two bottles of champagne. We toast to our growing friend circle, and I lean into Heidi for a hug; she squeezes me in the way only a very best friend can squeeze you. I reposition myself between Parker's legs, and he wraps his arm around me in a way that makes me feel like my entire existence has been waiting for this very moment, time stops and says you've made it, you opened all the right doors, and this is precisely where I was leading you. As the sun begins its descent, the once-blue sky gradually morphs into a kaleidoscope of pinks, purples, and oranges, casting a colorful backdrop against the houses on the street, each one adorned with its unique blend of colors. It's like an artist's palette, with an endless array of colors that defy description. Nestled against Parker's shoulder, I let myself relax and absorb the sights, sounds, and scents that surround us.

Chapter 13: Friendsgiving

The morning of Friendsgiving includes the clanging of pots and pans, lots of coffee, and shouting from both Heidi and Thomas. Parker comes downstairs last, and I admire the Abercrombie & Fitch joggers I gave him that he is wearing. He stretches his arms over his head, and I see the peak of his happy trail and notice the prominent outline of him behind the heather gray sweatpants. Chase, Brian, Felix and Jessica gathered on the porch smoking ridiculous cigars Chase found at the preppy shopping center. I see from the near-empty bottle on the counter that they are also sipping on Hennessy. With all the doors and windows open to vent the cooking steam, Alice is enjoying a book on the couch, covered with a blanket. I smile at Parker, and he plants a kiss on my forehead before announcing to Heidi and Thomas, "I'm ready to suit up, team." They eye him and eye each other, not used to a third chef.

"Can you cook?" Heidi asks, waving a spatula at him. "I'm Italian," he says as if that is an acceptable answer. I see the look that passes between them again and the most subtle nod from Thomas. Heidi nods and shoves a recipe at him. "Start here," she says. "We weren't sure if we were going to get this one across the finish line, and now it's up to you, hero." "Aye, Aye," Parker responds, combing the counters for his ingredients. I watch them in awe, their organized shuffling and sharing of spices, the casual tastings, and I fall in love with the scene, wondering how I can bottle this moment or freeze it and keep it forever so that on those dark days, I can pull it from memory and live in it again.

The moment has arrived to convene at the grand table, where we express our gratitude to the talented chefs for the extraordinary feast that graces our presence. Felix and Jessica chose exquisite china adorned with intricate gold ribbon patterns, adding a touch of elegance to the visual spectacle before us. I remember that Heidi and I bought four bottles of the best wine we tasted yesterday, and I rushed to grab two bottles from the separate wine fridge. The cognac drinkers keep with that while the rest of us enjoy the wine. The perfect day and evening unfold, and I can't help but feel my heart growing in size. Our stomachs full to the brim, we regrettably forgo the opportunity to watch the sunset at the park. Felix proposes a leisurely stroll, citing the benefits of digestion. After a long day of indulging in drinks and feasting on delicious food, exhaustion settles upon us like a heavy blanket. With weary bodies and contented minds, we slowly disperse to our respective havens within the house. The air is filled with the faint scent of alcohol and the lingering aroma of the scrumptious meal we devoured earlier. Each step we take is accompanied by the creaking of tired floorboards, a symphony of weariness.

Thomas and I walk up the stairs together and poke him in the ribs. "How's that noncommittal relationship going?" I pester.

He pats my head and returns a condescending, "Awe, I'll tell you when you're older."

I roll my eyes in return and head into my room. It seems I missed Parker's premature departure entirely, as I stumbled upon him looking absolutely flawless in the room. Perched on the built-in seat under the large window, he immerses himself in the pages of Whispers by Dean Koontz. As I stand in the doorway, my heart aches for him, even though he's only a short distance in front of me. Finally, I disrupted him by shutting the door behind me. "I will 100% be running tomorrow morning," I say, unbuttoning my pants and letting them fall down my legs. Digging into Parker's suitcase, I discover a faded band T-shirt that has seen better days. I carefully pluck the shirt from its neatly folded spot, then proceed to remove my sweater and bra before pulling it over my head. I stand, and the scent of sandalwood, cedar, and citrus wraps around me, creating a fragrant embrace. He looks at me, eyebrow raised. "You're seriously going to dirty my shirt when you brought a month's worth of clothes?" I clutch the t-shirt by the collar, lift it over my nose, and inhale boisterously. "But nothing I have smells this good!" He looks around before plucking a decorative feather from a vase, using it as a bookmark, and setting it back on the shelf. He sits back on the window seat and pats his lap for me to join him. I swing one knee beside his leg and place my other wide across him until it settles on the bench across his opposite leg; I slowly settle myself into a straddled position, letting my chest skim his nose and lips, and my hair falls onto his face before resting my lips on his forehead. He pulls me into him by cupping my ass and presses his lips to my neck before giving it a soft nibble, he tips his head back, and I kiss him deeply on the mouth; once I pull away, he grabs my ass in both hands lifts me to stay around his waist and then drops me softly on to the bed. When morning comes, I am still wrapped in him, curled in the space he makes, winding around my small, by comparison, body. I turn to face him and lay my head against his chest, feeling the soft rhythm of his heart, my head rising and falling gently with his breath. I feel him tighten around me, and I know he's awake, but he hasn't opened his eyes until the rapping at our door.

"Rise and shine, love birds!" Felix sings at the door: "It's morning run time!"

He snaps his eyes shut and whispers, "I'll see ya in a bit." I punch him softly on the chest before hearing,

"Sarah! Get your fine ass out of that bed now!"

"Coming,"

With a groan, I reluctantly retrieve my running clothes from my bag. As Parker lay half asleep, I blew him a kiss, and in response, he gave me a sleepy thumbs up followed by a playful air kiss.

Felix and I are joined by Heidi in the foyer. As we step outside, the cool morning air envelops us, carrying with it a refreshing breeze. The sun is just beginning to rise, casting a golden hue over the landscape. It takes me a moment to find my rhythm, but by mile one, I feel a sense of perfection, as if my body has been rejuvenated. As we keep thumping along the climbing and falling streets, I hear:

"However far away, I will always love you
However long I stay, I will always love you
Whatever words I say, I will always love you
I will always love you"

Chapter 14: Coit Tower

We bundle up and head to the wharf, meandering the stores, sharing warm sugared doughnuts from wax paper bags, and filling up on Ghirardelli-flavored hot coffee. We talk to the sea lions off the pier, enjoy the aquarium, and buy matching trinkets to commemorate our time. Brian surprises us all by purchasing a trip to Alcatraz, and we busy ourselves before our boat departs. Once on the ship, we huddle together because the temperature drops at least ten degrees on the bay water, and the ship's windows do little to keep the enclosed area any warmer. The only difference is you just aren't being sprayed with mist, adding to the frigid temperatures. During the tour, we capture goofy pictures and converse about the reasons for our hypothetical imprisonment in Alcatraz. The mist from the bay traps dampness in Alcatraz's interior, and chipped paint or rust covers much of the metal. The combination of mildew and the musky smell of damp people hangs in the air, making me feel uneasy as I quickly survey the surroundings for any available exits. Standing in front of one of the despondent-looking prison cells equipped with a petite, depressing ceramic sink and toilet, Alice quips that the love of her life probably lived and died in one of the cells. Thomas emphatically assures her it may be better that way. As we explore every corner of the island, our eyes soak in its breathtaking beauty - the shimmering blue waters, the lush greenery, and the towering cliffs. The chilly wind whispers through our ears, reminding us of the frigid temperatures. Our noses catch a whiff of the salty ocean air, while our freezing bodies long for the comforting warmth of a cozy restaurant. The thought of steaming clam chowder tantalizes our taste buds and fuels our determination to make it back to our boat.

We find the first place to accommodate us all and shake our jackets free of the spritzing rain that has begun to fall outside. Everyone consumes their bread bowls in shivering silence, and conversation only starts once we become adequately thawed. "No more outdoor things today, cool?" Chase announces, teeth chattering, and we all agree in unison. Then Felix follows up with, "Hey guys, I know this is your Friendsgiving, and I'm new here, but I'm actually taking Thomas to a proper queer outing. Hope you don't mind." Brian takes Heidi's hand and announces he made them dinner reservations. Chase explains he met someone on a dating site who's in the area. Alice wants a night with her book. Lastly Jessica will be third wheeling with Thomas and Felix for a ride to the Castro. Parker squeezes my hip, and his face fills with delight; he looks at his watch and hands a twenty-dollar bill to Brian. "Will this cover us?" Brian nods, and Parker grabs my hand. "We've got somewhere to be," he says, bending to coax me out of my seat. I hastily throw back on my nearly dry but still too thin jacket and give questioning looks to the table. Parker leads us outside and waves down a cab cruising by. "Coit Tower," he says, and the cab roars off, sending us to the back of our seats. Not that I am an expert in cab drivers, or driving in general but I've never feared for my life more than whilst in a cab climbing the vertical streets of San Francisco. While at a red light heading out of the wharf, Parker insistently asks the cab driver if he can pull to the side. The cabbie obliges, and Parker hops out, darting to a gift store. He grabs two sweaters adorned with San Francisco on the front, and we throw them on under our thinner rain jackets. We get to Coit Tower, and miraculously, there's no line, which ordinarily prevents me from going. He paid for our tickets, and we headed up.

When I finally made it to the top, my breath caught in my throat as I took in the incredible panoramic view. As we arrived just before closing time, we were fortunate enough to witness the mesmerizing transformation of the Bay Bridge as it slowly lit up, contrasting beautifully with the fading daylight. The bay's breathtaking beauty captivates me, but Parker's frantic search shatters my tranquility through his pockets, causing a knot to form in my stomach. He then pulls out an iPod from his pocket and carefully untangles the earphones, gently placing one in my ear. Jimmy Eat World 23 begins, and I'm struck with the sudden urge to cry. I look up at him, and he smiles at me. "I wanted to give you the gift of the parking garage, Parker's version." He looks away, and I place my hand on his cheek, turning him back to face me. "I love you, Parker. I am so in love with you." He smiles and places his hand over mine on his cheek. With our gaze fixed on the bay, we witness the sun's descent, its fading light reflecting off the water in a breathtaking display. We stay until security forces us to leave.

As we approached the house, darkness blanketed the surroundings, and an eerie emptiness filled the air, leaving us bewildered. As we ascend the stairs, Parker gestures towards our bathroom.

"I've been meaning to ask if you'll join me in that killer bathtub?"

"Are there any bubbles for it?"

"I think just some lavender salt," he shrugs.

"That'll do," I say, and with that, he starts the bath, which takes time to fill. Dipping into it, I am grateful for the hot water around me, and Parker slowly dips himself across from me. Like the house, the bathroom is white, but even whiter somehow. White cabinets, chrome fixtures, a glass shower, and a large square of glass blocks make a privacy window that lets fractured streetlights illuminate the bathroom into an orange glow. We leisurely converse about what we will do back in Reno, and Parker proposes Christmas dinner with his family. While I'm still not completely over the situation with his sister, I am anxious about another shot at getting to know his warm and loud family.

The water turns lukewarm, and I show him my wrinkled hands. He nods and pulls himself out of the bath while I watch water drip from his skin. He shakes a towel before me, and I pull the bath chain before exiting to join him.

Shortly after, we're lounging in bed while Parker is reading and I am watching a competition show where two couples are racing to design the ultimate fixer-upper house. After a couple of hours, we hear the laughter of many male voices fill the room across our hallway. I turn up my show while Parker strategically places a rolled-up towel under our door to block out some of the noise. Once their door is closed, the sound is muffled enough, and we return to what we have endearingly named old couple time.

Chapter 15: With A P-H

I walk out of my and Parker's room, head downstairs desperately seeking coffee, and am met with two men, not any of the men I would expect. I stopped to take in my surroundings and rule out anything like time travel or perhaps not drunk but drunk and didn't know it Timeshare swapping. Nope, I think I am still in the place I have been in for the entirety of our trip. One man seems to notice my confusion and cuts into my thoughts.

"Coffee?" The other turns.

"Ooh, this one is adorable!"

Gay, I think to myself, that one is gay. Still confused, I walk into the kitchen and take the cup from the stranger's hand. His face sharply narrows, and his chin comes to almost a villainous point. Underneath the blonde and pink hair, his bright blue eyes soften, and his features appear less sharp. His pale skin is flawless, like porcelain, which suddenly makes me self-conscious because I don't know if I remembered to wash my face last night.

"Thanks," I say, still confused. "Who are you?"

A familiar voice cuts in, "Oh Sarah, you are up," and I'm met with a kiss on the cheek that startles more than comforts me.

I snap to the cheek kisser and find Felix twirling through the kitchen. "This is Chord," he says, placing a hand on the gruff-looking man with a full beard and man bun. Twirling again, he finishes. "And Stephen."

"With a P-H," says the porcelain-skinned Stephen, cutting him off.

"Hi," I manage, and it sounds more like a question than a greeting. "She's Thomas' bestie," Felix finishes. "Oh," the two men say, as if it answers anything at all. Deciding I can't stand in the kitchen anymore for fear I'll black out from the overload of confusion, I finish my coffee and step to the balcony, where I find Alice with her coffee and Chase with a cup of what I'm assuming is coffee, both muted and looking out at the park.

"How was it in there?" Chase asks, nodding his head to the inside of the house.

"I'm lost," I respond. "Who are they?"

"Guys Felix and Thomas brought home," says Alice. "Sometime early morning me and Chase ended up in the living room avoiding the noise." She says, gesticulating pounding with her fists.

"Loud?" I question.

Chase shudders. "It was like an all-male orgy."

I let out a laugh that surprised all of us, and then they both joined. As I turn to Chase, I say, "good for them. I thought you had a date?"

"I did, and then I came back. Alice was already asleep in the living room, so I tried to sleep in her bed and couldn't, so I ended up on the other couch." I nod.

"Where did you guys go?" asks Alice

"Coit Tower. It was amazing. We stayed until the sun was almost down when they kicked us out."

"That's so romantic!" she squeals delightedly, and Chase frowns in her direction.

I hear the roar of Thomas' deep voice as he descends the stairs and turn to see a yawning Parker absentmindedly scratching his abdomen. This reveals his toned stomach and low pants, which scores him wolf whistles from the three men in the kitchen, and I see him snap to attention, lowering his shirt. All gay, obviously.

Our new friends and Felix prepare an extensive breakfast, and we all serve ourselves buffet style and sit between the kitchen living room and large table. Heidi and Brian come out of their room fresh-faced and dressed while the rest of us are still wearing pajamas; Jessica is the last to wake up and give everyone she crosses, including Stephen, with a PH and Chord, a fist bump, and a grunt.

Our two guests say their goodbyes, and it's back to our original crew making plans for our last full day in San Francisco, which includes more time in the city at Haight-Ashbury, Union Square, and the Museum. We all stay together, and the weather remains sunny, allowing us to walk to most of our destinations; we decide to stay in and play cards for the evening, which turns into heavy drinking for the bulk of us while Brian and Chase assume their roles as the responsible adults and remind the rest of us loud drunk children they will be driving us home tomorrow morning.

The morning drive home is awful due to our hangovers and need for Gatorade, ginger ale, and frequent bathroom breaks. This causes the drive to take twice as long as it did originally. Once we are finally dropped off at the townhome that belongs to Thomas and me, Parker and I head upstairs and crawl into bed to sleep off the hangovers.

Chapter 16: Bathroom Ain't Big Enough

Christmas Eve has arrived, and Parker and I are in the loud, warm home of his and his parents; we have maintained a steady schedule of visitation, and I've gone to all his shows, often neglecting other bands I need to see, and thanks to the article that dropped in the local paper on the website his audience has grown giving Reverberation Breakdown more notoriety in the area. For my part as a band girlfriend, I busy myself making sure they sound their best, getting great photos taken, and having opportunities with better venues and openings for better bands.

Parker brings in my overnight bag and puts it in his bedroom, which I will stay in alone as his parents aren't into bed-sharing with couples who aren't married. He will instead stay across the hall from me, bunking with his cousin, who is in town for Christmas. The house is guaranteed to get louder tomorrow with the influx of the rest of his family members, which begins promptly with a traditional Christmas breakfast. I agreed to the sleepover instead of just coming early because the thought of sleeping in Parker's childhood bedroom with the smell of him clinging to me was too alluring to pass up, in addition to the fact that I feel utterly emptied of something when he's less than a couple feet away from me. The touching between us is incessant; a hand, arm, or leg is constantly flung over the other. It's like there's no threshold in which we reach a satisfying amount of physical touch.

After an intentionally light dinner, I am now severely limiting the number of carbohydrates I eat because it seems there's no satisfying threshold for that either. Parker holds me for a long time in the hallway, kissing me and telling me how badly he wants to be sleeping next to me with my body tucked into the curve of his. When, finally, his mother shouts something in Italian, he reluctantly releases me and watches me settle into his bed. He releases his breath, and I watch him close my door. Then, it's just me and his four walls.

I am surrounded by his unmistakable scent in the room, which serves as a comforting reminder of his presence. Above me, the Farrah Faucet iconic bathing suit photo hangs, a treasured possession said to have been passed down from Parker's grandfather. His walls are robin egg blue with white shiplap cutting them in half, a design feature he says has existed his entire life. There is a small desk with a few pens and a notepad where he does his homework, and two white accordion doors hide his messy closet. It's plain and tidy, a demonstration of the fact that he scarcely spends any time here, and yet, it smells as if he is right next to me.

I wake drowsily to a hand cupping me at my center and then feel the brush of Parker's lips against my neck. Every movement is hurried until he's kissing me hard, his lips leaving a lingering warmth on mine as he quickly retreats into his room, leaving me breathless and questioning the reality of the moment.

In the morning I crack open the door and peak down the hall to see if the bathroom is in use. When I confirm the door is open and the bathroom is dark, I dart across and down the hall into the open bathroom door, hugging my bag to my chest. I walk in backward and pull the door shut. Relief leaves my body like a cannon being shot. Intense humiliation replaces it as I back into Parker's cousin, who is standing mid-stream over the toilet. He lets out a sharp yelp, causing me to let out a high-pitched shriek, as I hastily lunge forward towards the door handle. My hand encounters an unexpected resistance, accompanied by a yipping sound. Giving up on pushing it open, feeling helpless and confined, I tightly shut my eyes and cover them with my hands for extra assurance. "Oh, my GAAWWWWDDD," I cry as the door squeaks on the hinges, followed by the voice of Parker bellowing a string of grunts and curses. "What is going on here!?" I hear a female voice cut into the hysteria, and I am just hoping that I am abducted by aliens or swallowed by the Earth. I feel a hand on my shoulder and hear a placid, "I'm just gonna go by you and get out of here." Without opening my eyes, I move to one side and feel a body shuffle past me while sensing another close in.

"Sarah?" I hear Parker's voice, and I open one eye and then the other. "What the hell is going on? Were you just in here with Victor?" He sounded suspicious and confused, which alerted my defenses.

In disbelief as my voice pitchers higher, I rebuke, that I saw the door open, and the bathroom was dark, so I hurried in here to get ready. Unfortunately it turns out it was already occupied. "I'm so embarrassed," I continue, "and what's worse is your immediate reaction was that I somehow planned this incident to be near your cousin!?"

"That's not what I said," explains Parker.

"Oh, but it was clearly implied," I say pointedly.

"You know I love you two, but you cannot shower together," I hear Parker's mom interject, and I just stare at the floor.

Parker groans and says, "I know, Mom, we're not trying to."

"Can I please get ready?" I plead. Parker shuts the door, and I lock it, then test it before showering.

When I return to Parker's room, he sits completely dressed on the bed, examining his foot and showing me the scrapes from my attempted escape. "I'm sorry for making you feel like that," he says, "I didn't mean to assume anything. I just can't imagine you with anyone but me, and it gets the better of me sometimes."

"I don't want anyone else, Parker, just you," I say, grabbing his hand.

"You will always win," he says. "There's not a single fight I would win."

"We don't need to fight, Parker." I say, unsure what he means, squeezing his hand tighter. "Let's go have breakfast."

I am greeted by family members I've already met and others I have not, each as warm and loud as the rest. They all cackle at Victor and Carla's retelling of the morning's incident, and while I find it funny now, I can tell it makes Parker uncomfortable, so I keep my laugh inside.

Between our meals and other Christmas activities, Parker, his father, and other members of the family play guitar or piano and sing. Watching him is mesmerizing, as he effortlessly manipulates the strings, creating a flow of music that makes its way from him to the inside of me. Being so enamored with another human being, everything they do enters your being and stays there, new cells coursing through your bloodstream. The rest of the day goes by smoothly, and when it gets late, Parker and I decide to head back to my house. We're both exhausted and in danger of falling asleep, which could lead to another sleepover. We couldn't bear the thought of spending another night in separate rooms, so we headed back to my townhome. Once there, we passionately make love, as if events like war has separated us for months. We then fall asleep in each other's arms, with my body nestled into the curve of his.

Chapter 17: New Year's Envy

My friends oppose going to the Knit's New Year's Eve Party after watching Parker's band play at a bar down the street.

"Sarah, we love you," says Heidi, "but we cannot go to another one of his shows; we are DYING to do something else—"

"ANYthing else." Thomas cuts in. "Listen, Parker is hot and talented, but his band is not, and if you make me watch them again, I'll ring your pretty little neck."

"Okay, okay," I concede, "Parker will just meet us at the Knit."

All my friends, including Brian and Chase, are giving a round of applause. I text Parker and let him know majority rules and that I'll see him at the Knit after his show; he texts back with a sad face.

> I can't believe you're choosing them over me
> It's not like that
> Then what's it like?
> I don't want to walk alone the extra blocks
> Ok, I guess

I love you. I'll see you after
K
Parker.... I love you.
Yeah, you too

Returning my phone to my pocket, I'm burdened with guilt, not because I'm not going to his show, but because I'm eager to be with my friends doing our regular hanging out and partying. We make it to the Knit and start our usual round of shots and drinks with Felix behind the bar. We dance to the DJ, and Heidi and I are putting on our regular pseudo-lesbian dance show, Brian at her back, which leaves Chase to scour the scene for any single and willing dance partners. I feel a hand grip my hips, and I turn to find a stranger trying to dance with me; I remove his hands and shake my head while shouting, "No, thank you!" he ambles forward. I try again to cut off his grip on me; he's not getting the message. Before I can break away from him, Brian moves around Heidi and places himself in front of me, Chase closing in next to him. "Back off!"

Brian shouts and the man raises his hands in surrender as he turns away. We walk back toward our table as I am wiping away the invisible handprints where he once had a hold of me. "You ok?" Chase asks in my ear. "Yeah," I nod. "I'm fine." I grab Brian's arm and gesture at my heart while I silently say, "thank you," and he gives me a brisk head tilt when I notice Parker cutting through the crowd looking for me, or so I assume. With a burst of energy, I sprint towards him and wrap my arms around him. He clasps me firmly and holds my face while kissing me. "I'm so happy you are here!" He gives me another squeeze. Spotting that he has brought the rest of the band, I beckon them over to the tables we have taken. As we sit together and grab a table, we exchange hugs and handshakes and order a round of drinks. I explain the scenario that just played out, and Parker looks at me more with disdain than concern. "Maybe you shouldn't dance like that unless I'm around." I ignore the jab and just nod in an attempt not to start a fight; I've learned over the weeks we've been together that Parker's insecurity often rears itself when there's another man involved, no real scenario, just another one who may or may not be interested in me. Because of the tension this often brings I have gotten good at keeping it at bay. Heidi and Thomas think it's somewhat trivial that I concern myself with his insecurities. Still, I challenge that I'm being respectful while he works through them.

The night continued without incident until the countdown finally began: 5, 4, 3, 2, 1! Parker and I passionately kiss, promising that this will be the first New Year of many we spend together.

Chapter 18: Too Old for MTV

Parker and I continued our relationship into the summer, effortlessly falling into a predictable and comforting cadence. We even survived the week-long trip Heidi, and I took to Chicago, primarily spent at our sales conference, with only one day dedicated to seeing the sights. Parker and I talked more than Heidi and Brian, which Heidi was friendly enough to point out each time.

We are all preparing for Thomas' and my 24th birthdays; we are always the last ones to turn the same age as everyone else, and even though our birthdays are a few weeks apart, we have always celebrated together. This year we've rented a cabin at the lake and will ring in year 24 with boating, swimming, barbecuing and drinking.

Parker fixed his Mustang some time ago, so he and I drove to the cabin in his beautiful car, which garners looks from everyone we pass. The car's engine roars through the dense forest as we ascend the winding road to our cabin. The scorching heat amplifies the discomfort of the leather interior, forcing me to repeatedly lift myself off the seat, yearning for a refreshing gust of air to alleviate the sticky sensation on my skin.

We are the last to arrive, but because it's a birthday trip, Thomas and I are guaranteed the best rooms available. In this particular rental best seems to have been determined by the fact that the bedroom has an adjoining bathroom, the only grading system available given the cabins lack of upgrades. The cabin, presumably built in the 80s, retains its original decor. With predominantly wood-paneled walls, the cabin exudes a dark and cramped atmosphere. The furniture, consisting of mismatched dining chairs and wicker sofas, adds to the eclectic charm. However, the reason we chose this was for the outside. The backyard abuts a soft sand beach with a dock, firepit, and chairs. The view is pure blue lake and sky, so much blue it's hard to tell where the lake ends and the sky begins. Currently, Chase and Brian are applying seasoning to the meat that they plan to cook later this evening. I hear something about it being something they hunted together. Promptly I choose to ignore that conversation to avoid getting grossed out. Alice informs Parker and me that everyone is waiting for us to head out onto the large speed boat Heidi and Brian rented for the occasion. We change into our swimming slash boating attire and Parker eyes my swimsuit and cover up skeptically. "I don't know if I can let you out of this room in that," he says teasingly while tugging at the tie around the back of my neck. "Don't start something we can't finish," I say. He gently slides his hands through the wide-flowing sleeves of my cover up to brush his fingertips delicately over the sides of my breasts; my skin prickles, and he smiles at the apparent reaction my body has to his hands. Hearing the calls from our friends we make our way to the dock where he gets in the boat and then helps me in steadying me by my hips.

We spend so many hours on the lake, by the time we have eaten our meticulously packed picnic lunch by Heidi and

Thomas we are sunburnt and calling it quits. The water seems to stretch endlessly as we make our way back to the dock. Parker announces he has to use the bathroom and first steps off the boat in a hurry to the outdoor bathroom on our cabin's property. Chase has positioned himself on the dock and is helping everyone off the boat. I urgently make my way to the area we're all exiting, and as I step off, a massive wave from another boat's wake catches the boat, and it violently moves backward. Chase yanks me forward, pinning me against his chest so I don't fall off the dock into the water. "Thanks" I say as I feel Parker snatch me out of Chase's grasp. "You okay?" he says, eyeing Chase, who appears utterly unbothered by Parker's territorial display.

"Yeah," I say, feeling my nerves settle. "That could've been way worse."

"I mean, he probably could have prevented the fall without rubbing himself all over you."

"Parker," I say, peeved. "He wasn't rubbing himself on me."

His look gives way to irritation, and I'm not ready to fight this out on my birthday trip, so I change my tone and flash him a smile while drawing a finger down his chest, "The only guy I want rubbing themselves on me is you." He wraps me into him, burying his face into my neck and enticing the earlier reactions that were dismissed by our boating time. We fall into our usual intensity, pulling the wet bathing suits from each other's bodies and masking the quiet room with our urgent moans and squelching of damp skin pressing against more wet skin. He wraps my legs around him and pushes me against the shower stall as he thrusts himself into me. He turns on the shower to muffle our sounds, so much water goes unused. We continue our interpretive display of power and ownership of one another, such that by the time we are washing, it is as cold as the lake. We dress and join the remaining group for dinner outside.

We receive a birthday cake adorned with an alarming number of candles, surprising Thomas and me. "24 for each of you," says Alice excitedly. I am staring into the flames, praying they don't start a forest fire in the time they take to sing Happy Birthday to us. Thomas must've shared my anxiety because as soon as they reached the end, we accidentally bumped foreheads, both leaning in sync to blow out the flames of all 48 candles. As we laugh at the absurdity of our run-in, the sound of cheers fills the air.

"Did you know we're too old for MTV reality shows?" I ask.

"What?" clarifies Alice.

"We're all 24 now," I continue, "and that is the cut-off to be eligible for one of MTV's reality shows; we're officially too old for MTV, and what's worse, I'm too old for my favorite song. It doesn't go: I'll be 24 or 25, it goes I'll be 23." I finish solemnly.

We all take a moment of silence for our perceived youth before Chase lifts a beer. "Here's to being young until 30!" We all laugh, toast each other to his decree, and continue smoking, drinking, and laughing into the evening.

Chapter 19: One Year In

Parker and I formally celebrate our first anniversary in October. We are sitting in the back of my truck, watching the sunset from the parking garage where it all started; 23 is playing in the background of my newly titled Parking Garage Playlist as Parker draws small circles into my upward-facing palm. We've navigated our lives intertwining for a year, and the intensity of our feelings still engulfs my senses; I'm so eager to be around and with him I've let so much of myself that isn't attached to him fall away. My friends are in some parts happy for me, but also express concern for my relationship, which they classify as obsessive. Out of everyone, Thomas is the one who is most aware of the things in my personal life that I have neglected. He's also taken up the role of advisor: quick to provide counsel during the blowout disagreements Parker and I have about nothing in particular, offering that the ferocity of love I have with Parker should be examined by a professional. "You're young," he says. "It's okay to take some time for you still."

"I can't remember a time before you," Parker interrupts my thoughts. As I turn my head, I catch him looking at me with a smile.

"Why would you want to?" I respond and close in to kiss him gently on the lips. We stay locked in our teenage-inspired make-out session in the parking garage, and the feeling of him abandons any pause I may have given to our relationship. There's no way we aren't meant to be when something feels like this. When people talk about fireworks, this is what they mean.

The night after, Parker has a show, a big one, and my friends reluctantly agree to come only because it is their most important show to date. They are opening for a more well-known alternative band in Sacramento, so we are all driving down to show support, including Will and Roger. Roger jumps at the opportunity to showcase a band that is climbing the local scene; he reaches out to some acquaintances and gets us an interview with the headliner to up the ante. Parker is at his absolute best before a show; he is amped up and excited, and falling further in love with him is inevitable when I see him light up practicing the chords on his guitar, singing the notes to warm up his vocal cords. He is irresistibly magnetic.

In interviewer slash rock journalist mode, a position I've always found exhilarating. I meet with the headliner before the show and confidently have my entire charming persona on display; I laugh at their jokes, make my own clever jokes, and am casually flirtatious when I ask my sequence of questions regarding their inspirations and relationship statuses. The drummer is distractingly good-looking, and our chemistry throughout the conversation is undeniable. However, I am cautious because I have a boyfriend I love. Still, the thought of his hands touching me and watching the tensing and release of his large, muscled arms visible through his cut-out tank top has chills lighting up my spine.

I leave the interview and return to see Parker and his band readying themselves for the stage. He catches my eye, and I blow him a kiss that he returns, and just like that, the drummer boy is out of sight and mind.

"Sarah, right?" I turn and am faced with Kyler, the clear weightlifter slash drummer of the band who's headlining tonight's shows with an impressive crowd.

"Yep," I say, popping the P sound.

"Your boyfriend is headed on stage now, right?"

"Parker," I correct. "Yes, he is."

"Buy you a drink while they play?"

A smile plays on his lips that I can't quite make out. I am so distracted by the intensity of his sharp blue eyes looming over my body that I forget words and instead nod my agreement. We head to the bar, and I catch the faces of all my friends following our path to the bar. Thomas gives a raised fist as I shake my head no.

We ordered our drinks, and after getting them, I introduced him to my friends. He shakes all their hands, and most of my table gives him long stares of approval, visibly comforting him while I feel my face flush. Thankfully, Parker's band began to play, and I assumed Kyler would leave, but he continued to stand at our table and turned his attention to the stage.

During the first song I noticed Kyler's hand absently drumming along to their music - ON MY ASS! Startled, I shout to the table that I must use the restroom and flee first in the wrong direction before correcting the course as Heidi and Alice catch up to me.

"Are you okay?" shouts Heidi.

"He had his hand on my ass!" I sputter, as Alice snaps her head back to look at him, "Damn, I wish his hand was on my ass."

"Not the point, Alice!" Heidi loops her hand through mine, and we enter the quieter bathroom. I promptly empty my bladder, wet a paper towel, and dab it on my face, careful not to ruin my makeup. "What are you freaking out about, anyway? You didn't sleep with the guy."

"I don't know," I say, panicked. "I don't know!"

"Okay, just relax and take a breath. You're going to go back out there, not let anyone know you're flustered, and when your also hot boyfriend gets off stage, you're going to make out with him, got it?" I nod, my hands braced against the sink.

"You're right; I'm being so weird right now."

When we head back out, I scan the area but Kyler is nowhere to be found, and a wave of relief washes over me. As I take the coaster from Thomas, I can't help but feel perplexed until I see the massive black numbers that have mysteriously appeared on it. I know it's his phone number; I slide it into my purse and think that judging by this crowd, he will find a distraction easily. Speaking of distractions, I see Parker singing, guitar behind his back, and he's making eye contact with a group of girls shouting and reaching for him as he reaches back to them in a serenade of sorts; instantly, my body heats with rage. I am staring at him, trying to will him to turn away and see me, sing to me, reach for me. No luck. Immersed in my silent fury, I search the room for Kyler, sweeping my eyes back and forth until I catch sight of his too-large tank top that barely acts as a cover to his muscled torso. I approach him with decisive steps; he catches me coming with that same searing gaze and wicked grin from earlier. He steps back into the darkness of behind the stage; when I reach him, I don't think, I don't breathe; I just press myself into him and feel his muscles clench around me, meeting me in a tacky kiss that goes on for less than a minute before I stop it and turn back to my table awash with colliding feelings of reproach and self-righteousness.

When Parker's band completes their set list and clears away their items from the stage, I see Parker emerge. He's met with a swarm of barely dressed concertgoers who stop him for photos, giggles, and what looks like autographs. Autographs on BOOBS, oh absolutely not. I stomp to his side and give my sweetest smile to the sluts standing before me. "Who are you!?"

One asks impolitely as her slur tells me she's had one too many of whatever drink sloshes around in her hand. Seizing the opportunity to make her spill it onto her unsuspecting friend, I apologize and respond, "Oh, me? I'm the girlfriend," I say, grasping Parker's arm and pulling him in for a forced kiss. He tentatively kisses me in return, and I stand watch as he completes his thanks to the now semi-disinterested girl group.

Because we drove separately, and my friends and I didn't have any band equipment to pack up, I make it to my place before Parker. A part of me assumes he's not coming over as planned, which infuriates me further but would've probably been better because when he enters my room, I immediately stand and greet him with, "What the fuck was that, Parker?"

"What was what, Sarah?" he says.

On impulse, I shake my head in disbelief. "Are you kidding me!? Am I somehow imagining all the attention you were paying to those barely dressed bitches?" My voice is shrill.

"Oh fucking please, Sarah, I saw you at your interview. Don't act like I wasn't playing the part JUST LIKE YOU!" He says this slowly, each word landing like a blow.

"So that's it then? We just make each other jealous until what? One of us wins?" I throw my hands up, prompting him for an answer.

"I don't fucking know, Sarah, I'm just trying to match you!"

"Me!?" I screech. This intensely amuses him and he guffaws maniacally.

"You KISSED him, Sarah! You fucking kissed that guy! Chris told me everything he saw with his own eyes."

I plop down instantly and cry inconsolably, my tears streaming down my face and filling my hands with salty liquid. I hear footsteps moving away, stomping down the stairs, and I wince as the floor beneath me shakes from the forceful slam of the front door.

Who the hell am I?

Chapter 20: Not Your Grade School Recess

It's been two whole weeks since Parker and I have had any contact with each other, and the distraction of missing him is so heavy my chest and head constantly ache with his absence. I am sitting at work using my thumbs to press circles into my temples when one of our senior leaders enters the building looking like someone just informed him that his grandma, dog, and brother all died in a train wreck. Asking for our attention, he shuffles us to the center of the room, where a sealed, plain white envelope is handed to us. He delivers the news, and I hear it in pieces with what feels like long stretches of static between market crashing, doors closing, severance, and applications being accepted for positions that will remain. A distant ringing is filling my head now as I contend with what's happening. Desperately I seek Heidi, whose face is twisted with dismay as she meets my eyes. We're asked to remove our belongings and leave immediately, but Heidi isn't leaving. She is being ushered into an office as I am being ushered out. She gives me a sign that shows she'll call me, and I load my things into my truck. I drive to my empty townhome because Thomas is still at work and clumsily place my box of items in the middle of my room. The emptiness feels like a deep cavern; there is no Parker, job, Heidi, or Thomas. I am utterly alone, and it feels sickening. Not able to face the magnitude of my walls and their imposing emptiness, I grab my keys and jump back into my truck, driving the familiar route to the parking garage. When I arrive, I arrange my cushions in the back and start my playlist. It'll be a few hours until the sun sets, but I suddenly have nowhere else to be and nothing to do.

I must've fallen asleep; my body's response to all the grief was to shut down. I woke to a breeze and abruptly started shivering as the sky darkens, giving way to the sunset's purples, pinks, and oranges. Needing to drown the silence, I reach into my truck and start my playlist again, which lands on Paramore's All I Wanted Was You, and the tears sting my eyes; I search with my blurred vision for the truck blanket, and instead, I lift a sweater, Parker's sweater. I stick myself inside of it, pulling the collar up over my eyes, and heave large salty tears into my chest. The anguish of all the loss overwhelms me as I faintly register a knocking against the side of my truck. I cautiously uncover my face, and through the fog of my sadness, I see Parker standing with his arms crossed on the side of my truck's bed.

"Hey," he whispers, and I return nothing. He lifts his chin, and I'm unsure if I actually nod before he jumps into my truck with me. "Heidi is looking for you; she told me what happened and thought maybe you came to me." He pauses. "I knew you were here," he exhales. "I thought about telling her but wanted to find you myself." Still, I say nothing, which urges him to continue. "Can you say something? Anything?" I shake my head no, and he places his arm around me, pulling me into the familiar nook of him, and I cry again, giant, heavy sobs that shake the bed of my truck. We don't speak while he holds me until it's so dark that you can only see black ahead unless you look down on the city.

He drives me home, walks me into my room, takes off all my clothes like he's bringing me home after a night of drinking, and can't manage to do so myself, except the stark contrast is that I am fighting tears instead of laughter. He tucks himself into my bed with me, and I sleep because he is here, because of all the wrong in my life; simply being with him corrects the universe enough that I can.

Chapter 21: Things We Never Said

In the months that follow my job loss, I live on my severance. Adding to my complete shit storm of a life, Roger from Rock Out Local receives the heartbreaking news that his mother has been diagnosed with terminal cancer. He heads back to Southern California, causing Rock Out Local to grind to a halt. I compose and publish a farewell article that shocks no one, as our little gig ending coincides with the impending recession that will engulf the entire US.

Thanks to a friend I met through Rock Out Local, I landed a job tending bar and began my shifts at the thriving Three Olives bar downtown. We get a steady stream of after-work drinkers who usually come wearing three-piece suits and briefcases, divorcees, and other feathered birds sprinkled in between, which often includes my friends. It turns out my charismatic personality, coupled with strategically planned outfits usually reserved for going out with my friends, lends itself well at Three Olives. I can make ends meet on my weekend tips alone. Thank goodness for small favors; I like the bar, chatting with the customers and getting compliments from the patrons.

I dramatically contrast my usual co-worker, Timothy Allen Gregory, who goes hilariously by Tag, making him sound like a college frat boy. Tag is 10 years my senior and is already graying around the edges of his hairline. Tag is classically handsome, like a James Bond type, with his thick dark hair styled with gel that mimics John Travolta in Grease; he wears a button-down shirt tucked into dark pants and different suspenders with a mostly matching tie every night. The ladies and gays who visit the bar, my friends included, adore him. At the end of the night when we are counting out tips, Tag usually has a wad of phone numbers that rivals the wad of cash. Tag even plays dice with Parker when he comes in.

If it's still light out during my break, Parker and I will saunter along the river, where we fall into old habits of holding hands, kissing, and laughing. Notably, a vast chasm of unspoken words stretches between us, growing wider as we avoid addressing what transpired between us. It begs the question of why we went from being inseparable, with only hours between visits and constant physical contact, to complete silence just a few months ago. From my perspective, the wounds from all the prior events are still too fresh, as if the skin hasn't fully healed and is sensitive to the slightest touch of air. So, to be the one who rips free the band-aid, keeping us solidly together, this version of acceptable happiness, would be like pouring alcohol on that scrape. Instead, I cling to his arm, lacing his fingers with mine, inhaling his citrus and sandalwood scent, and telling him regularly how much I love him, because I do. Our lovemaking is intense, but it has evolved with more hands around necks and pinning me against the bed. He now exudes a sense of primacy over me, which occasionally confuses me with my newly appointed status as prey. I am the stupid girl who kissed the drummer boy who meant nothing because, for Parker, I felt everything.

Chapter 22: My Song

Tag and I are shuffling quickly around each other with our bar back zig zagging between us on one of our busier weekends; some large conference is at the casino nearest us, and we were lucky enough to receive their business, which is already promising to be over a thousand dollar night in tips for each of us. Tag and I both know our strengths in the crowds that come in and have gotten used to sharing tips on our shift, something of a rarity at Three Olives, but we both have confidence we've earned them equally. If I have a group of gals at my end of the bar, I'll swap places with Tag so he can talk them up and perform juggling acts with bottles and shakers while he pours their drinks; this, of course, is the show they came for, not me. I have two parts: always leaning, bending over, and deliberately placing bills in my shirt while feigning interest in the latest market trends because of the recession or the smack-talking cool girl who can dish it and take it.

While the prospect of tonight's tips has undeniably put me at the top of my game, I am praying for enough of a slowdown that I can sprint, literally sprint, the two blocks to an acoustic show Parker is doing at a place called the Blue Room as a surprise. Tag is on board. The crowd just needs to be subdued enough for him and our bar back to handle. Thankfully, the conference goers, who are not proving to be the all-night party crowd, are the ones headed back into the casinos for gambling. Finally, the crowd drops enough that Tag gives me the okay, and I hastily exit the bar, clutching my high heels I will exchange with the ballet flats I am currently running in. I practically hurl the cover charge at the person standing just inside the doors after being told the show is almost over. "That's fine," I say while throwing my heels on. I am in the very back of the room but can see Parker and his bandmates between the crowd if I stand just so. My heart is thumping from the race here, and I unconsciously place a hand on my chest as I stare between the people directly at Parker.

His song plays, and the melody is somber and unrecognizable; it strikes me that Parker has a new song, and I'm wounded at the fact I didn't know. He sings, and his voice, as usual during slow songs, is a beautiful, melodious dance between bass and tenor. I pull my hair behind my ear to catch more of the lyrics and recognize with a sudden gut punch that I am the subject of this song. This song describes how some broken hearts are unmendable. As the song continues to illustrate shattered expectations, I feel a stinging behind my nose that threatens to give way to tears suddenly. The music crescendos before ending in the soft, somber way it started, and everyone bursts into applause.

As my thoughts replay part of the bridge and chorus, muffling the applause, I can hear the lyrics of our torment. Parker stands and scans the crowd; duck, I think, but I am cemented to my position. As if willed by some unworldly power, he spots me through the sea of people, and it's just me and him for a string of moments before I turn and bolt for Three Olives. I sprint the entire two blocks in my high-heels and burst through the door to a hushed crowd. Tag spots me with a look of concern stretching across his features. He signals me to the back, and I swiftly move, afraid that my face will betray me and display the hurt coursing through me like tidal waves.

Tag hands me a shot, I down it without a thought. He gestures, satisfied that he made a good choice by pouring it. "I just need a minute," I let out. "Take your time," he says, leaving me alone in the small office but returning immediately to inform me that Parker is here. I look up, and Tag demonstrates his willingness to kick him out if I say the words. I shake my head no, stand, and straighten myself up, using the tiny mirror on the wall to see how blotched my face is. Tag brushes off my shoulder in a gesture that mimics rappers in music videos before saying, "You look beautiful, not at all like you were crying." I look at him sidelong and take a deep breath before heading to the bar. Our bar back has set Parker up with some kind of drink, and he is impatiently or nervously tapping his fingers against it. When I approach, he wrings his hands around the glass, and I decide its nerves, not impatience, that ails him. "You were there?" he starts, and he seems dazed.

"I was," I respond precisely.

He blows out a loud puff of air. His shoulders noticeably deflate before stating, "I should've told you." He doesn't meet my eyes. Instead, I am watching him continue to squeeze the glass in his hands.

I let a long pause settle between us before asking, "About the song?"

He nods in agreement as his phone vibrates, flashing the name "Not Sarah," on the screen. Quickly, he ignores it and explains "it's a girl Chris is seeing; her name is also Sarah, but not you, Sarah, so that's why—" he stops. "Anyway, I should have told you there was a song that even existed about us, about you. You shouldn't have been surprised."

"Surprised," I say, enunciating each syllable with the hesitation of someone learning English for the first time. "I wasn't surprised. I was hurt. I AM hurt."

"That's not better," he laughs inwardly. "That might be worse. Actually, no, that IS worse."

I look at Tag and then back to Parker. "Can we maybe talk about this somewhere more private?" He also looks around the bar. "Oh, yeah, okay. What time are you off?" I slide him my apartment key and say he can wait for me there and return to my regular duties before we close in the next few hours. Tag doesn't press me for much, but I give him enough that when I tell him about the song, he grimaces in response. "Good luck," he says as we both enter our cars, and I give him a thumbs up.

I chain smoke two cigarettes on the way home and stand in front of my door, willing it to fall from its hinges and mush me into the pavement in some cartoon-like accident that prevents me from talking with Parker or doing anything ever again. No luck. I open the door and find Parker sitting on the couch drinking what appears to be whiskey in a rocks glass with Thomas at his side.

"And how was the night?" Thomas chirps, which tells me he has no idea what has transpired. "Thousand-dollar night," I respond animatedly, flashing a smile and sashaying my hips in celebration. He raises his glass in a toast, offering me one.

"No whiskey for me. Thanks," I say.

"There's some raspberry vodka and club soda in there." he points with his glass toward the kitchen.

"That, I will do."

After making my drink, I sit on the patio and light my third cigarette in the brief span of 15 minutes. As I blow a cloud of smoke into the air, Parker steps out, sliding the door closed at a ridiculously slow pace. Given this, I have minutes to calculate all the points at which I could still dash through the door and run away before the opening becomes too tiny to accommodate me.

"Sooooo," Parker says with the same speed that he closed the door.

"Soooo," I repeat.

"Are we going to talk about what happened?"

I laugh upwardly at the sky and then face him. "Which part, Parker? My mistake? your irreparable heart? The part where we can't fix each other?"

"I don't think we're unfixable," he says.

"Okay, so let's say we're fixable. Obviously, we aren't fixing it; we haven't even talked about it; we've been avoiding it for months, and I did not know how damaged things really were."

"That's not true," he says, pointing a finger at me. "You have just been doing what Sarah always does, avoiding the conflict and just shoving it down until the repressed emotion detonates. Or does it ever detonate?"

"I don't know," I say defensively. "Listen, Parker, I appreciate you sparing my feelings because of everything I've been going through, but that apparently has helped nothing, so maybe just let it out."

He paces in front of me. "Truthfully, I was waiting for it to happen; somehow, I knew it would, and not because I think you're a terrible person, but because I knew if I played with the fire of your jealousy even fractionally, you would win. I couldn't make you as jealous as you make me."

"What do you mean?" I say confused.

"I always thought that you would eventually find someone better, someone you were more interested in."

"I've never wanted anyone else; I've always wanted you."

"Well," he sneers, almost amused, "kissing some random guy at a show because I was flirting with some girls doesn't exactly make that clear."

"Ha-ha," I mock. "It is without question that was wrong; I don't even know why I did it. It was like I was watching you ignore me, watching you sing to all those girls. It reminded me of that night, the one when I wore Coca-Cola." I pause and take a long drag from my cigarette. "How I felt knowing there was someone there before me, someone who could take your attention from me, and something inside me snapped." I look up. I can see Parker's face twist at the mention of him. "You'll never understand how sorry I was, how sorry I am that I did that, and then I find out I hurt you so much you wrote a song about it?!"

"I love you," he says resolutely, and I feel that familiar sting as the tears slowly drop from my eyes.

"I've only loved you," I cry. "I don't want to lose you, Parker; what can we do to be good again? How do we get past this?"

"We start from here. You are sorry, I forgive you, and we start again." He nods and stands with his hand out. I take it, stamping out my cigarette, as he leads me up the stairs to my room, where he closes the door behind us. He tenderly lifts my chin to him and kisses me, this time with none of the force from the last couple of months. I embrace him tightly, and he lets go of my face to draw me nearer, sliding his hand up my shirt and tracing his fingers along my back, undoing my bra as he moves. He then reaches to my front and unbuttons and unzips my pants before attempting to squeeze his hand into my underwear. "Too tight," he says into my mouth. Hence, I release him and forcefully pull my pants down past my hips, causing them to fall without hindrance. I feel him open his belt and pants between us, also allowing them to fall. I remove my shirt, unclasped bra going with it, while he is moving us backward to my bed; his lips leave mine again as he removes his shirt and then kisses me again, pressing his bare chest into mine. He tenderly tucks his arms behind me, and we land smoothly on my bed, tangling each other with limbs before

I feel him push my underwear aside. Slowly, the pressure of him builds inside of me. No loud moaning, no heavy gasps of desire. Everything is tender, like an apology and forgiveness being written by our bodies.

Chapter 23: Not So New Year

Days turn to weeks, weeks to months, and our second anniversary, birthdays, and holidays pass without special celebrations, including friend trips - thanks to the recession. Parker and I are together, but the need to be near him isn't as fierce as it once was; long gaps stretch between us, and the ache I used to feel when he was away never comes. We've managed to stay together despite the intense challenges we face when the topic of cheating arises, causing Parker to become visibly tense and unable to meet my gaze. I feel as though I'll never be able to return to the girl I once was to him, forever marked in some way. My friends have all noticed the difference, and for their part, they're here to support me, but suspect our new relationship isn't the healthiest. Heidi points out that I'm different around him, like a little kid who's always in trouble, and Felix points out that he spends more time on his phone than ever. They never recommend that I leave him out loud, but I feel it looming over our conversations.

On New Year's Eve, I am working in the busy bar with Tag as my friends drink at a table, if only so we can pretend to celebrate together. Parker comes in with Chris after his show and joins them; the tension when I visit is palpable. Felix will work well into New Year's morning, and the party he is tending bar for has a one-hundred-dollar ticket price, which is why I am in the company of our friends and not him. I lean over the bar to greet Parker with a quick kiss and let him know I'll bring drinks over. I rapidly make them drinks and run them over, kissing him again, wrapping my arms around his neck, and catching Chris rolling his eyes. Heidi catches it, too, and Brian gives her a brisk shake of his head, displaying his unwillingness to have any drama tonight. Ignoring Chris, I return to land another string of kisses before joining Tag behind the bar. We are busy, and the bar patrons have filled the jukebox with upbeat, mostly pop songs. Then I hear an alternative beat begin and recognize it as Theory of a Deadman's Bad Girlfriend; I consider little about it until I spot Chris and Parker chuckling amongst each other at the table. Thomas and Heidi appear to be frowning at them.

Wait, I think abruptly, am I the bad girlfriend? I take a deep breath and continue to do my job through the song, which ends, as another song less belittling to my ego begins. Tag springs to the bar and is now energetically performing some kind of Chippendales-style dance to the pop song, then suddenly stops to wave me onto the bar. I vigorously shake my head in disagreement. He chants my name, causing the rest of the bar to chant "Sar-ah, Sar-ah!" as well. Finally, I roll my eyes and climb onto the bar, careful not to knock anything over. I dance ridiculously and offbeat as Tag raises an eyebrow and then clutches his stomach in exaggerated laughter. Our mismatched dance-off carried on until a slower song came on the jukebox, resulting in a burst of applause from the bar. It is a relief to observe that even Parker is clapping and laughing. As I approach their table to check on my friend's drinks, Parker unexpectedly pulls me in and remarks, "Well, that was entertaining."

With a smile, I ask him, "What do you mean?"

"Well, I half expected you to really dance, like you used to, and like ON Tag."

I shake my head. "I'd rather not dance on Tag ever; besides, I wouldn't want to be the bad girlfriend, now, would I?"

His face plummeted at the comment for a split second, only noticed by me, but he swiftly recovered. Maybe he thought I missed the dig, but I did not, and I wasn't about to let it slide. I exchange conversations with my friends, and then we are all looking toward the banging sound of Tag once again standing on the bar. "10!" he shouts, and we all join in the countdown; at one, Parker grabs my face and kisses me, then whispers, "Here's to our New Year, babe."

Chapter 24: Not Sarah

I am lying across Parker's bed on my stomach room as he takes a shower before we head out for the night. Since Parker decided he would be more comfortable living at home until he finished school, we decided not to move in together. Having a non-judgmental girlfriend makes living at home much easier - we've even joked about it. I am avidly flipping through a magazine from his mother's coffee table, admiring mostly the pictures of food and well-decorated homes. A buzzing sound fills the muted room so I splay my fingers out, searching the space near me on the bed for my phone. When I make contact with the vibrating square, I bring it to my face and see that I have an unread message from "not Sarah". Panic spikes immediately. My heartbeat races. The air thickens with tension. I release Parker's phone as if I had just grabbed a live rattlesnake. I stare at the traitorous phone, willing it to burst into flame, removing the stomach-twisting desire to open it and read the message. Hearing the water still flowing from the bathroom, I carefully pick it back up and click open the message.

I miss you

I feel sick and lightheaded as a lump forms in my throat while my heart pounds loudly in my ears. While quickly scrolling, I skim through the small computer-like text displayed on the tiny screen.

Did you break up with her?
No, it's complicated
You know I'm always here :)
I know, thank you
More….
Thank you for last night, I needed that
I couldn't imagine not being there
More….
Thought you'd like to see what you're missing today a photo of a woman whose piercing eyes are staring back at my own; this woman, "not Sarah," has her bare chest displayed while a bashful smile plays across her face.

:) mmm I like that is the text with a returned photo of Parker shirtless.

I hear Parker's bathroom door open. A high-pitched ringing has joined the relentless thumping sound in my ears, my whole body feels hot. As Parker emerges in his towel, I use my softball skills from grade school to throw the phone at him with remarkable velocity. He braces himself as the small black box of foreboding hits him squarely in the chest, the impact reverberating through his entire being.

"Ow, Sarah, what the fuck!?"

"What the fuck!?" I shriek crazily. "What the fuck!? Fuck you, Parker, that's what!"

Recognition flashes on his face, and he stands in the doorway, yanking his boxers and jeans up in one quick motion. "Sarah," he says, beseeching with his palms up.

"No!" I shout, "Move!"

He approaches, and I back away until I'm stopped by his desk. He grabs my biceps, wrapping his hands around my entire arm, and lowers his face to meet mine straight on. "I can explain."

"No, you can't," I say. "There's no acceptable explanation. I need to leave, and you need to move."

"Sarah!" he shouts, shaking me slightly. "Listen to me!"

"Let. Me. Go. Parker," I retort with a forced calmness that catches him off guard. I can feel my face hot with anger, tears that feel like lava streaming down my cheeks onto my shirt as his eyes plead for me to relent. We stay in this face-off until he lets me go and steps to the side. I stormed out of his house, only to realize he had driven us here. "Fuck!" I exclaim to the dark air as I dig for my phone and dial Thomas. "Can you come get me?" I blurt out frantically and breathlessly as I walk away from Parker's house. "Sure," responds Thomas with no hesitation, and I tell him where I think I'll make it on foot.

The walk has done nothing to smother my rage, and when I see Thomas' car pull up, it provides little more relief than just getting me further from Parker. I jump inside, slamming the door, realizing my hands are still shaking with rage as I instruct him to take me to Three Olives. On the way, I tell him what happened, and he cuts in only to say things like "What a stupid little bitch" or "straight men are embarrassing." When we pull up to Three Olives Thomas points out, "This is too obvious," and drives away; we end up at a familiar spot we used to frequent because they offered things like dime draft and dollar drink nights. It's actually where I met Zach for the first time. He parks, nods to me, and we enter the now extensively remodeled bar with its single male bartender, Matt. We ordered two drinks and shots before Matt told me he remembered me from Rock Out Local. Raising my glass, I take the shot in one gulp. Only now do I register my phone has been vibrating consistently since I left Parker. I open it briefly to see missed calls and messages from Parker and then one from Zach; the devil sure knows when to make his entrance.

Is this still Sarah's phone?

I shoot a quick text in response **Yep**

Where you at?

Funny you should ask, the drinks are still strong but a bit more than a dollar.

Less than a half hour later, Zach is walking through the door, and Thomas is turning on his barstool, tilting his head at me, eyebrows raised; he follows it with a soft whistle that indicates danger is approaching. Zach sits on the barstool next to me, and his face gives way to a half grin, the dark blue eyes warning me to stay away. Matt reaches out to shake Zach's hand and says, "Turkey?" Zach nods, and I realize he still comes here; all these years later, I've stayed away, and he's been here precisely where I left him.

"What are you doing?" Thomas asks pointedly.

"What do you mean?" I say distractedly.

Matt and Zach engage in conversation.

"Sarah, I can see this poor decision being made, and I just think you're not going to cure one broken heart with another."

"Well—" I say, sighing, "you're not wrong."

"Just maybe, don't go total atomic bomb on the situation, okay?"

"Okay," I agree, but know I am lying; the level of hurt I feel has exceeded the kind where I'm sad and want a few sad songs in the back of my truck with a blanket and cushions. This hurt feels vacant of sadness; replaced only by indignation and fueled by a demand for reprisal. All I did was kiss another man, a stranger! That's it. His number was trashed and never spoke to him again. I wasn't about to turn to another man for advice on my troubled relationship, especially one who had obvious intentions of sleeping with me. That guy meant nothing then and still means nothing today. I was paying a penance that did not match my crime, and it unhinged me.

In a low voice, I hear Thomas ask, "Do you need me to stay?"

Confidently, I declare, "I'm a big girl."

Zach places a hand on my back, leaning across me to Thomas. "I promise I'll get her home safe."

Thomas eyes him and then me and shakes his head uneasily. "Are you sure you want to stay here with him?" Graciously providing me with another out.

"I'm sure I don't want to go anywhere else. I appreciate your obvious concerns, but I am here for a good time, not a long time."

"He's never really cared about you," he whispers to remind me.

"And finally, I don't care if he cares," I say with amusement fueled by my still simmering anger.

Thomas, finally conceding, asks for two shots from Matt; we clink them together and throw them back; he kisses me on the cheek, looks at Zach, points a finger at him, and warns, "Get all of her home in one piece, heart included." Zach nods and raises his glass in agreement, and Thomas turns for the door. Despite Parker never being here with me before and the unlikelihood of a run-in, the satisfaction of witnessing the hurt and surprise on Parker's face is worth pondering. Maybe he wouldn't feel surprised at all. Perhaps he would just expect it because I am the bad girlfriend. Fuck it. With Zach beside me, I lean over and kiss him, and he reciprocates as if it's the most familiar gesture between us. I pull away. Zach's eyes darken, a mischievous smile forms on his lips and he nods to the door.

"Are you up for some more nostalgia?"

Gratefully, I gaze at him, reminiscing about the familiarity of his charm, yet the warning bells ring loudly as his magnetic pull entices me. "I'm up for anything."

As Zach leads me to his 80s Ford Bronco, which he has steadily improved over the years I've known him, I loop my arm through his. He drives to a convenience store, goes in returns with a brown paper bag, then drives us off the road up a hill until we are overlooking the whole city from a distance, he hands me a small can from the bag which I see is a canned long island. I crack it open and take a long drink before squishing my face in disgust as it moves down my throat.

"These are terrible," I laugh.

"I disagree," he says, finishing his. "So what's going on, and how am I still enemy number one?"

I laugh again, surprising myself. "Long story."

"We've got time," he says, cracking open another drink.

I sigh. "Let's keep it easy; a year ago, I kissed a guy who was not my boyfriend and never saw him again, we got back together. and tonight I found out he's been having this, at least, emotional relationship with another girl, named 'Not Sarah' in his phone, with weird boobs, so here I am with you, strategically avoiding him."

"Weird boobs?"

"Yeah, she sent him a picture of her boobs, and they're weird. Is that all you got from all of that?"

"No, I just was curious how you knew they were weird, so you saw the messages between them?"

"Yeah, pages of them, so many pages." I frown into the can of the Long Island.

"Fuck," he exhales, "and you're sure you want to be here with me? Considering?"

I hear the implication in his voice. I was a jerk who cheated on you, too, remember? "Zach, in this scenario you are purely a distraction, a welcome one, but that's it. Don't read too far into it."

"Fair enough," he replies. "I can do that."

We continue to drink our canned Long Island as he plays classic rock radio, which reminds me that my dad will be here in a few days. He's on a break from teaching and driving here solely because he wants to take a road trip. He's supposed to be meeting Parker while he's here, Parker, who I've been raving about for two whole years, explaining how in love with him I am and how perfect he is. Yes, Zach is, in fact, a very welcome distraction. We fall into conversations and arguments about who was the best band or what the best songs were in the 70s. We are surrounded by darkness now, and I know we can't leave this spot until one of us is sober. I check my phone and realize I have no service, which only bothers me because I can't let Thomas know I'm okay; not that he's waiting around worried about me; that's not his way, but it would be nice to let him know I'm not falling apart. Zach is busy experimenting with the backseat-less area behind us, inflating what sounds like a raft up with air.

"Air mattress," Zach announces. "I frequently end up sleeping back here in the hills a lot."

I bet with many girls, too, but say cooly, "Oh really?"

"It's—I'm not, I'm not suggesting," he says.

"Alright then, what are you suggesting?" I inquire as he spins the cap on the air mattress, pulling out a couple blankets and tossing them haphazardly on the mattress. As he turns to respond, I throw my shirt and bra on his face. I am awkwardly yanking my pants down my legs, clumsily balancing against my back in the passenger seat. Zach doesn't wait for further instructions, pulls his shirt over his head, and undoes his belt and remove his pants.

The moment I open my eyes, I am greeted by the blinding light of the early sun. I spin my head and discover that Zach is using a shirt to shield his face from the brightness. I'm also dimly aware that of all our time together, this is maybe the third time in total we've actually spent the night together, and just like all the others, it somehow feels amiss, maybe more so. My eyes still adjusting to the bright sun, I locate my clothing and Zach's sweater that I throw on over my bra and step out of the Bronco to relieve my too-full bladder and have a cigarette. While walking back, I hesitate to glance at the city and determine that it is the last occasion I will witness it in such a way. Zach drives me home, and I send off a couple of urgent texts to my friends, assuring them I am alive and completely fine. When I enter my townhouse, I am relieved that no one is there, no Thomas, no Parker; I am alone. I pull out all my bags and suitcases and pack things in them without any true comprehension of what I'm actually doing.

Once I'm done, I call my parents and tell them I'll be driving back with dad to the Pacific Northwest; it takes some back-and-forth discussion before they are on board with my decision. "Love you guys, too. I'll see you soon." I experience a sense of relief, but also a tinge of sadness, when I think of leaving my friends. I messaged all of them, saying that there's something important I want to tell them, that we need to make plans because I am only telling everyone once, I'm not repeating this information in spurts, or I may lose the nerve to genuinely do it. I scroll over Parker's name and all the missed messages and voicemails I haven't had the nerve to read or listen to. My finger hovers with indecision before I delete everything, every voicemail, every message, and every picture stored in my phone. Then I block him. The removal of him feels like an exorcism. Before I finished, I cried so much that my tears soaked my phone and the carpet beneath me.

Chapter 25: Miles Between Us

It's the day before Valentine's Day and the five of us have done all of our favorite things together: visited all our favorite bars, as well as dined out places that haven't been forced close because of the recession. Now, sitting with our half burgers and baskets of fries, which we all agree tastes mediocre in the cold light of day versus after the night of partying, which usually preceded this meal. We have exchanged tears and laughter in excess, and there's not much left to say or do other than make promises of future visits. Because my determination is well known, nobody doubts my certainty or whether I've changed my mind.

As we return to what used to be my townhouse, I gaze at Frank's, where I'd been eating near homemade meals for the last four years. Unfortunately, Frank Sr. passed away a few months ago because of a heart attack. We pass Benedict's, a place that holds many memories for me, now closed and unoccupied. I settle onto the couch, surrounded by all the places in the city that I've spent years in, late nights, and memories. Felix will move into my old room, so we've already cleared my bed. However, I left my old pull chain lamp and blush-colored velvet recliner from my grandmother behind, which already makes me feel homesick. I removed all the posters, which left the walls blank and dismally white. The process started nicely, then morphed into the smooth paper being torn from its places during an outburst: against them, against the music, the memory of him, the sheer will it's taken me not to call him, not to beg for us to be different. This home, once the sanctuary that brought me warmth and comfort and housed so many sensations, is now just the storage for my things that will later be packed into my dad's car. This box of things are the only things that will come with me when I leave. Tonight, while my dad sleeps in his hotel room, I will sleep, or try to sleep, on my couch, which has always felt more like Jessica's than ours. I could sleep in my nearly empty room on the floor, but that just feels too depressing to end with. As I lay staring at the white ceiling, the quiet room fills with my phone ringtone, and I charge for my purse, scooping through all the contents before finally revealing my phone; flashing on the screen is a number I don't recognize, and I assume it's the room my dad is staying in.

"Hello?"

"Sarah, don't hang up." Instantly, I recognize Parker's voice, and my chest tightens. Words cannot form; I hold the phone strangely away from my ear but can make out his voice. "Please, can we talk? I heard you were leaving; I just—I just don't want things to end this way." Still, I say nothing. "Jesus, Sarah, please say something. Look, I'm sorry. I'm sorry about her. I'm sorry I didn't tell you or end things. I just—I don't know what I was thinking; it was wrong. I guess I just felt like I deserved to have options, too," he continues to beg in the background.

At that moment, a realization dawned on me. I recognized that the part of our relationship which I thought I had come to terms with has instead evolved into bitterness and hostility. We would always get even with each other. He needed options, too, because, in his mind, I had them; I was just dangling them in front of him until I got bored. This, of course, wasn't true, but his perception, my indiscretion, and my night with Zach made it so. Turns out, I was the bad girlfriend, after all.

"Parker," I clear my throat.

"Thank god," he exasperates., "I was starting to think maybe I was talking to myself," he sounds relieved and I know what I'm about to do is going to destroy us.

"Parker," I repeat, getting right to it. "I slept with someone else. I slept with Zach, actually, and I don't want to hate myself for it, but I do. I hate that I am the winner of your shitty bad girlfriend game." I don't stop. "I am putting hundreds of miles between us so we don't do this again; I just want to be done." I hear a moment's noise of rustling, and then my phone shows the call has ended.

Unable to sleep now, I press a series of numbers into my phone and listen to the rings until I hear, "Hey Sarah, what's up? Everything ok?" "Dad? How far could we make it tonight?"

Within minutes, my dad is at my townhouse, methodically packing away the remaining bags that I have left. It's a bittersweet feeling, as I am both eager and sad to leave this place that I have called home for the past few years. As I peer out of the window, I notice that the bright city lights have transformed into a serene landscape of brown and snow-splotched hills in just a few minutes. I can't help but feel a sense of calm wash over me as I bid farewell to the bustling city and prepare to embark on a new adventure.

Chapter 26: Fast Forward

I arrived in the Pacific Northwest on Valentine's Day, and now it's been two Valentine's Days since then. I am standing impatiently in the airport, waiting for my plane to board. Holidays and school breaks have passed, so I will miss two full days of classes, which I blamed for my anxiety this morning. "Why are you so wound up?" My mom asks as I paced around, waiting for the appropriate time for my dad to drop me off at the airport. I am actually confident it won't put me far behind as I've always been pretty good at keeping up with schoolwork and getting good grades; I surmise this is what happens when your dad is a college professor for all the parts of life you can remember, and now the college professor at your school. I will graduate early with my journalism degree and concentration in communication. My motivation to get this degree only came when I started working at a trendy apartment complex outside of Seattle. Thanks to living with my parents at 27 and falling into a comfortable routine of school, dinner, homework, work-work, sleep, and repeat, I haven't made many real friends. I have the odd coworker lunch date, classmate study session, or a random work party. I met a couple of guys and one of them I even called my boyfriend for a few months but would now refer to him as an accidental blip. What's even more comical is that he was supposed to be traveling with me to my hometown, but he won't be getting on this plane, and he probably has no idea that this was even supposed to happen today.

Tomorrow, the day after Valentine's Day, happens to be Heidi and Brian's engagement party in Lake Tahoe. This trip will unceremoniously mark my first return trip to Reno since I left. Maybe even more hilarious than my now solo trip is that Zach is picking me up from the airport. We have somehow become bizarre friends in my time away, even passing each other relationship and life advice over the last two years. Also, he was the only one who would not be at work when my plane landed and offered to pick me up since I would no longer be renting a car since it would just be me. We begin boarding, and my heartbeat quickens under my sweater. I place a hand on my chest, mindlessly rubbing it as I pass the lady my boarding pass. When I find my seat, I put my headphones in.

"And I'm the one you can never trust
Because wounds are ways to reveal us
And yeah, I could have tried
And devoted my life to both of us
But what a waste of my time
When the world we have is yours"

After I land in the familiar airport, I am walking with my carry-on bag toward the exit, fumbling with my phone when I see Zach standing with his hands in his pockets before I can dial him. He's thoughtfully waiting in the area just before you will get tackled by TSA agents if you don't have a ticket. I smile and wave, and then, in seconds, he smoothly loops his arms around me and lifts me a bit before effortlessly taking my bag.

"That's totally unnecessary," I say. "It rolls. I can manage to your car."

He maintains possession of my bag and pulls me into his side. "Hungry?"

"Starving, actually."

"Great, there's a new brewery around the way I'll take you."

"Brewery," I say. "Alright, fancy pants."

He loads my things into his old Bronco, which again has seen several improvements since my last time in it; looking over my shoulder, I see that it now includes a proper back seat.

"Awe, what happened to your bed?" I joke.

He looks behind him from the front seat, almost confused. "Oh," he laughs. "Yeah, the seat has been back there for a bit now."

We arrive at the parking lot of a two-story brick building, and we can see large stainless steel equipment through windows that resemble the grain silos in Washington my dad used to show me during our road trips. We walk in, and instead of waiting for the hostess, he moves right past, taking my hand and guiding me through the filled seats. Then I spot them: Heidi, Alice, Jessica, Thomas, Felix, Chase, and Brian, all seated at a large table near the glass-enclosed equipment. Delighted with surprise, I shrieked and they shuffled me in and out of hugs, even Brian and Chase gave me one. I turn to Zach with tear-soaked cheeks and punch him in the arm.

"You should've told me!"

"This was way more fun," he says, pulling out a chair for me to sit.

A taller blonde server with her hair in two French braids comes by the table as Zach stands to kiss her before turning to me, offering "this is Sarah."

She takes my hand. "Hi, I'm Rachel; I heard this was going to be a loud reunion."

"Yes," I agree, taking her hand. "Rachel, it's so nice to finally meet you in person, and thank you for letting Zach grab me today; these idiots all told me they were busy," I finish by glaring at all my friends.

"Oh, sure thing," she says. "I love a good surprise when it's not me." She takes our drink order, and I nudge Zach in the ribs. "She's even prettier in person. Don't screw that up, huh?"

He grins and sits, opening the menu and telling us "you can't go wrong with anything here."

After lunch Zach winds me through some parts of the city that are coming back to life and finally drops me at my hotel; I was considering staying with one of my friends but then chose a hotel so that I could maintain the feeling that I am a visitor here. This is not home. Zach walks me to check in, and I hug him long, thanking him for the lunch surprise; he leaves me waiting in line, and I watch him go, marveling at how unusual we are. My room is like most standard casino hotel rooms, with a beige color scheme with a few hints of red throughout the pictures and one red chair positioned next to a small side table with the hotel's list of services in a trifold printout on top. I look out the window and see a few different areas under construction, other casinos, and a part of the snowy Sierra mountains. Unsure of what to do with myself until we meet for dinner later tonight, downstairs from where I am staying, I grab my computer and check over some of my homework; after that, I plug some random searches into Google and then give up when nothing piques my interest. I explore the room, opening and closing different storage compartments, taking in the scents of soap, shampoo, conditioner, and lotion. I then return to the window and look out at a place that used to be familiar but now feels strange. I don't think of him.

Finally, dinner time comes and I can't wait to see my friends again because being here alone is mildly torturous. We collide again in a mashup of hugs and greetings before finally being seated and catching up in person. I know what they're all doing: Heidi stayed at our old job for a while longer as she was one of only two people who were offered positions to remain in the company but has now moved on to a better company based out of the Bay Area making twice as much, I will always marvel at her ability to completely dominate her career; Alice and Jessica are working in real estate together as the market is skyrocketing, and Jessica has formally come out, as we all suspected. She is currently seeing a paralegal named Rowan (who is studying for her JD). If they stay together, they will be an unyielding power couple, I'm sure. Alice occasionally dates but strongly prefers going home to an apartment that operates solely with her interests; Thomas and Felix are still together, and Felix is now a Nurse Practitioner. Thomas, a nurse by profession, finds more fulfillment in utilizing his technical degree in imaging, less messy he says. I presume Chase is still working on his parent's ranch as a professional cowboy. I don't know, I haven't ever asked. He's just usually around for Brian's entertainment. I found out a few months ago that Brian has started his own electrical company, which is gaining momentum with a new contract he just scored with a builder purchasing a few properties in the area to build residential units. Even though there is no change in time between the Pacific Northwest and Lake Tahoe, I feel exhausted after dinner. As the night concludes, we make arrangements for them to bring me to the engagement party tomorrow.

Chapter 27: Engagement Party

I wake up in the morning and decide to head out for a run, which is my usual start these days; I pass both unrecognizable and familiar places along the river before turning to retrace my path and cutting down an old alleyway to my hotel. Running these streets feels like gliding on autopilot, my legs instinctively navigating the combination of brick and cement beneath me. Something akin to a force-field abruptly stops me from moving forward and there I am standing outside the Knit, but it's not the Knit anymore. It's nothing, and curiously, I ponder, neither are we. Leaving the memory in my wake, I run back to my hotel room.

I haven't spoken to Parker since that night. I have no substantial information about him. The only exception was about a year ago When I was feeling weak and curious and typed his name into a social media search revealing a photo of him and a girl, the girl I can only assume was that girl. After digging back through a few photos, I saw one of him and the rest of Reverberation Breakdown all playing over what looked to be a large crowd in an impressive-looking venue, it had several comments but the one to grab my attention said **glad we made it brother no bad girlfriends stopping you now**. The comment had several likes, with coinciding comments ranging from **yeah! Fuck that bitch** to **hear she moved because she ran out of dudes to sleep with**. I deleted my profile a few moments later and vowed never to look again.

"Shit!" I exclaim when I check my watch for the stats of my run. I had less than an hour to get ready and would need every moment; I pulled out my cocktail dress and hung it to get some steam while I showered and dug through my bag for my makeup and hair supplies. My once dyed jet-black hair is now a natural light brown with some blonde streaks, something my mother talked me into one day when we passed a salon. I shower quickly and, while my hair is twisted up in a towel, I apply my makeup. I meticulously followed a video tutorial and assembled a face makeup look, which left me feeling satisfied. I begin to slide my dress over my head, feeling the smooth fabric against my skin. The sage green color is soothing to the eyes, and the mock-neck design adds a touch of elegance. Its tea-length and long sleeves provide a sense of modesty. As I pull it down, I notice the sheer overlay, delicate and ethereal, adding a subtle allure. But now, I realize that this choice comes with a downside. The sheer fabric snags on everything I brush against, creating an annoying tugging sensation. To save myself some time, thanks to the mock neck, I chose to pull my hair into a high pony, drying and curling the ends. Good enough, I think, and I hear my phone ringing. I hop slash walk toward the noise while pulling on my nude-colored pumps. "Hello?"

"Hey bitch, we're down in the lobby. Let's go!" Thomas says into the phone. "I'm on my way," I say, grabbing my purse and peacoat before checking to ensure I have the hotel card key and closing the door.

"I'm literally running to the elevator."

"Good," he says before ending the call.

We arrived at the clubhouse in Lake Tahoe earlier than we needed, which is no minor miracle, considering we should've careened off the mountaintop several times with the way Felix was driving. I forcefully fling the back door open and exit the vehicle in a hurry, swearing to never enter it again. My first view after almost dying is Heidi. Her face beams as she comes toward me. Heidi undeniably radiates in a long burgundy dress with a daringly high slit up the thigh. Her hair is tied back in a high ponytail, and her blunt bangs hang just over her eyebrows, accentuating her bright blue eyes that seem unreal.

"Hi," she squeals. "Isn't this beautiful!?"

"You're beautiful," I say, and she does a slow twirl while Felix catches up and gives her a wolf whistle.

"Come, come," she says. "You have to see inside; everything is perfect."

As we all walked in together, Brian smoothly replaced my hooked arm in Heidi's, and they gracefully made their way towards other partygoers. I spot Chase tugging at his collar and then his tie before taking a long pull of his beer; even seeing it now, I cannot picture Chase in formal wear. I walk over and tap his beer with the white wine I got from the bar.

"So they're finally doing it, huh?" I say while he continues to tug at his collar.

"Do you think I can wear the same suit to the wedding?" He asks taking another drink of his beer.

"Don't they pick the suits for the groomsmen?" I ask and see him shrug.

"Let's hope it's more comfortable than this one."

He squirms again, and I see a small tag sticking out from the back of his collar. "Oh, I think it's a leftover tag," I say, handing him my wine glass. He leans down as I stand taller on my shoes, and I swiftly extract it and then fling it to the ground. He sighs with relief. Handing me back my glass. "You owe me," I say, and we stand in comfortable silence, the same silence we have all these years as the best friends of our corresponding best friends.

I don't smoke anymore, but something about being here makes me want to. I state aloud that I need some air and inquire about an outdoor space. With a nod, he guides me through the bustling room adorned with wine-colored table runners and golden accents. Crystal centerpieces adorn the tables, featuring burgundy flowers and delicate baby's breath, surrounded by gold accented decorative pieces that resemble the barren, winter grass. Chase walks me to a patio that appears to be the separation between our banquet room and an adjoining restaurant. I stand under the patio heater, and again, Chase and I are standing in our customary silence, looking out over the golf course, which is steadily darkening with the setting sun.

I see all the patrons in the sparkling restaurant and imagine they have elected to celebrate their Valentine's dinner today since it is Saturday. They all appear so in love. Their wine glasses brimming, devouring an exquisitely presented expensive meal, and after, they will probably have mind-blowing sex. Afterwards, the relationship will revert to its dull, uneventful state, just like yesterday and the preceding days and weeks. I can't help but smirk to myself, finding it ironic that a future journalist major possesses such cynicism.

My smirk abruptly descends to a frown. "Holy shit!"

"What?" questions Chase, making me jump slightly, reminding me he was here.

I see him; Parker is standing across the way. Too far to yell out, "why the fuck are you here?" However, close enough I can see his deep dimple as he laughs, doing a funny bow before taking a lady's hand, bringing her to her feet, and spinning her into him. Chase waves his hand in front of my face, and I blink rapidly; I'm hallucinating, I think, but when I refocus, I'm not. With the open doors before him, Parker's gaze seems to meet mine, despite the darkness that engulfs us. Yet, the fact that he is a brilliantly lit diorama casts doubt upon this fleeting connection.

I wobble, and Chase steadies me by the arms. "That's Parker, isn't it?" I nod, not taking my eyes off him. "I thought the douchebag looked familiar."

"Huh?" I say, confused.

"I've heard the stories; I'm not a fan; Brian said if he ever saw him again, he'd deck him," and I'm now distracted by the warmth of this declaration. "Brian said that?"

"Yeah," he says undoubtedly.

I loop my arm through his and have him take me back to the party. When we got inside, I saw Brian and Heidi talking to an older, well-dressed man, and before Brian could gesture, I hugged him tight. Stiff and awkward, he returns my embrace with a one-armed hug. "Uh, Sarah, there's someone I want you to meet," I release him and turn to the stranger with an outstretched hand.

"Mark Miller," he says confidently, "I'm getting ready to break ground on a group of high rises in the downtown area, the first of which will be The Views."

"Oh wow," I say, impressed. "That's incredible."

"Brian here was telling me you do some property management work up North?"

"Yes," I say, "I work for a complex near Redondo Beach, the Washington one, not the California one," which has become my habitual follow-up statement. "I'm finishing my degree at the community college my dad works at and hope to do more of the marketing or resident experience stuff."

"I saw your videos," he says.

"My videos?" I assert in total perplexity.

"You did a local band thing, right?"

"Oh!" I say with a mix of surprise and embarrassment, "Yes, I did."

"You've got something special, kid, charisma; I'd like to stay in touch if we can talk you into heading back south?"

"Sure," I say, taking the card he's extended.

He leaves, and I look at Brian, who wears a satisfied smile, and Heidi, whose eyes are filled with anticipation.

"Wouldn't it be so great if you came back?" She exclaims with excitement.

I nod because I don't have it in me to tell her that seeing Parker outside just a few moments ago still felt horrendous, and moving back here would mean deliberately avoiding that forever. Deciding to keep quiet on the matter, I shift the conversation towards their engagement and let Heidi eagerly chatter away about wedding details - this is, after all, their special night.

As the evening wore on, I wished for it to linger longer, prolonging my time with my friends. The moment of farewell had come, and we awkwardly collided into a jumble of hugs and tears, paying no mind to our formal attire. Heidi holds me tightly. "It's time to come home."

I clasp her tightly in return, trying to stop the tears from flowing. Chase offers to drive me back down to my hotel and I agree for the sake of my life and so I'll stop crying.

"Will you at least think about it?" Chase asks.

"Think about what?"

"The job."

"I miss everyone so much." I respond honestly.

The rest of the trip is our customary silence and I look out the window at the dark trees as we make our descent back into the city. As he parks in the valet area of my hotel, I offer a warm smile, but he only responds with a curt nod. Just as I'm getting out of the car, my dress snags and tears, a surprising twist of fate that I am surprised didn't happen sooner.

"Oh damn," I curse. "Well, it finally ripped."

Chase calls out from the driver's seat, "But you still look like a princess," and gives me a shrug.

"Thanks, Chase," I say and shut the door, smiling again. This time, he smiles back.

I intentionally made my flight early in the morning to avoid the part where I consider moving back here, back home. This is my home, and I miss it; I love my parents, but I miss my friends and the familiarity of everything around me. I undress, toss the now ripped gown in my suitcase, and put everything away. Then, as if time had sped up, my dad was waiting for me dutifully at the airport and took me back to their home in Washington.

Chapter 28: Coming Home

Mark Miller emails me every other week to provide an update on The Views and, on my graduation day, emails me with an offer for the Director of Resident Experience at The Views. This offer, of course, comes with an apartment of my choosing, a substantial pay increase, and an opportunity to live near all my friends again. I show my parents, and each gives me the "we love you BUT" speech because after close to three years later, I still have no friends, one known failed relationship, and will be 28 years old in a couple of weeks. Of course, they finish with the sentiment that I am only a plane ride away.

On the day of my birthday, Thomas and I make the slow, because we have to stop at every little place along the way, trip back to Reno in my old truck. At our last breakfast stop, we confidently walk into a small restaurant, which unquestionably contains the townsfolk, because we gather side glances from almost every table we pass before being seated across a table of two senior men having a heated debate about something happening overseas. The walls are adorned with trains, planes, and automobiles, as if they were part of a deliberate theme. I feel relieved to have something else to focus on, rather than another homage to the railway that once connected the east and west. While assessing the room, I spot Thomas and one of the elderly men wearing the exact same button-down short-sleeved shirts. Thomas's face contorts with horror as he gazes down at his shirt.

"I will be throwing this away immediately," he says, his features twisting in disgust as his eyes dart between himself and the man banging his cane into the floor.

Upon our exit from the museum of the Old West, disguised as a restaurant, he does just that. The shirt is left in the same town as its matching counterpart while we embark on our great Western journey back to my new and rightful home.

A perk that came with my new boss and job is that they hired a decorator to fully furnish my apartment before my arrival. When we spoke about her design ideas for the apartment, I'd never seen in person, I told her, "contemporary, I guess." Because of all the options she rattled out, it was the only one I thought I knew. All I had to do was move my clothes and other accompaniments, meaning that no one had to actually physically relocate any furniture on my behalf, an announcement that got actual applause from Brian on the other end of the video call.

We make our way over the last hill into the city, and the familiar view makes me gasp. I drop Thomas off at the remodeled townhome we used to share as a very tired-looking Felix, who has apparently just finished his last 12-hour shift, gives me a quick wave.

Finding my numbered parking spot as stated in my welcome home email, I find my way to Ray, who works in the lobby. Ray is a tall, friendly walnut-skinned man who doubles as a piano player at a nearby bar on some nights. He points out the similarities I dare not to by winking and saying, "but at least I've still got my sight." Ray has a group of employees come together and help get all my belongings into the elevator up the 15 floors to my apartment.

Once inside, with no more visitors, I collapse onto the couch, swaying back and forth before realizing it isn't the most comfortable, but I don't mind. My new one-bedroom apartment has a soft gray color with white trim and baseboards. The medium brown hardwood floors may be real, but it's hard to tell. Overall, the space has minimal decoration with clean lines and a few geometric wall art displays that complement the geometric-designed area rug. The coffee and dining tables match and are sleek black with glass tops. My new kitchen has navy cabinets with stainless steel appliances and a simple subway tile backsplash that matches the shower. The designer modeled the large king-sized bed according to a catalogue, featuring a white comforter, high thread count white sheets, and an abundance of decorative pillows that are sure to give me daily panic attacks about how to arrange them. The key point is that the cloud-like bed rapidly sends me into a deep slumber.

I wake in the morning to the sun, which compels me to never forget to close the giant floor-to-ceiling curtains ever again if I plan on sleeping past 5:30am. Since I'm awake, I decide to call my parents and update them on how everything looks, including my wish for a more comfortable couch. Nevertheless, I am fully settled and will start work on Wednesday instead of Monday. I head into the kitchen and see I have a coffee maker and just enough coffee, creamer, and sugar for about two cups, and I start it. Once it's finished, I head to my terrace, which has a small table and two red Adirondack chairs. I watch the remaining sunrise before the sky settles on its bright robin's egg blue. Queen plays in my mind.

"*I wanna be there in my city,*"

Chapter 29: Ladies Who Lunch

It's been just about 10 months since I've been back and having my friends back has been phenomenal, the job is great, and I'm finally feeling as if all the turbulence from the past years have led to this clarity in time where everything is just right. I dated a guy I met from another one of Mark Miller's locations for about three months before learning that denying him entry to my backside was reprehensible, causing him to end things. The five of us chatted about this over one of our now regular lunches that sometimes extends to dinner. While two of us didn't see a problem with this particular act, the rest of us were steadfast in our belief that is an exit only.

"Brian doesn't like the idea of it," announces Heidi.

"I actually orgasm super-fast when there's a little play back there," Alice hums, and Thomas shakes his head in agreement. "I think you're all doing yourself a disservice by not just trying it."

Jessica explains that she and Rowan don't even experiment with strap-ons, which gets an audible gasp of surprise from Thomas.

"Well, it wouldn't have been with him anyway," I say with finality.

"Oh, so you're not against it," says Thomas. "It would just need to be the right person to go up your butt."

"Well, no, that's not what I meant." I take a drink from my wine and finish. "I guess what I meant was that he wasn't a long haul boyfriend. Just a run-of-the-mill void filler."

"Void filler?" Alice inquires with her head tilted.

"Yes, void filler, you know it will not be serious or lead to anything, but you don't want it to so it's easy and just fills a need for the time being, no one is sad when it ends, no big deal," I say waving my hands dismissively.

"Huh," she says thoughtfully "I guess that's my preferred relationship."

We all laugh when Thomas says, "You can always just keep it open, like me and Felix. Sometimes we share a little, sometimes we group it up, and sometimes he and I see the same guys separately. It's a win, win, win," he displays three fingers on his hand.

"I don't think straight women are capable of that," I laugh when Jessica chimes in, "lesbians either."

As Thomas and I walk together toward my apartment, which he'll eventually pass to reach his apartment, I remind him of the concert tomorrow night. "Saving Abel!" I shout while shaking his arm. "Can you believe it!? We never got to see them when they were first starting out but look at us now!" Still shaking his arm, he looks at me with mock excitement. I poke him jokingly. "Gosh, I haven't been to a concert since..." I calculate mentally and hold my fingers up one by one in a mock gesture of counting. "Oh yeah, since I heard Parker singing that terrible song about me!" We both laugh and he stands with me as I open the door to my building.

"Will you be okay?" I ask.

"Walking home?" He clarifies. "Yeah, I'm a big guy, Sarah. No one is willing to risk getting their ass kicked trying to kidnap someone, plus I'm gay, so it would be additionally embarrassing for them." I chuckle and wave as he continues to walk toward his place.

Chapter 30: You, Again.

A band was already on stage when we walked into the poorly lit and loud concert hall, which I believe doubles as a ballroom. We purposefully came late, having dinner beforehand, in hopes of skipping the opener so we would just see Saving Abel. Thomas has reminded me umpteen times that he has had his fill of listening to bands he didn't like to make me happy. Even so, this wasn't like old times when I had to be at the show before everything started and long after it ended. The band playing was pretty good, making me give a nod of approval to Thomas, who agreed. The nostalgia of being back at a concert surrounded by the music was intoxicating; scanning the surrounding area, I saw a group of girls hovering over a merchandise table, telling Thomas I would check it out while he got our drinks. Combing through the piles of merchandise, I find a Saving Abel shirt that will go home with me, and then I see one that says Reverberation Breakdown. Unbelievably, it's my size, and I briskly shove it at the lady who looks at me, confused. "This too?"

"Yes, please," I say, and she gives me my total.

While it's still dark, I swap shirts for the Reverberation Breakdown one and meet Thomas back at the bar just as the lights come on, signifying an intermission. Blinking against the now blinding bright lights, I see items being hauled from the stage and wonder to myself why they just don't use the same equipment.

"Thomas! Check this out," I say, pulling my shirt out so he can read it. He squints at it and then rolls his eyes dramatically. "Where the hell did you find that?" he says disinterestedly. I point toward the merch table. "How odd," he comments. In that moment, the world around me becomes a blur, my focus solely on him as everything else fades away. Parker emerges, his silhouette cloaked in shadows, as if he were a fallen angel, stepping through the backstage door. Time freezes as I observe him gracefully navigate through a sea of eager admirers, exchanging warm greetings and posing for countless photographs.

Thomas follows my gaze and blurts, "Whoa, is that fucking Parker!? He got impossibly better looking." I'm rooted in my place, and my body has equal sensations telling me to run to and away from him simultaneously. His attire for shows was consistent: dark blue jeans and a button-up shirt with rolled-up sleeves. But now, his more muscular body makes the shirt cling to his arms and chest. Absently, I take a sip from my straw and find it dry, momentarily diverting my attention from Parker as I clank the glass against my empty cup. Thomas removed my drink from my hand and ordered another round. By the time I clocked Parker again, he was staring unwaveringly at me, mouth agape, the slow rise and fall of his chest indicating he saw a ghost—me. Parker made his way towards Thomas and me in what seemed to be an eternity. He was smiling apprehensively, which sent my nerves into a frenzy. Before I could collect myself, he was here at arm's length, and all my blood was surging directly into my center. Funny how memories work.

"Hey!" I speak in a higher pitch and elongate the word awkwardly.

"Hey?" Parker responds, but it's more of a question.

"Hey!" Says a now overly entertained Thomas.

"Wa—Was that you?" I croak. "Up there on the stage just now?"

"Yeah, it was," he answers sternly, still searching me for something that answers whatever question is playing behind his features.

"Wow," I say, drawing it out. "Gosh, you were outstanding; I—"

Thomas cuts in. "What she means to say is your new band isn't a pile of shit like your last band."

This briefly interrupts Parker's gaze from me, and he turns to Thomas. "Well, that actually means a lot coming from you, so thank you."

"What do you think of this shirt?" I cut back in, pulling it out like I did for Thomas.

His face softens a bit, and he chuckles. "Where in the world did you find that?"

I point to the girls over at the merchandise table, still holding the shirt. Parker looks at me when a small smile forms at the corners of his mouth. Unconsciously, I reach for his hand, clasping it hard in my own, and lead him away from the bar. My eyes frantically darted around me, and I zeroed in on the men's restroom, which, to my astonishment, was completely empty upon entering. Parker, awakening from his coma, desperately tries to free his hand in protest as I forcefully continue to lead him to the very end of the stalls, then swiftly lock us inside of one. "Uh, Sarah," he says, but I interrupt him by crashing my lips onto his. He reciprocates warily. Then, he holds on to my waist, pulling himself away from me. Parker is searching my face again, and it registers that we should not be in a bathroom or ANY room kissing and, finally, that I am an insane person. "Sorry," I murmur to the floor, and in an instant, I find myself engaged in a more desperate kiss that I'm certain I didn't initiate. While my brain races to catch up to an event that solely involved my lust, I feel Parker's arms wrap around my back and unclasp my bra. He then reaches one hand to the front of me, grasping each of my breasts, pinching my nipples between his fingers. I let out a frustrated noise and sink my hands into his waistband, finding him hard and squeezing him in one hand, to which he responds by turning me around abruptly. He firmly presses both my hands against the stall door; I then register that he is yanking my pants down letting them fall freely once under my hips. Parker pauses only to press himself into my backside, letting his erection settle there. The only sounds I hear are hearts thumping in rapid succession.

I feel him leaning down, and with his lips against my ear, he asks, "Protection?" "Bir—birth control," I stammer, and he rasps, "Good enough." As he moves my thong to the side, allowing his fingers to slide into the warmth between my legs, I buckle slightly. Before I can cry out, he covers my mouth with his hand, predicting I will reveal our sordid activity. Next comes the unmistakable sound of jeans unzipping. There are fumbling movements, I suspect due to our height differences, and my hips are being held tightly pressing me further against the door that is straining at his hinges. Struggling to maintain my tiptoe stance, I feel him penetrating me, his grip tightening over my mouth, stifling my muffled squeal as it slips through his fingers.

We have a rushed and greedy performance, where no one fully considers each other's needs until our releases come one after the other as if on cue. Parker's head is hanging next to my own. Slowly, Parker releases my mouth, and I swallow and swirl my tongue around my dry lips; he pulls out and away. In my attempt to pull up my pants, I realize they remained buttoned, causing me to unbutton them first, shimmy them back over my butt and thighs, and re-button them again. Parker had himself cleaned and righted by the time I had thrown my hair on top of my head with the hair tie I kept on my wrist for this occasion, the concert, not the sex in the bathroom part. Now we are just staring at each other, stupefied. Yes, we did, in fact, just have sex in the bathroom of a concert hall where his band had just played.

Finally, he declares, "I'll go first, so you can do whatever. No one will believe it took me that long to piss." He's right and I want desperately to clean the mess between my legs, so once he exits, that is precisely what I do. I am pained with unbuttoning my pants again, and at the same time, realize that things are eerily quiet in the stall. I wonder if my lungs are filling and expelling air, so I take a deep, voluntary breath and stand to button my pants up again, cursing them. I explode from the stall, oblivious that I am in the men's restroom, a men's restroom at a concert where my ex-boyfriend's band just played, and where we JUST HAD SEX! As the thoughts topple out one over the other, I look up to make eye contact with a perplexed male concertgoer using the urinal diagonal from me. I feel my cheeks flush in an instant, and I cover my face as I skirr the bathroom, exclaiming, "I'm so sorry, I must've—" I don't finish.

Once I recalibrate myself with the now dark concert hall, the headlining band plays. I find Thomas seated at the bar with my empty chair, holding all our belongings. I slide our jackets and my purse over the back of the stool and sit. "Worth it?" he teases, raising both eyebrows, "I mean, I don't blame you; I would take that new and improved version of sulky Parker on a ride, too."

Before I can answer, Saving Abel blares through the room, starting with the only song that would make everything that just happened completely scripted.

"I'm so addicted to all the things you do when you're going down on me in between the sheets. Oh, the sounds you make with every breath you take. It's unlike anything when you're loving me"

"I have to go," and I whirl around, collecting my things as Thomas downs his drink. Once outside, he looks at me and says, "We should at least do Five Queens since we're already out."

Nodding my agreement, we walk to Five Queens and enjoy a night out with just the two of us, intensifying the evening's nostalgia. We laughed and swayed, finally coming to a stop at our usual crossing. He carried on walking, while I headed towards my building. As the evening progressed, the significant developments of this night slipped from my mind.

Chapter 31: The Morning After

I wake up to an apartment that reminds me it is perfectly positioned for the rising sun to be a problem when I forget to close those damn floor-to-ceiling curtains. My head throbs a little, but nothing a soup bowl sized coffee, a quick run, and a nap later won't fix. Standing to make my way to the bathroom, I see myself in the mirror, which reminds me that, yes, you did have sex last night, Sarah. Returning to the side of the bed and without closing my curtains, I sit on my bed and clasp my hands together, hanging my head in disbelief. My attention is drawn to the floor where I see my work phone flashing, leaving me feeling puzzled. I rarely get anything on my work phone on weekends because my manager, Cora, is a beast at her job. I slide myself onto the floor and open it, unread email; this makes even less sense; who's emailing me personally on a Sunday. New message from ppag@mavenads.com, really? Sales pitching on a Sunday? These agencies are truly desperate for our attention. I open it, leaning against the side of my bed, and blink rapidly as if the mixture of sun and hangover have tricked me into thinking I see a message from Parker.

What the fucking fuck was that Sarah?????You fucking left with no explanation, no contact information, no fucking reason you're back in town, and I find out through my contacts that you've been back almost a year and are the Director of Resident Experience at The Views? Do you know what it took to get your work email address? Do you know all the lies I had to tell to get through your gatekeeper of a manager? You better write back to me with a phone number or an address. I swear to God.

I secretly praise Cora and fumble with my heart and brain's disagreement on whether to respond. You forcibly yanked the guy into a men's bathroom and made him have sex with you, I think, yes, but you also broke his and your heart into a million pieces about 4 years ago. The other half of me contests. I shake both sides away and decide I owe him about a thousand explanations, but for now, my contact information will do. I type in my name and address, hit send, and then retreat to the shower, starting my coffee maker on the way. Exiting my shower and wrapping myself in a terry-cloth robe, I hear buzzing from my apartment's doorbell system. I push the button, "hello?"

"Sarah, could you please tell the nice man at the front desk I can come to your place?"

"Parker!?" I unintentionally speak louder than intended, possibly hurting poor Ray's eardrum.

"The one and only." He says peeved.

"Let him up, Ray," I respond quickly. Wondering what had caused Ray to stop him in the first place. "Yes, ma'am," He says politely, and then I hurry around because I have only 15, or maybe less now, floors before Parker is at my door. I dart into my closet, thankful I showered, and hastily throw on sweatpants, a sheer bra, and a white tank top, rustling my hair with my towel. To finish, I throw on some ChapStick and give myself a mirror check. Good enough, I think. The knocking comes, and my heart flutters, a frantic bird trapped in the confines of my chest.

"Parker," I say, naturally while opening my door as if it's perfectly normal to see him on the other side; a short 15 minutes after I sent my information.

"Sarah." He says, which tells me he has not thought of anything to say on his drive nor on the 15 floors up.

"Coffee?" I suggest and open the door wide enough for him to walk through.

"Yeah, okay," he says tentatively while nodding. He steps in and takes in my one-bedroom high rise that overlooks the river and out towards the ski resorts. A beautiful layer of early season snow covers the mountains, making them glitter in the morning sun. "This is really nice. Good for you."

"Thanks," I say. "The view at night is even better. Do you take your coffee the same?"

"Yeah, I do; some things haven't changed." He chides as he looks back at me; I point to the breakfast bar and gesture for him to sit.

"Can we sit outside?" He asks, nodding toward my balcony.

"Sure, let me grab a sweater." Briskly I retrieve a long sweater to wrap around me before grabbing both our cups and handing him one as we make our way to the balcony. He chose the Adirondack chair furthest from the door, and I sat in the closest one. We look out to the mountains, and the moment feels strangely surreal and comfortable all at once. Finding speech first, I looked at him and says, "Parker, I'm really sorry. I wasn't expecting to see you there, and when I saw you, nostalgia and vodka took the wheel."

He blinks as if this explains nothing, and I feel my cheeks tingle with color. "Okay, Sarah," he says patiently. "That literally explains one of the million things I deserve explanations for; let's start somewhere four fucking years ago when you left me here with my literal heart in my hand." The words feel like a slap, and my calm persona is quickly relieved of its post by the tears that are now filling and flooding my cheeks. "Oh, shit." He says apologetically, "Oh shit, Sarah, I didn't mean for it to come out that way. I had been preparing speeches on the walkover, and I guess they all formed into one sentence."

I wipe my tears with my sleeve and say, "Walk?"

"Yeah, I stayed at the hotel where the show was, so when I got your message and realized how close you were. I more accurately ran here." This explains how quickly he could make it here. We sip our coffees in silence for a bit before I exhale. "Parker, it would take more than a morning over coffee to explain the last four years. Also, I never told you I was back, number one, because I know I hurt you; number two, you really hurt me; and three, because I heard through multiple people you were in a happy relationship. Actually, some of those people warned me more than informed me, so," a pause, "I avoided you."

He nods and chuckles a little. "Addy?" I nod and fix my eyes on the mountains. "We are together, but I wouldn't say we're happy. She's actually been trying to find a place so when I have the opportunity to, I stay at friends, hotels, or my parents," he exhales and continues, "I told her she could have our place, but she says she can't live in a place where our love used to live." He shakes his head. "I feel like an asshole." I place my hand over his and give it a squeeze.

"I'll always beat you in that category, Mister Pagano." He smiles genuinely, making my stomach flip-flop. "Any chance you'll stay for some breakfast?" I ask. "The cool thing about my job is I essentially get room service from the cafe downstairs. They're pretty good, and you can't beat the convenience."

"Alright," he smirks, "but only because you're paying."

"I'll make the call," and I return inside. He stays outside while I order breakfast, and I can see him staring contentedly at the mountains. I hang up the phone and announce to the open door it should be up in 30 minutes and ask if he needs a refill of coffee. I observe him stand, noticeably breathe in and out, and walk in the door.

"How are you so calm?" He asks while absently running his hand over my couch. With my stomach roiling and my chest bird still flapping wild, I utter, "therapy."

"Is that some kind of joke?"

"Not really," I say sheepishly, then finish, "I'm just trying to be careful."

"Careful!?" he chuffs. "Careful is not dragging me into a bathroom and having sex with me, not saying goodbye, or having the decency to give me a way to reach you over the last four-fucking years, or standing here acting like everything is normal."

My body reacts as if his hands are clasped over my arms, and he shakes me. I steady my breath before finally offering, "I don't know how to apologize for everything, and you know I was always better at avoidance."

"What about therapy?" He says contemptuously.

"You know what?" I exclaim, as if I'm speaking of my sins to a congregation. "Yes, I've been in therapy, and yes, I put a couple of states between us when things got messed up, but you're not innocent, Parker; you messed up, too!" I set my cup down hard before going on. "Yes, I regret never speaking to you over all this time, but you know what? Every time I thought about it, I was reminded; of her, of how I was the bad fucking girlfriend, of how little you all thought about me, so I stopped myself."

"So then what the fuck was last night, Sarah!?" He shouts exasperated, "You can't avoid someone when their dick is inside you, you know that, right?"

I grumble in frustration. "I'm soooo sorry that all 5'3" and 130 lbs of me could put all of you," I bemuse, flailing my arm in a wild circle in his direction, "in some kind of chokehold that forced you to have sex with me! MAAAYBE you should work on your own self-control, Parker."

He charges forward, and I retreat to my kitchen counter, watching him come. He grips my face firmly and stares intensely into my eyes before crushing his mouth to mine. I shove him backward. "Don't!" I say firmly. "Don't do something you're going to regret; I can't be the person who comes in and complicates everything." He grabs my face again, and I look at him, pleading. "Please," I whisper. "Don't let me mess up your life. I don't want to be like the girl that ruined us."

The sound of urgent knocks startled me with a pleasant voice calling through my door, "Miss G, I have your food from the cafe."

I hastily rubbed my eyes and fluffed my hair before answering the door. Tina reads my face and looks beyond me to Parker. She meets my gaze again, and I give her a nod that we're okay. I swing the door wide open, and she comes in, placing the assortment of breakfast on my small table. Parker and I stand in awkward silence. Tina nods at us both and leaves, closing the door behind her. We both stare at the food on the table, and Parker motions for us to sit. I walk past him, sitting at the table, he chooses the empty chair across from me.

"This may be too much food," he announces, looking at the spread.

"I thought maybe we could just eat our feelings," I say, shrugging.

"So," he continues hesitantly, "therapy?"

I laugh, "Yes," I nod and scoop some food onto a plastic plate. Tina was friendly enough to leave. "Turns out I'm no good at dealing with emotions," I smile.

Parker raises his eyebrows. "You don't say."

"Alright, mister perfect," I tease.

"How about you? Who's the girl?"

He expelled a long breath. "Shayne, and what do you want to know?"

"First off," I say, "Why does she have such a cool fucking name?" He rolls his eyes.

"We've been together for over two years, and the last few months, she's been pressuring things to—I don't know, go somewhere, and I'm like, where? Where should things go? I'm not thinking marriage right now, and two years feels a bit fast for that, anyway." I look up quickly, and he notices but says nothing. "Here's the thing, and I'm sorry for how this is going to come out." Setting my fork down, I focused on him. "All the parts of her I like are because they're nothing like you, but all the things that I imagine myself being with for the rest of my life are—well, the parts I like about you."

I feel the stinging behind my nose again, the bird's wings picking up their pace. This is why I stayed away and found ways to remain invisible all these years. I even managed to stay invisible in this very same town. "Parker," I say softly, "I am really sorry about last night; I honestly didn't even know you would be there. I mean, I saw they had an opener, but I had no idea that was your band. I got the shirt and didn't think anything of it; I was just so excited to have a piece of you, and then—" I pause and look upward to force the tears forming to roll backward. "There you were. I just couldn't be invisible anymore; I needed to see you, needed you to see me."

"We did a little more than see each other." He says, stabbing some food and putting it into his mouth.

I hang my head and push my palms to my forehead. "I know," I groan with resignation, "I promise you, I am not going to complicate your situation, okay?"

"What about you?" He asks.

"What about me?"

"Are you—" he starts.

"No," I interject. "No, I dated a bit up north, but nothing since I've been back." I decide to leave out "up the butt," guy.

"Why?" He asks curiously, and his eyes are so sincere that I don't know how to answer him. Well let's see, Parker, I was already pretty messed up when you got a hold of me, and we both know how that turned out, so I kind of decided maybe relationships aren't for me. I think it but don't say it. He discerns the discomfort in my hesitation and says, "tell me like I'm your therapist," while leaning back and using his hands to demonstrate a notepad and pen.

"If my therapist looked like you," I say, "I would be in big trouble."

"Just say it, Sarah," he demands, "if you do, I won't hold last night against you."

"What if I want you to?" I dare.

"Dammit, Sarah, for once, don't avoid the question, please," he says impatiently.

"Fine!" I say, irritated, "But you asked; our relationship made it impossible for me to have another one; we were on fire together, constant fireworks, everything the good and the bad, just one fuse setting off another; by the time all that happened I was too scorched to recover."

"I would've understood, you know?" He says softly, "if you would've just stayed and told me."

I meet his gaze. "No, you wouldn't have; you understand now because the fire is finally out."

He pauses in his thoughts. "Okay, then why not reach out sooner, send me a message, and get some closure?" He shrugs.

"Because I knew not to," in that moment, he leans forward, dropping his utensils. "Once, I looked you up on social media, and there were all these terrible comments about me on your page, so I deleted my profile right then and there." I hesitate, "I was here a couple of years ago visiting everyone, and I was doing real good again finishing school, working at a place like this up north by the sound, I missed everyone so much because I had stayed away for almost 2 years at that point," I break again noticing his eyes are fixed on me, willing me to continue; I clear my throat, sipping water. "Brian and Heidi were having a real engagement party in Tahoe, Parker. I—" I stop again, wondering how I say it. "I saw you at the clubhouse on the golf course; you were with a girl, and you were helping her up from the table, and I watched you spin her around and—"

"We had just started dating officially." He says, then looks up at me. "You, were there? You were right there?" he says, desperately.

"I was."

"Why didn't you? Say anything?"

"What was I supposed to do, Parker? You looked so happy, and you spun her around like—like you used to do to me." I say, letting the tears fall freely now.

"I think I was," he says almost apologetically. "I guess I understand, you know, why you wouldn't, after everything."

I give a half smile and can feel the red blotches forming on my face from so many bouts of crying and not crying. We finish eating and don't talk about anything more in the past. Once we are done, I courteously show Parker around my small place, and he tells me how he misses the posters and magazine cutouts I had spread all over my walls, which makes me laugh. I explained a decorator designed my place, so I chose none of its decor. We continued to exchange basic information about our jobs and his advertising agency, which surprisingly had not pitched a campaign to our complex. He tells me about how he will buy into a partnership with Maven. I explain to him our strategy to manage two more high rises, which will increase my workload significantly. He asks about Washington, and I fill in some of the gaps: jobs, missteps with boyfriends, how I started prioritizing myself by seeking therapy, and finishing my degree.

When it is finally time for him to leave, he stands at my doorway, holding me for a long time before he promises to keep in touch with me and throws in that he will put together a pitch for the company. I promise to put it in the right hands and stay in touch with him. "Sarah, I'm going to kiss you again because if I don't, I'll just wind up back here to do it later, and I think maybe for now, until I figure things out, I shouldn't be back here."

"Parker," I say, but it's meaningless as we're already locked in a kiss that says everything we've repeated and everything we won't say. Everything has changed. I am the kind of person who could keep it all together this time; he's still the only person I think can love me, and yet, the timing is still, somehow, off. He leaves through the door slowly, glancing back as if to make sure I'm still there. Once the door is closed, I return to my room, closing the curtains so I am consumed by darkness. Memories swirl around, projecting against my eyelids like movie clips: Halloween, San Francisco, the parking garage, walks, talks, kissing, sex, and the end. A strangled sob escapes, and I rub my eyes to stop the images from playing and replaying. I reach for my phone and dial Heidi.

"Hey, what's up?" She says, concerned because I never call. Through stifled sobs on the other end, she says, "I'll grab Thomas and head over." The phone clicks, and I set it beside me, willing myself to pick my head up. The center of my chest heaves in agony, insistent that I release the caged emotions wreaking havoc like millions of bats coming down on Bruce Wayne in that one Batman movie. Finally, I break down and grab my pillow, wailing into it; corpulent tears and vociferous sobs between gasps of air are my only companions for the thirty minutes it takes Thomas and Heidi to arrive at my door.

None of us smoke anymore, so we're all just crowded on my porch, looking out to the mountains and sipping wine while I tell them about the morning events. Thomas shakes his head in disbelief and comments on how he's got to hand it to Parker for being so bold last night and this morning. Heidi looks at me sorrowfully, as if she can't put me back together satisfactorily.

"So what now?" she asks. "What does he expect from you? You're the one who's been trying to stay away from him; I mean, aside from whatever crawled into your drink last night, which, by the way, he could've totally said no."

"I'm not sure." I say, "I guess a part of me always knew that there was some kind of chokehold that would always exist for Parker, but I genuinely don't feel good knowing that he will have to go back to her and either lie or tell her the truth. And then where does this leave me?" I look between them. "Am I just supposed to be alone because I'm waiting for him or because I'm afraid I'll never love anyone like him? That seems cruel."

They both nod but can't provide me with any realistic or helpful responses, so they don't. I finish off the last of my wine, and Heidi stands abruptly. "Hot tubs are open, right?"

"Yeah," I answer.

"Great! Hot tub time it is!"

"Do you even have suits?" I ask.

Thomas replies with a wink, "We literally only came here for the hot tub."

Chapter 32: Spoons

A few days pass before I hear anything related to Parker, which comes in the form of a formal pitch presentation sent by, I'm assuming, his assistant, David Spoons, who obnoxiously signs off as "Spoons" in his email. I roll my eyes and promptly pass it to our marketing team, who respond within an hour that they're interested and would like me to make the connection.

Spoons, we'd like a meeting. Please send me your best available days, and I'll make something happen. Sincerely, Knives. (haha)

I hit send, then forcefully dig my pointer fingers into my temples, massaging them generously. In 20 minutes, Spoons has already provided me with their availability. I set up the best corresponding time for our team and reserved our best meeting room. The room we use to either impress people we'd like to work with or intimidate people who don't want to work with us. Two days from today and eleven days since that morning.

I tell Heidi, Thomas, Felix, Jessica and Alice about our meeting over dinner. Felix squeals with delight, telling me to wear my sexiest professional outfit and make him sweat. I laugh and remind them he's in a complicated relationship that I need zero part of being involved in.

"Why would I want to create drama?" I say over my wineglass.

"Umm, because obviously you still love him!" Shouts Felix.

"Also, I think he obviously still loves you," Alice adds politely.

"Guys," I level with my friends. "While I appreciate the romanticism, this is not a fairy tale get-back-together moment. There was a momentary lapse in judgment leading to sex in a bathroom."

Heidi faces me straight on. "I'll admit you two had your problems, but like you said, you're both different now; maybe things could work out."

Thomas huffs. "I'm not convinced. Is he hotter now? Yes, is his band better? Yes. Do I think you guys are meant for each other? I don't know," he shrugs and finishes, "I just don't think love has to be a battlefield." Felix grabs Thomas's hand and gives him a look of appreciation, maybe at the song reference or because they wrote this rule themselves.

The next morning nervously standing before my wardrobe, I feel the familiar pangs of nostalgia and think back on the first time I stood in my closet, preparing to meet him. At the same time, I can't stop hearing Thomas' words. Was our love a battlefield? This time may be different; we've learned and grown, right? Why don't we deserve another chance? I find a rose-patterned pair of black nylons to pair with nude closed-toed high-heeled pumps and a black knee-length fitted skirt with a slit up the back, and I decide on an argyle-styled blouse to complete the top. Feeling pleased with my outfit selection, I shower to wrap my hair in overnight no-heat curlers.

When morning arrives, I do more pacing than necessary. I am so nervous that I add extra deodorant to my armpits because I can't stop sweating. Perfect, I think; not only am I nervous and sweating, but I've taken triple the number of steps than usual and am sweating from the exertion. I was relieved that I opted for heat-less curls, as adding any more heat would only exacerbate sweat forming under my arms, at my hairline, and in the creases of my elbows.

What little confidence I have mustered in the elevator is forgotten when I see Parker; he's so handsome, so grown-up. This makes me feel like I am still that young 23-year-old girl, not the professional I've become. In the meeting room, I spot a shorter man, presumably Spoons, shaking hands with our marketing team. Physically, I shake my nerves away and stride in as I would any other meeting. I greet my coworkers, testing the pitch of my voice before turning to Parker, and we shake hands and introduce ourselves cordially before I turn and ask, "Spoons?" The stout crewcut sporting man wearing khakis and a forest green polo starts from my shoes and makes his way to my hand before taking it and finally reaching my face. We're almost eye level. "Yes, Dave—David Spoons," he says, choking the words out. Parker shoots him a side look, his face turning slightly red, showing his embarrassment or lack of appreciation for how long Spoons holds my hand. My marketing team, oblivious, kicked off the meeting and swiftly fell into a professional back and forth that resulted in a signed deal with Maven Advertisement. My team thanks me for making the connection, and I courteously excuse myself from the remainder of the meeting.

Upon reaching my office, I sit down and proceed to reconfigure my laptop in order to connect it to the larger displays. I intensely shake my arms wide to my sides, still conscious of how sweaty I've been. My eyes shut to a vision of Parker seated across from me, his suit expertly cut to size, pen flipping over his fingers in a skillful motion, the way his eyes would slowly swing to mine, focusing on the pen I kept twirling at the edge of my lips. Remembering him, something I tried for four years not to do, had become infinitely more arduous. I hear a sharp knock on my office door, which slices abruptly into my thoughts, and I sit at attention. Parker is leaning against my open door frame, arms crossed over his torso, one leg over the other, and I spy a dimple forming as his grin widens. I think very suddenly that I feel naked, so I begin to rub my hands back and forth over my legs, reminding myself that I do, in fact, have clothes on.

"Can we talk?" he asks. I point to the white leather seat in front of me. He closes my office door and scoots the chair uneasily, as if it's the same weight of a compact car he's pushing uphill before finally seating himself.

"Can I be frank?" He doesn't wait for a response. "I don't know why I am in here."

I smile and tilt my head to the side. "Oh?"

He groans and slides both palms over his face, "you look great, by the way. I think Spoons is hoping this arrangement will end with him, you know?"

I raise an eyebrow. "Are you coming in here to tell me your coworker wants to sleep with me? Because I will tell you right now, I don't want to sleep with him," he smiles at the floor.

"Thank goodness for small favors, but no, I'm not here to tell you who you can or can't sleep with, or even who wants to sleep with you."

Seeing his apprehension, the courage I fervently sought is flooding my system. I stand from my chair and move toward him, placing my hands on the arms of his chair, bending to meet his gaze. "So if it's not to inform me of potential sex partners, why are you here, Parker?"

His deep brown eyes fix on mine, and the charge in them tells me we both know why he's here. "You live here, right?" he asks indicatively.

"What are you suggesting?" I return.

He leans into my ear, and the smell of sandalwood fills my senses. "Take me to your apartment and find out."

We head out of my office together, and to the unsuspecting eye, it looks like a typical interaction between business partners. The instant we enter the empty elevator, platonic niceties are replaced by a fever. We are a cataclysm of ragged breaths, hands in hair, nails dragging into the sleeves of our business wear, then Parker cupping my ass, pulling me against him while kissing and biting at my neck. We reach my floor without stopping, and I fumble with my key card before it finally flashes green. We shove ourselves through the door into my room. He throws his coat over my bar chair and grabs my hand, leading me to my bedroom. He spins me into him, pressing my butt against him. I feel his erection through the suit pants closer to my back because of his height, but it still sends electric spasms up my spine. Once near the side of my bed, he boldly bends me forward, hiking my skirt up around my waist. Parker runs gentle hands up my pantyhose, tracing some of the rose patterns before tugging them over my hips and butt, leaving me in a laced thong, breathing erratically. His breath is ragged, and he snarls with frustration as I hear the buckle of his belt release, his pants drop, and he moves my thong to the side. He firmly grabs the bottom of my ass and forcefully pushes me onto the bed so that, on all fours, he can effortlessly coax himself inside me. With a reciprocating motion, he continues to thrust himself into me, rocking us back and forth. I collapse onto my bed, thoughts blurring, countless sensations coming to a crescendo.

I come to in a haze of barely undressed rapture and look to see him staring at the ceiling but not contented; feeling self-conscious, I stand and head for my bathroom. Closed inside, I clean myself up, throw my hair in a ponytail, and fold a robe around me. I return to him seated at the edge of my bed, looking over the hills, shirt still unbuttoned but pants back in place. I sit beside him and squeeze his hand.

"I have the distinct feeling I've done something I promised I wouldn't do."

He looks at me and smiles. "You're not the only one; you're like a magnet." Rocking his head back and forth, he continues, "And her, I don't know what she wants, but it hasn't been me for a while; I even thought maybe she was seeing some else because she started sleeping in the other room."

We're suspended in time as Parker stays silent, and I have no advice to give. I'm studying the painting hanging over my bed, a floral canvas that looks like hundreds of poppies peeking out between thousands of colorful dots that conspire to make wildflowers. In fact, this is my favorite piece picked by the designer. It reminds me of a meadow of wildflowers, an image, a place, so clear in my mind it's like I've visited it a thousand lifetimes before even though I never have in this one.

"Yesterday Shayne said that we should figure this out, and part of me wants to, but part of me—ugh, I don't know."

I place my hand on his shoulder and shake my head in understanding. "Love doesn't have to be a battlefield." I say, smiling at him.

Parker's face hardened, the once handsome grown man of earlier diminished by the deep grooves of his forehead and darkness under his eyes. "You know," he says harshly, "I'm not like you; I can't just remove my emotions and make jokes about us."

I laugh despite myself, "jokes Parker? I'm not joking, but while we're on the subject, do you and your buddies still refer to me as the bad girlfriend? Or what am I now?" I throw my hands out to the sides in a gesture of disbelief.

"Oh god, Sarah, really? This again?"

"I wasn't the only one who was bad," I remind him. "Where's your credit, Parker? Who even was that girl!? Shayne!?" I set my jaw and clenched my fists, struggling to keep my tone from rising to the octave it wanted.

"You want to waste time talking about something from four years ago?" He asks preposterously.

"You do!" I scream, "That's your favorite part about this; making sure I remember what I did, how I fucked up; well, Parker, you were the bad boyfriend."

He murmurs, "I am sorry for that; I'm sorry I let everyone think that about you." He chuckles, disbelieving, "And now look, I am the bad boyfriend again."

"Ex-boyfriend?" I clarify.

"Yeah, I guess you're right, bad ex-boyfriend."

"If I had stayed, would we have made it, Parker?"

"I don't know, but I loved you for years after. There were days I would look for you, but I could never reach you and your friends." He pauses and shakes his head. "They weren't going to let me get to you; they loved you too much to watch you hurt again."

As I exhale, I can taste the saltiness of my tears on my lips, and I carefully brush away the remaining drops from my cheeks. "I don't know what any of this means, Parker, but none of it feels exactly right; I can see it on your face, too." I sigh longingly. "We can't see through the trees right now, and I can't be a complication; we spent so much time complicating things; if we're going to be anything, we're going to do it right."

We sit in peaceful silence, and I am back in that field of wildflowers, so entranced by them I imagine their smell. When Parker finally stands to button his shirt, "you're right, you know, you can't be a complication, and this doesn't feel as right as it should, if we're going to do it. It's going to be exactly right." He exits my room, grabbing his jacket before turning to face me and then again out of my view.

"That view, Sarah. It's worthy of an iPod mix."

I smile at the memory. "Why do you think I have it?"

He studies me warmly with an intense look.

"Sooo," he drags out, "I guess I'll be seeing you a bit here and there, but I'll try to let Spoons handle this one, so it's easier, at least until I can figure things out."

"Thanks," I say, meaning it.

We graciously smile at each other, and I let my hand linger on his as he stands in the doorway. Once he leaves, I lock the door, grab my phone, and text Cora. **Done for the day. See you tomorrow.**

Feeling like the moment calls for a song, I search through my playlists. Landing on the one lovingly named "breakup songs" that Heidi made for me, I play Roxette. Using my robe and undergarments as the obvious choice for this number, I dance around my house, belting to the cathartic lyrics.

"It must have been love
But it's over now
It must have been good
But I lost it somehow
It must have been love
But it's over now
From the moment we touched
'Til the time had run out"

Chapter 33:
Keep The Music Alive

Parker kept to his word. Our contact over the next few days into the weeks before the Gala is minimal. My contact with Spoons is also curiously minimal, but I have no real complaints. Thanks to the help of Maven Advertising, this Gala will be our biggest yet.

Slowly, I pull the stretch crepe fabric, its deep red color resembling that of a fine wine, up my body. I held my breath, making sure not to snag or tear anything on the 950-dollar Saks gown I had splurged on for this event. One shoulder remains free while the other boasts a billowing silk chiffon open sleeve to match the accented billowing train starting at the waist. The gown hugs my body until it flares out in a mermaid style design at the bottom. The caution with which I am dressing myself in this makes me regret it entirely. I consistently ran 5 miles daily, attended 3 Pilates classes weekly, and diligently lifted weights for months to prevent any possibility of gaining weight. My hair is curled to perfection and gathered to one side thanks to my salon-owning neighbor, Gabriel, who insisted he prepare me for the evening; grateful now that he did, my planned updo wouldn't have been elegant enough to match this beautiful dress.

Electing mournfully not to buy the two-thousand-dollar Swarovski decorated heels also from Saks, I finish my look by strapping on my sequined stilettos from Dillard's that came in at just over one hundred dollars. The Views Gala, "Keep the Music Alive," is being held basically across the street in a stylishly remodeled casino ballroom decorated in white hues, with glowing lamps giving it an ethereal feel. Cora, myself, and our marketing team hit the nail on the head when I mentioned the theme should feel classic, like the instruments we are trying to save. Maven Advertisement brought in all the right people with deep pockets with their perfect marketing strategy.

A rapid knock echoes through my bathroom, and I assume it's Heidi and Brian coming to escort me across the street. Gestures such as these are what I think of now when I remember Brian four years ago. Despite his dullness, he always ensured our safety, particularly for Heidi and me, without any complaint. Brian would walk me blocks away from where he needed to go because Heidi cared for me, so, by default, Brian cared for me, too. He fixes things around my place that I don't get maintenance to do; he reminds me about oil changes and tire rotations, sometimes taking my car while Heidi and I have lunch and doing them for me. I grasp why she never left, not for the reasons she always told us, but because he was an undeniably good man. Besides all of that, her best friend was a walking cautionary tale.

I swing open the door. "Thank goodness you're here! I cannot get this zipper up," and I spin around so Heidi can zip me before stepping through the threshold. When she finishes zipping, I walk forward, allowing them in while I gather what I need to leave. When I turn, I'm shocked to see a fourth well-dressed person in my house. "Chase!?" I say with surprise. "I didn't know you were coming, and wow, you're in another suit!" The suit enhanced his attractiveness beyond my expectations.

"Sarah, I know you insisted on going to this alone, but you simply cannot go to a Gala hosted by your work without a date!" Heidi asserts, "So we brought Chase." Chase grins in a way that tells me he wasn't given a choice in the matter.

"Oh, for heaven's sake, Heidi, I would've been fine, but thank you, Chase, for getting all dressed up, anyway." I say pleasantly.

"Just call me arm candy," he says, a bit too lively, making it sound purely sarcastic.

Heidi turns and eyes him before clapping, "Shall we go then?" and we're off to cross the street.

Hooking my arm through Chase, inwardly thankful now to have a date to "my" Gala, we step inside, and with lights dimmed and everything sparkling perfectly, I am taken aback by just how stunning this all is. Chase looks around the room and gives me a nudge. "You did good, kid." I smile and silently praise my team for being AWESOME. Chase and I followed Heidi in search of our table, which should contain Thomas, Felix, Alice, Jessica, Rowan, Cora, and Drew from my team. As we approach the table, Chase receives several long stares from women in the room. It's completely unsurprising. Thanks to his square, rugged features, dark blonde messy hair, and stubbled cheeks, he looks every bit the hardworking cowboy, even when cleaned up. Chase stands right around 5'10 or 5'11; he's not quite six feet. I know this because Felix is precisely, and Chase comes right in underneath him. He is broad-shouldered but slimly built; you can tell he's strong because his clothing tightens around him as he shifts and moves. The guy hasn't an ounce of fat on him; I've seen him in swim trunks; it's all ranch muscle. He's forever reminded me of a cowboy, which is mainly because his parents own a very successful ranch, the ranch he works on and is in line to inherit; more than that, though, he's quiet, polite, and has all the charm you would expect from a southern cowboy, so the shoe has always fit. Once we find our table and friends, Chase politely pulls out my seat, and I take it, wondering why none of these girls have ever locked him down.

As the evening gets underway, we all pour a glass of champagne and toast. I exclusively dance with my friends, Chase methodically makes his way around the room, being as attentive as I would expect my forced date to be. He stands with me in photos for the event and shares comments about what he knows of me personally throughout our time as the shared best friends of Brian and Heidi with people conducting interviews for the evening; he makes sure for anything I am publicly involved in that he is at my side being the perfect date. We have a few keynote speakers and an auction to raise money, so in time, we are all taking our seats, listening to the auction, and inspirational talks begin. The last keynote speaker takes up her post and gives a poignant and inspirational speech about how having the opportunity to learn and play an instrument saved her life. As she speaks, I think about how important music has been for me, too, and wipe away a few stray tears as her feelings are mutual. We all stand to applaud, and one of our sponsors announces that in honor of her speech, they will donate $20,000 to "Keep the Music Alive." Cora ushers Chase and me to meet the keynote speaker for a photo opportunity as the hosts of tonight's event, with the most noteworthy speaker. They will use this photo for marketing in the coming months. Following Cora to her position near the stage, where she is thanking other event sponsors and posing for pictures, I watch as a familiar man leaves her with a kiss on the cheek, then on the lips, and my stomach wrenches. I feel Chase steady me and hold on to my hip as I force my hand to extend.

"Sarah, with The Views," I choke out.

"What a speech," comments Chase, to fill my silence.

"Oh, you're too kind; it was all true," she says, and I see her give Chase a once over, eyeing him gratefully, which provides me with a strange stab of jealousy. She is absolutely gorgeous, towering over me by at least 5 inches, with long platinum hair that suits her features better than any other platinum blondes I've seen. She definitely has some lip filler, I can tell, and her boobs are most likely fake but the way she carries herself, it says classy and expensive more than fake and trashy. A photographer comes back to snap a photo of us together, and then she says. "Wait one more with our dates!" I see her turn and wave someone over. "Parker!" She shouts right as I think it. Knowing my discomfort, Chase descends and pulls me to his other side, placing himself between the keynote speaker and me, which places two bodies between me and Parker. I smile for the photos and implore the holy being above that I don't look as tense as I feel. When the photographer leaves, she introduces us to Parker. I am frozen; my hands and legs are filled with lead. Chase fills my silence once more with pleasantries, and Parker calls her Shayne, Shayne............ The name echoes, swirling around in my skull. It is now just an empty cave battering her name around before Chase stops it by violently nudging my side. I come to, and Parker's face practically begs me to fix the uneasiness.

"I… er," I stammer, my mind going blank for a moment. "I am so sorry; I think the champagne and crowd—" I stop and stammer again. "If you'll excuse me." Regaining control of my limbs, I wander toward the exit that leads to a terrace. I breathe in and out on counts of four, which is as useless as a screen door on a submarine. Momentarily this makes me consider how I would rather be floating along the depths of a bottomless ocean trapped in a small tin tube. My whole body is trembling as I walk through the doors to the terrace, empty, likely because it is snowing and easily 20 degrees. The door swings open abruptly behind me, and I assume it's Chase coming to stand guard.

"I'll be fine," I say to the night.

"That's good news." Comes a voice that is distinctly not Chase's. I spin around and throw my arms out on a guffaw. "What in the FUCK are you doing here, Parker?"

"I came to check on you," he says in earnest.

"No!" I shout back, "No, you do not get to check on me; I am not yours to check on."

"Sarah," he says despondently.

"No," I say and start to move forward, but he shifts to block me. "Sarah," he repeats.

"Parker," I say forlornly, "I am not owed anything from you; we are not together; you are obviously still with her, which is confusing, yes, maybe even hurtful, but NOT my business."

"Hurtful?" He shouts, baffled. "It's not like I'm cheating on you, Sarah, but maybe now you have a taste of how it feels."

I look at the snow falling from the sky, letting out an exasperated breath. "Is that why you're here with her? Is that why you followed me outside? To exact some kind of revenge for something that happened four years ago?" I turn to face him, and he replies after meeting my gaze.

"No, Sarah, that's not why I'm here. I'm, yes, with her, and yeah, okay, maybe it does make me feel good just a little bit that you are so bothered that I am here with her."

I laugh incredulously. "Always a competition, I see, except this time I don't think I get the title of bad girlfriend," and start again for the door back inside.

Parker stops me by my arm and whirls me so that I face him. The height of my heels makes me an easy target for his lips, which crush against mine hard enough to give me whiplash. I retreat and he thrusts into me with more force and urgency, shifting his hands from my arms to my back. "No!" I assert into his mouth, but I know already that I'm returning the kiss because my brain is full seconds behind what I'm telling it to stop doing. The door forcefully opens again, and he releases me as if I've just caught fire, which causes me to stumble unbalanced, so he steadies me by my arms.

"Sarah," says Chase, "They're looking for you."

I briskly wipe my mouth and walk past Parker, saying nothing. Chase places a calloused hand, causing the uncovered skin on my back to prickle, then whispers, "You good?"

"No," I say darkly.

We head to the table first, and I grab my purse to check my small mirror. I fix my face and add some lipstick, then make my final rounds, shaking hands, embracing people, and posing for more photos. In turn, I am explaining to each that I am simply exhausted and will cut my evening short, but "thank you so much for coming to support our Gala" is on polite repeat for a full 45 minutes longer.

Once back at the table, I hugged my friends for their support and told them I was tired and ready to go home. Brian and Heidi insist Chase walk back across the street since they got a room here for the night and he obliges with no argument; he also accepts no argument from me when I tell him how unnecessary this is. We walk side-by-side across the street and down to my entrance. He then further instructs that he'll see me to my door. We stand in the elevator in our customary compatible silence, and I am grateful that he is Chase; otherwise, I would get bombarded with questions.

When we're at my door, I use the keycard and push it open; he asks if he can use my bathroom while waiting for a cab. I point him toward the bathroom outside my bedroom; as he walks in, he goes too far into the living room, passing it, but stops to comment on the views from my still-open windows. He looks back at me, and I point again to the bathroom, and he doubles back. I was standing in my closet, fighting with my zipper, when I heard the familiar flush that sounded like a wind tunnel inside my closet.

"Chase," I yell.

"Yeah," he says.

"Could you maybe unzip me before you leave? I'm sorry that's such a girl thing to ask. However, I figure if you're still on date duty."

I hear a snicker of amusement as he attempts to follow my voice until I meet him at the large entrance to my room. I turn my back to him, and he holds my zipper and slides it down until his hand is resting on the small of my back. He doesn't let go, the skin warming underneath his hand. "I'm drunk," he states absolutely.

"Chase?" I inquire.

"You just look like a princess, and I'm too drunk to let go of this zipper, I think."

I spin around, causing his hand to free itself, holding my dress to my chest, and thank him for the compliment. He gives me a half smile and continues to eye me before hissing.

"Shit, the cab" I watch him pull out his phone, then press it to his ear, and he groans.

"Something wrong?" I say.

"No cabs for an hour." He groans again.

"Just stay on the couch, Chase; it's no big deal. I have plenty of blankets."

"You're sure?"

"I'm sure," heading to the closet for spare blankets and pillows. "It's not like you've never slept on my couch before," I tease and hand him over the pile of blankets.

"Who didn't sleep on that couch?" He questions, and I laugh. "I think I may be the only person."

He takes his suit jacket off and tosses it on my barstool, frees his neck from the bowtie, and un-tucks and frees the buttons on his shirt before falling onto my couch. "I hate dressing up."

"Well," I say with projection as I head to my closet, "you don't have to do it again until the wedding, right?"

He raises his voice so I can hear him saying, "I may not do it then either."

I laugh and return in pajama bottoms and a tank top, "do you need anything before I head to bed? There are cups in that cabinet, and water comes from the fridge, but the ice maker doesn't expel the ice, so you have to grab it from the inside." He shakes his head, and I move to close the large curtains, explaining that he'll be up at dawn if I don't.

"I'm always up at dawn," he says, and then I give a small laugh, thinking duh before I turn out the light.

"Hey, Chase."

"Yeah."

"Thank you for being my date tonight."

"I literally tried to say no several times until my life and hunting trip were threatened, so no thanks are necessary; it was self-preservation."

"Well, thanks anyway," I say again; I think I see something like a salute in the dark and then walk into my room.

Waking the following day, I noted Chase had already gone; he wasn't kidding. As I entered my kitchen, I noticed a scribbled note near my coffee pot: **stole a cup and some coffee. Hope you don't mind. P.S. your couch sucks!**

I laugh and slip it into my notes, cards, and whatever drawer.

Chapter 34: Three's a Crowd

The texts, emails, and phone calls come in torrents from Parker. I lack the inner strength to ignore them all and have intentionally had late dinners and even sleepovers at Brian and Heidis since they have a spare bedroom to avoid what I fear will evolve into a pop-in visit to discuss what happened at the Gala, now almost three weeks ago.

When I think back on all the moments, I was chasing the memory of ecstasy that used to consume my and Parker's togetherness; instead, being around him has flooded my system with sadness and regret. Looking back on our electricity, I see with all too much clarity the overcharged, errant love story. What if we weren't supposed to fix it? Maybe things weren't supposed to go back, and perhaps those feelings we had all those years ago were just who we were and not who we are now. Did I love him? There was no doubt. Did he love me? I'm positive. But four full years had passed. Every instance of encountering the same electricity served as an unmistakable warning, indicating the inevitable consequences if we gave in to temptation. That wasn't how love should feel, was it? If we were meant to be together, it would be easy, right? Like Thomas said, love doesn't have to be a battlefield, and this absolutely felt like war. I couldn't talk to anyone about it anymore; let's face it, I was annoying myself with the endless loop. In reality, the only person who could answer these questions was me alone, and if I were going to be free of him, I needed to let him go and place him back in the past from which he came.

I emerged from Brian and Heidi's spare bedroom and made a beeline for the restroom, desperate to relieve my full bladder that I had been holding in to avoid abandoning the cozy warmth of the blankets. I snuck a look at myself in the mirror and thought about how tired I looked, how badly I needed to color my hair, and should probably give my eyes a break from contacts and use my glasses for a few days. "Phew," I breathe, blowing air through my lips, and left the bathroom to collect my things and head back to my apartment.

Heidi, Brian, and Chase were all in the kitchen pouring coffee. Heidi greeted me with a cup, placing it in my hand and patting my shoulder. "Parker called," she says apologetically, "I told him you were just trying to sort things out, and he said you were just classically avoiding conflict." She shrugs "I think the sooner you talk to him the sooner you can move past this chapter and rid your system of him."

Funny, I think I was just saying the same thing to myself. Accepting the coffee with a nod, I take a generous sip, feeling the warmth spread through my body, and playfully roll my eyes.

"Hey, listen," she continues, "Brian and Chase are going to the range today to get ready for hunting season, and I'm just doing lunch with my mom but if you need me, I'll cancel."

I shake my head vehemently. "No, oh gosh, Heidi, no. You're right. I need to talk to him and get this all over with, shake free of him and all that."

Brian interjects and says, "Only if you feel like it's a good idea; I think it's a little weird he's trying to hunt you down, so if you're not comfortable with it, don't do it." Chase signals his agreement.

"Guys," I deadpan. "This is Parker, he's not going to hurt me, well not like hurt me hurt me, you know what I mean." They both hold my gaze and I concede, "I will call the moment I feel different."

They return to their coffees, and what I think is a map. Heidi pulled me into a side hug, and I placed my coffee down to leave. I take the winding road down Heidi's Hill back into the city, which is much smoother in the new X5 than my old truck, I note. For a moment I considered selling the truck that is too tall, but almost immediately decided against it, so now I have two cars a BMW X5 and an old Toyota.

Once I exit the elevator to my hall, I see a body slumped against my door. Parker, I realize immediately. I walk up, and he looks up at me, surprised, but exhaustion looms over him, too. I nod, he stands, and I let us in my apartment. He sits on my couch, which I only now realize is still adorned with the blankets and pillow I gave Chase weeks ago after the Gala. Parker looks at them skeptically and moves them into a pile away from him. He rubs the heels of his palms into his and, on an exhale, says, "I've been trying to get a hold of you."

I solemnly nod. "I know."

"How can you just avoid me like that?"

"I'm upset, Parker," I say flatly, "You slept with me twice, all the while telling me you were over, and then I see you at the Gala with her, clearly together, and when I question it, you essentially ask me how it felt. I've never done complicated, Parker, you know that, and THAT is the definition of complicated."

"I'm not like you." He retorts.

"What is that supposed to mean?" I snap.

He aggressively stands and vigorously throws his arms in front of him. "I can't just sleep with you, remove all emotion, and wake up okay the next day."

"You think that there's no emotion here, Parker!? Really!?" I say aghast, "That's ALLLLLL there is; my emotions are supercharged here, but you are WITH an entire lovely human being, and if there were nothing there, truly, you would be broken up, but you're not, are you?" I pause and take a deep breath before finalizing. "Me and you cannot exist in a world where you and her do."

"You don't always get to set the parameters of our relationship, Sarah."

I exhale sharply and put my hands on my face. "Parker, I am not yours. You are not mine; YOU ARE HERS. I'm not setting parameters because there's nothing here."

"Nothing here!?" He shouts so loudly I take a large step back from him. "You cannot stand there and tell me there's NOTHING here, Sarah. Don't you fucking lie to me."

"There's nothing here," I reiterate calmly. "There's nothing here because there's no you and me. We broke up four years ago, and no matter what, you are with her." I take a breath. "Go home, Parker."

Parker stands and walks past me to the door; before turning the handle, he sighs audibly. "I'm not doing this again, Sarah; if I leave, I'm gone." I make no move to console or discourage him, and when I hear the door click closed, I exhale a breath that I've only just realized I was holding. A finality inside of me has not yet existed where Parker was concerned. He was always a loose end trailing me, the lyrics in the songs I would sing, the thing I couldn't put my finger on in other relationships, and the one I never quite forgave myself for. Yet, in this moment, the chapter had inexorably ended.

Chapter 35: Christmas on Vinyl

On Christmas morning, my tree was adorned with three small presents: one from my parents, one from The View's team, and one mysterious package with no label, except for my address. With Mouse, the black and white cat I recently adopted, by my side, it's just the two of us in this empty room. One evening, by the time we reached our third bottle of Prosecco, I was in a fit of laughter and spontaneously suggested naming the cat Mouse, much to the amusement of Felix and Thomas. We all laughed until tears streamed down our faces and our sides hurt from the uncontrollable mirth. So here he was, leisurely strolling across my wooden floor, basking in the warmth of the sun's rays that flooded the living room before the anticipated snowfall.

My oversized Christmas tree, which was far too big for just one person, illuminated my modest living space with brilliant rays of light. During the nighttime, it became my cherished view as the vibrant hues resembled explosive solar flares, cascading across the walls. The twinkling lights, following their pre-programmed patterns, whimsically danced, captivating

Mouse as it sought their elusive movements. Meanwhile, I basked in a state of tranquil appreciation, relishing the enchanting spectacle.

I make my cup of coffee, savoring the rich aroma, before bending down to retrieve my gifts from under the tree: crisp dollar bills, cozy slipper socks from Mom and Dad, and, of course, my eagerly anticipated annual favorite vibrant patterned pajamas. A plush blanket was adorned with an adorable pattern of black and white cats, resembling Mouse from The Views team. Then, there it was, the last unopened present, a perfect square and surprisingly light to the touch. With curiosity building, I meticulously examine it, taking my time to assess its weight and dimensions, attempting to unravel its secrets before I rip the paper to shreds. It's a record, which first struck me as an odd gift because I don't have a player. As if waking abruptly to a blaring alarm, I suddenly realize that what I am holding is none other than Jimmy Eat World's "Futures" on vinyl, signed by the band themselves. My fingers trace the cover delicately, exploring its texture as I turn it over. A post-it note, bearing the words "verse 3" and a small heart, awaits me on the back. Parker. My intuition clings to the thought of him buying this and I know it like I knew from the first moment I met him I was in love with him. I also discern this gift, this gesture, is not a representation of a beginning or resurgence, but the end.

"I won't always love what I'll never have
I won't always live in my regrets"

I place it on the shelf above my electric fireplace and admire it for a long while before finally letting the memories and the feelings pass and fade. Retreating to my room for my phone to make all my "Merry Christmas" phone calls, I don't mention the record. It's not for anyone else to contemplate its meaning; I know, and that's enough.

By the time I am done, the snow is falling, and I turn down both Heidi and Thomas on their offers for Christmas with their family. I don't want to drive back into the city after it's snowed and I feel awfully cozy in my tree's glittering lights, the fireplace's warmth, and for once with myself. Mouse has now retreated to the chair I've strategically placed near the fireplace, and his loud purring fills the quiet room. I shift to unfold and toss my new Mouse blanket wide over me, taking care to cover the length of me in one go. I pick a holiday movie and keep the volume low. I wait as the room turns dark, giving way to the colored lights' melodious dance again.

Chapter 36: Hero and a Distressed Damsel

It is now New Year's Eve and we make a promise to ourselves that we will remain classy, less swaying back and forth while walking home holding our heels drunk, and more heading out while we're still able to say the alphabet without giggling. Thomas, Felix, and I are within walking distance of downtown; specifically, I am smack in the middle. Everyone else decides to get rooms so we can be out until well after midnight and safely tuck ourselves in at night's end without sliding around on the snow and ice-filled streets. Chase, as always, has decided to take his chances with a date downtown instead of actually getting a room, but Heidi and Brian assure him the second bed in their room is available if that doesn't pan out. It will pan out for him; it will always pan out for men who look like Chase.

We go to the adjoining casinos from their hotel and start our first round at a bar with a Billie Holiday-style band playing a mix of upbeat and holiday-themed jazz. Flickering fake candles and dark furniture adorn the bar, while maroons and purples make up its colored carpet. The stage, surrounded by slot machines, features two large, crushed velvet curtains tied open with thick gold rope. The almost distracting lighting almost makes you forget that it is in the middle of a casino gaming floor. Our first round of shots comes, and we all toast to the New Year and Brian and Heidi's upcoming wedding. Brian formally proposed in an even year, but there wasn't enough time to plan the wedding. Heidi didn't like the idea of getting married in an odd year, so instead, she had ample time to plan and re-plan her dream wedding, which would take place at the same clubhouse where their engagement party was. Conversation spills over the music, and we make our way to the second stop of the evening, where we girls and Felix take to the dance floor, switching between regular dancing and then doing ridiculous dances like the sprinkler, lawn mower, and shopping cart. At the same time, Thomas whoops from the tables, and Chase and Brian look embarrassed.

As 11 o'clock hits, we make our way to the last stop, an invitation-only party that promises to be the hottest spot in town to ring in the New Year. Walking inside, it's as if you've entered a Cirque du Soleil sideshow. Aerialists are floating above small circular landing positions. Female and male dancers are scattered throughout, embellished with glittery makeup and large stuck-on gems across their sculpted bodies; we make our way to an open table, and each plucks a champagne flute from the passing waiters. I sit beside Thomas as Felix drags Alice and Jessica to the dance floor. Rowan shoots Jessica a look that says she'll be passing and starts thumbing through her phone.

"My feet are killing me!" I shout into Thomas' ear.

"Not used to all this walking in those bad boys anymore, are you?" He shouts back.

"No," I say, laughing. "This is terrible; do you think they would mind if I went barefoot here?"

"If you go barefoot here, Sarah, I will personally escort you out."

I turn to smack his arm, and that's when I see her, Shayne, the might-as-well-be Victoria's Secret model wearing a scrunched red shimmery dress paired with red strappy heels, her long blonde locks flowing over her shoulders. She's laughing with a group of people, making them all look like mere mortals against her exquisite features. My eyes are now anxiously darting around the room searching for Parker. Thomas must notice because he tracks my eyes and continues to turn to find what I'm looking for. "Sarah!" he pokes me and says into my ear, "I see him." He grabs my hand underneath the table and points toward Parker, now walking across the room, headed to Shayne. Once he reaches her, he drapes his arm over her shoulder, flicking her hair and then tracing the stitching of her dress down to her lower back. He kisses the spot on her neck where her hair once laid, and my stomach twinges. The DJ announces everyone should make their way to the dance floor for the last few songs of 2013. A remixed version of Rihanna's Stay begins, and I scoff as Thomas pulls me from my seat. I catch a glimpse of Chase with his arms around a pretty brunette as we make our way to Brian, Heidi, Felix, Jessica and Alice. The mix explodes into I Knew You Were Trouble, and we are all (beside Brian) shouting the lyrics to the sky and dancing wildly. I am back to life with my friends, enjoying the evening, Gangnam Style, Die Young, and We Can't Stop play. I am making my best impression of Miley Cyrus twerking on all of my friends when the DJ spins Happy New Year by Abba, beginning the count down from 20.

All of us are counting in unison. Then, as I yell five, throwing my head back, I face forward only to be staring again at Shayne and Parker, smiling, and counting to each other. I become acutely aware of how alone I am. "ONE!" the crowd shouts. The sounds of people cheering and ABBA disappearing, leaving me a vacuum of stifled noises. I watch helplessly as they lock lips with one another, the room blurring; my vision tunnels on them as I stand alone amongst a crowd of people making out. I start to close my eyes when I am being spun around. I feel lips press against my own. Someone's rough hands on the skin of my arm pulling me in while they bring one hand to my neck and the other to my cheek; my lips part, and the gentle entrance of this person, man I assume when I feel the stubble, tongue distracts my sensations. I am torn between glee and aversion. Suddenly, the sound rushes back into my ears, and I can hear the echo of shouting as the enigmatic man slowly withdraws. I blink to first see a look of complete surprise on Heidis's face, then Brian's; looking across the blurred face in front of me, I see an agape Thomas, who may be slow clapping? Then I see Parker stupefied, grasping at Shayne to pull her opposite of where I am standing. It's like a reverse optical illusion where the closer things take longer to come into focus, and the person in front of me is Chase. His square features, messy dark blonde hair, and hazel eyes bore me with uncertainty.

"What is going on?" Heidi says with evident confusion, and Chase speaks up before I can make words or thoughts happen. "I couldn't just let her stand there, alone, with that going on." He points his beer bottle to Parker and Shayne. Heidi looks over her shoulder, then looks back and exaggerates a shudder. She grips Chase's hand and gives him a wink. "You're so thoughtful sometimes!" Before grabbing both my arms and dragging me back to dancing, "Come on bitch," she shouts wildly. "This is our last year in our 20s and my last year unmarried!" She snakes her hands up and down the outsides of my dress, and then I dip below her waist, straddling one of her long legs. I notice that more than one pair of eyes has become fascinated with our show, and I can't help but feel the moment and play into this sexy mingle. We continue at it until Brian becomes overtly uncomfortable with the amount of attention on his fiancée and makes a stance to step behind her as he's always done. A slow song plays, and we head back to the table to rest our tired and aching feet. We pluck our last flutes of champagne from the server as this party begins its 2AM wrap-up. There are plenty of other clubs that will be hosting the partygoers until the sun comes up, but I am spent; I hug my group. Brian and Heidi are going to use this opportunity to exit as well, while the rest of them will find their way to Five Queens to end the night.

We say our goodbyes in shouts, and to Heidi and Brian, I maintain that yes, I will be fine stare. "There are so many security guards out tonight!" I shout, "I'll be totally fine! I start making my way against the crowd of noisy, joyful, intoxicated party attendees when someone grabs my hand. I pivot suddenly and see Chase next to me.

"At least let me walk you out and across the street," he says.

"You really don't have to do that," I insist.

"Well, I wanted to apologize, too, for earlier. I didn't ask or think, I just felt like you could use a distraction."

I look sideways at him, blushing a bit, and say, "I did, thank you for coming to my rescue," then finish, "see, if you walk me home that will be too much rescuing for the evening, and I can't pay that kind of debt." He chuckles and continues to see me outside, where the snow is falling, making quite the display against the city's neon lights.

Chase groans, "I bet cabs are a mess."

"What about the brunette from the party?" I tease.

"Oh, her? Yeah, she wasn't interested after I kissed you and all. She said it looked more than friendly." He laughs and continues, "I guess I was too convincing." Shrugging, he digs his hands into his pockets.

I shiver as the cold air penetrates beyond my jacket. "I'd offer my couch, yet I distinctly remember a note saying it sucked."

"It does." He says genuinely, "I've got Heidi and Brian's room if home isn't an option. Hell, maybe I'll wander around and party a bit more."

I hugged and thanked him again before the walk sign signals, and I slowly crossed. SLAM! My unsuspecting heels slide apart. The sound of a slight scuff against the ground fills the air. I feel the pressure as I forcefully cram my elbow into the unforgiving earth, followed by the sharp impact of my knee and hip. "Fuck!" I shout and am being hoisted from the snow by Chase. "What was that about no more rescuing!?" He ridicules. I elbow his ribs with less force than I want because the throbbing in my body has now taken over as the foremost sensation, the cold coming in at a distant second.

"You would mock me right now," I say painfully.

"Come on, ice princess, I'll walk you home."

Stepping into my apartment, I can sense the pain starting to fade away, providing me with a flicker of optimism that I've only sustained some bruises. But it's not until tomorrow, when the alcohol's effects wear off, that I'll be able to confirm it. Chase takes my jacket and hangs it on the coat rack along with his.

"You got anything to drink? Looks like I'm giving your couch another try."

"Everyone at The Views got a bottle of champagne," I answer.

"That'll do; where's it at?"

"The fridge and glasses are on the bar."

"Would you like one?"

"Sure."

He places a champagne flute in front of where I sit on the couch to unbuckle my shoes, and I massage my feet against the rug's coarse fibers. "Hell of a view," he says. I grab my glass and join him by the expansive window, where the soft flakes of snow create a mesmerizing scene. As we stand there, it's as if we are enclosed in a magical snow globe. "Isn't it?" I cherish admiringly.

He turns and holds his glass, and I clink mine against it. "You know our best friends are getting married this year?"

"It feels like they always have been, but now I have to wear a suit for it."

I laugh. "It just feels like we're all hitting that next chapter, you know?"

He nods at the falling snow and changes the subject, "You got those blankets? I'm gonna see what I can do on your floor here and watch the snow fall," he snickers. "Gotta be better than that couch."

"The couch is not that bad!" I nudge him playfully and wince. "Actually, can you grab the blankets and stuff? My arm is pretty sore." He nods, and I lead him to my bedroom with an almost equal-sized window capturing the falling snow.

"Damn!" Chase exclaims, "It gets better?!"

"Perks of the job."

I point to the place in my closet where I sloppily threw all the blankets from his last stay, and he gathers them all in one arm, heading to the couch. I try to bend my arm for my zipper. The pain is intense, causing me to wince as I make another attempt to hold it using my less injured arm. No luck: I try to twist my dress. No luck: I try to pull it up higher, yeah right, down, not a chance over my wonder bra inflated boobs. I exasperate and make my way to the living room, where Chase has precariously placed pillows and cushions on the floor before my window.

"Chase, I have one more rescue mission."

He turns. "Zipper?"

I give him a self-conscious grin and spin around, so my back faces him. He unzips me with an effort that makes all my prior efforts seem absurd, and I turn to thank him again for coming to my aid. He nods a polite "you're welcome" and returns to his assembly. I shimmy myself free from the dress and remove my patterned nylon stockings, noticing a giant tear that reveals a remarkably red raspberry from my knee to the middle of my thigh.

With no additional thought, I scramble to the living room and find Chase now seated on my couch. Throwing my bare leg over him, I say incredulously, "Can you believe this?" He steadies my calf and places a hand on my other leg as I wobble in my odd flamingo stance. "Damn!" he concurs. "You really did it." He sweeps his rough hand up my leg, careful not to cross the rash, and then we both realize that his other hand has found itself cupping my bare ass.

My heart thumps and either excitement or alcohol forces me to lower onto his lap, giving a full face of my breasts spilling out of the push-up bra I chose for tonight's cocktail dress. Now holding both my legs, one more gently over the tender open skin, Chase stills beneath me, his chest rising and falling. Staring at each other, I clasp my hands around his neck and lean into his ear. "Carry me to my room?" Without an answer, I feel him grasp the bottom of my ass with his two calloused hands, and he carries me, with zero effort, to my bedroom; the bottom of my thighs skim the tops of his unbuttoned pants. My chest grazes against his scarcely haired, bare chest through his unbuttoned shirt. The gentleness in which I feel him encourages my skin's response to prickle. He tries to place me on my bed, but my hands remain clasped, so he has to lift me higher and descend with me, performing the motion slowly and in control, showcasing his ranch strength.

Once he's over me, I grab underneath the collar of his button-down shirt and open it further to peel it away from his chest. He lifts one arm at a time so I can pull it off of him before finally tossing it to the ground. Seemingly okay with the proposition, he kisses me on the neck. I exhale as my body tenses at the thrill of it. He moves to my lips and fumbles with his pants, shoving them off with his socks. His feet are dangling off the bed, so he scoops underneath me and moves me higher again so that my head can rest on a pillow. He passionately returns to kiss my lips, savoring every moment and taking his time to draw the fingers of his free hand up and down my skin, attentive to the areas that respond in goosebumps and shivers. Finally, he reaches behind me and unclasps my bra, pulling it easily away from my chest and discarding it to the side. He takes my full breast in his rough hand, removing his mouth from mine, then dips his head to my nipple, licking small circles at first before ending with a small nip that sends a sting directly to my center. I feel myself moistened with desire; I roll my hips upward and press into him, permitting me to feel his stiff arousal. He answers by grinding back into me, pressing himself directly between my slit, and I release a pleading moan as he continues to suck and flick at my other nipple; all his movements are cursory and intentional, causing indescribable sparks and sensations through my body.

Finally, I hear the tear of a condom wrapper, I assume, and feel his shuffle with his boxers before painstakingly removing my thong one hip at a time. Placing his lips over mine, he uses his free hand to gently insert himself inside me, and the motion stops as he fills me completely. I moan and angle up, urging him to move, and when he does, he slowly backs out before slowly entering again. I am all anticipation and impatience as he thrusts more deeply, not fast but methodically; he thrusts all the way in and then retreats all the way out. "Chase" I say impatiently, and he just takes my nipple in his mouth, teasing and nipping as I continue to beg for more of him. On another slow entrance, he grips underneath me and spins us, effectively replacing me on top of him; his hands are now guiding my hips back and forth as he sits up to kiss and bite my breasts, my collarbone, and the lower parts of my neck. His guidance is hasty now, and I throw my head back, arching into him. I hear him moaning and breathing heavily as his grip tightens around my waist. He begins to add pressure upward as I continue to grind against him. I place my hands on his chest, feeling the sensation of each fingertip increasing the pressure on his skin. My orgasm continues for minutes as he continues to guide my hips on top of him.

At last, Chase lets out a guttural moan before burying his face into my chest. He throbs inside me, and we stay close, breathing heavily, skin slick with sweat, my body responding to all his touches as if its sensitivity is tuned to be acutely aware of nothing else but Chase. He slides his hands carefully to avoid my gigantic scrape and lifts me from his lap. I head to my bathroom to clean myself up. As I return to my bed, he passes me toward the bathroom, delicately skimming his hands across my stomach, waist, and hip; again, my body responds with prickled skin. I slide my rumpled covers over my body, and Chase joins me on the other side; we don't say anything, but he draws small circles on my shoulder as I face him, the snow falling in large flakes behind him. The only light seeping in comes from one soft yellow lamp in the living room, which only highlights the square jaw and rough features. Cowboy, I think again and close my eyes.

Chapter 37: Snowed In

The sound of curtains being closed wakes me up, and the room grows noticeably darker. I open my eyes into tiny slits and briefly make out Chase's naked body, hauling the curtains all the way until they are closed. "Nope," he says, "absolutely not, too early for all that bright white and sun." He scoots back into the bed, pulls the cover high over his face, and I stifle a laugh. I am, however, grateful for the darkness and descend back into sleep before the dull pulsing in my head becomes a full-fledged hangover.

We wake together a few hours later, and I'm undeniably hung over. Mentally, I calculate that a coffee the size of a soup bowl, four large cups of water, and two Tylenol may back it off to a low rumble. Chase must be feeling similar because he has immediately started rubbing his temples. "I'll make the coffee," I say and receive a thumbs up. I slide out of bed, grab my robe off the closet door, and throw it over me. The white from the snow and the sun is an agonizing combination that forces me to make a detour and close the second curtain option available, which is a soft cream-colored sheer curtain to dull the incoming light and keep it light enough that I don't have to turn on any artificial light. I start the coffee, drink one full glass of water with two Tylenol, and bring Chase the same remedy; he downs it all and sits to look at me, only one eye open. From this angle, he looks boyish and adorable instead of rugged, further exacerbated when he tilts his head.

"So, we did that, huh? It wasn't a spicy dream?"

"No," I reply, meeting his head tilt with my own. Instinctively, I squeeze my legs together to ward off the tingle that has arisen and take a step back away from him. He bicycles, then swings his legs to touch the floor, steading his throbbing head again. I reach for his boxers from the bottom of the bed and hand them to him. He pulls them on and stands. "Coffee done?" he asks, still cradling his head. "Should be," I say, and Mouse strolls in, meowing insistently for his morning wet food, a chore I do every day despite the full dish of his dry food. I turn, walking out to feed Mouse, and Chase follows, pulling the blanket still strewn across the couch. Twisting it around him; while he sits at the breakfast bar, I turn the fireplace on. I decide to turn on my Christmas tree and see the snowflakes make tiny shadows on the curtain as they fall.

"How do you take your coffee?" I ask, while gathering a large cup from the cupboard.

"Black," he responds evenly, and I turn to face him, appalled. "Ew, really?"

"Yes, less work for everyone," he says, making a grabby hand in my direction.

I pour his cup and set it in his hand, then turn to make my own, which I then hold steadily, head to my couch, retrieve another blanket, and toss it over my legs; he takes a seat next to me and sidles up next to me like a child preparing to ask for ice cream for breakfast. I give a side glance as he rubs his shoulder against mine.

"Thanks for giving me a proper place to sleep this time," he jokes.

"Chase!" I say, laughing. "The couch is not that bad!"

He pokes me in my side, and I slap his hand away. "Don't you dare try to tickle me while I have coffee in my hand," I warn.

He settles next to me, taking a long sip of his gross coffee. "Thanks for not making it weird," he says more seriously, looking ahead at the fireplace.

"We're both adults," I say, and anytime I say that phrase, I immediately feel like a child. I shift uncomfortably, then say, "We don't have to be weird about it."

He gently taps my coffee cup with his own, declaring, "It was pretty fucking good, too."

I blush and feel the heat generate like little sparks across my face and in between my legs. "Uh-huh." I manage, and he leans forward to see my face.

"Sarah Gillespie, are you blushing?" He razzes me, attempting more jabs at my side.

"Chase!" I screech, placing my coffee cup down before it is involuntarily tossed from my hand. "Sarah!" he mimics, and I am flailing while trying to fend off the swarm of fingers attacking my sides. In an attempt to free myself, I lie backward and try to scoot myself away but am jerking more than escaping. Breathless with laughter I beg him to stop. Finally, he relents, cackling with pleasure; when I turn to scoop my coffee, he meets my face, and his eyes search mine.

"What?" I say, still catching my breath.

"Just checking to see if you're still blushing, but now you just look like you ran a long time." Seemingly satisfied, he nods and returns to his cup. We drink the rest of our coffee, watching The Food Network, and Chase peeks through the window.

"Man," he announces, "It's really coming down out there." He checks his phone, and the road to the ranch is closed until it can be plowed and crossed safely. "I'll call Brian and see where they're at," he says.

"Chase," I say, "roads closed, it's snowing like crazy. You can stay here, unless I'm terrible company."

"You're not," he blurts.

"Then stay," I say, patting the couch. "We have plenty of food. I can probably order up from the cafe and just be lazy, hungover people like everyone else on the first day of the new year."

He sits back on the couch and nods. "Okay, I will."

I order from the cafe because we both decided hungover people on the first day of the new year should not oversee cooking their own meals. We ate and chatted, and I made Chase swear on a bagel not to tickle me anymore. We laugh so much throughout our conversation that I virtually forget that we've never spent time together, just the two of us. He's so funny and laughs at the quips I toss, which makes me appreciate we are becoming acquainted as Heidi and Brian's corresponding best friends. He has his own theories on why Brian has always been the quiet, "boring" type, and I tell him how I've started to appreciate him more as we all grow up. Then, he effectively dampens the mood by casually asking, "What was the deal anyway, with the broody bad guy?" as a wave of uneasiness settles in.

I delicately shake my head. "Do you really want to talk about that?"

"Why not?" he shrugs. "We're here a while."

I start with the basics, and when I mention our connection, I glance at him with a hint of embarrassment, anticipating a typical response like "girls and their sparks," but he remains silent. He just keeps nodding and making eye contact, popping in to ask clarifying questions or say things like "Yeah, I can see that."

"Anyway," I conclude, "Love burning that hot has no choice but to fizzle out, eventually. It's like we were flames, consuming all the fuel until there was nothing left to burn. Everything was so intense and passionate, especially at first, but in the long run, it wasn't sustainable."

I look at him for a long beat, waiting for him to burst out laughing, call me crazy, or worse, tell me that I am a horrible bitch for doing what I did, but he doesn't. Instead he blows out a long burst of air.

"Shit," he says, looking in front of him bewildered. "You think you'll ever get back together?"

"No," I answer with certainty, "he's with someone else, and she seems amazing. It's safe to say we've fizzled out. What about you?" I ask, bumping his elbow with mine, quickly remembering my tumble form the night before. "Any love stories?"

"Nah," he says, "I don't get that far in, you know? I think there are girls who wanted to, but since I've never spent the time properly getting to know anyone for longer than a night or two. We fizzle out much faster," he winks, and I push him playfully.

"Why not?" I ask, "Why not get to know anyone properly?"

"Dunno, really," he says with a shrug. "What do I really have to offer? I live at home, work on the ranch, and that's it; I'm not going anywhere cool, don't have big dreams, and I'm fine with it."

I look at him, searching for the gotcha that never comes. He's being genuine about his reluctance to get into a relationship, and something inside me warms to him. "At least you know where you're headed," I say after a beat. "I'm not unhappy, but I don't know if this is what I want forever, you know? Like, here in the city, doing this job forever? That seems absurd."

"Why?" he asks with curiosity.

"I honestly don't know; it just doesn't feel final." He nods in understanding, then looks at his phone, "All right," he slaps his knees, "we've wasted a few hours on that, and I'm here for a while; what else ya got?"

I tap my pointer finger to my chin as if contemplating deeply, "Oh my gosh!" I shriek, and Chase winces like I'm going to slap him. "I have a Nintendo 64. My parents just sent it back to me, and I had no idea how to hook it up."

"Sarah," he says, looking at me with a sudden seriousness, "You've been hiding an N64 this whole time!? What games?"

"A bunch, actually," I say excitedly.

"Well, go get it; hopefully, you have everything to hook it up."

"Oh, it's all there," I say, "knowing my dad, he threw in extra cords so I could start my own random cord box."

I take his arm, lead him to the closet, and point to the tall shelf the box is sitting on. "How did it get there?" he asks. "I asked one of the maintenance guys to throw it up there for me." He looks me up and down before reaching for the box, and I tighten my robe; suddenly feeling self-conscious. He pulls it down carefully, balancing it on his fingertips and then his full palm before he's able to let it rest on his forearms. He brings it to my living room, emptying its contents and plugging wires in various locations. After a few hushed curses, the TV comes to life with the gaming system. He picks Mario Kart and chooses Mushroom as driver one, and then, before handing me the remote, chooses Princess Peach as player two, "Alright princess, let's see whatcha got."

The day darkens into the evening, and we break to watch the sunset behind the snowfall. Briefly, I am back in that parking garage listening to music with Parker holding and drawing into my hand. Chase, who's still using a blanket as clothing over his boxers, cuts into the memory. "You mind if I shower?" I shake my head, no, so he turns toward my bathroom. I wonder what he's planning on putting on after; unlike me, who lives here, his choices are a nice set of trousers, a button-up shirt, or my blankets. I snap my fingers, bring myself to attention, and throw sweatpants under my robe, making my way to Gabriel's. I tap on the door, and Gabriel answers, glancing over me with horror. "I cannot fix this," and his Hispanic accent only extenuates that he thinks I look like a bridge troll; he continues to point a finger up and down me while I say, "no, jerk, do you have some, like, sweatpants I could steal from you for my house guest? He's stuck until the roads open," "Hmmm," he says suddenly, looking mischievous, "what is he like?"

"What do you mean?"

"Is he a big man or a small man?" He's raising his eyebrows suggestively, and I respond, "he's like 5'10ish, I think." Gabriel looks at me completely unimpressed, leaving me in his doorway; he returns with some black sweatpants and a white v-neck t-shirt. "Why are we dressing this man in your apartment?"

"We're just—it's not like that," I say hurriedly and thank him while rushing back down the hallway.

Upon closing my door, I was surprised to see Chase standing naked in the bathroom, with the door open and drying off. He turns and makes eye contact with my mouth, which has settled wide open; gaping at him. I hurl the clothes in his direction, spinning around so that I can't see him.

"These are from my gay neighbor," I shout. "So, you don't have to wear boxers the rest of the night."

I hear him chuckling before he says, "Sarah, we had sex; you've seen me naked."

"No, I haven't," I say defensively. "It was dark, and there was lots of champagne involved; that is completely different,"

"Well, you might as well get a look at it now; come on, get it over with so you can stop acting so damn shy."

"Oh, my gawwwd, Chase!" I say, flustered, "stop, you're being ridiculous," still standing with my back towards him.

He responds composedly. "Okay, Sarah, I'll make you a deal," and I can hear the playfulness in his tone. "You look, or I'm not putting those clothes on, or any clothes for the rest of my time here."

"Chase!" I insist, my chest tightening as the trapped butterflies bounce around in my stomach. I begin to turn slowly, one hand covering my face. "Penalty!" he makes a sound like a buzzer. "Remove the hand!" I groan and open my eyes to find him dressed in borrowed clothes that fit him remarkably well. As if to test my will, they also reveal the outline of his penis. Where my eyes promptly affix themselves before I snap them shut and shake my head.

"I can't believe you were going to look!" He chuckles.

"Chase, I'm going to murder you!" I say with an uneasiness that I'm praying is not presenting itself on my face. He laughs and replaces himself on my couch, patting the spot next to him and winking. I approach him and position myself next to him, creating enough space to conceal the pounding of my heart.

"Why do I make you so nervous?" He asks curiously. "I don't bite, unless you ask." He winks. My memory flashes to him nipping the sensitive skin of my breasts. My nipples pinch instantly under my shirt, which draws Chase's eyes directly to them. Instinctively, I cover my chest, causing him to tilt his head with a grin. "Don't," I say with a warning. "What?" He says innocently, leaning back and clasping his hands behind his head, a cheesy smile plastered ear to ear. I'm saved from myself when a knock sounds at my door, causing Chase to jump to attention as I move to open it.

"Heyyyyy girl," says Felix, peeking around me, "Thomas and I decided to walk over because we knew you would probably be eating some sad microwavable food and thought we'd bring you pesto pasta from Franks for—Oh!" He stops short, and Thomas barrels in with the bag of food. "I've gotta sit down; I'm not built for trudging through snow." He dumps the bag with a loud thump onto my countertop, then, noticing the obvious quiet, looks in the direction of Chase. "Oh shit!" He exclaims at an octave too high before attempting to recover. "I'm sure there's enough for four."

Felix hasn't even tried to recover and hands me a bottle of wine without taking his eyes off Chase. He pans back to me, then back to Chase. "My two favorite gays!" Chimes in Chase, seemingly unbothered by their entrance into our sleepover, going for handshakes that further set the awkward stage for my best friend and his noncommittal boyfriend. Thomas shoots me a glance that conveys I have some explaining to do before settling on the couch, "Ooh, Mario Kart!" He says, already distracted. Chase returns to the couch, handing him my controller. Felix busies himself in my kitchen, and I come over to help him unpack the steaming hot, mouthwatering bag of food. "Ahh," I inhale as I empty its contents comprising pasta, salad, bread, and dessert, "Aldina is still the best around," I say. He leans over to me and whispers, "What's this?" Tossing a nonchalant glance toward my couch, I whisper back, "I fell last night in the snow, like really bad, so he helped me home, then he found out the road to the ranch is closed due to, you know, the weather, so he stayed." Felix gives me a sharp look. "That's it?" "That's it," I lie. "Check out my beat-up leg," and I pull my sweats away from my hip far enough so he can see the rash and bruise. Raising an eyebrow, he doesn't press further and resumes pulling plates down from my cabinets, sets my oven to heat the pasta, and pours us both a glass of wine.

In time, we all gather at my small table to eat and drink wine. My small place fills with laughter as they recount their harrowing adventure to my apartment from the one Thomas and I used to share.

"It was cruel and unusual punishment, and I should've let him schlepp over here all alone, quite frankly." Chides Thomas as Felix gives him a side-eye.

"He was down to watching horror movies set in winter with subtitles. I couldn't take it anymore and needed to socialize." Felix says, pantomiming how bored he was.

"Should we have called Heidi and Brian?" I ask.

"I did," says Thomas, "But Heidi said they were already soaking in the in-room hot tub." Probably for the best, I think. Then, wistfully say, "Some girls have all the luck."

Chase glances up from his place a small grin curls his lips at me with an unreadable face, I raise an eyebrow back, and he returns to looking at his plate. Thomas and I move together to clear all the plates while Felix and Chase are in a deep conversation about sustainable farming; once in the kitchen, we clean up, side by side, just as we used to.

"Tell. Me. Everything." Thomas says out of the side of his mouth.

"There's nothing to tell," I lie again. "He walked me home because I fell," volunteering the large raspberry on my outer thigh, "and then couldn't get home because of the weather, so he stayed."

"Sarah," Thomas whispers. "I lived across the hall from you for enough years to know sex happened." I immediately blush, which betrays any lie I try to preserve.

"Holy shit, you did," he says, surprised.

"I thought you could tell!" I hiss.

"I was just trying to bully you into telling me, but you really did, didn't you?"

"Yes," I say softly, "but it's nothing, it's not anything."

"So how was the farmer in no clothes?" He probes with curiosity, now rinsing the dishes and placing them in my dishwasher.

"Thomas!"

"What!?" He says innocently. "I've always been curious, all that rugged manliness paired with how he fills out those jeans, and he probably does a lot with his hands, mmm."

My face falls, and I am staring at my best friend like he's become inhabited by a stranger, a still gay stranger who's obviously fantasized about Chase. "What?" he says again, "Chase is criminally handsome, and you know he's handy, and when he comes in at night after working long on the farm, I bet his tan skin glistens like in those country music videos." Now I know an alien has replaced him; someone stole his skin and is wearing it around. I wonder if Felix knows his noncommittal boyfriend is a skin walker. He's gazing at me with anticipation when I sigh. "It was good, I guess; I don't know, there was a lot of champagne involved." It was better than Frank's pesto pasta, my favorite wine, driving through a winding autumn leaved street, windows down, crisp air blowing through my outstretched fingers all my favorite songs playing on the radio I think to myself, as blurred images play out in my mind. "Nothing has happened since; it was a onetime whatever," I say, flailing my hands wildly.

"Too bad," says Thomas suspiciously before joining Chase and Felix back at the table with a deck of cards.

After we played a few rounds and finished the wine, Thomas and Felix exited my place and headed for their walk home. Felix gave me a knowing wink, and I shut the door on him with a glare.

"Well, that was fun," says Chase from behind me. "Shall we?"

I turn to face him, "Shall we?" I prompt, willing him to finish.

"Go to sleep, Sarah," he says matter of fact as if I am implying something.

"Yeah, okay," I say, "Yeah, we should."

Chapter 38: The 100 Acre Ranch

The next morning we briefly argue about me driving him home, some part of his polite gentleman personality threatened by my reasonable and also polite offer. Once he finally agrees, he changes back into his New Year's dress clothes and leaves the borrowed clothes in a pile next to my laundry basket.

"I didn't know what to do with those," he explains.

"I'll deal with them later," I respond and fold them carelessly.

On the 45-minute drive to Chase's ranch, it springs to mind that I'd never been to a ranch or Chase's house and would be doing both today. The ride is predominantly silent, punctuated by conversation reserved for strangers on a subway. He explains as we pull in that, over the years, they've sold some of their acreage but still have close to 100 acres, which stretches back and up some of the surrounding mountains. I turn down the drive he points to, and he starts to name all the beautiful homes I see; that's my parents' house; that's Grams and Gramps, which is the original, and then that way back there is me, so you'd have to follow this dirt for a bit. "I guess it's a good thing I brought the big boy truck!" I say and start heading down the road in awe of the surroundings. We reach his house, which is a two-story cabin-inspired home with a small porch in the front. I put the truck in park, and he regards me with a puzzled expression.

"What?" I ask.

"Are you staying?" he asks slowly, and there's a twinge of anxiety in the question.

I decide to level with him. "Chase," I begin seriously, "I've never been on a ranch or near this much open space unless you count when I was driving to Washington; you spent two nights in my apartment; I am seeing this cabin."

I see a grin curl the corners of his lips, and he nods. "Alright then, come on out."

Despite my assumption that farm animals would be noisy, the surroundings are peacefully silent. We walk up to his door, and as he places his key in the lock, I hear something with a motor pulling up, causing Chase to pivot; a man and lady approach on an ATV, and I recognize Chase in their features immediately, especially the man.

"Your parents?" I ask, and he nods. As they step out, I greet them part of the way, "Hi, I'm Sarah," and hold out my hand; they each take it.

"Trisha," says his mom, "Cliff," says his dad, "we were wondering who was coming up the drive, didn't recognize the old truck," Cliff says nodding at my Toyota.

"Well, Chase was marooned at my place until the snow let up, so I offered to bring him home. This place is incredible," I say, looking around again.

"Hey Mom, hey Pop," he says and greets them both with a hug, landing a kiss on his Mom's cheek "Sarah just wanted to see the cabin."

"And maybe stay forever," I say joking. Chase looks like he may faint so I continue, "kidding, of course, this is just my first time on a ranch and I—"

"Well then you'll have to show her around Chase," says Trisha. "Come by the house for some lunch and then Chase can take you on a proper tour."

I see Chase half agree and I think ah, my turn to make you nervous. "Sounds lovely," I say, giving him no out, and they take their leave.

Chase guides me indoors, and to my surprise, it's a modern space featuring white kitchen cabinets, a stunning marble breakfast bar with matching countertops, warm-toned wooden floors, dark beams, and large windows that create a charming and bright ambiance. Positioned by a real wood-burning stove, there's a three-seat couch and a recliner set adjacent to each other. He directs me to take a seat anywhere in the living room while he goes to shower and change.

"I don't get to see your room?" I joke, and he turns, and his face shows hints of red.

"How about I get to at least look at it first, and then you can come see it? I doubt I'm as clean as you."

"Fair enough," I say, and sit on his couch, which is wildly more comfortable than mine. I shuck off my boots and curl my legs underneath me, looking out the large windows to the mountains. The shower initiates and I surreptitiously reflect on what he looks like underneath the falling water.

A few minutes after I hear the water turn off, my invitation to come upstairs is hollered down at me. I take the stairs, which curve subtly to a mostly open loft on the back side of the cabin. To my surprise, even more windows are looking toward the back of the property. There's a skylight above the bed and I wonder how many girls have looked up at the sky with him in his immaculately made bed. The fragrances of rain, cut grass, and something smoky that reminds me of a campfire fill the room. There's a large closet and bathroom that is all white tile with accents of a tile that almost looks like blue geodes; I gasp when I see the big clawfoot tub underneath another skylight. "Lucky" I tease. Then come back near his bed where the stairs lead back down. I see something pointed out the window. "Chase!" I squeal with delight. "You have a telescope!?" He meets me next to it. "You can see practically everything out here; would be silly not to." I look up at him beguiled, his shaggy hair still wet, the ends curling as it dries, his hazel eyes taking on the same colors as landscape out his window, golden browns and shades of green. His beard was longer, more frayed than Parker kept his but the brush of it against my cheeks two nights before made it my favorite texture. Abruptly snapping myself out of staring at him, I run my fingers over the telescope.

"Maybe one day I'll get snowed in out here, and you can show me." He doesn't respond, making me feel silly for hoping. He effortlessly pulls on his boots, skillfully lacing them. "Ready? I've gotta show you around now, or my mom will whip me." A snort laugh rockets out of me and Chase tilts his head in that boyish way before we head back out to the drive. I start to open my truck door when Chase clears his throat and points to another ATV next to his place parked under a carport along with a big four-door truck that has two back tires. "That why you don't drive much?" I ask, hooking a thumb at the big truck. "Definitely," he says, and we hop in the ATV, making the trek back up the road to his mom's. We savored her expertly crafted lunch, and I silently noted the profound stillness in this location. Usually, I'm at Thomas' deafening house, so this is much different. She hands us a basket to pack, holding some cookies and snacks. I wonder how long my tour will be precisely because of the weight of the monstrous basket. Does it require rations that weigh as much as a small toddler?

Chase knowingly takes the basket; obviously aware it is over-packed and heavy. "I think she's just excited," he remarks.

"About?" I ask.

"You're the only girl I've brought here in, like a decade. My older brother is married and gave her two grand babies, but that is not enough, and then Jenny was late, so she's still in high school; I'm her only hope."

"Ahhh," I say, "so she thinks I'm going to be her grandbaby maker."

He laughs hard and loud, and it makes me laugh, too. "You don't have to take me on some grand tour, Chase. This is just an amazing place, and I can't believe you get to live here."

"Honestly, it's the least I can do."

We pass his cabin and venture out into the vast meadows that stretch across the rest of their property, the ATV kicking up dust behind us. Scattered throughout are groups of large Oak trees, and he points out a small creek that widens into a swimmable area toward the mountains. He shows me their horses, cows, pigs, chickens, and ducks. They have a Llama and an Alpaca, but according to Chase, they're both pretty mean so we don't say hi. We pass by some goats, and then finally, the majority of the land is occupied by Bison, which they raise and nurture until they are sold for food. This sight evokes a feeling of sadness, and Chase notices the long face I have. He then proceeds to explain how their ranch follows ethical practices, which sets them apart from many others.

We head back to his place, and once parked, I check my watch. "I should probably get out of here before I'm driving in the midnight lighting of 5 o'clock."

"I'll walk you," he says, leading me, his hand resting softly on my lower back. He opens my truck door, places a hand on my elbow, helps me shut my door, and gives me a wave before I start the engine and head back. I click on the power of my radio, chuckling at the song that plays through the speakers.

"You sit there in your heartache
Waiting on some beautiful boy to
To save you from your old ways
You play forgiveness
Watch it now, here he comes"

Back in my post snowed-in, post coital, wrinkle in normal life apartment, I click the twinkling lights of my tree back on. Watching them dance across my walls, mesmerizing Mouse, I wonder what this feeling is.

Chapter 39: An Embarrassment of Flowers

The first couple of weeks after the holidays are always clumsy; everyone is decompressing from family time, trying to remember how to work efficiently, and generally slower than usual. Exhausted from the effort of trying to organize some kind of resident engagement day in February that will have a Valentine's Day theme. I promptly dismiss thoughts of bake sales and Sadie Hawkins dances as elementary, as I will my brain to think more creatively. Groaning audibly, I put my forehead to my palms and then lowered my head all the way down to my desk onto my crossed arms. I breathed in and out deeply as a subtle knock came before Cora's small voice emerged. This contrast to her tough exterior and no-bull attitude always catches me a little off guard. Lifting my head sluggishly and take in the embarrassing display of varying white-colored flowers she struggles to hold in the vase. I stand and help her place them on a small table in my office.

"Wow," I say teasingly, "what did you do right? Or—" I pause, "what did he do wrong?"

She steadies me with an expression of confusion, tilting her head around the gigantic bouquet, "They're for you."

"Me!? Who's getting me flowers!?"

Cora again looks at me with confusion and a minor annoyance, like, how the hell would I know? My hands are delicately probing through the pedals, searching for a card. Cora clears her throat, and I glance at her hands still inside the bouquet. "Can I go? I have a meeting."

"Oh, sure," I say, forgetting she was there, "sorry, I'll see you at the 3?" She nods and takes her leave.

Finally, I pluck the small square from its trident-shaped holder and find it blank on one side. Carefully flipping it over, I could feel the blood buzzing through my veins as I eagerly anticipated the sender. My excitement grew as I read the typed letters.

Meteor shower this weekend. Since you've never seen one through a telescope, and my couch is the definition of comfort, I expect to see you before dark. PS I hope the flowers make everyone spread rumors about you. -Chase

I sink back further into my chair and smile adoringly at the little card before picking up my phone, realizing I don't actually have his number. Do I just show up before dark like the card says? Do I ask Brian and Heidi for his number, and what would I tell them? *Hey, uh, Chase and I slept together and may do it again, but I'm not sure how to reach him?* My phone rings, and my whole body reacts as if a ghost has just manifested in the room and yelled, "Boo!" I look at my phone and see it's Heidi calling, so I take a moment to refocus and answer, "Hey."

"Hey," she says quickly "You know how Brian was supposed to come by today and look at the truck?"

"Yeah," I say, realizing I forgot about that weird sound my truck was making.

"So I made our dinner plans completely forgetting, but I didn't want you to be left hanging, so Chase is going to come by and look at it, or at least he will be once I call him. Is that okay?"

"Chase?" I say like I've never heard of him.

"Yeah, Chase," she says, laughing. "You know, blonde messy hair, Brian's best friend? That Chase." I nod, but she can't see me, so she follows up with, "Are you there?"

"Ye—Yeah, sorry, I just."

"You're busy, I know; I'll let you get back to it. I just wanted to make sure you knew Chase would be swinging by. Less than three you!"

The call ended, leaving me feeling like a tornado had just picked me up, spun me in circles, and placed me in another universe. My computer pings that I have an upcoming meeting. I groan in frustration when I see it's with David Spoons from Maven Advertising. "Gee, thanks," I curse the ceiling and get up, hauling my laptop under one arm.

The meeting turned out to be surprisingly productive instead of annoying, as we now have a wine-tasting and expert pairing demonstration scheduled for our Valentine's-themed resident event, courtesy of Maven Advertising. The best part is they love us so much they have offered to manage the whole thing; all I have to do is say yay or nay. Mark Miller, my boss, has also been so impressed by the relationship with the advertising company that he now uses them for several of his properties. He's sure to give me kudos each time they do great work since I was responsible for making the connection. I also suspect some of my recent pay increases are due to how happy he is with them, if only he knew how much that relationship cost me. Parker has faithfully kept his word, and I work solely with Spoons, while Mark tends to work more closely with Parker, keeping them both away from The Views. Spoons has persistently pursued his quest to take me on a date, but thankfully, my pitch of not mixing work with pleasure keeps him at bay, for the most part.

I peek at the embarrassing display of flowers once more before flicking out my light and am thankful that the day turned into a win overall. Once back inside my apartment, I throw all my work clothes into the hamper, exchanging them for the cozy matching pajama set my mom sent me for Christmas. Imagine if your grandma's couch went on an adventurous rendezvous with a lumberjack - that's what these pajamas are like. Thus, creating the soft monstrosity of fabric now hanging unflatteringly over my body in the worst fashion statement. Still, they are so delightfully cozy I can't be bothered to care how unattractive they make me look until—the knock comes. "Fuuuuuck," I hiss to no one in particular; Mouse barely picks his head up before settling back into a more impossible position on the couch. Opening the door, Chase's hazel eyes scan me from head to toe, taking in every detail before a warm smile spreads across his face, transforming his typically rugged appearance.

"Now those are sexy pajamas," he steps in around me, walking over to scratch the top of Mouse's head, "get my flowers?"

"I did," I say, folding my arms over the pajamas in a futile attempt to cover the flannel flower pattern that covers every inch of them.

"I asked for the most over-the-top display of all-white flowers they could make," he says proudly.

Despite my embarrassment, I laugh, "They delivered, so you got your money's worth, in my opinion."

He smiles again; a zing travels my spine. "Where's your keys?" He says in a more serious tone.

"Oh, they're hanging over here," I say, walking toward my kitchen counter that has three small hooks for my keys underneath a cabinet: plucking the correct set from the hook. I hand them over and then open my freezer to dig out ice from the container inside, adding it to my glass. I close the freezer, get water from the door, and find Chase staring at me, stupefied, "Uhm, what was that?"

"Oh, my ice maker doesn't drop the ice from the door for some reason, so I just get it from the top."

He raises an eyebrow. "Don't you have maintenance?"

"I do, but I don't bug them unless I really have to."

"How long has it been like that?" He quips.

"Umm, like a year or so?" I say with a shrug, and Chase blinks at me rapidly as if retrieving my ice this way for a year, or so, is possibly the most ludicrous thing he's ever heard, therefore needing more time to process. "I'm going to drive your truck around, and then I'll take a look at that." Chase spins on his heels and is out the door.

Returning in just under an hour, Chase tells me he thinks he knows what's wrong, but he'll need some tools to be sure, tools he has at his house, which then makes him say, "So about my invite, you interested?" I don't immediately respond to stop myself from shouting YES! In the overexcited way my body seems to want me to react, and he continues, "Look, no pressure, I just thought maybe you'd like to look through the telescope, and you would be doing me a favor, testing the sleep-ability of my couch, which would hopefully inspire you to get a new one."

I smirk at the comment, "All right, but only if you have something good to drink."

"I've only got cognac, I think, but I'm sure my mom's got something you'd like; I'll swing by on my way back and have it ready, so Friday then? Bring the truck!" I nod my agreement, and he hangs my keys back on the hook, winding back around to scratch Mouse again, who stretches at the contact and yawns. "Bring those pajamas," he says with a wink. Then Chase is out the door again, leaving me reeling somehow from the interaction.

Chapter 40: Connections and Constellations

Thankfully, or perhaps unfortunately, I have absolutely no plans to dodge, allowing me the complete freedom to spend a night at Chase's. Which has left me presently stalling in my bedroom while I remove and replace every item I am packing into the black and pink weekend bag, the bag I got for free because I overspent at Victoria Secret which only earned me 1% cash back on the credit card I used to cover it and this bag. "It's our exclusive weekender bag," said the overly buoyant woman at the cash register. Leaving me to smile stupidly, as if to convey that earning this bag gave me an exorbitant amount of pleasure. Now the unremarkable bag sits open, its contents: a toothbrush, toothpaste, hairbrush, and the embarrassing pajamas my mother bought me. Finally, I decide on some jeans, a tank top, a baggy shirt, a sweater, and standard pajamas, throwing them all into my bag carelessly before checking to make sure Mouse has enough food in his feeder. He does; he either has enough food for a month or none because that's how I choose to fill it.

I am parking in front of Chase's house before sunset. Trisha rolls past in the ATV, waving wildly at me; I wave back politely and grab my bag from the passenger seat before dropping out of my truck. Chase opens his front door, approaches, and takes my bag before I can protest, leaving me to make fidgeting gestures with my hands while following him into his house. He sets my bag near the couch and then points to the breakfast bar. "That's what my mom picked out; she brought a glass and warned me not to pour into any of mine." I laugh and see a bottle placed thoughtfully on ice next to a beautiful wine glass with a long delicate stem. The setup is so lovely that I don't even care what it is, I'm going drink the whole damn thing and be thankful for it. When Chase jokes about serving me Bison, I can't help but make pitiful whining sounds. He reassures me it's just a dish his mom prepared and tells me again how eager she is to see a girl in his house. He adds, "I break her heart every time I have to tell her we're just friends." I pantomime my heart breaking and pout as if I am just as hurt by the news. We are friends, right? Or at least becoming friends? His friendship is like the one I have with Thomas in our banter and the ease of being around each other, with one minor difference: the sex part. It's true; Thomas has undoubtedly seen me naked on MANY occasions, but we've never engaged in anything sexually. Chase and I, well, we undeniably did, and now I can't stop thinking about it, but nothing even remotely sexual has happened since.

His face reddens at my reaction, and he promptly changes subjects. "I've gotta get some wood in there before we freeze to death," he points to the wood-burning stove. "Once the sun goes down, the temperature drops like twenty degrees, and I don't think you're ready for something like that."

"Ahhh," I say, "but that's where you're mistaken. I brought my warmest jammies." Knowing the reference, Chase chuckles at the wood he's loading into the stove.

"I can't wait to see those again. Probably the best thing I've ever seen on a woman, truth be told," he says, dripping with sarcasm, "and I've seen a lot on and off of em," he finishes.

"Which reminds me," I say coolly, "Why don't you bring any women out here? It is enchanting and, dare I say, romantic? A real panty dropper, in my opinion." Chase looks directly at my lap before returning to my eyes, clearing his throat. I also look at my lap; yep, panties are secure; why would I even say that?

"Like I said before, I get in and out before anyone has time to get bored. I've got like five tricks, Sarah, and you've seen all of 'em."

I make a quizzical face. "All five?"

"Yep," he responds, popping the P sound.

"But since none of them include being here, obviously, there has to be more," I say genuinely. He looks at me for a long while, something like appreciation playing across the rough edges of his face, and then finally, "Fair."

We eat and chat; I remark that the wine his mother picked is delicious and pairs well with the meal, no coincidence. Then we're sitting on a small platform outside his loft room, which Chase reveals in the best view of the sunset on the entire property. I nudge him and accuse him of fabricating that fact because there are 100 acres. Surely this isn't the best. The sky transitions from soft blues and pinks to a vibrant display of deep reds, oranges, and purples, creating a breathtaking backdrop. As we watch, he leans back playfully, drawing me closer, while the gray clouds gradually fade into the darkening sky. He leaves to refill my glass and says we should wait another couple of hours before using the telescope; he says it's best when the sky is as dark as possible.

Back downstairs, he sits in the recliner. I sit on the couch where I pretend it's outrageously uncomfortable, and he doesn't pretend to believe me.

He goes upstairs, leaving me with something about living off the grid before returning in a matching flannel snowman set of pajamas. I'm so surprised I do a spit take, thankful that most of it ends back in the cup and am raucous with laughter. He waves his hands in a gesture that says let it out before explaining this is why he wanted me to bring mine over. "My mom got me these for Christmas; they're hideous but so damn soft," he explains, raking his hands up and down his torso revealing a small patch of hair above his waistline. I bound up to pull mine from the bag and use his loft to throw them on, modeling them as I return to the living room, sashaying theatrically while Chase doubles over with laughter. He enthusiastically pulls his phone from his pocket and stands next to me, a wide goofy grin on his face while he extends his arm to capture us both in the frame of his phone's camera. I stick my tongue out as he takes the photo, then he shows me before returning his phone to its place in his pajama pants.

"So, you ready for another refill and some stars?"

I respond, "Absolutely, been waiting my whole life, in fact."

It takes Chase thirty minutes of listening to me ooh and ahh before he realizes I am indeed fascinated with this experience.

"Do you want to look?" I say, stepping back.

He shakes his head no. "I get to do this all the time, and you seem to be enjoying it."

"Are you sure?" I confirm, and he gestures for me to keep looking, with my eye focused on passing meteors coming every few minutes. "Aren't you bored, just watching me? Seems like a fairly solo activity if you're not going to look."

"Nah, I'm actually entertained by your enjoyment."

A few more minutes pass and I'm tired of standing. My back aches from hunching over the telescope, so I take a seat cross-legged on the floor next to his bed and face him. "I think you should consider adding this to your list of tricks Chase."

With a sly smile, he traces his jawline with his thumb and pointer finger, stopping when they meet at his chin. "Alright, I have six tricks."

Without warning, he jolts upright and motions for me to join him on his bed. When I shoot him a confused glance, he responds with an exaggerated eye roll and instructs me to come closer. Obediently, I scoot next to him on the bed. Placing two pillows underneath it, he gestures towards the skylight. Lying side by side, we gaze up at the stars, mesmerized by the sporadic flashes darting across the night sky. "Seven," I say. He turns to look at me before using his thumb to trace my bottom lip. "I want to kiss you right now." "K," I breathe. He does, his soft lips contrasting against the rough callouses of his hand. His movements are deliberate and methodical, building up pressure until he suddenly stops and returns to the skylight. Keeping my gaze on him forgetting about the meteors slicing through the sky I think, eight.

Chase wakes up at an ungodly hour, leaving me lying on his bed in my uncomfortably warm pajamas, covered with a carefully draped blanket. By the time I make my way to the now cold pot of coffee he proudly announces that he's already fixed whatever sound my truck was making, made a loop around the animals with Cliff, and completed a million other tasks that needed tending because of a storm coming. Feeling moderately embarrassed by my complete lack of task completion compared to his, I reach for a coffee cup, and he announces everyone is waiting in the big house to see if I'll come for breakfast. "Sounds great," I say and head back up to pull my clothes on, brush my teeth, and do something with my hair. When I glimpse my watch and notice it's barely past 7:30 AM, I come to the realization that they must be completely out of their minds. On our quick ATV ride to his parents, Chase places his hand on my thigh gently, and I cover it with my own, not really holding it but an acknowledgment that it's there and I have no intention of moving it. From the outside, his parents' house looks worn down, with crumbling bricks that give the impression they may not withstand a strong wind. However, once inside, everything appears fresh and as if it were just built. In the open floor plan, the floors are uniform and complemented by dark exposed beams set against a light blue-gray painted wall. The contemporary black fixtures and recessed lighting create a stylish atmosphere. The aroma in the air is reminiscent of a bakery, with a sweet, buttery warmth enveloping everything in a perfectly baked embrace. Unlike Parker's house, the family breakfast is filled with quiet conversations, the soft murmur of voices floating across the small table. Jenny passes occasional looks between me and Chase, then grins tauntingly at Chase when she thinks I'm not looking.

Full and happy with blueberry pancakes, we're back on the ATV when Chase says, "so, would you consider this a date?" Caught off-guard by the sudden need to label our time together, I nervously make a popping sound with my mouth.

"I'm no expert but, if one needed to define this, then one hundred percent." I say, and in response, there's a profound silence, broken only by the tender gesture of Chase intertwining our hands.

Before leaving, we officially exchange phone numbers and linger outside my open truck door for a long while before he bends and kisses me gently. As he pulls back, I catch a fleeting glimpse of the golden flicker in his hazel eyes before he swiftly turns and guides me into the truck, his hands gently resting on my hips, and then closes the door. Driving away, I hear his deep, smokey voice repeating like echoes in my mind, "So, would you consider this a date?" The radio's song barely muffling it.

THE BOY IN THE BAND

"I said No one has to know what we do
His hands are in my hair, his clothes are in my room
And his voice is a familiar sound
Nothin' lasts forever
But this is gettin' good now"

Chapter 41: Does Wine Pair with Ex-Boyfriends or New Ones?

In appreciation for Trisha's contribution of wine to my sleepover with her son, I reached out to Chase and sent an invitation for both her and Cliff to attend a wine pairing and tasting mixer at The Views, hosted by Maven Advertising. Amidst our nonstop texting throughout the day, Chase informs me that Trisha is thrilled about the idea of a romantic evening with Cliff.

I think my parents like you more than even I do; it's going to be impossible for us to break up

Are we dating?

I don't know, haha, maybe?

Exploring other options?

Definitely not, although now that I have more tricks, maybe I should?

Definitely not!

=)

Maven Advertisement is truly showing off its marketing skills with this mixer, and I am both impressed and relieved that they did everything with very little involvement from me. They diligently reached out to every distributor and caterer, ensuring a seamless evening. The air was filled with the mesmerizing glow of sparkling lights, casting a magical ambiance. The tables were artfully adorned with tasteful decorations in shades of pink, red, and purple, creating an inviting and romantic atmosphere for an unforgettable Valentine's night out. On my first glass of wine, I shower praise to Cora and Spoons for collaborating on the magical evening. Chase walks in with Trisha and Cliff, who begin making their way around the little tables. Chase stands near a blank wall and doesn't move to interrupt my conversation until I wave him over; I introduce him to both Cora and Spoons. Cora's laughter echoed throughout the room as she exclaims, "OMG! The awful bouquet guy!?" Clasping his one biceps in appreciation, she tossed her head back, roaring again before taking a deep breath. Again, I'm shocked by the volume her small body can reach. Once she gathers herself, Spoons, who looks confused and jealous, shakes Chase's hand, and I see his knuckles whiten. In an instant, he pulls back, shaking his hand in pain as Chase gives him a brisk nod.

When he leaves, I ask, "What was that?"

Chase shakes his head as if it's nothing. "Oh, I just don't think he knows how strong a born rancher's hand is and was trying to exercise some kind of authority."

I laugh and nudge him in the ribs. "Drink? I hear there are even some exotic meat pairings, if you're interested?" He shakes his head, yes.

We join his parents, moving between tables until we are seated with none other than the beautiful Shayne, Parker, and, because there's no better explanation than some historic karma-like debt being paid right now, my boss, Mark Miller.

With no better ideas for my free hand, which to my horror is shaking, I forcefully shove it into Chase's back pocket and look at him apologetically. Chase remains composed, as if he's encountered this uncomfortable situation daily, effortlessly navigating it with the expertise of a seasoned veteran. The faint hum of conversation fills the air, mingling with the aroma of cheeses and wine. Parker's eyes are shifting between Chase and me in such haste he looks like he wants to pick up the charcuterie board and hurl it at us while Shayne, also unbothered, is casually rubbing his back and chatting with the remaining table attendees. Chase, a master of cautious composure, seems to pick up on the apparent friction and whispers, "We can go, no difference to me." He places a gentle hand on my back that makes my spine react as if it's been struck by lightning. I jolt and let out a strangled laugh that sounds like I'm saying brrrrrr in the way they do on television shows to inform the audience it's cold. This makes Chase laugh and apologize for forgetting that I'm so ticklish; he actually says the words, "I'm sorry, I forgot you were so ticklish," and now Parker's face is a crimson color, his eyebrows knitted tightly together in displeasure. "Excuse me," says Parker, who leaves the table abruptly, with no further explanation to anyone. In his absence, the table engages in conversation about the pairings, which they liked better, and I relax under the steady stream of praise for a job well done by Mark Miller. Parker returns kissing Shayne on the cheek which Chase responds to by pulling up my hand and pressing his lips to my knuckles announcing that we've had a great time and will be calling it a night. Not wanting to appear genuinely confused by this announcement, I stand, hug Trisha and Cliff, who thank me again, and say polite goodbyes to the remaining table, including Parker, who nods hastily.

 We walk through the courtyard and into the building before Chase sighs. "Ooof," I look at him as he grabs one of my hands, "couldn't take another night ending with Parker," he seems apologetic, which forces me to think of all the times Chase has been in the background of mine and Parker's tension. I nod; something is emerging between us, and I cannot let the night end on this note. Straightening, I say, "Let's not go upstairs; let's go somewhere else, anywhere; we're in the city. We've got loads of options." He smiles, and I finish. "Maybe I can show you some of my tricks?"

"Alright, Sarah," he says in his now typical cavalier drawl, "let's see what you got."

Since it's the weekend corresponding with Valentine's Day, everywhere we go is primarily filled with couples, making us another twosome passing through. We indulge in playing the sprawling board games amidst the lively ambiance of the brewery, surrounded by the clinking of glasses and laughter. We shout at the thrill of throwing axes; the thuds echoing through the space. As the night progresses, we make our way to my beloved Five Queens, its warm and familiar atmosphere embracing us. Upon our entrance, I hear "Sarah!!!" over the loud music and see Jessica, Rowan, Alice, and Thomas all gathered at a table. Thomas eyes me, and his face fills with devilish satisfaction when he sees I am pulling Chase behind me. If memory serves me, Chase has been here before but was usually hunkered with Brian in their own protected bubble. When we joined their table, Felix returned, and the look of suspicion and surprise made Chase laugh against my shoulder.

"Well, well, well," Felix says eyeing us speculatively. "Are we official?" With a more mischievous look, Alice turned towards us, pointing a finger between the two of us and innocently blinking as she rested her chin on her knuckles.

"I—" I stammer. "I don't know what you mean."

Chase fills in, "We're taking a page from your book," pointing between Felix and Thomas, "No labels or strings, you know, stuff like that."

The table comes alive with laughter, transforming the rest of the night into a carefree and merry atmosphere, with jokes, drinks, and dancing to keep the energy high. I was determinedly trying to make Chase dance, but he firmly disagreed.

Back in my hallway, we stumble into each other, our laughter echoing off the walls as we catch our breath. Chase takes hold of me, his touch steady and strong, and kisses me deeply. He pulls back and says breathlessly, "Don't have sex with me tonight, please." My brain and body clearly interpret two opposing messages, so I say, "HA!" but I think I meant to say, huh? Which he interprets, maybe correctly, as, yeah right, and proceeds to tell me if he's going to have sex with me again, it will be sans a night of heavy drinking. So, we don't; we crawl into my bed after Chase ensures the curtains are secure, and we sleep, my body pulsing with the need for him.

Chapter 42: Three is STILL a Crowd

Ppag@mavenads.com writes: **Was he in the background all along? Always picking you up when something went wrong just lurking and waiting for an opportunity to snatch you up?**

Wondering if the fact that it's Monday and a whole week since the mixer has somehow scrambled the words of an advertising campaign into this message, a message that sounds undeniably like an accusation of infidelity from someone who is very obviously in a long-term relationship with a woman who is also very obviously not me. Pinching the bridge of my nose and counting to five, I check again. Then, I slam my laptop closed and push it away from me. "I don't have fucking time for this, Parker," I say to the empty office before exiting. I need to go anywhere, really, just not be here.

"Hey Sarah," Cora pokes out, "Mark wants to see you in the war room," I wave and head in that direction when I am met with who other than Parker fucking Pagano and David

Spoons. "Grab your stuff, Sarah, we're going to lunch," says Mark and I nod politely, no strength to argue.

We're seated together at a spot Mark takes everyone to that overlooks the river. Because I've been here so much the server knows what I am ordering. With tension suffocating me like a vice, I fixate my gaze on my food, evading any chance of making eye contact with my accuser. Between polite nods and one-word answers, I am fervently praying to the merciful heavens that this restaurant burst into flames, forcing us to leave immediately. No such luck. Thanks to Spoon's incessant talking, which is typical of a marketing guy, my negative demeanor goes mostly unnoticed, except by Parker, who has been fixated on me since we ended up in this unbelievably dreadful situation. Maybe I can shout, "it seems I've started my period!" Allowing me to leave without question. I don't, however.

We leave the restaurant, and I am relieved at the sight of the picturesque high rise, my home, my freedom from this claustrophobic car ride. Panic washes over me, causing the blood to drain from my body, and I mutter curses under my breath as I notice my purse is missing, likely still hanging on the back of the chair at the restaurant. In an attempt to stay composed, I explain the situation and reassure them that the restaurant is within walking distance, just a few blocks away. Just as Mark was about to turn around, trapping me in this personal hell for longer, Parker kindly offers to walk me. In an instant, my entire body ignites with a fiery heat, replacing the flow of blood with scorching hot lava. It takes every ounce of my wavering professionalism not to scream out "THE HELL HE WILL!" When Mark praises him for this act of kindness. The moment we stepped out of the car, I knew I had no chance of out-walking Parker; his stride was three times longer than mine, making my efforts seem futile.

Parker frantically gets in front of me and shouts, "Sarah, look, I'm sorry, I don't even know why I sent you that, it—it's not even my business."

Despite trying to face the opposite direction, I couldn't help but spin back towards him, my face contorted with fury. My voice erupted, filled with intensity and rage. "You're right, Parker, it's NOT your business." Shocked by my reaction, he takes a step to the side, allowing me to pass.

Keeping my pace now he asks, "Well, are you happy at least?"

I send him another look—daggers. No longer willing to express my frustration aloud, I quicken my stride. Swinging the door open quickly, I hurry inside, leaving him to catch it before it closes on him; this gives the few people left in the restaurant the unmistakable impression I'm not happy with my companion. My purse, as I assumed, is still hanging on the chair. With nowhere else to channel my anger I forcefully whip it off, nearly yanking the chair with it before storming back out, leaving Parker again to follow pathetically behind me.

"Sarah, you're acting embarrassing!"

This strikes a nerve, and before I can do that thing where you think and then speak, I'm pointing a finger at him. "I don't care what you think, Parker, I do not care! I cannot do this!" I wave my arms between us, "This thing, where we revolve around each other as if other people don't exist and why—" I'm pleading now, tears forming that sting in my nostrils. "Why do you care who I am with? When you are with someone else? Someone who seems pretty fucking wonderful?"

He stares at me, his face guilty and I can't keep looking at him. Once more, I set off towards my building, a sanctuary where I can find refuge. I feel his presence, his footsteps echoing softly behind me, as I catch glimpses of his silhouette in my peripheral vision. I sense his steady breaths, the faint rustle of his clothing, and the warmth radiating from his body. Despite knowing he could easily match my pace; he chooses to stay just a step behind. As we were on the cusp of rounding the corner to my entrance, his apology finally broke the silence. I couldn't bring myself to turn around.

During the short walk in the hall from the elevator, I crossed paths with Gabriel. "Oh hey, that attractive vaquero you had over, the one you insisted wear clothes, he's back." He winks mischievously, clicks his tongue, and gracefully sidesteps me, unveiling Chase with a bouquet and a trusty tool bag.

"Hey, I just got here, and your—Cora, she said you were at lunch, so I thought maybe I'd just wait until you called?" He stammers. "I was going to fix your ice maker, maybe; I don't know, I'm not great at the surprise thing, it turns out. Also, I think I forget other people work like normal hours," he's still rambling. The sentiment engulfs me completely, and I can't help but burst into tears, which instantly fills him with horror, until I rush into his arms. He holds me until I let us in my place. "Are you okay?" he asks. As I took several deep breaths, I struggled to explain the current events, my words catching in my throat due to sheer exhaustion. Chase takes everything stoically, nodding in silence. When I'm done, I hiccup, "The flowers are beautiful; I should get them in some water." With unwavering patience, he watches me attentively as I fill a vase with water and arrange the flowers, ensuring they are perfectly positioned on my breakfast bar. I sniff, "I've actually gotta head back to my office. Can I leave you here?"

"Yeah, of course," he says, those hazel eyes filled with concern as he lightly grabs my hand.

I look at our hands together and give his a squeeze. "Mouse, keep an eye on him, okay?" Mouse does nothing, and I leave.

Still recovering from the torrent of emotions of the day I am grateful to be entering my apartment, relieved that I can soon put this all behind me. Entering, I notice Chase on the balcony, so I place my things on the edge of my table and he his way. Hearing me slide the door open he says, "Which is better?"

Momentarily taken aback by the question, I clarify, "Plunging to your death or living?"

He laughs with great enthusiasm. "My view or yours?"

"Ohhhh," I say, "that's what you meant, of course. Well, that's easy, mine is better."

He pokes me in the rib "Liar."

I smile, nodding toward the kitchen. "How'd it go in there?"

"You can now retrieve ice without using your grubby hands."

Now it's my turn to poke him. "Thanks, and thanks for earlier; you have no idea how great it was to see you here after all that."

"About that," his voice is serious, too serious. There's an ominous thud in my stomach. "If that is going to be a complication for you, then maybe I shouldn't—we shouldn't. You know, be?" He shifts uncomfortably before continuing, "I don't even know what this is, but I like hanging out with you. I think you're funny and you like my—" He slowly displays seven fingers, "tricks."

I rest my arms on the weathered railing, absorbing the breathtaking view. My gaze fixates on the graying clouds, looming over the majestic mountains, as if ready to engulf them. "Eight," I say softly, "so far, I've counted eight, and I'm not sure if I've actually seen the first five."

As we both lean over the railing, I can't help but notice the smug expression on his face. "Oh, yeah?" he questions, his tone dripping with satisfaction.

Facing him, I say with a smile, "I think you're funny, too. And, if I am being totally honest, I want to see how many tricks I can count."

"Will you tell me? I mean, would you tell me if he is back in your life?"

"He'll never be back in my life like that again, but I will be honest about everything, Parker, and anything else." I take a deep breath. "So far, Chase, you know all my secrets."

He looks at me with immense gratitude and examines my face for a beat. "If it wasn't a weekday, I'd stay, but I've gotta get back; you'll be okay?"

"Yeah, of course. Mouse and I will be fantastic."

Standing in my doorway, he gently intertwines his fingers with mine, his touch sending shivers down my spine. As his lips meet mine, a soft melody of our breaths harmonizes with the faint sound of distant raindrops. The scent of him fills the air around me and I breathe him in all musk and smoke. In that moment, his tender kiss melts me, turning every fiber of my being into water, flowing with a mixture of desire and warmth.

Chapter 43: Yes to Undress

"I'm like really surprised you haven't been dating anyone," Heidi says as she spins in a dress that makes her look more like a pastry than a bride. "And a little impressed, you're like really taking your time." She shakes her head no to the bridal shop employee. Being freed from the puffy white dress, she continues on. "The good thing is, if you don't have a date to my wedding, we know Chase won't, at least until after, and you guys can just—" she clasps her hands together "be each other's date as the best man and maid of honor." Observing Alice's wide-eyed expression, I covertly mouthed no shaking my head. Jessica, uninterested, rolls her eyes and returns to her rapid texting. "You know? Heidi finishes staring at me, waiting for my response, but before I can answer, another white dress, making a sound reminiscent of a sped-up version of jingle bells, is hastily lifted over her. Before they can clip it to her size, she shakes her head no, and it's coming off again, leaving her standing in her bra and underwear until they bring the next dress.

"I can't wait to see you all try on the bridesmaid's dresses; since they're all the same color, maybe we'll just do whichever style looks best on you." We beam broadly and agree with her as she continues talking. "Then you'll all have a unique style of black dress. That would be so cute, but would it look good in pictures?" We all dutifully tell our soon-to-be bride friend that anything she does will be perfect when another dress is hurled over her head; as she spins back and forth, my phone buzzes with a text.

Chase: are you being forced into cake tasting later?
Me: yes, you?
Chase: yes, Brian doesn't want to go alone but has to go
Me: what a good friend you are
Chase: I'm the best man; I'm just doing my duty
Me: con of being the best man but free cake!
Chase: and I get to suffer with you

"Hello," I look up to see an annoyed Heidi snapping toward me, "what do you think? And why are you smiling like that? OMG are you—seeing someone? Is that who you're texting? Let me see!" She holds out her hand and I throw my phone into my purse which such force and precision it makes an audible knock against the floor. "No, Cora just said something funny about a resident, anyway," I lie. "That dress looks beautiful. It's definitely a strong contender unless they find something in the same silhouette that has more of an open back. I mean, it is a spring wedding."

This distracts Heidi enough that she nods at the bridal consultant who with the help of an assistant unclips Heidi again hauls the dress over her and is off for another one. The dress they carefully drape over her is a mesmerizing trumpet dress. Its back gracefully plunges, adorned with delicate pearl-like beads that begin at the mid-back and cascade all the way down to her knees. As it fans out, it reveals a captivating sparkling accent piece that widens with the dress's elegant end. The dress exudes an enchanting aura, leaving a trail of awe and anticipation in its wake.

"This is the one," I say stepping onto the platform with her. Alice and Jessica both clap and cheer loudly when she spins around. The room falls silent as our bridal consultant, hidden behind the mirror, rings a bell that resonates with an obnoxious noise, earning her a collective glare from all of us. Following that, we each try on our dresses, not really minding as long as Heidi is pleased, and within one more hour, everything is sorted out.

Heidi and I are pulling up to the cake tasting when I see an elated to see his bride-to-be Brian, and an also delighted but not too happy-looking Chase. I hug Brian. Heidi tells him she found the dress, and I chime in that she's never looked so beautiful before, which he then explains is impossible. Chase makes a mock face of disinterest before saying, "How about them cakes?!" A laugh rockets out of me, a laugh that makes Heidi look confused, Chase look like we just got caught naked and Brian asks Heidi what was so funny. In an attempt to prevent further awkward moments, I hold the door open for everyone, only for Chase to sneakily take a swipe at my hand. Here's the thing: would our two best friends be upset by whatever Chase and I are doing? Which genuinely isn't much more than kissing and hanging out; I don't know, truth be told, but our dynamic is so precious. If they thought we'd ruin it somehow, that would make things weird, and with their wedding coming up and the fact that we've unintentionally hidden it this long, we've just decided to keep it this way.

Once we tasted a sufficient amount of cake that our stomachs hurt from the sugar, Heidi and Brian finalized their cake order. Chase delicately traced the tops of my jeans with his fingers, pushing me into a corner out of sight, then softly and lovingly placing his lips to mine to continue to tease the bare skin underneath my jeans' button. We hear Brian and Heidi both say Thank You. Like teenagers caught red-handed by their parents, we instantly break apart. "You guys are being strange," Heidi announces, splitting a look between us. We stay silent and she looks to Chase. "Chase, would you mind dropping Sarah? Brian and I are going to do some extra errands together before heading home."

What she really means is this is the most fertile phase of her menstrual cycle. Therefore, they need to go "do it." Trying to have a baby has never made Brian happier or Heidi more organized. Chase and I speak in perfect synchrony with varying answers, which wins us one more puzzled look from Heidi. Then Chase says, "Sure." and we exit.

Helping me into his truck, we make our way to my apartment. As we pull closer Chase points to the construction along the curb where he normally parks because his behemoth of a truck doesn't fit in the parking garage. I pointed him to a small park, or at least what could pass as one, with a single bench and a narrow path meandering between buildings. I mentioned the presence of a small, empty parking lot, so he decided to pull in. Once he put the truck in park, I close the gap between us by pushing the console upright and sitting in the small center seat. Awkwardly, I configure myself so one leg was on either side of the cup holder under the radio; he looks only at the area between my legs before returning his eyes to the road. I may be mistaken but, I hear an audible swallow as he places one hand on my thigh. We've been doing this thing for weeks, maybe even a couple months now, where we kiss, usually at the end of a visit, and he barely skims his hands over my body through my clothes, and I am charged with temptation. Today marked the first time his touch ventured beyond my face and arms, igniting a fiery longing for further exploration. It takes all my self-discipline to stop my arms and hands from ripping off my clothes, throwing myself at him, and begging for him to do more than just kiss me, do more than touch me, but there's something about his tentativeness that always stalls me. However, today I decide to throw caution to the wind. Grabbing his hand, still sitting on my thigh, unmoving, I assertively pull it to the seam of my jeans that sit perfectly at my center. He observes me vigilantly. Using my hand, I curl his fingers to cup me and lean my head backward expelling air. Chase places a kiss to my collarbone. "Home," I whisper, and he nods against my neck.

In a flurry of motion, we scramble out of the truck and dash across the street, our feet pounding against the pavement. Above us, the sky rumbles with thunder, echoing through the air. The first raindrops fall, creating tiny specks on the glistening asphalt.

Crossing the threshold laughing, Ray nodded at us both, and we scurried into an elevator. Once we entered the elevator, Chase pulls me close to him, balling the center of my sweater into his fist, and the gentle kisses of the past slipped from our minds. Eager, rushed, deep thrusts of his tongue match the rhythm of our groping hands until the elevator sounds. We spill onto the 15th floor, righting ourselves to a couple just holding hands; nothing to see here.

It takes me seconds too long to fumble with my purse and find the key before Chase yanks it from inside a pocket, nearly spilling its contents, and shoves us inside. I'm barely moving at will toward my room. Instead, Chase has my hips securely in his grasp and is kissing and forcefully shoving me backward. Once he's over me on the bed and I feel the weight of him settled between my thighs, it's as if my brain has forfeited everything else for this one thing: him and me having sex.

He pulls my shirt over my head, and I do the same to him, marveling at his chest and torso, the way his muscles flex as he works the button and zipper from my jeans and tugs them until my legs are free. I'm left only in a bra, thong, and socks, which I shuffle off with opposite feet. He stands back to undo his belt, slides out of his pants, and is now revealing the unmistakable outline of his erection through his tight briefs. I'm staring, probably eyeing it like a predator, but I can't stop; I've been kissed to near ecstasy for too long. I want him so much that anything else but this act, in this moment, seems superfluous. I've shifted to a comfier spot on the bed where we can both relax without our limbs dangling off the sides.

Chase rasps something inaudible, then clears his throating trying again, "Sarah, we can't take this back; the first time, we could've chalked that up to drunken whatever. This is me and you, no excuses." I arch to unclasp my bra and drift my panties down my legs, eyeing him as they go before tossing them at his feet. "Gosh okay," he chirps, wringing his hands together. I chuckle at the boyish uncertainty. Taking his face in my hands, "this is just me and you." He lets his last article of clothing fall and settles between my legs. Chase trails kisses from one breast to the other, then sucks one nipple into his mouth before the other as I writhe beneath him, feeling his erection pushing against my thigh, hip, and stomach as he sucks, bites, and kisses from my neck to breasts and back again, the area between my thighs is becoming so slick with desire that I grasp him in one hand, sliding him inside me with no thought; he thrusts instinctively.

I cry into his chest, pleading that he persists. Holding him against me as he thrusts, digging my nails into the firm skin of his muscular back, I feel our skin skating across each other, making unattractive noises until his release comes. He places a firm bite on my extended neck. I arch up to him, sending my own release like a flood, compelling my hips to press themselves further into him, and he dips his head to kiss me gently as before. My heart rate slows, reminding me of the times in yoga when you finally release that challenging yoga pose, the one where your body is shaking from the sheer pain of it, but then when it's over, the pain immediately dissipates, and you are calm again; that is me, I am calm again. Chase's sudden backing off of me shattered the calm. He jerked himself away so suddenly it feels like someone threw a bucket of ice on me. "Fuck!" He shouts, "I came—I came inside you."

I look to acknowledge the lack of a condom and nod, now feeling every bit of his discomfort. "I—Uh, I'm on birth control; I take it like you're supposed to, so I think," I clear my throat "I think we're okay there. I'm not; I mean, I haven't since you; before you, it was like a while. I've had a thing with the doctor since then, so, I'm uh, I'm okay with the other stuff too, STDs and such." Now, feeling a bit too cold and naked, I find a corner of my blanket to drape across me. He grabs a throw blanket that made its way to the floor. In one motion, he tucks himself next to me and pulls it over us both.

"I'm just not ready for babies, you know, we're—" he shakes his head. "Well, what are we even? Feels like that conversation should at least come before babies."

Placing my head on his chest, I am comforted by the rhythmic beating of his heart. "We can be whatever we want, I think, friends who sleep together occasionally but kiss a lot?"

He stokes a calloused hand against my cheek, "We're not friends anymore, Sarah; I don't think we ever were."

"We'll have to tell them," I say.

"I know," he agrees, "maybe let's wait until after the wedding?"

"I think we're starting to seem suspicious," I admonish.

"True, you can't keep your hands off me," he teases.

"Ha-Ha," I mock.

We're opting to leave things undefined for now, embracing the excitement of the unknown as we revel in our connection. Coiled around him, captivated by the melodic thump of Chase's heartbeat. I love the way he effortlessly runs his fingers through my hair and gently strokes my face. As Chase seeps into my skin, I become overwhelmed with feelings that I'd long since buried.

Chapter 44: Emails Are Like Boomerangs

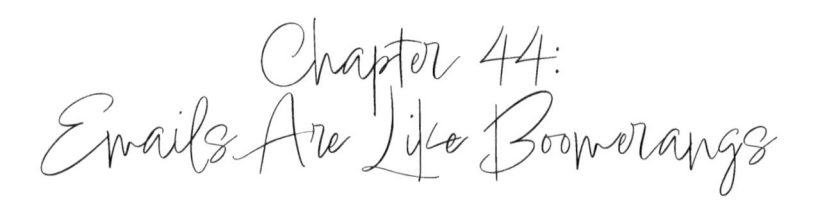

It's like an automatic reflex - I can't help but read Parker's emails from time-to-time, pondering how to bring an end to everything between us. We haven't seen each other in months; it's weeks away from Heidi and Brian's wedding, and I'm nearly positive I am in a relationship that is a secret to practically no one at this point. But here I am, reading them both again, as if I don't have them memorized like all the other parts of us.

Parker, I owe you an explanation or an apology.. delete

Parker, there's something I've always wanted to say to you... delete

Parker, maybe to understand what happened all those years ago

"Sarah?" I jump in surprise at the sudden knock on the door and the sound of Cora's voice echoing through my doorway. "Oh, sorry, didn't mean to startle you,"

I shake my head. "No, it's okay. I was just daydreaming, apparently," and closed my laptop. "What's up?"

"Felix and Thomas are here to get you for lunch?"

"Oh!" I say, remembering suddenly, and grab my things.

The spring weather makes today too beautiful for lunch indoors, so we walk to Urban Bistro. Their table availability more than triples in the warmer months because they are otherwise stacked and chained together outside. Inside, the bistro is vibrant and warm, permeated with the scent of just-baked loaves of bread and the lingering coffee for the afternoon drinkers. At the entrance, a narrow pathway leads to the line where you can order your preferred fancy sandwich. Adjacent to it, a petite pastry display catches your eye, usually brimming with delights during breakfast hours. However, now it holds a meager selection of leftover scones and muffins. After retrieving our distinct orders, we take seats outside at one of their wrought-iron tables.

The conversation begins with a swinger's party they attended just a few days ago, by accident, at The Chad, a well-known, usually male-only gay bar.

"It was outrageous," exclaims Felix. "I mean, we're all for open sex or whatever, but this was too much."

Thomas nods his agreement and explains, "We received this very fancy invitation that explained it was an invitation-only event at The Chad—"

"A chance to explore your fantasies," cuts in Felix.

"That's what it said," Thomas agrees, "but nowhere in my fantasies are a bunch of naked heterosexual married couples!"

I guffaw loudly. "Oh my gosh, I would have been mortified! I probably would've fainted right there on the spot. Who knew there was such a large market for that kind of thing here?"

Thomas points a fork at me. "What about you? Since you're not attending swingers' parties, what are you doing?"

"Or who?" finishes Felix

"Just staying busy with work," I say into my sandwich. Both of them look at me, disbelieving.

"You've never gone this long without a boyfriend," says Thomas. "So, I know you're getting it from somewhere, and my money is on Chase." I blush and choke on the bite I've just taken.

"There it is," says Felix boastfully. "How long?"

I stare at them both imploringly, and Thomas motions me to continue.

"I don't know," I continue flushed. "A while, but we're trying to keep it low-key because we don't know what Brian and Heidi will think."

"Heidi will take all the credit for being the matchmaker," says Thomas. "As a matter of fact, she'll be thrilled."

I shrugged. "I guess I'm worried if it doesn't work out."

"We're adults, Sarah," says Thomas. "This isn't the dramatic relationship you and Parker were engaged in; this is a healthy normal relationship, and if you both are keeping it secret and neither of you are freaking out about that alone, I'd say that's a good sign." I furrow my brow. "What I mean is," he continues, "you and Parker were so unrealistic, everything was either so hot everyone was getting burned or so cold that everyone was getting frozen out. You were never neutral, never able to just be."

I turn back to my food and take a deep breath, feeling the anticipation build in my chest as I prepare to reveal the secret I've been longing to share. "I've been thinking about sending him an email for like closure? I don't know why, maybe just so every time we see each other, it isn't weird?"

As I lock eyes with Felix, his eyebrows knit together in a puzzled expression. "I don't think he needs an email after all these years, babe. Y'all been done."

I split a look between the two and marveled at how their expressions said it all without a single word. Then, Thomas clears his throat and speaks with a meaningful tone. "I do think you should tell Heidi, though, before she finds out on her own." In that moment, I knew he was right.

Seated back in my office, I open my computer and have several unread emails, perhaps the most notable one from ppag@mavenads.com, which has an RE: in the front, which is impossible because I haven't emailed him.

ppag@mavenads.com writes: was there something specific you were trying to say here, Sarah? Not sure I understand your message.

Unfortunately, the chances of my computer spontaneously bursting into flames in the center of my desk, causing this to mysteriously disappear, is low, so instead, I take a deep breath and scroll to the message he received: **Parker, maybe to understand what happened all those years ago.** Oh great, I must've accidentally sent the message when I closed my laptop. Perfect, absolutely perfect, now what? How do I recover from this? I bury my head in my palms, the sound of my breath filling the silence as I desperately try to figure out what to do. My desk phone explodes in a ring, making my chest collapse as if Parker has crawled through my email, making me answer with a strained, "He—Hello. The Views, Sarah here."

"Sarah, it's Heidi. I tried reaching you on your cell, but you didn't answer; your dress came in, and you need to do a last fitting. When are you free?"

"Oh, OH!" I say louder, too loud. "Hi, uh, I can do tomorrow. Is that okay?"

"Are you okay? You sound funny?"

"Oh, I just," I pause, then squeezing my eyes shut say quickly. "I accidentally sent an email to Parker that I didn't mean to."

"What?" she says, dragging out the word, and definite sound of worry in her tone. "Spill."

"Ugh, I had this dumb idea that I should write him a note for like closure." I emphasize the question in my action.

"Why?" she says, again emphasizing the word.

"I don't know," I groan, clearly mortified. "And now I sent him a weird half-email, so I like to have to respond, right?" I can feel myself bouncing with anticipation in my seat while I hear her inhale sharply on the other end of the phone. She asks me about the severity of the situation, and I suggest reading her both emails for a better understanding. When I finish reading the email I sent and his follow up, a sharp, agonizing sound escapes her lips, perfectly mirroring the gravity of the situation. Heidi instructs I do nothing, there's nothing to do until we see each other tomorrow and we can strategize. We end the call with her explaining that because she knows me, she understands why I thought this an important step in moving on and is always there for me, no matter what.

Chapter 45: Disappointing a Friend

The scratching sensation against my cheek brings me out of my slumber, and I realize it's Chase, slowly nuzzling into my neck. Sensing my wakefulness, he boldly slips his hand between my legs, expertly teasing his fingers along my dampening slit. When I respond with a gasp, he skillfully slides one finger inside me, followed by another, causing a rush of desire to course through my body. With his palm pressed against me, he moves his fingers in a way that has me begging for more, uttering his name in between short, rapid breaths. As he trails kisses from my shoulder up to my neck, my senses are overwhelmed with pleasure. Chase hovers over me, sliding himself between my legs before lacing his arm behind me and rolling me to his top. He grasps my hip, urging me to move against him, as his other hand steadies my chest, keeping my torso upright. Filled with a sense of exposure and timidity, I reflexively attempt to shield my body. Yet, when his eyes capture the full image of me atop him, he releases a seemingly impossible amount of breath and utters, "You're so damn beautiful."

We shower together, Chase drawing me in holding my face and kissing me as the water trickles between us. We drink coffee, his black, mine barely coffee after everything I add to it. The morning unfolds leisurely, with every window ajar, inviting the gentle caress of the spring breeze to dance through my apartment, carrying the sweet scent of blossoming flowers. When it's time for me to meet Heidi, we walk to the elevator together, sharing kisses the whole way down. The door opens, and a voice pierces through our banter, forcing us to stand at an immediate attention. My stomach drops at the sight of her.

"What's going on?" With a look of irritation and confusion, Heidi stood in the lobby, tapping her strapped sandal impatiently beneath her Capri pants. I focus on the tattoo, the one on her ankle that I have, the other half of which splits me in two, the guilt so heavy I am frozen. Chase finds words first and says, "I spent the night." This announcement stitches her brows even closer together as she pans to me, "Heidi, I've been meaning to tell you—"

"Tell me what?" She inquires sharply but doesn't let anyone speak. "That you're sleeping with Brian's best friend? Does he know?" She switches to Chase, who shakes his head no, and she switches back to me. "How long?" I say nothing. "How long!?" She demands.

I look at Chase, ever the diplomat, holding my hand steadily. "Since New Years, maybe?" I murmur barely audible He nods in agreement. "So, months!?" She says with an irritated guffaw, and I grimace, wincing as if she slapped me.

"We've just been seeing how things go; we weren't hiding it; we were just trying to make sure, before—before saying anything."

She looks at me, but it's somber now, the disappointment being replaced by something akin to grief. "I can't believe you both think so little of us as friends that you would have to hide your relationship. Your appointment is in 20 minutes. Please don't be late." And just like that, she's walking out the door, the sound of her footsteps echoing through the empty lobby. I am aware that pursuing her is not a good idea. She needs space and time.

The car ride with Chase to my final dress fitting is filled with quietness, punctuated only by the sound of the engine and the occasional sigh. Still, he's kept his fingers laced through mine, only allowing us to separate to get out of my SUV. We walk into the bridal shop, where they make a couple of meticulous adjustments to my dress, leaving me to change out of it on my own, Chase jumps to unzip it and assists me in cautiously stepping out of it. He extends my arms out to the sides taking in the full sight of me, and tsks, "Too bad we have somewhere to be." Then allows me to take my arms back to put back on the maxi dress I wore to make this exchange easy.

"We have somewhere to be?" I ask, not remembering any plans today that involved Chase, as I was supposed to be here with Heidi.

"Yeah, we're going to Heidi and Brians." I start to protest, explaining that I know Heidi and she needs more time as he holds up a hand. "I already talked to Brian. We're going."

Chase confidently enters the four-digit code into the gated community, granting us seamless access with no prior indication of our arrival, except for Chase's conversation with Brian. As we make our way to their place, we meander past neighboring houses that obstruct glimpses of the vast emerald golf course. The air is filled with the distant swish of clubs hitting golf balls and the faint aroma of freshly cut grass wafts through the open windows of the car. The closer we get to their door, the more my hesitation grips me, causing my legs to feel increasingly burdened. I had a plan to resolve this, and this isn't the first time Heidi and I have disagreed; we always make up, so why does this feel different? As I'm lost in my thoughts, I suddenly feel a firm grip around my hand and meet Chase's intense gaze, making me realize that there's more than just hurt feelings at risk.

Heidi opens the door, splits an annoyed look between us, but opens the door wide and walks away, leaving us to walk through. Chase closes it behind him. Brian stands from the couch and shares a nod with Chase. He gives me a tight-lipped smile and they head for the garage, leaving me to trail behind a silent Heidi. She makes her way to the back porch with a glass of wine; seeing the wine on the counter, I help myself to a glass and down a quick 4oz from a coffee cup then walk out to find her sitting at their swinging chair watching the bustle of the ninth green. I perch uncomfortably on a brittle wicker chair and silently pray it doesn't collapse beneath me.

"Heidi," I finally muster, "I should have told you; in fact, I don't really know why I didn't." She doesn't bother to turn in my direction but scoffs, disbelieving. I regroup. "At first, I didn't even really know it was happening, and then when I realized it was, I didn't know how to tell you." She scoffs again, this time looking over to serve me a half eye roll. "Look," I say, more agitated than I mean to "what do you want from me?"

Facing me now head on looking offended and wronged. "Jesus, Sarah, you think I'm mad about Chase?" I look at her and take a deep breath so my features will soften. "I'm not mad about Chase. You and Chase are adults, and if it all blows up well, Chase and Brian will probably make it, and so will we." She pauses, "Why didn't you think you could tell me? I'm your best friend."

Gazing towards the ninth hole, we sit, silently captivated as a player gracefully sinks a remarkable long shot into the awaiting cup. The air fills with the joyous cheers of his exuberant friends, echoing through the vibrant green surroundings. When I see her features again, she looks dejected. I take inventory of all my thoughts and realize what I need to say. "I—" I start, but the words bottle in my throat, and I feel a sting in my nose. She looks at me and tilts her head ever so slightly, willing me to proceed. "It happened without me realizing it was happening, then I became protective of this tiny ember that was trying to ignite, and it felt safer to hide it, like if we just stayed in this bubble, just he and I, nothing would or could come along and take up all the oxygen." I quickly wipe at a falling tear before continuing. "Yes, I was afraid what you would think, and what Brian would think? I've always been so messy in relationships. Why would he trust me with his best friend?" A small sob escaped from me, and I hastily wiped away the remaining tears on my cheeks. "What if I hurt him, Heidi?"

She walks over to me, an arm wrapping me in a side hug that conveys her understanding. With Heidi by my side, I sat in silence, taking in the sight of the golfers as they came and went, while she held onto me with a gentle grip. A strangled quiet laugh escapes from Heidi and she releases me abruptly. "You like, really, like Chase," she quips, trying to contain her laughter. "I always wondered why he never really had girlfriends. It's like I met girls occasionally, but I could always tell they weren't serious. I always felt a little sad for him, protective too, I guess, so I get it." She faces me. "Who would've thought, you and Chase? Life is so funny sometimes."

I shrug and exhale my relief at her reaction. Now that we've moved past the part where she hates me for this, I have to ask again. "Heidi, what happens if I hurt him?"

With a serious expression, she leaned in and gently placed both hands on my shoulders, locking eyes with me. "You are not the bad girlfriend; you and Parker were complicated for no reason other than, well, there was just too much of everything." She made a large circle with her hands. "Even if you and Chase don't work out, it still doesn't mean you are or always will be messy." She paused again, eyeing me with a smile. "Yes, I'm still kinda sad you didn't tell me earlier, but I am a little proud of you too, being so protective and quiet about it; that is sooooo not you and Parker already." She gives me a long look and then releases my shoulders; checks her watch. "We should probably eat; gotta keep Brian's energy up for my fertile window that starts tomorrow."

With a squished face and a frown, I make it clear that I am not pleased with the excessive sharing. Turning back to the kitchen, her laughter lingers in the air, adding a sense of warmth and happiness to the room.

The boys, now relieved of their safe space in the garage, begin to rummage through the refrigerator for things that can go on the grill. Chase eyes me with a smirk and a nod before keeping in conversation about the latest catalytic converter thieving happening around the neighborhood adjacent. Brian explaining how the homeowners' association voted for the gates to be closed all day instead of the normal 5:00 PM. Heidi opens a fresh bottle of wine as I pepper her with questions about wine-drinking alongside fertility windows. "Today, we are celebrating," she says.

As Heidi and I share our own idle conversation about baby making and work. In a sudden burst of laughter, she hastily placed her wine glass on the table, desperately attempting to swallow what she had in her mouth before it erupted, spraying out in all directions. Between gasps of air and attempts to regain composure, Heidi catalogs all the times she has asked Chase to stand in as my date. As predicted, she takes credit for our blossoming relationship. I nonchalantly remind her that, to my knowledge, he is not my boyfriend. Heidi peeks outside, her voice hushed, taking note that the boys are out of earshot before whispering, "What about the Parker email?"

I try to mimic her hushed tone and respond by rolling my eyes and hastily hissing. "I have no idea why I even was trying to email him in the first place."

She places her glass down and holds up her hand. "Interested in my theory?" I nod, and she keeps the muted tone. "Maybe you thought if you answered the question of why you and Parker failed, every time, as a closure email." Making air quotes when she says closure, "It would give you confidence in this relationship."

I meet her gaze and then eye the bottle of wine, judging her statement by its contents, "Maybe. So, what do I do? I really shouldn't be emailing Parker, right?"

She shrugs, "probably not, but you might as well wrap it up, get it over with, do whatever you need to do. Because if you continue running into each other, it cannot keep ending in public arguments." I groan and take a long drink of my wine before sighing in agreement.

Chase and I stay through dinner, and although he's more reserved here, his touch lingers on the small of my back or gently rests on my thigh. When I look at him and see the whirlwind of thoughts, I know I have one more tough discussion to tackle. After our goodbyes, we walk toward my car, and I stop Chase from holding my hand by forcefully pinning my arms to my sides. Assuming my nerves are still on high alert, Chase winks at me once we're in the car and tries to take my hand which I've now pinned under my leg to stop it from shaking. I look at the space in front of me and before he can turn the keys in the ignition blurt out, "since we are confessing our sins today." Seen through my peripheral, he gives me a wary look but waits for me to finish. I recount the same story I told Heidi and inform him of my email to Parker, then relay part of the conversation I had with Heidi about me and him, explaining my reservations about being open with our relationship for fear I will inevitably ruin it by just being me. For the entirety of my monologue, Chase remains stoic, an expression of understanding on his rough features, and when I stop, a small smile turns up the corners of his mouth.

"Got yourself in a real pickle, didn't you?" I laugh despite my nerves and lean back into my seat, nodding, "I don't have any useful advice here, but from my vantage point, you're not messing anything up, at least not yet."

I look over at him, and he raises his eyebrows flirtatiously. "You'll let me know, right?"

"What?" he says, turning over the engine.

"If I do, start to mess things up?"

He regards me with compassion but doesn't answer. Instead, he just simply says, "ready to go?" I nod.

Chapter 46: Something Like Closure

To my utter horror but not surprise, I have a follow-up message from Parker. Just one word: **lunch?** Desperate for advice aside from the swirling incoherent screaming in my head, I send texts to Heidi and Thomas in our group chat. Then, because I swore I would tell Chase any Parker related news, I texted him individually, also asking for his opinion. The first ping comes from Chase almost instantly and I see the first three words: **I trust you.** Holding my breath, I open it, looking for the "but." **I trust you, but let him know I wrestle bison daily;** he follows it up with: **he's no match for me :)** Smiling; I send back: **the babies or the adults? It's an important distinction.** Another quicker-than-usual message comes through, and he's responded: **;) ;) call me after, please.** There is a subtle undercurrent of worry in his messages, prompting me to make a silent promise to never lose his trust. Minutes pass and the next pings are Thomas and Heidi, and I'm delighted for the reprieve from tapping my fingers against my desk.

Thomas: ugh whyyy are we still talking about him?
Heidi: rip off the Band-Aid

Thomas: Not your clothes
Heidi: right, keep it public and clothing mandatory
Thomas: although a bit of goodbye sex may not hurt, he is pretty hot now
Heidi: and we're done listening to Thomas
Thomas: it's too early for this, anyway
Heidi: Just try not to scream at each other in public
Me: Wow guys this has been truly unhelpful
Thomas: I only take crises after lunch
Heidi: Good Luck?
Me: I'll let you know how it goes

In just a few brief hours, Parker and I find ourselves sitting face-to-face at a bustling and noisy buffet-style lunch restaurant. I selected a glass of wine, while he went for something on tap. Our aluminum trays and lunches provide a moment of respite amidst the hustle and bustle of the industrial space, where the mingling scents and sounds transport us back to the days of school cafeterias, but with far superior cuisine. So far, our conversation has been limited to superficial topics like businesses and weather, with no substantial exchange.

"So," I clear my throat, "that email." Parker swallows and nods expectantly. "I uh, I think I wanted to just finally give you an answer for everything, but more for me than you." His repeated nods, accompanied by his refusal to speak, plunge me into a disturbing state of unease, as if I am being subjected to a psychological torment, compelling me to continue confessing to a crime. "You didn't deserve me up and leaving like that, and I don't think I deserved—" The memories trickle in first like dots of rain after a thunderclap then it's like I'm standing under a waterfall I have to stop talking. Not wanting to relive the heartbreak of all those messages, being named the bad girlfriend, images of us good and bad but never neutral. When I meet his gaze, he looks distant, like he's somewhere else entirely, perhaps trapped under the same waterfall of memories. My fork slips from my grasp and clatters onto my tray, jolting us back to the present.

"Sarah, I've forgiven us for being young and too in love to understand the gravity of it. We were two people who felt too much of everything between us; in some ways, it was a competition when it shouldn't have been." I give a half smile in acknowledgment. He finishes, sounding lighter. "Our relationship then and now has been a lesson in what not to do."

He looks at me apologetically and I nod my agreement, "I never thought I would get over you, but now I think I needed you to figure out me."

"So, you're over me now, Sarah?" A mischievous smile appeared on his well-groomed face, and my laughter erupted unexpectedly. He laughs too and downs his beer while I compose myself. A few apologies are exchanged, accompanied by dismissive hand gestures, and suddenly the atmosphere shifts into an everyday business meeting. The end of our encounter approaches, and we both pause, bringing ourselves to a halt. In a professional manner, he takes my hand and shakes it, signifying our parting.

"Sarah, I'll see you around; good luck with—with everything."

"Mister Pagano," I return, "Thank you for lunch, and good luck to you too."

We leave the noisy restaurant, our footsteps echoing on the pavement as we venture off in opposite directions. It's as if the bustling city around us serves as a metaphor for our diverging paths. The aroma of food from the tight row of restaurants wafts through the streets, mixing with the scent of rain to come. The afternoon breeze brushes against my face, carrying with it a sense of freedom and uncertainty. As I walk away, I resist the urge to glance back, knowing deep down that there is no turning back.

I pull my phone from my purse and dial Chase, who doesn't answer. "Hey, it's me. You're probably wrestling bison, so give me a call when you get this." With a buzz of energy coursing through me, I make my way back to my office, realizing there's not much to occupy my time. In a swift motion, I gather my belongings and notify Cora of my early departure. She nods and reminds me of tomorrow's meetings.

Standing in the elevator, there's a lightness in me like I finally shrugged off the heavy layers of emotion I'd been carrying for years; I can forgive myself now. Smiling to myself, I round the corner to my door and find Chase standing apprehensively next to it. "Hey" I say, smiling, noticing an edginess to him. "Hey" he returns, and I use my key card to unlock my door; he opens it for me, and I walk in before him, he follows clenching and unclenching his fists.

"Chase? Is something wrong?" A knot forms in my throat.

"I couldn't stop thinking about you being at lunch with him," he says almost apologetically.

I take his clenched hand in mine, unrolling his fingers from inside his fist. "Chase."

He raises his hand to stop me. "I've never been jealous, Sarah. I trust you, but I don't know how to be—be like this."

The uneasiness lingers, yet a smile involuntarily creeps onto my face when I look at him. "Chase, I can't imagine a worse time to tell you this," I pause and correct. "Actually, yes, I can," I shake my head and continue. His eyes meet mine with anxiety as he nervously taps his fist against his leg. "I am falling in love with you, or maybe I already am." I chuckle softly, my shoulders lifting in a carefree manner. My joy hangs in the atmosphere as a warm feeling of amusement washes over me. "All I know is there's nothing I want more than to keep falling in love with you."

His face went through a rollercoaster of emotions before finally settling into a state of calm and happiness. His shoulders visibly dropped, letting go of all the tension they had been holding. "So it went terrible?" He jests.

"Well, once I mentioned the bison wrestling, all bets were off." He rolled his eyes, and I continue. "This town is going to be big enough for the both of us." Laughing at the remark, he pulls me into him, "and Chase," I say, serious now, "I'm sorry you've been stuck dealing with all this; I haven't been fair to whatever this is between us."

The moment he grinned in acknowledgment, a wave of his musky scent, reminiscent of wet straw, washed over me and I breathed him in before he I heard his low voice. "Speaking of, maybe to make things easier for you, so you know what we are and all. Let's just call me your boyfriend, huh?"

"Are you sure you want me as a girlfriend?"

He pulls me into him, his embrace firm and possessive, as he whispers, "I don't want you to belong to anyone else."

Chase lifts my chin so our eyes meet, then presses one of his gentle kisses against my lips. I collapse into him, blissfully happy. With a slight tug, I pull my blouse away from my waist and over my head, feeling the cool air against my bare skin. Chase does the honors of promptly unbuttoning my trousers, then pulls his shirt over his head. Still fixed on me, he unclasps his large belt buckle, unbuttons, and unzips, then maneuvers expertly, hoisting my legs around his waist, and carries me to the bed where we coalesce in a swell of affection limbs tangling as we consummate the next chapter, in what will now be, the story of us.

Chapter 47: The Wedding

In an almost comical fashion, our faces are incredibly close, yet neither Heidi nor I dare to look into each other's eyes. Gathered into an armful of white and lace I am in an impossible squat holding the train and bottom of her dress high over the toilet as she empties her bladder one last time before we cinch her up. It's a scorching 400 degrees in the small bathroom, I surmise, and I am worried that if we stay like this any longer, I won't have any makeup left on my face as it will have melted off along with my skin. Each passing second my hair becomes heavier, weighed down as sweat accumulates over every strand of hair and every inch of my body. Once we exit, Gabriel, the salon-owning neighbor and hired help for the occasion, will be hysterical at our ruined coiffes. It was par for the course, really, when I consider the barrage of vivid expletives he hurled at me while criticizing my restlessness, while elegantly piling my curls atop my head.

"Finished," Heidi says, and we're so close I feel her say it. "Okay," I say breathlessly. "Why don't I try to flush before we stand, just in case?" I shuffle uncomfortably. "Water would be better than pee, right?"

"Sarah, no part of my dress better hit that toilet water, do you understand?"

"I do," I confirm quickly. "I'm just in a precarious situation here."

I feel around behind her until I find the handle and flush. We wait in silence for it to finish and then stand together as I maintain hold of the pearl white gown primarily gathered around her waist. Heidi walks forward, penguin-like, with her underwear seated on her calves as I walk backward. Finally, when I think we are free of the toilet, I shimmy to her side to check that we have enough clearance. "Can you pull them up while I hold all of this?" She does an impressive forward fold and places her underwear back in its rightful place. With caution, I lower the surrounding dress, mindful of the challenge posed by the minuscule bathroom and the risk of it touching any part of the toilet. Heidi opens the door and I walk behind her as she gingerly exits the too-small door of the too-small bathroom that doubles as an oven, making sure nothing drags or snags. The main room of the historic cabin, once owned by the golf course namesake a century ago, exudes a chilly breeze through its drafty logs and brick walls, providing a refreshing respite from the heat. Carefully dabbing at my sweat with a napkin in my dress's handy pockets, I notice Heidi and Brian's mothers crying, and they both nod at me in understanding. It's not worth correcting them; in truth, they have been crying in spurts since we arrived, which is as bothersome as it is adorable. Jessica, a notorious non-crier, is glaring at them in revulsion, and Alice is futilely attempting not to join them.

Gabriel claps frantically, exclaiming, "Ay, Caramba!" Then snaps at us all to help get her ready; we are doing buttons and zippers, fluffing the train and bottom of her dress, which fans out in a trumpet just below her knees. Gabriel places her shoes before her, guiding each foot, then stands and fixes a bit of her hair and makeup before saying, "¡uau! Mira a esta hermosa novia." We all just clap idiotically along with him. He stops me before I head out and clicks his tongue, gesturing at me to wait while he grabs the gigantic pallet of makeup and fixes whatever is wrong with my face. Gabriel, frustrated and exasperated, fusses with my hair in a flurry of ha-rumps and huffs before finally conceding that it's a lost cause and motioning for me to leave.

As we step out of the room, now ground zero for the pre-wedding wardrobe changes, a fragrance of varying perfumes, hairspray, and damp forest follow us. With eager anticipation, we depart together, then everyone's eyes are on us, the bridal party, as we head opposite the seating entrance. Giddy with delight, the four of us line up and Alice looks to Gabriel for the nod signifying we're about to walk. The first song cues, an instrumental version of 100 Years by Five For Fighting, and Alice is the first to exit, joining arms with a family member of Brian; they begin the choreographed walk down the aisle; Jessica goes next, joining the arm of Brian's older brother, who nods respectfully. A surge of emotion consumes my body, igniting a fire of unspoken words within me as I steal one last glance at Heidi. "Don't." She says faintly, her voice and features softened by the beautiful veil. "I'll cry." I nod in understanding, the unspoken language between us saying more than words ever could. We know the love of our friendship will withstand many more events to come, like a sturdy ship sailing through stormy seas.

The usher guides me through the elegant white doors, decorated with golden script that reads "Carlisle Wedding."

As soon as our eyes meet, it's as if a swarm of hummingbirds takes flight inside me, their wings beating rapidly against the walls of my chest. Chase's hazel eyes shimmer like gold, and his unruly gold-brown locks stubbornly resist the hair gel that Gabriel likely used in an attempt to tame his wild cowboy hairstyle into something more appropriate for a wedding. The well-fitted dark suit hugs his muscular body, accentuating his broad shoulders. A wide grin spreads across his face, revealing his square jawline framed by a neatly trimmed beard. This is my boyfriend, I think, and as I walk towards him, my legs tremble like jelly. As we approach each other, he leans in and presses a tender kiss against my cheek, prompting me to entwine my arm with his. Beginning our choreographed walk down the aisle, I see phones and cameras everywhere and wonder if my face is as red as it feels. At the end of the aisle, I improvise my hug to Brian, and he surprises me by saying, "Thanks, I'm so nervous."

With the start of the wedding march, Heidi steps forward, her pearl white gown glimmering in the light, and Brian's face cracks, his eyes shimmering with unshed tears. Alice loses her battle against crying and I can unmistakably hear Jessica sneer at her next to me. When you witness someone you love walking down their wedding aisle, you're caught off guard by the intense emotions that wash over you. I can feel a hiccup forcing its way out as I try to suppress a sob. Chase's eyes meet mine with warmth, while Jessica's frustration is evident in her sigh. Heidi and Brian take their places before the minister, and their vows begin.

After the ceremony, we find ourselves standing for extended periods, professional photographers capturing unforgettable moments against a backdrop of enchanting landscapes. The course provide a feast for the eyes, with their scenic offerings of the shimmering lake and majestic mountains. The air is filled with the invigorating scent of nature, while the distant sounds of rustling leaves and chirping birds serenade our senses. On a break from the bridal parties, participation in photos; Alice, Jessica and I take in the breathtaking beauty that surrounds us.

"Do you think I'll ever get to have a wedding like this?" Jessica ponders audibly.

I look at her dumbfounded, "Why couldn't you?"

"Because I'm a lesbian jew."

"I won't pretend to know enough about either of those things unless you count that weird year I only made out with girls, but why would those things matter?"

Jessica shrugs and pushes a pinecone around on the ground.

"Hey," I nudge as I bump her bouquet with mine and face her, seeing the glint of tears in the corners of her eyes. "You deserve a wedding as magnificent as you want, and if anyone thinks you don't, they can kiss your ass."

A corner of her mouth lifts. "Rowans' parents still aren't completely on board with the idea of me, you know."

"Then they have no idea how fucking extraordinary you are."

"Thanks, Sarah."

"Smile and say Carlisle Wedding!" Shouts the photographer, and we lean in together for a candid.

"I think I'll limit the photos, though," says Jessica indisputably.

"I would be forever grateful," I say, gently nudging her with my elbow.

After the string of pictures taken after the ceremony, we are now in the same room we were in for their engagement party. The room was transformed into an elegant setting, with round tables draped in white and gold cloth. Burgundy flowers, accompanied by decorative feathers, served as centerpieces. Little gold stands, displaying name tags, helped everyone find their assigned seats. The bridesmaids and groomsmen are all seated together except Jessica's, aisle mate, who has switched with Rowan so he can sit next to his wife and daughter. Chase and I, now a full-fledged couple, openly express our affection through playful banter and passionate kisses. "Get a room!"

I hear from behind me and find Thomas and Felix, who are scooting themselves snuggly into our table. As we captured the essence of the moment through our own amateur photography, raised toasts to our friend Heidi, and marveled at the depth of our friendship, everything felt harmonious. That moment when you know the stars and everything had aligned just right.

Chase and I join the dancefloor for a couple's song. I am pleasantly surprised by the graceful movements of his dancing, my curiosity piqued as he effortlessly spins me out and then pulls me back in. The melodic strains of a waltz fill the room, a sweet and romantic tune that floats through the air. As he whispers, "My mom always said it was important for boys to know how to dance," a warm smile spreads across my face. In a tender moment, he plants a gentle kiss on my lips continuing to guide me in a slow waltz. The closeness between us heightens my senses, and a fiery sensation spreads through every inch of my body that longs for him.

"I keep meaning to tell you how gorgeous you look in that suit."

"Truth be told, I can't wait to get it off."

"I like what's under the suit, too," I say with a wink.

He spins and then dips me to the end of the song, "I'll show you later," he winks back.

The DJ's voice reverberates in the room, commanding everyone's attention for the upcoming speeches. I stand nervously, preparing to deliver my maid of honor's speech. Even though I've spoken to groups this size before, this is so personal and my body trembles as I begin; "Brian," my throat catches, making an embarrassing sound into the microphone, garnering a few laughs. Mortified and feeling the heat spread across my cheeks like a brush fire, I begin again. "Over the years, I have come to know how truly wonderful of a man you are and how we are all so lucky to have you in our lives. You've diligently watched over us and provided unwavering support even when we didn't know it, and it has been an honor and a privilege to share the love of our beautiful Heidi with you. Cheers." I raise my glass, and Heidi wipes away a stray tear while I see Brian's eyes glisten as he nods to me with appreciation.

Ending the wedding extravagance, the crowd sees Brian and Heid off as they head to their room, giving long hugs and congratulations as they go; they'll be off to Costa Rica in the morning, so it's unlikely the rest of us will see them again until they return. Chase and I are the last to walk with them, and Heidi pulls us both into a hug. "You're next!" She sing-songs and hands me her bouquet in place of the traditional toss. I give her a curious look and hold the bouquet up so Chase can inspect it; he shakes Brian's hand, hugs him, and then Heidi. Brian moves around them to pull me in for another hug, our second tonight and probably third or fourth in all the years we've known each other, "take care of him, okay? He's one of the good ones." I give him a knowing nod, "I know," and we watch them walk away for a few moments before heading to our room.

The first thing I do is kick my heels off while I watch Chase loosen his tie and undo the buttons of his suit vest, then undo a few buttons of his button-down shirt. He snaps to look at me, "Don't you dare touch that zipper, Princess." I laugh and wait for him to walk over; he stands behind me as I scoop the flowing curls away from my back, and he slowly unzips me until his hand rests on my lower back. "The best part of this is now, when I let go of this zipper, I get to touch you again." Speaking directly into my ear from behind me, his breath is hot against my neck sending sparks down my back where his hand is still resting. "The first time, I didn't want to let go."

"You slept on the couch," I mumble.

"Then there was New Year's Eve," he continues, "and I knew I had to kiss you again, but I didn't know how."

As I feel the smile involuntarily appear on my face, a rush of warmth travels through my body, bringing us closer together as his chest presses against my back. "You wanted to kiss me?" I ask teasingly.

"I do now, too."

With a gentle touch, he turns me in his arms and lifts my chin, his eyes filled with tenderness, then he does and I know I will always want him to.

Chapter 48: Thirty

Seated side by side on the balcony of Felix's family time share in San Francisco, Thomas and I, the eternal children of the group, are enjoying the view as our birthday dinner is being prepared. Felix and Thomas took the room they had during their last visit, while Heidi and Brian took the room that Parker and I shared on our previous visit. I suspect this was done intentionally, but I don't mention it to avoid highlighting its significance. Chase steps out with Brian and Jessica, all marveling at how the small cigar shop weathered the recession and all these years. He bends to kiss the top of my head, handing a cigar to Thomas, who scrutinizes it as Jessica badgers him to become a man.

"Don't boys among your people become men at 13 or something?" He replies.

"You're not one of the Chosen, so unfortunately, your time has come at year 30." He mocks laughter and plucks the cigar from Chase's hand. They banter back and forth until Heidi and Felix call to come eat. Everyone heads in, leaving Thomas and I seated together. A familiarity sets me back to our townhome on the river, seated side by side, just us.

"Remember that guy," I say, looking out to the park. "The one with the dog?"

"The gentle lover," he says without pause.

"What do you think he's up to now?"

Without looking at me, he answers. "He still comes to the river, but there's a different dog and a baby."

I face him, startled at the disclosure, and vaguely hear our names being called from the inside. "Do you think—" I don't finish.

"It's been what, seven, eight years," he responds decisively.

"Oh," I say, feeling a surge of tender emotion for the man I'd never met, suddenly conscious of the time that has passed.

Felix steps on the porch, clapping wildly to corral us back into the house, while Thomas shoots me a playful glare, clearly unimpressed with his noncommittal partner. I snap too, and as I begin to cross the threshold, the sound of laughter and chatter fills the air, creating a lively atmosphere.. With memories swirling in my mind, I find a seat between Alice and Chase, reminiscing about the precious moments we've experienced together. Alice warmly places her arm around me pulling me into a side embrace saying, "Welcome to thirty!" Chase leans into my ear, his warm rasp sending sparks down my back as always and whispers, "I'll be wearing your favorite suit later, happy thirty princess." Shaking away the thoughts of Chase feeling the red on my cheeks, I raise my now full glass of wine to Thomas. "Thirty, flirty, and thriving, right beeyotch?" He raises his glass in return, and we all toast to year 30.

In the midst of our morning run, the fog hung heavily over the pastel-colored narrow homes of the affluent but gloomy neighborhood, creating an eerie atmosphere. Distracted, my gaze misplaced, I misjudge the curb, my foot hitting it with a jolt. A sharp, searing pain shoots through me, followed by a numbing ache that pulses with each beat. Felix, his touch firm yet gentle, examines my foot, flexing it in various directions, as I feel the pressure and movement, trying to assess the damage. After taking a brief rest, Heidi and Felix extended their hands to help me up. With their support, I cautiously placed my foot on the ground to test how much weight it could bear. It's uncomfortable but not concerning so Felix decides that it's probably not anything serious. Still, we're reduced to walking the remaining distance to the house.

"You and Chase, how is that going?" Felix announces too casually.

"Good," I say honestly.

Felix passes a look to Heidi, and she follows up, "Just good? Come on, we never hear anything about it."

I look to the sky and back down again; it's not lost on me that the last time I was being batted back and forth, the tennis ball in this Wimbledon-style interrogation, was here in San Francisco. "I don't know how to explain it; we're just good like everything is always good. It's not dull or anything, but we're just good."

They pass another look between them, and it's Felix's turn to press, "Are you in love?"

I stop splitting a look between them and quip. "I love everyone on this trip, so I don't know if I understand the question."

Another smirk passes between them like they are communicating in secret. "Is that all?" I ask, a bit vexed.

"That's all," they say in tandem, and we continue walking.

"Well," Felix says finally. "Actually, how's the, you know?" I guffaw in disbelief. "What!?" says Felix. "I see those rough hands, that lean muscular body; I've always been a little curious."

"It's also good," I say resolutely.

Heidi awes in admiration. "This is the real deal, isn't it? I mean, you're not giving us anything."

I gesticulate, zipping my lips. They both link their arms through mine, and we hurriedly, as hurriedly as I can, retreat to the house as the raindrops start to fall, creating random splotches on the sidewalk.

Inside, Felix informs every one of my wrong step. Chase eyes me knowingly, thinking back to that fateful New Year in the snow. With ease, he effortlessly lifts me, his brawny arms embracing me as he settles me onto his lap in the plush recliner. Nestled against him, I am enveloped by his warmth, finding comfort in his presence. In my ear, he whispers that Thomas and Jessica interrogated him about our relationship; I share how I was subjected to a similar round of questioning. "So," he says, drawing it out softly, "do you love me?" I shift, but only to place my head more comfortably on his shoulder.

"What did you hear?"

"That you were tight-lipped."

I smile, "with absolute certainty."

His heart makes a little pitter-patter of appreciation against my ear, and he says, "Me too."

Chapter 49: Endless Wildflowers

As a strong breeze blows, my hair is whipped around, tickling my cheeks and obscuring my vision. Trying to steady the oversized picnic basket behind me, I swiped strands of hair out of my mouth while Chase's laughter echoed as we sped up the bumpy hill on his ATV.

Once he stops, he reaches for the basket, then comes around to my side and helps me out.

"We'll just walk up this way a bit toward that tree." He points with the basket and I steady myself on the loose gravel.

While we hike frequently around his family's property, I've never been to this spot. As the scent of vibrant wildflowers engulfs my senses, a rush of nostalgia washes over me upon reaching the hill's summit. As I stand there, I am captivated by the sight of endless wildflowers swaying in the late summer breeze, much like the framed painting that adorns my bedroom wall. The explosion of colors in every imaginable hue is accentuated by sporadic bursts of vibrant red. Just like the painting. The painting that has been my source of comfort and refuge all these days and nights is finally here, in tangible form, on Chase's ranch.

Moving my hair across my back to one shoulder, Chase kisses me on the now bare spot on the neck. "Wanna eat?" I faintly nod. "You okay?" He murmurs, breathing warmly against my ear.

"It's just—" I stammer, my voice catching. "It's my painting, the one above my bed."

"I know," he replies, his tone filled with certainty.

When I caught sight of the playful grin forming on his lips, I immediately clapped my hand against his arm in delight. "Are you deliberately burning through all your tricks to get rid of me?"

Chase's laughter fills the surroundings, reverberating as he shakes his head in amusement and guides me towards the picnic spot, hand in hand. Settled on the tattered blanket picking through the assortment of food his mom packed for us, always too much. I can feel his gaze fixed on me, like a warmth against my skin. As I soak in the breathtaking panorama, it's reminiscent of those starry nights spent stargazing with a telescope. Like his contentment hinges entirely on my happiness. I am more than willing to be the only person he chooses to share his life with if this is what he means by his statement that he is not going anywhere and doesn't have anything to offer. This love was uncomplicated and came naturally. Simple. Love is like the mesmerizing fields around us, with delicate flowers swaying elegantly in the summer sun, warm and comforting. Not a battlefield.

Chapter 50: Matching Pajamas

The Views, in partnership with Maven Advertising, are hosting their first tree lighting at one of Mark Millers' newest properties, which was an essential part of the build. He wanted a large enough area to have a Christmas tree that would rival Times Square. It doesn't, but it's exciting all the same. Thomas gathers all of us together and pops the champagne cork, sending it flying into the crowd, likely bouncing off an unsuspecting victim. We all hold our glasses out, and Thomas looks at Heidi. "Where's your glass, babe?" She shakes her head no, and we all stare at her silently before Alice cries out, "Holy Moses, she's pregnant!" I pin a look on Heidi, and she nods a cautious yes. We all join Alice in her scream of delight, gathering her and Brian in a group hug. Chase declined the group hug and instead gave her a sweet congratulation before returning to place his hand in my jacket pocket with mine. As we retreat to an average distance apart, I see Mark Miller approaching us with who else but Parker and Spoons. Chase squeezes my hand a little tighter. Mark presses a firm handshake into Brian's before introducing him and Heidi to

Parker and Spoons, "Brian, I insist that you let Parker here take a look at some advertising options for you. Guys, an absolute whiz." Mark gives Parker a pat on the back while he extends his hand to an apprehensive Brian.

"Sure, we'll take a look," says Brian politely.

"It would be my pleasure," says Parker. Mark then turns. "You know Sarah already—" and he's cut off by, "Chase," says Chase, holding out his hand; Parker takes it as if his hand is acting of its own accord, staring at it with curiosity. "Chase," he repeats with a pause. "Nice to meet you," he finishes politely. Shaking hands with everyone else, who seems to think this is a weird simulation we've entered, we round off the parallel universe when Shayne suddenly appears by Parker's side, displaying a very pregnant belly through her unzipped jacket. In the normal universe, I think maybe this would upset me. Yet, in this universe, I catch myself smiling at her swollen middle, then at Parker before saying, "Congratulations, you both must be so thrilled." Shayne flashes me her gorgeous, white-toothed smile and holds her belly gingerly, "We're waiting until the baby comes to know the gender, like a last surprise kind of thing." "Amazing," I say, "my best friend Heidi is also pregnant," turning to my equally gorgeous dark-haired bestie. Exuberantly, Shayne lets out a loud squeal and pulls Heidi into a peculiar stomach-hugging embrace. Once Heidi detaches herself, we all stand in an awkward silence while the glimmering, smaller than Times Square tree, stands illuminating us. I give Parker a nod; he nods back and turns the pregnant Shayne away from us toward the tree. Chase squeezes me in and kisses my temple, "ready to get out of here?" I nod my agreement, and he drives us back to his place, where we will have Christmas tomorrow with his family.

When we arrive at his house, we both eagerly tear into our Christmas Eve presents from our parents, guessing what they are. We both raise our new pajama sets in unison and promptly put them on, showcasing them to each other before ultimately discarding them to make love under the star-filled skylight. Tangled together, I rested my head on his chest, mesmerized by the rhythmic and ever-steady thump of Chase's heart. His rough hand glides up and down my back, leaving a trail of tingling warmth in its wake, until it finally comes to a rest. His quiet, sleepy breathing fills the room with a gentle, rhythmic sound.

Christmas morning comes, and I wake to a matching pajama-dressed Chase sitting anxiously at the edge of the bed. Sleepily, I shuffle out from under the warm covers and slip into my cozy pajamas. "You have to go downstairs, sit on the couch, and close your eyes."

Exhausted and unable to muster the energy to ask for clarification, I comply with Chase's instructions. I can hear him leave through the front door and return shortly after. "Okay, open," he says.

Tension filled Chase's hands as they tightly gripped a basket, inside of which a small black fuzz bobbed about. "I'm naming him Jimmy after that band you like, the one you have the signed record of."

My face lights up with a mixture of surprise and excitement as he acknowledges the album that I'm sure he's never heard. The joy in his eyes twinkles like the Christmas tree standing vigil over the moment. There's a faint scent of pine from the real tree cut from the farm that fills the air, adding a touch of holiday spirit to the moment. With the soft glow of the rising sun casting a warm and cozy ambiance, I wrap my arms around him, while the puppy tries to wriggle free from his grip.

"Brian and I decided it was time for bird dogs, so Heidi looked up the breeders, found this one, practically did a background check on them and their extended family before deciding this was the right litter," he pauses. "He'll stay here, obviously, but I thought we could make him something that's ours."

"Jimmy," I whisper, my thoughts momentarily drifting to the man by the river as I gently stroke the squirming puppy. It feels as though a surge of electricity ignites within me, connecting pieces together like a jigsaw puzzle. There's something I want, need, to do right now. Jimmy Eat Worlds 23 roars into my synapse, coursing through me loudly, dominating my thoughts; *"what are you hoping for?"* Afraid that the lyrics playing in my head might make me shout, I whisper cautiously.

"Chase" he looks directly at me, more accurately, inside me. I stumble out the words "Will you ma—" he puts his thumb to my lips and stops me, placing Jimmy on the floor. My throat tightens, a lump forming as the weight of the words threatens to suffocate me. Every muscle in my body freezes in anticipation as he reaches into his pocket, the sound of 23 still echoing in my ears. I become acutely aware of him, his sharp features etching themselves into my mind, as the faint scent of his cologne lingers in the air. Time seems to stand still as he carefully withdraws a cigar box, it's meticulously carvings being traced by his fingers. "Sarah" he clears his throat, "I was going to do this later when our friends came, but if you're trying to beat me to it I may as well—" He takes a deep breath. As he opens the cigar box, I can't help but notice his hands joggling, anticipation evident in his eyes as he unveils the hidden treasure within - a small velvet box. With a slow and deliberate motion, he opens it, and a mesmerizing vintage ring comes into view. The ring is decorated with sparkling diamonds that catch the light and intricate carvings that add to its elegance. As he holds it up, the ring seems to glow in his hand, radiating its own beauty. He looks at me, and I can see the emotion and surety in his eyes. "Will you marry me?" The song explodes in my senses again.

THE BOY IN THE BAND

"I'm here, I'm now, I'm ready
Holding on tight
Don't give away the end
The one thing that stays mine."

About the Author

Kerri Lynn, a healthcare pro by day, mom by night, and animal lover 24/7, is now spicing things up as a storyteller extraordinaire! Raised in the pulsating heart of a vibrant city, she blends her sizzling experiences into tales of love, friendship, and resilience, infused with wit, charm, and a dash of unapologetic sexiness. When not diving into her writing or rocking her career, Kerri treasures moments with her family and furry friends, living life with gusto. Her debut novel, "The Boy in the Band," marks the start of a scintillating new chapter, and she's inviting you to join the fun! Connect with Kerri for a wild ride through a world brimming with passion, allure, and tantalizing tales.

Milton Keynes UK
Ingram Content Group UK Ltd.
UKHW051343140724
445326UK00014BA/628